FIREBUG

® **IMAGE COMICS, INC.**

Robert Kirkman—Chief Operating Officer
Erik Larsen—Chief Financial Officer
Todd McFarlane—President
Marc Silvestri—Chief Executive Officer
Jim Valentino—Vice President

Eric Stephenson—Publisher
Corey Hart—Director of Sales
Jeff Boison—Director of Publishing Planning
& Book Trade Sales
Chris Ross—Director of Digital Sales
Jeff Stang—Director of Specialty Sales
Kat Salazar—Director of PR & Marketing
Drew Gill—Art Director
Heather Doornink—Production Director
Branwyn Bigglestone—Controller
IMAGECOMICS.COM

FIREBUG. First printing. March 2018. Published by Image Comics, Inc. Office of publication: 2701 NW Vaughn St., Suite 780, Portland, OR 97210. Copyright © 2018 Johnnie Christmas. All rights reserved. A portion of FIREBUG originally appeared in issue #7 of ISLAND comics magazine (2016). "Firebug," its logos, and the likenesses of all characters herein are trademarks of Johnnie Christmas, unless otherwise noted. "Image" and the Image Comics logos are registered trademarks of Image Comics, Inc. No part of this publication may be reproduced or transmitted, in any form or by any means (except for short excerpts for journalistic or review purposes), without the express written permission of Johnnie Christmas, or Image Comics, Inc. All names, characters, events, and locales in this publication are entirely fictional. Any resemblance to actual persons (living or dead), events, or places, without satiric intent, is coincidental. Printed in the USA. For information regarding the CPSIA on this printed material call: 203-595-3636 and provide reference #RICH–780735. For international rights, contact: foreignlicensing@imagecomics.com.
ISBN: 978-1-5343-0494-9.

FIREBUG

CREATED BY JOHNNIE CHRISTMAS

JOHNNIE CHRISTMAS
STORY & ART

TAMRA BONVILLAIN
COLORS

ARIANA MAHER
LETTERS

FLATTERS:
FERNANDO ARGÜELLO & LUDWIG OLIMBA

COLOR SEPARATIONS AND ADDITIONAL FLATTING:
STELLADIA

DESIGN:
JOHNNIE CHRISTMAS & ARIANA MAHER

SPECIAL THANKS TO BRANDON GRAHAM.
WHO LOVES COMICS MORE THAN ANYONE I KNOW.

*DEDICATED
TO MY MOTHER,
CONSTANCE.*

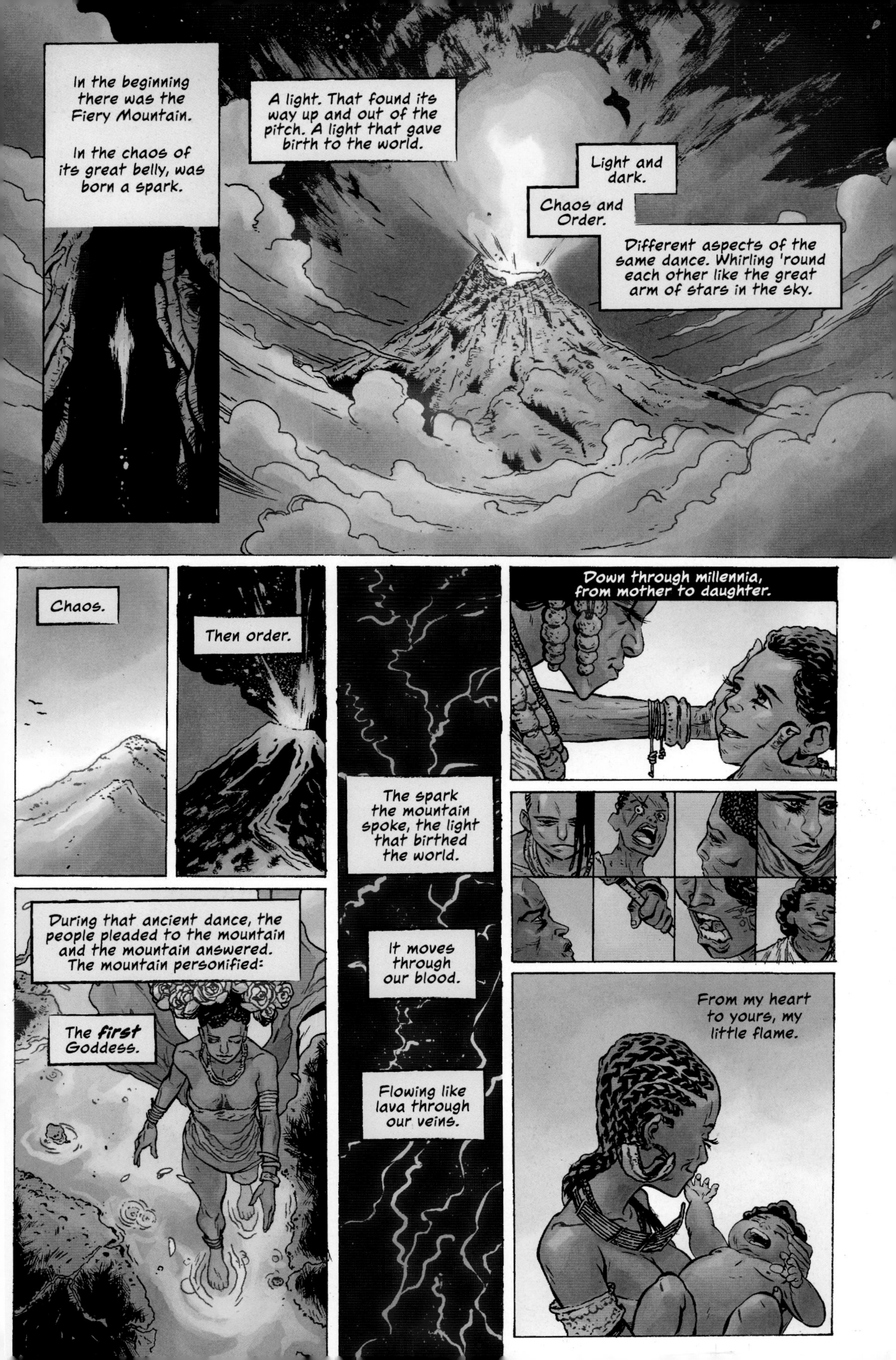
In the beginning there was the Fiery Mountain.
In the chaos of its great belly, was born a spark.
A light. That found its way up and out of the pitch. A light that gave birth to the world.
Light and dark.
Chaos and Order.
Different aspects of the same dance. Whirling 'round each other like the great arm of stars in the sky.
Chaos.
Then order.
The spark the mountain spoke, the light that birthed the world.
It moves through our blood.
Flowing like lava through our veins.
Down through millennia, from mother to daughter.
During that ancient dance, the people pleaded to the mountain and the mountain answered. The mountain personified:
The *first* Goddess.
From my heart to yours, my little flame.

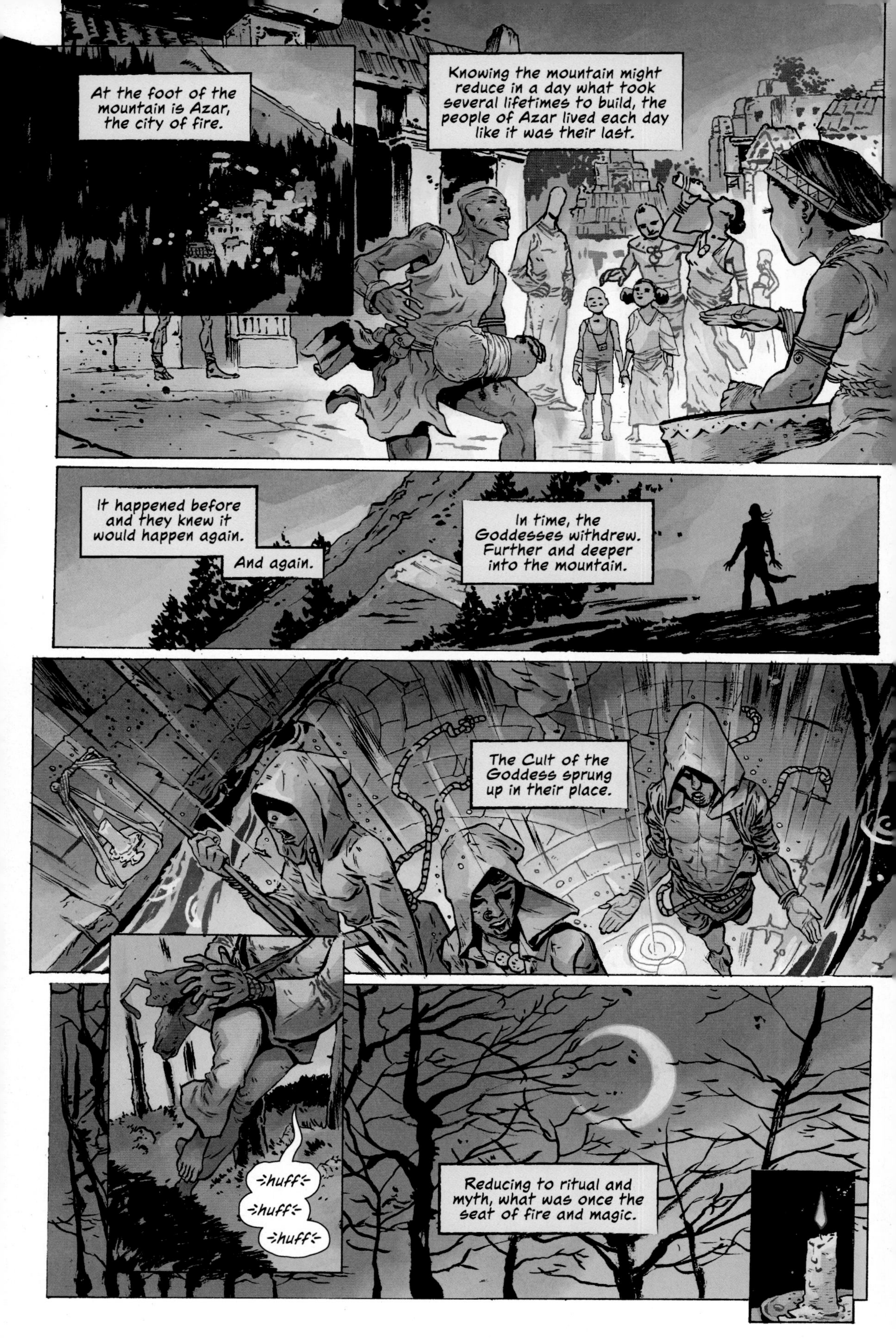
At the foot of the mountain is Azar, the city of fire.
Knowing the mountain might reduce in a day what took several lifetimes to build, the people of Azar lived each day like it was their last.
It happened before and they knew it would happen again.
And again.
In time, the Goddesses withdrew. Further and deeper into the mountain.
The Cult of the Goddess sprung up in their place.
huff
huff
huff
Reducing to ritual and myth, what was once the seat of fire and magic.

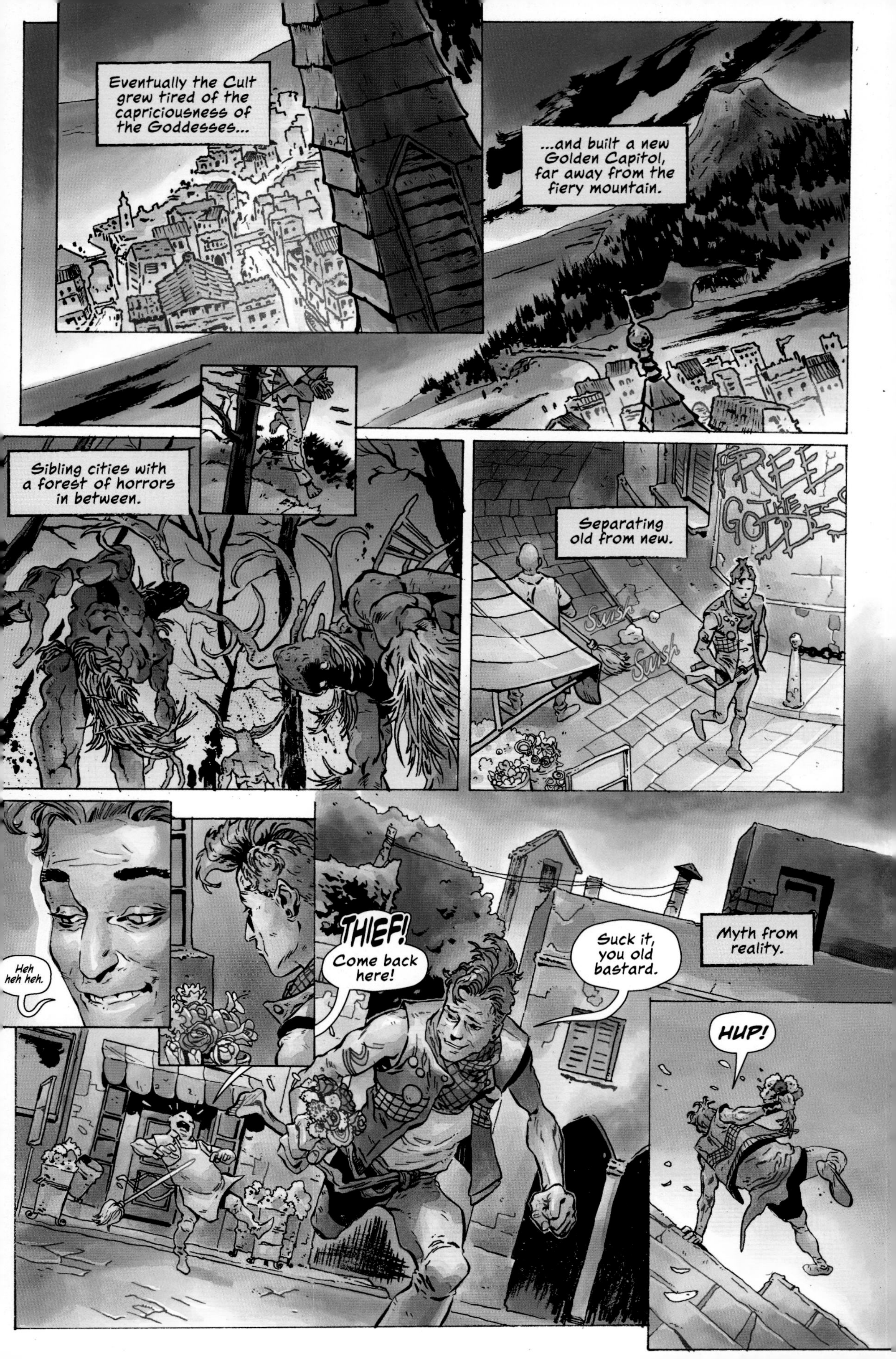
Eventually the Cult grew tired of the capriciousness of the Goddesses...
...and built a new Golden Capitol, far away from the fiery mountain.
Sibling cities with a forest of horrors in between.
Separating old from new.
FREE THE GODDES
SWISH
SWISH
Heh heh heh.
THIEF! Come back here!
Suck it, you old bastard.
Myth from reality.
HUP!

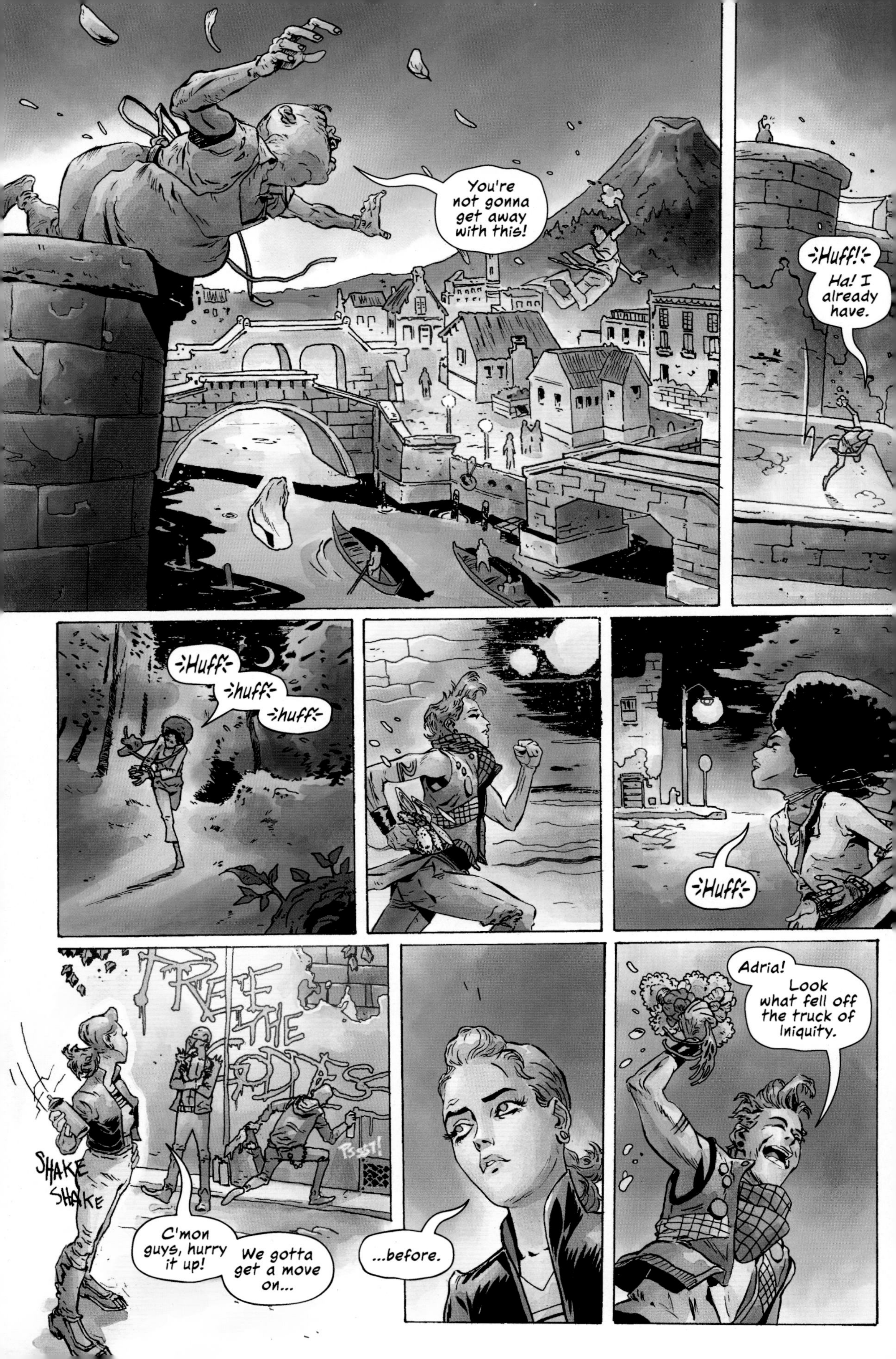
You're not gonna get away with this!
-Huff!- Ha! I already have.
-Huff-
-huff-
-huff-
-Huff-
FREE THE GODDESS
SHAKE
SHAKE
PSSST!
C'mon guys, hurry it up!
We gotta get a move on...
...before.
Adria! Look what fell off the truck of Iniquity.

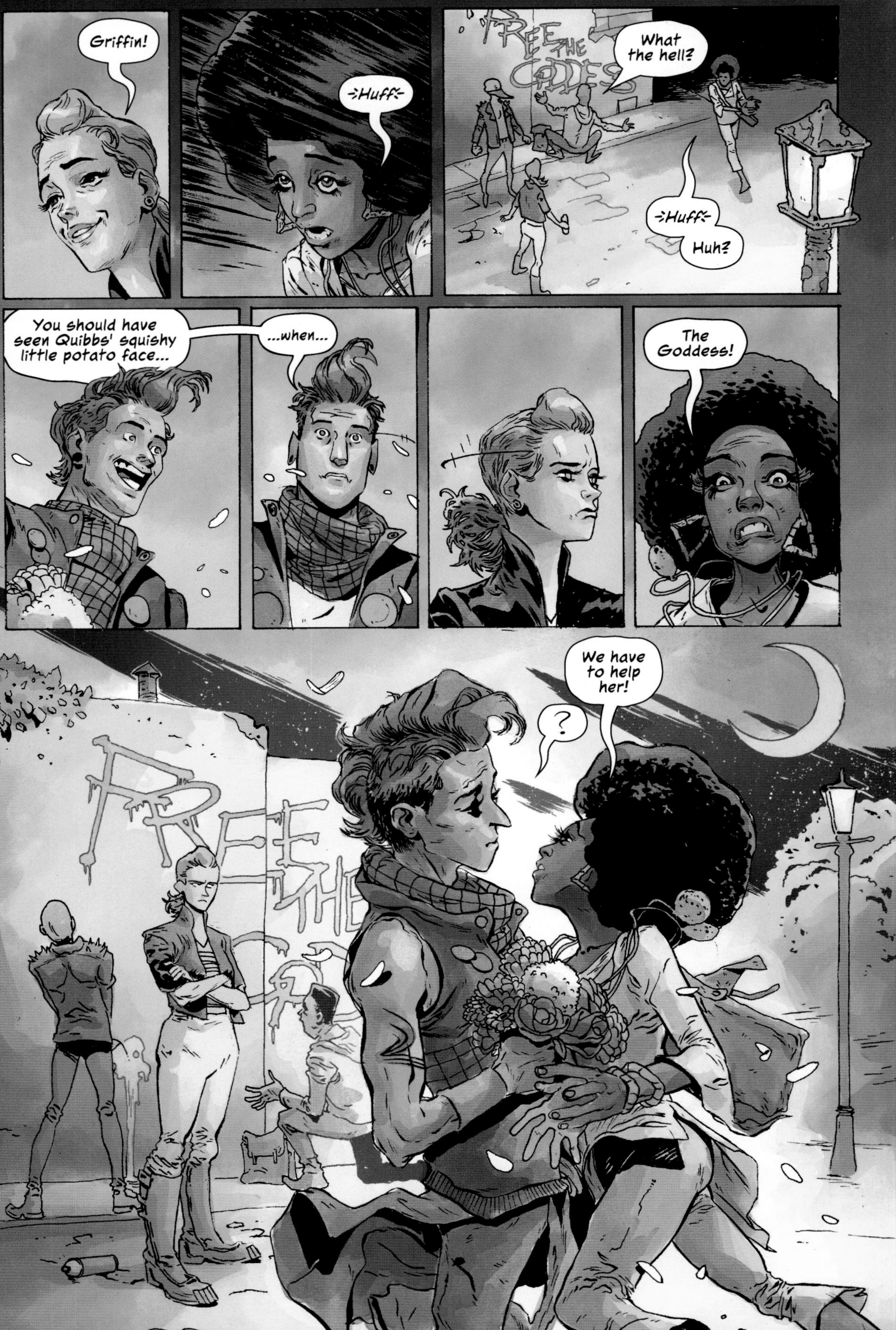
Griffin!
Huff
FREE THE GODDES
What the hell?
Huff
Huh?
You should have seen Quibbs' squishy little potato face...
...when...
The Goddess!
FREE THE
?
We have to help her!

1

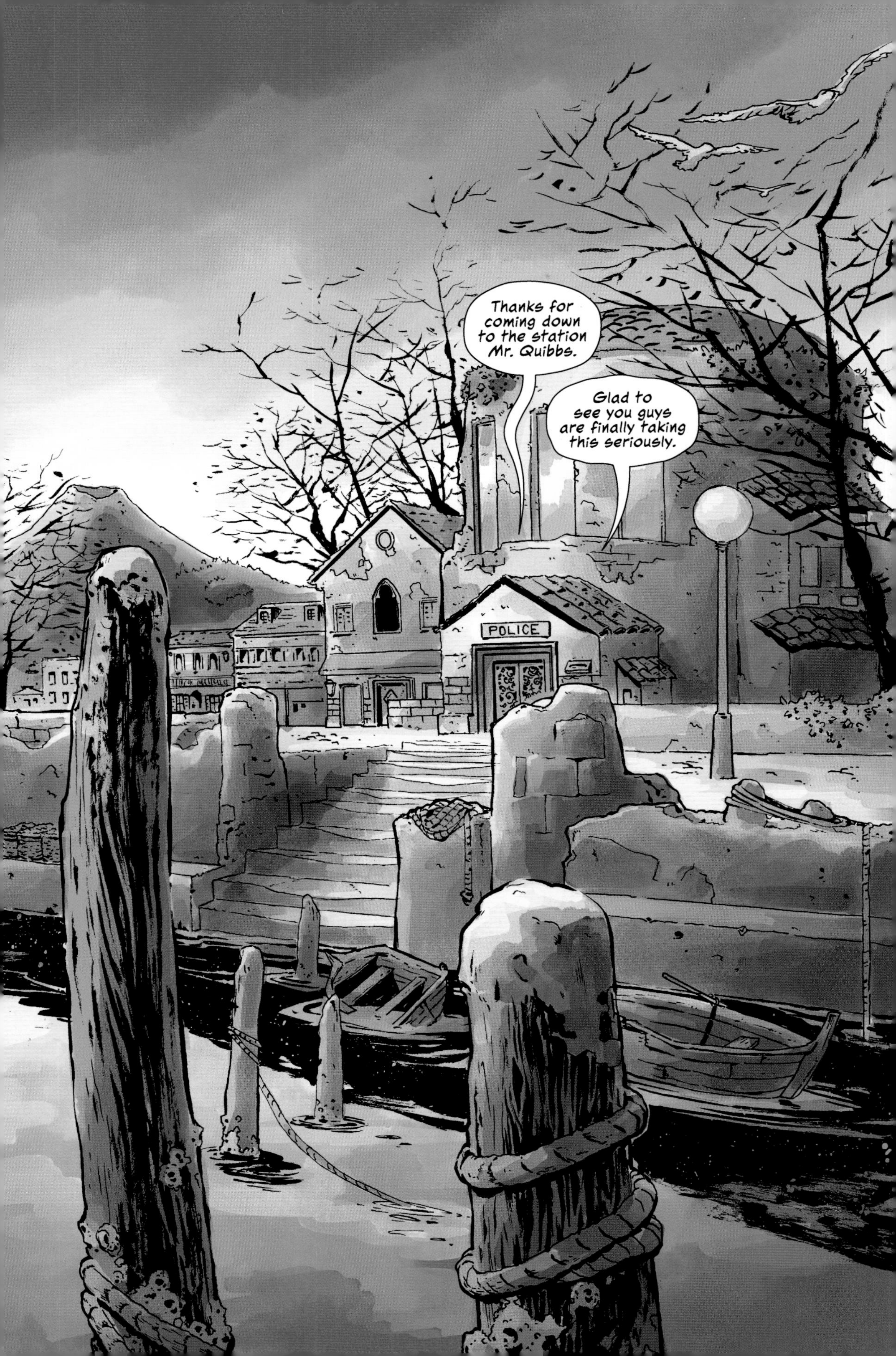
Thanks for coming down to the station Mr. Quibbs.
Glad to see you guys are finally taking this seriously.
POLICE

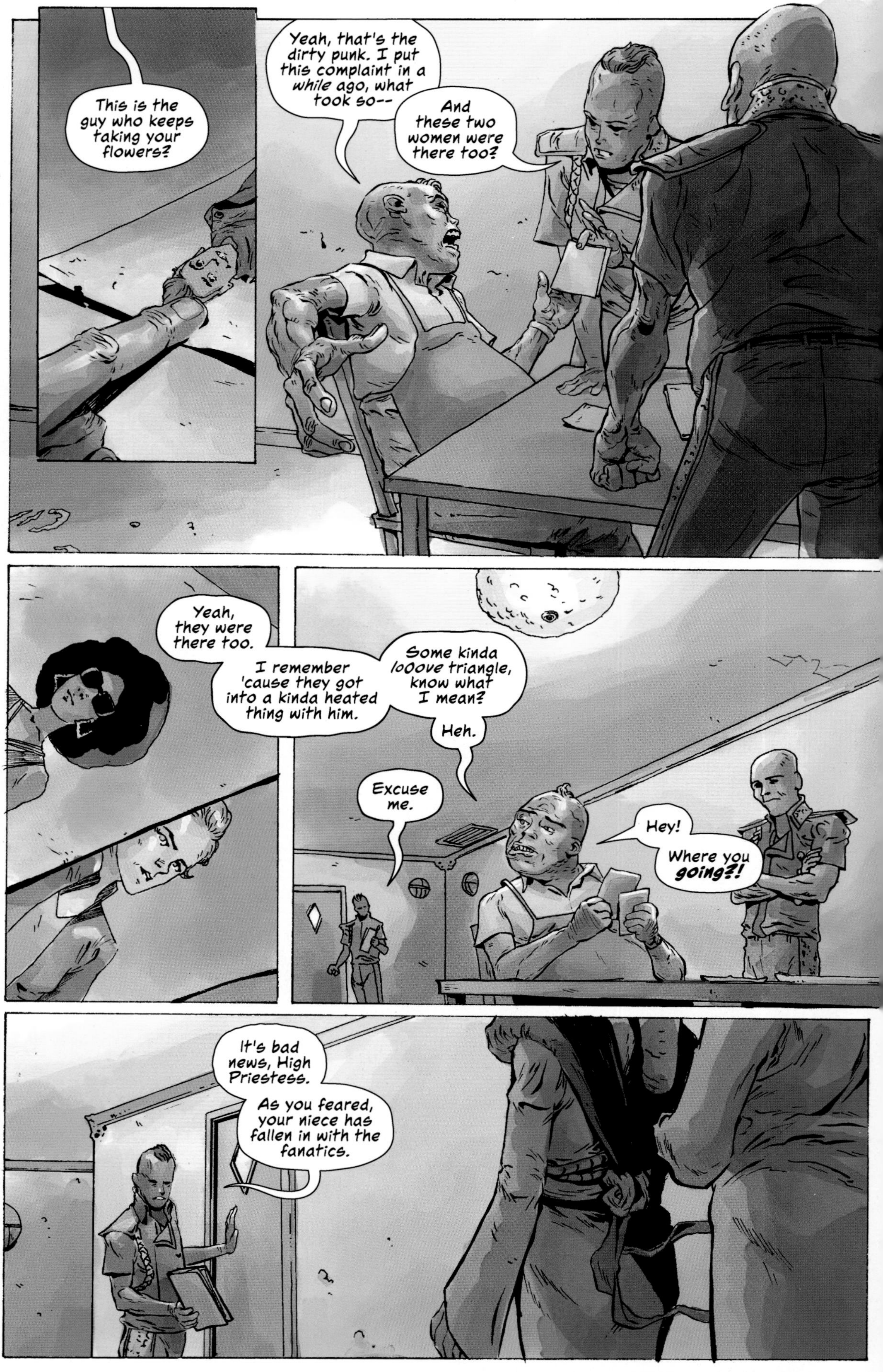

This is the guy who keeps taking your flowers?
Yeah, that's the dirty punk. I put this complaint in a *while* ago, what took so--
And these two women were there too?
Yeah, they were there too.
I remember 'cause they got into a kinda heated thing with him.
Some kinda looove triangle, know what I mean?
Heh.
Excuse me.
Hey!
Where you ***going?!***
It's bad news, High Priestess.
As you feared, your niece has fallen in with the fanatics.

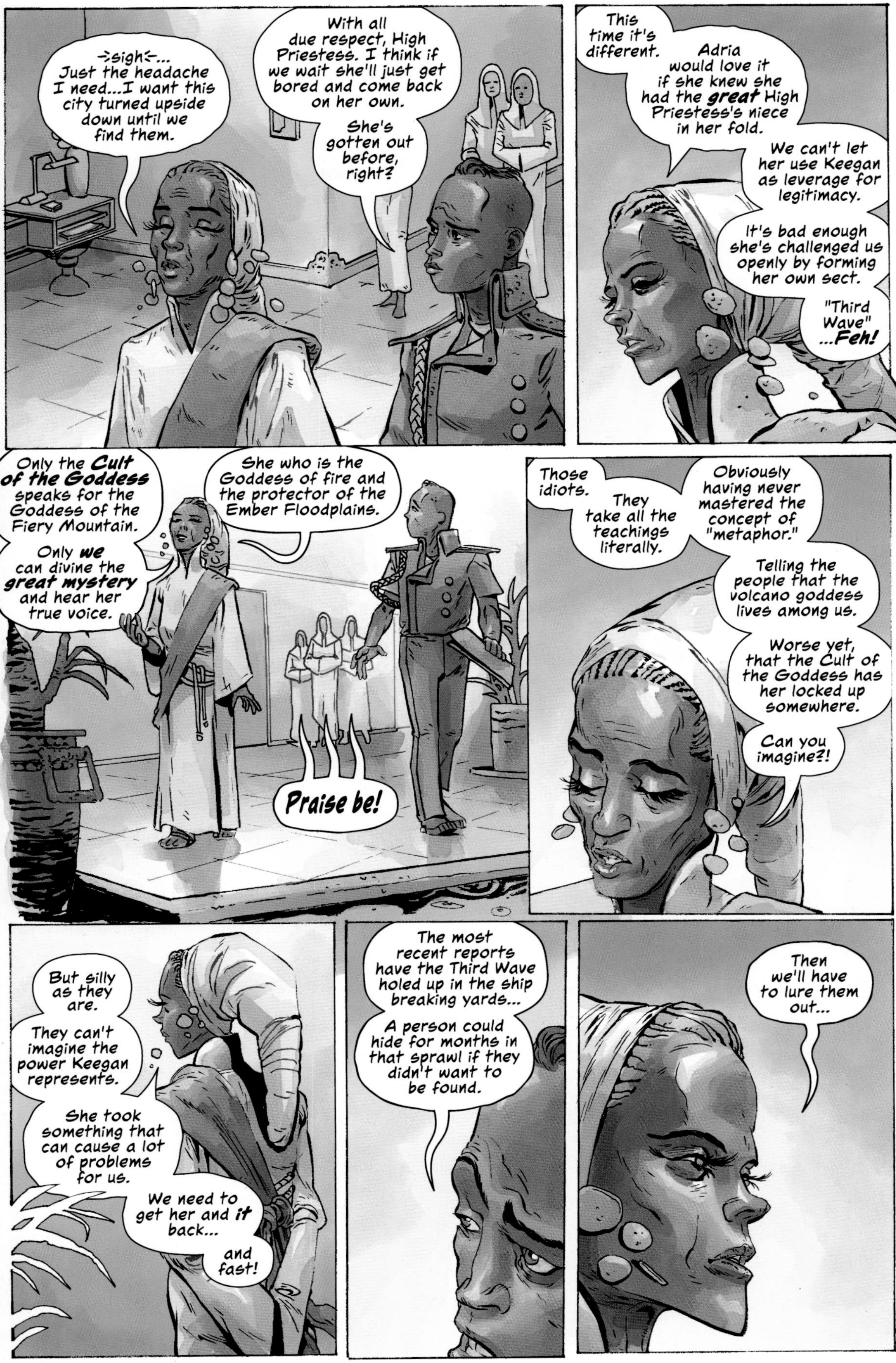

->sigh<-... Just the headache I need...I want this city turned upside down until we find them.
With all due respect, High Priestess. I think if we wait she'll just get bored and come back on her own.
She's gotten out before, right?
This time it's different.
Adria would love it if she knew she had the great High Priestess's niece in her fold.
We can't let her use Keegan as leverage for legitimacy.
It's bad enough she's challenged us openly by forming her own sect.
"Third Wave" ...Feh!
Only the Cult of the Goddess speaks for the Goddess of the Fiery Mountain.
Only we can divine the great mystery and hear her true voice.
She who is the Goddess of fire and the protector of the Ember Floodplains.
Praise be!
Those idiots.
They take all the teachings literally.
Obviously having never mastered the concept of "metaphor."
Telling the people that the volcano goddess lives among us.
Worse yet, that the Cult of the Goddess has her locked up somewhere.
Can you imagine?!
But silly as they are.
They can't imagine the power Keegan represents.
She took something that can cause a lot of problems for us.
We need to get her and it back...
and fast!
The most recent reports have the Third Wave holed up in the ship breaking yards...
A person could hide for months in that sprawl if they didn't want to be found.
Then we'll have to lure them out...

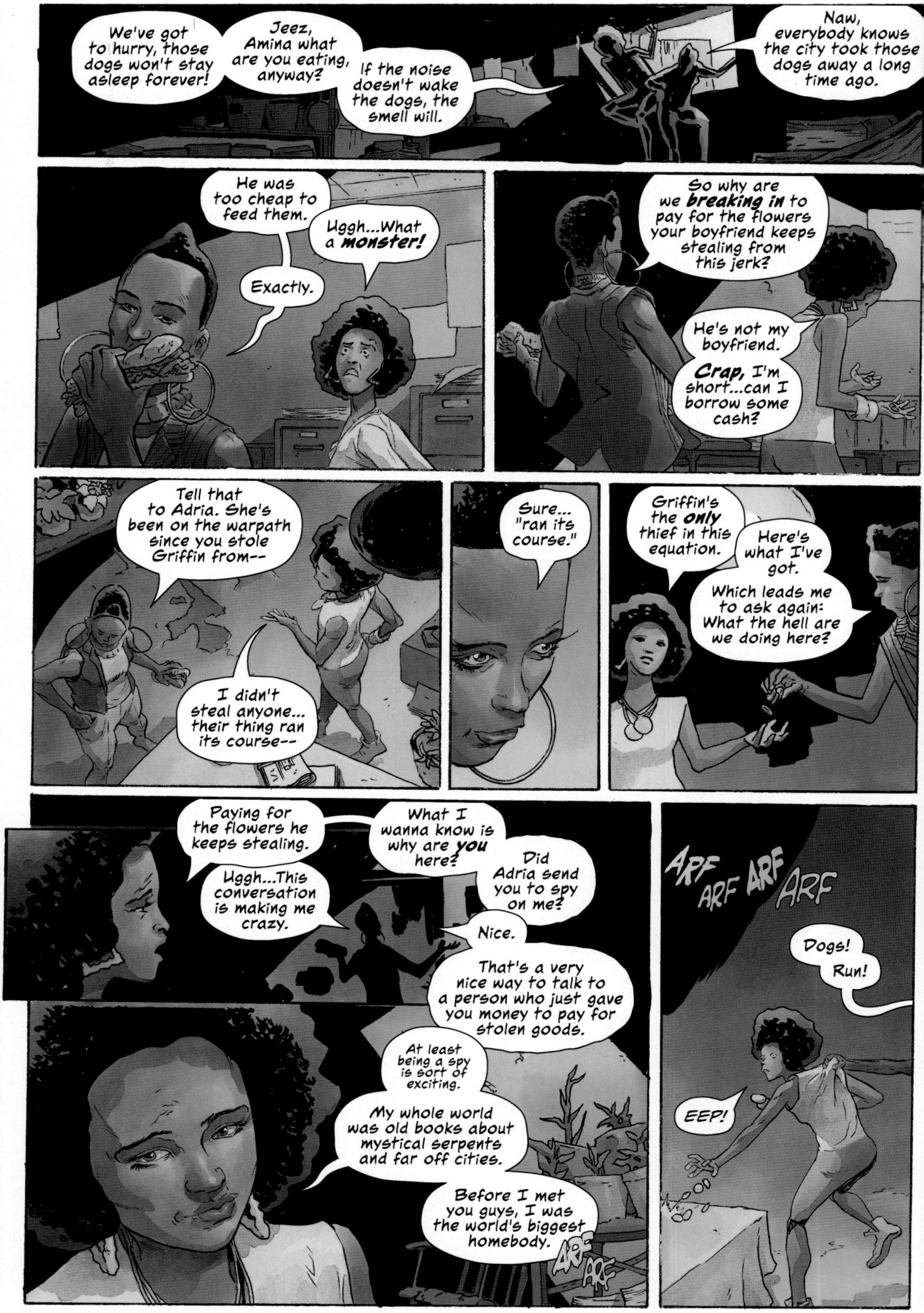

We've got to hurry, those dogs won't stay asleep forever!
Jeez, Amina what are you eating, anyway?
If the noise doesn't wake the dogs, the smell will.
Naw, everybody knows the city took those dogs away a long time ago.
He was too cheap to feed them.
Uggh...What a **monster!**
Exactly.
So why are we **breaking in** to pay for the flowers your boyfriend keeps stealing from this jerk?
He's not my boyfriend.
Crap, I'm short...can I borrow some cash?
Tell that to Adria. She's been on the warpath since you stole Griffin from--
I didn't steal anyone... their thing ran its course--
Sure... "ran its course."
Griffin's the **only** thief in this equation.
Here's what I've got.
Which leads me to ask again: What the hell are we doing here?
Paying for the flowers he keeps stealing.
What I wanna know is why are **you** here?
Did Adria send you to spy on me?
Uggh...This conversation is making me crazy.
Nice.
That's a very nice way to talk to a person who just gave you money to pay for stolen goods.
At least being a spy is sort of exciting.
My whole world was old books about mystical serpents and far off cities.
Before I met you guys, I was the world's biggest homebody.
ARF ARF
ARF ARF ARF ARF
Dogs!
Run!
EEP!

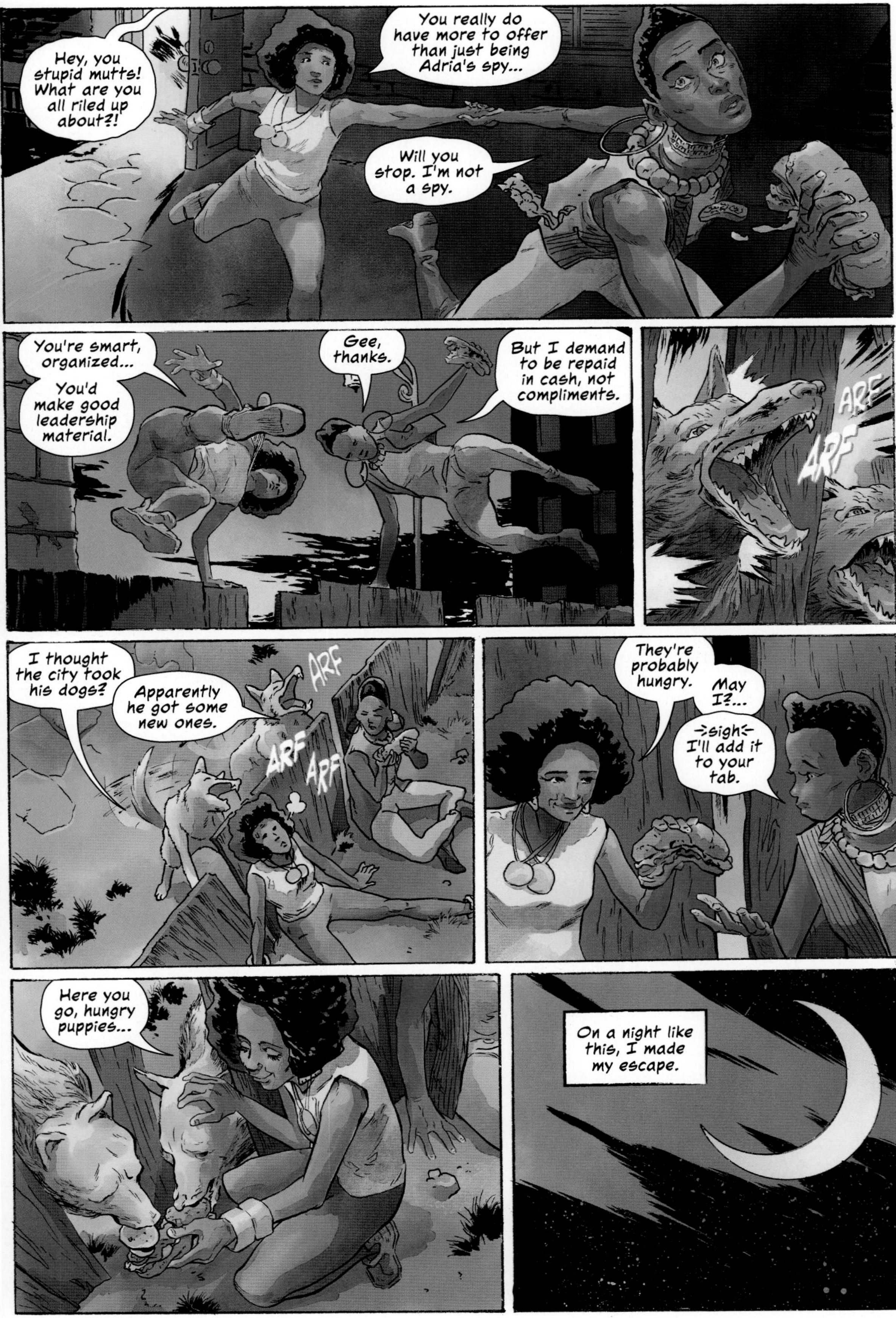
Hey, you stupid mutts! What are you all riled up about?!
You really do have more to offer than just being Adria's spy...
Will you stop. I'm not a spy.
You're smart, organized...
You'd make good leadership material.
Gee, thanks.
But I demand to be repaid in cash, not compliments.
ARF
ARF
I thought the city took his dogs?
Apparently he got some new ones.
ARF
ARF
ARF
They're probably hungry.
May I?...
sigh
I'll add it to your tab.
Here you go, hungry puppies...
On a night like this, I made my escape.

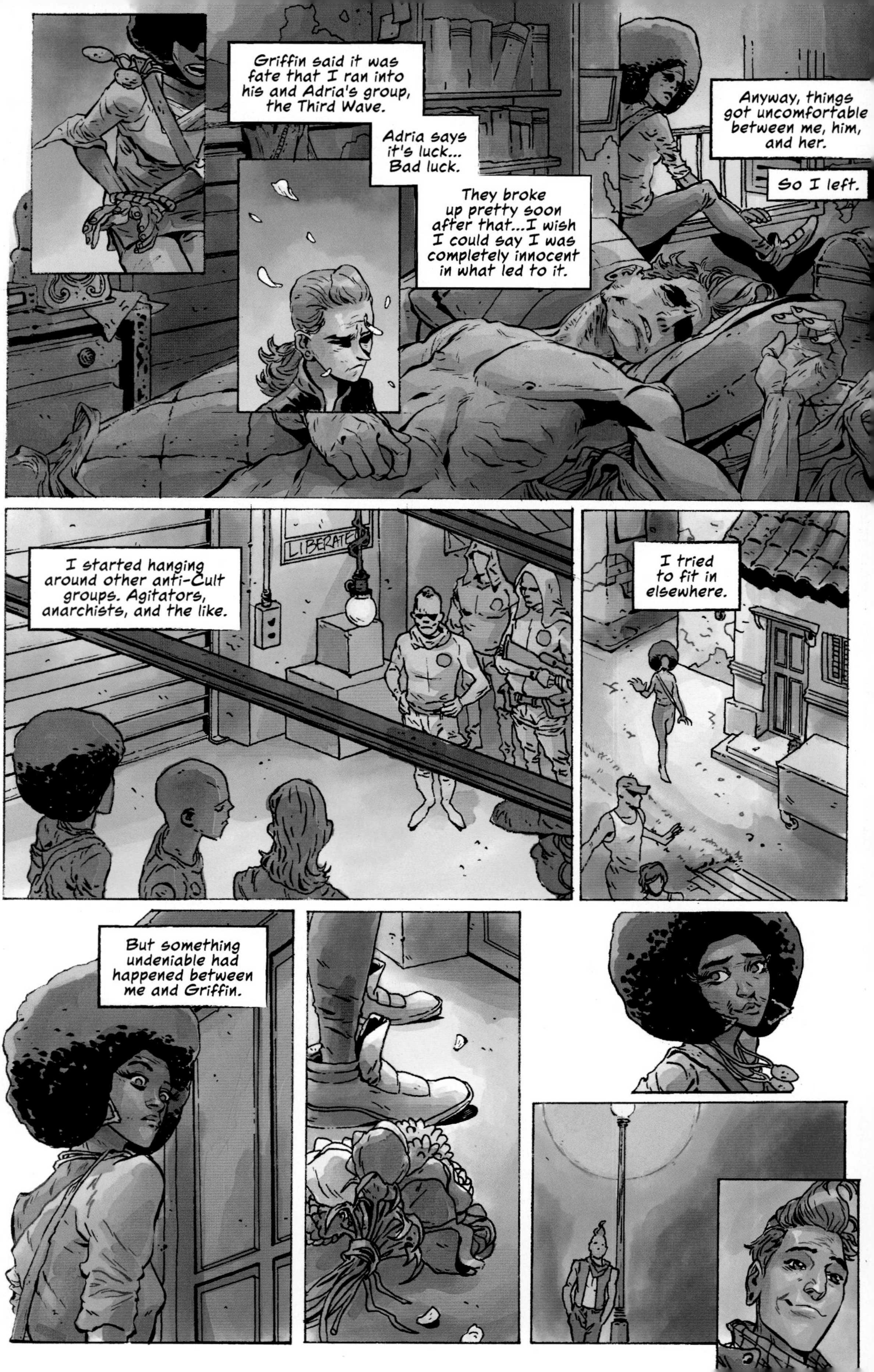

Griffin said it was fate that I ran into his and Adria's group, the Third Wave.
Adria says it's luck... Bad luck.
They broke up pretty soon after that...I wish I could say I was completely innocent in what led to it.
Anyway, things got uncomfortable between me, him, and her.
So I left.
LIBERATE
I started hanging around other anti-Cult groups. Agitators, anarchists, and the like.
I tried to fit in elsewhere.
But something undeniable had happened between me and Griffin.

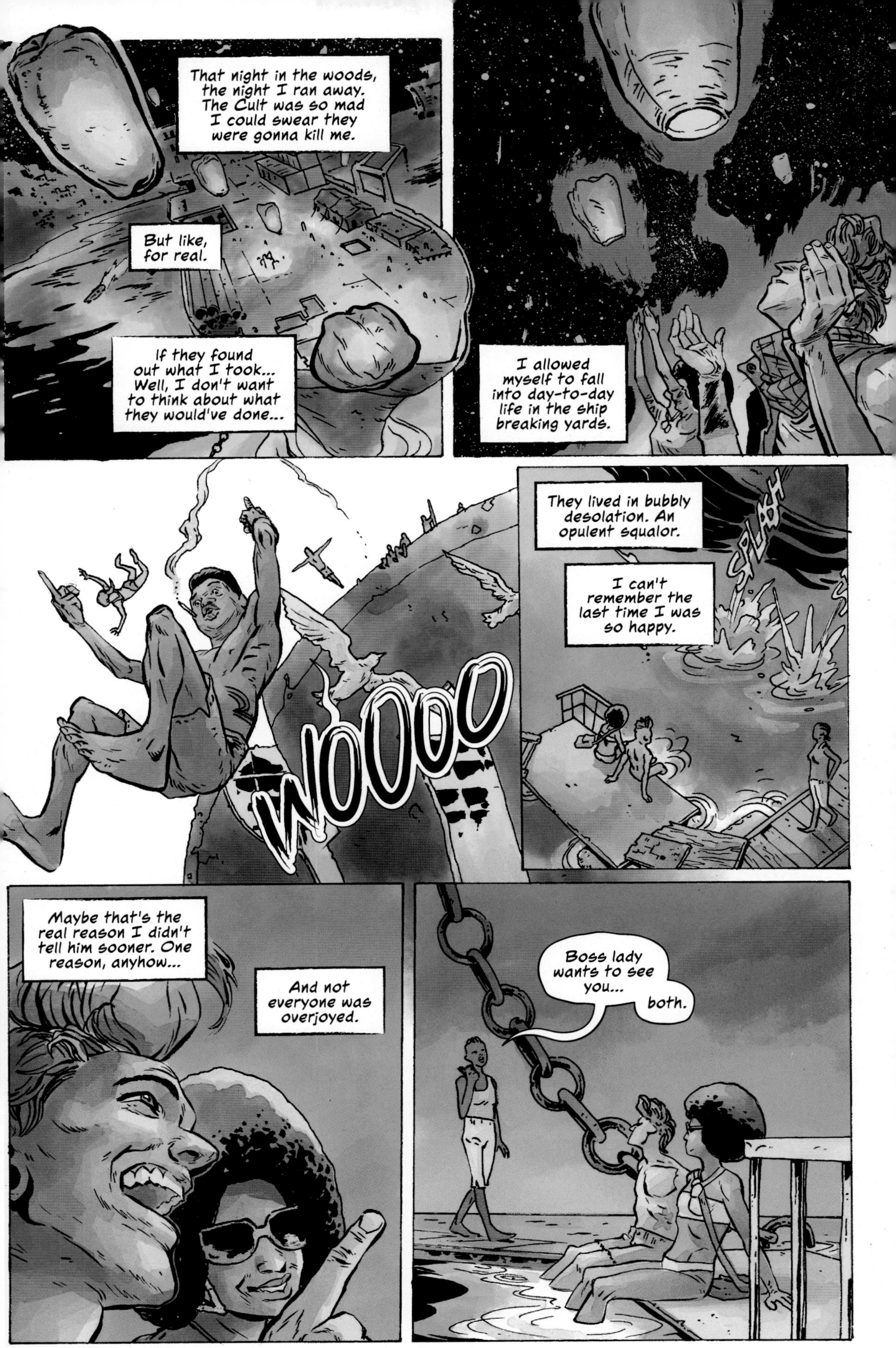
That night in the woods, the night I ran away. The Cult was so mad I could swear they were gonna kill me.
But like, for real.
If they found out what I took... Well, I don't want to think about what they would've done...
I allowed myself to fall into day-to-day life in the ship breaking yards.
WOOOO
They lived in bubbly desolation. An opulent squalor.
I can't remember the last time I was so happy.
SPLASH
Maybe that's the real reason I didn't tell him sooner. One reason, anyhow...
And not everyone was overjoyed.
Boss lady wants to see you...
both.

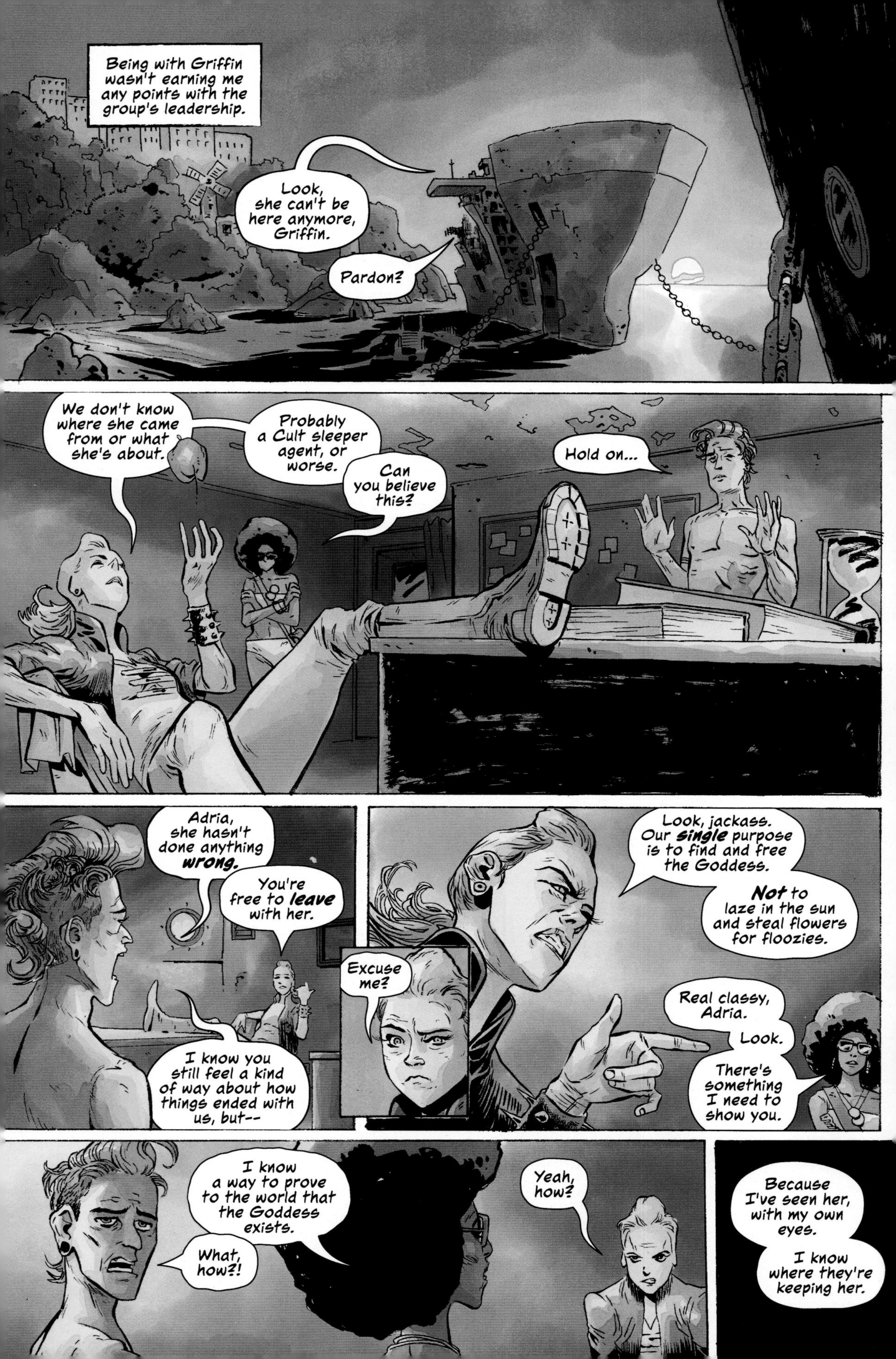
Being with Griffin wasn't earning me any points with the group's leadership.
Look, she can't be here anymore, Griffin.
Pardon?
We don't know where she came from or what she's about.
Probably a Cult sleeper agent, or worse.
Can you believe this?
Hold on...
Adria, she hasn't done anything wrong.
You're free to leave with her.
I know you still feel a kind of way about how things ended with us, but--
Look, jackass. Our single purpose is to find and free the Goddess.
Not to laze in the sun and steal flowers for floozies.
Excuse me?
Real classy, Adria.
Look.
There's something I need to show you.
I know a way to prove to the world that the Goddess exists.
What, how?!
Yeah, how?
Because I've seen her, with my own eyes.
I know where they're keeping her.

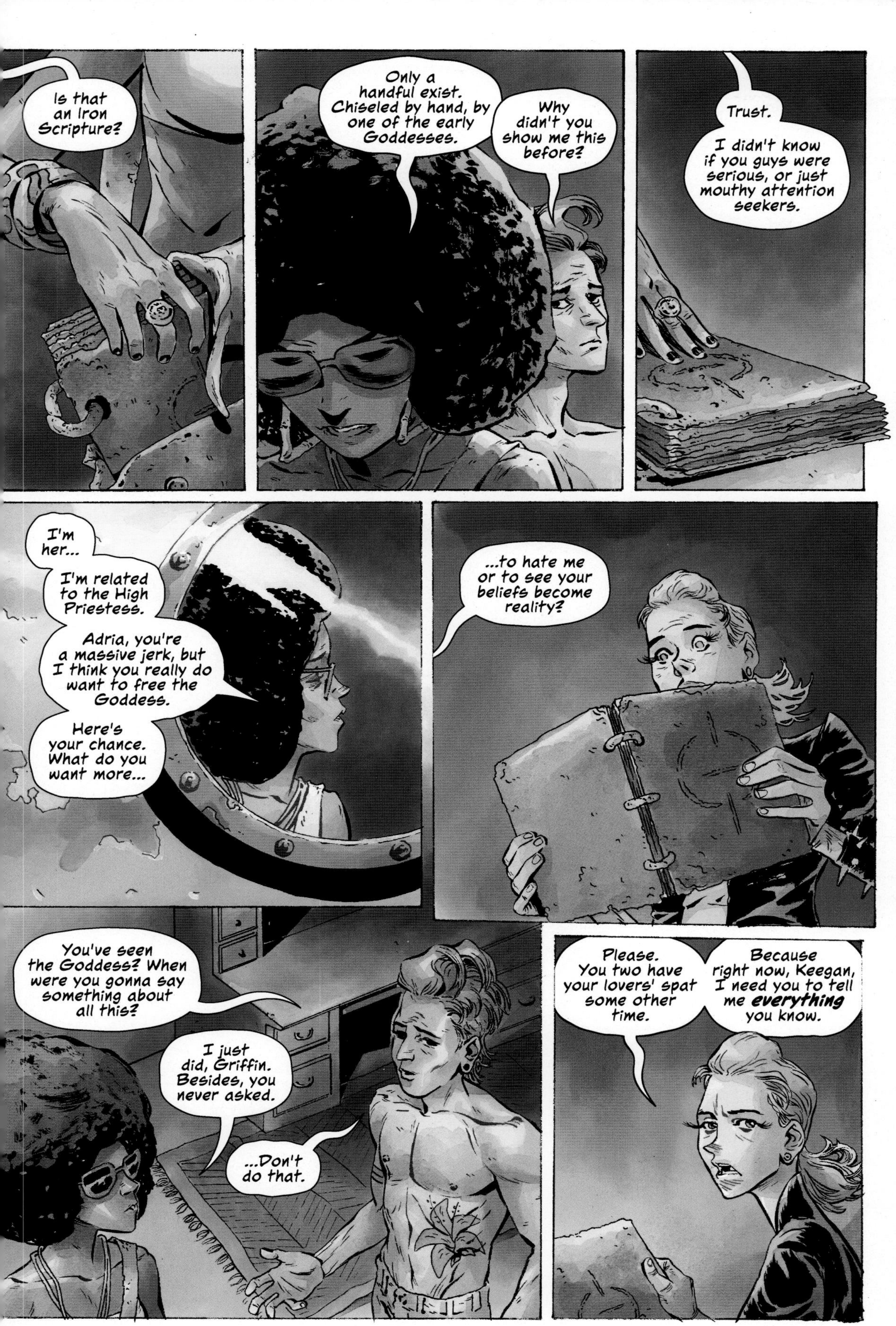
Is that an Iron Scripture?
Only a handful exist. Chiseled by hand, by one of the early Goddesses.
Why didn't you show me this before?
Trust.
I didn't know if you guys were serious, or just mouthy attention seekers.
I'm her...
I'm related to the High Priestess.
Adria, you're a massive jerk, but I think you really do want to free the Goddess.
Here's your chance. What do you want more...
...to hate me or to see your beliefs become reality?
You've seen the Goddess? When were you gonna say something about all this?
I just did, Griffin. Besides, you never asked.
...Don't do that.
Please. You two have your lovers' spat some other time.
Because right now, Keegan, I need you to tell me ***everything*** you know.

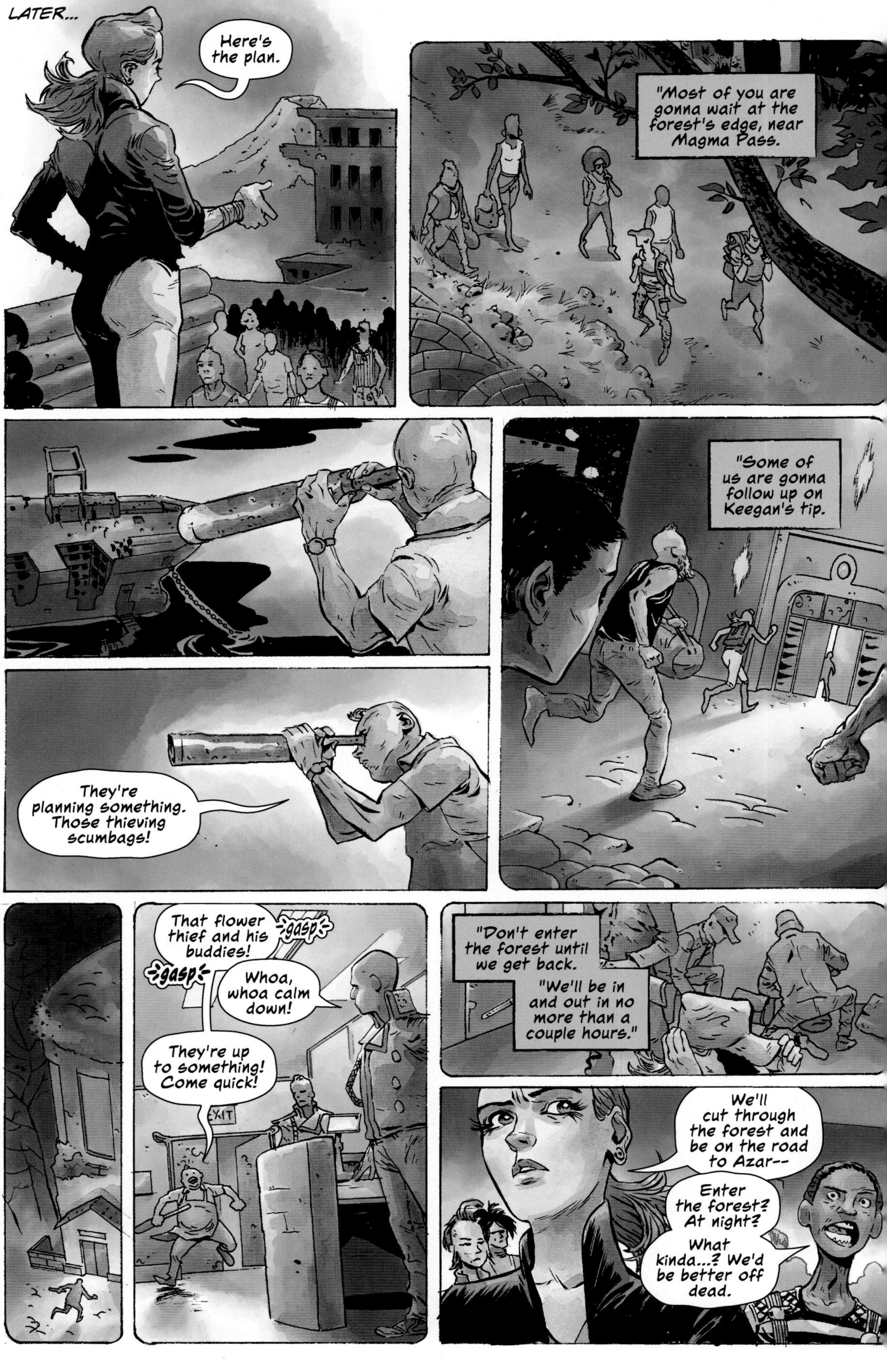
LATER...
Here's the plan.
"Most of you are gonna wait at the forest's edge, near Magma Pass.
"Some of us are gonna follow up on Keegan's tip.
They're planning something. Those thieving scumbags!
That flower thief and his buddies!
gasp
gasp
Whoa, whoa calm down!
They're up to something! Come quick!
EXIT
"Don't enter the forest until we get back.
"We'll be in and out in no more than a couple hours."
We'll cut through the forest and be on the road to Azar--
Enter the forest? At night?
What kinda...? We'd be better off dead.

If Keegan is right, tonight we'll walk under the protection of the Most High.

We'll have nothing to fear.

Her footsteps will light the dark and treacherous path.

Praise be!

But if Keegan's plan is some kind of trap...well...not even a goddess will be able to save *her.*

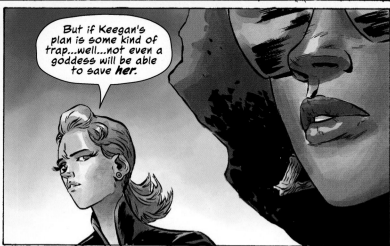

Concentrate on not messing up your end of this, and we'll be just fine.

Griffin, you're coming with us.

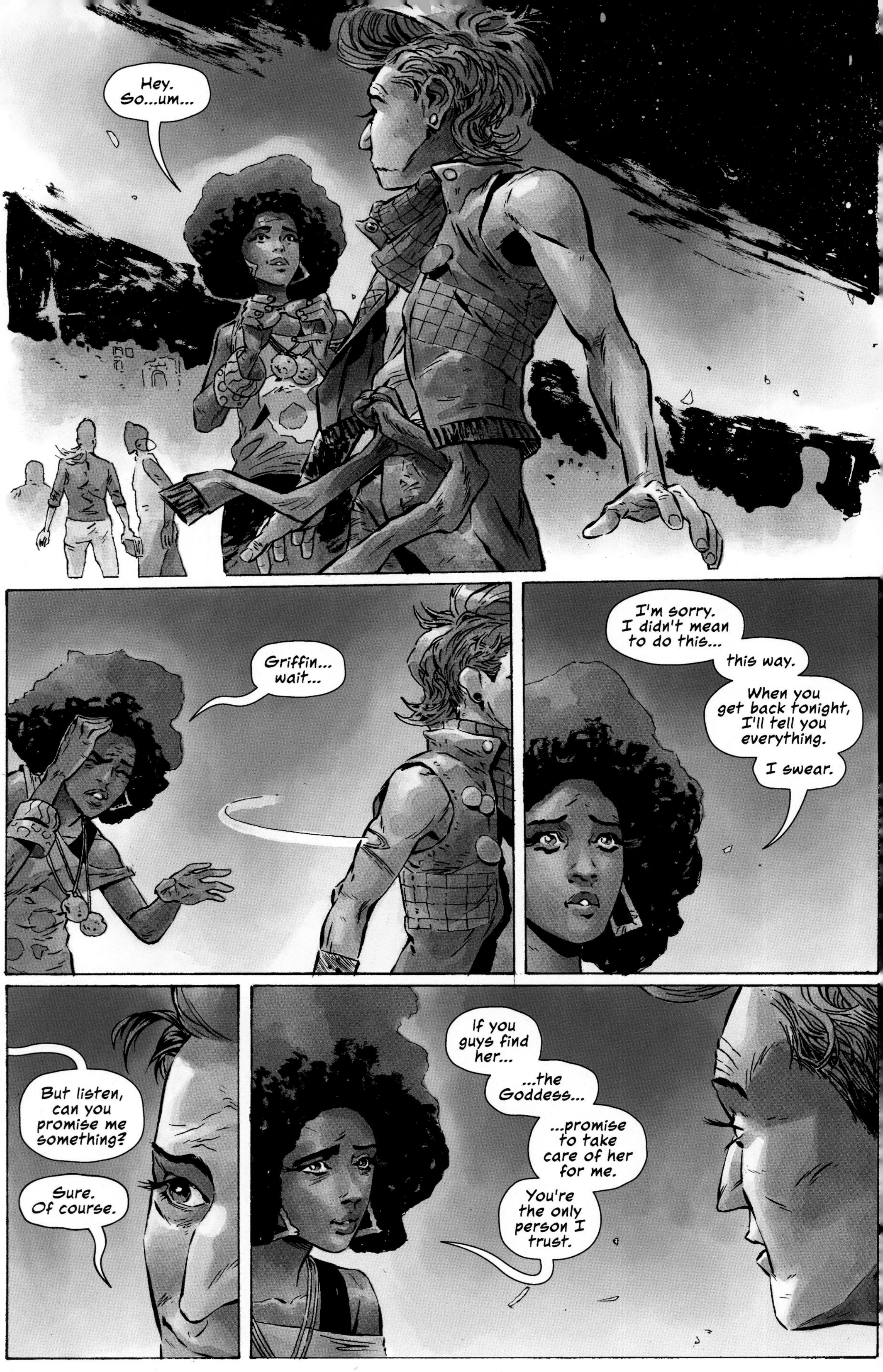
Hey. So...um...
Griffin... wait...
I'm sorry. I didn't mean to do this...
this way.
When you get back tonight, I'll tell you everything.
I swear.
But listen, can you promise me something?
Sure. Of course.
If you guys find her...
...the Goddess...
...promise to take care of her for me.
You're the only person I trust.

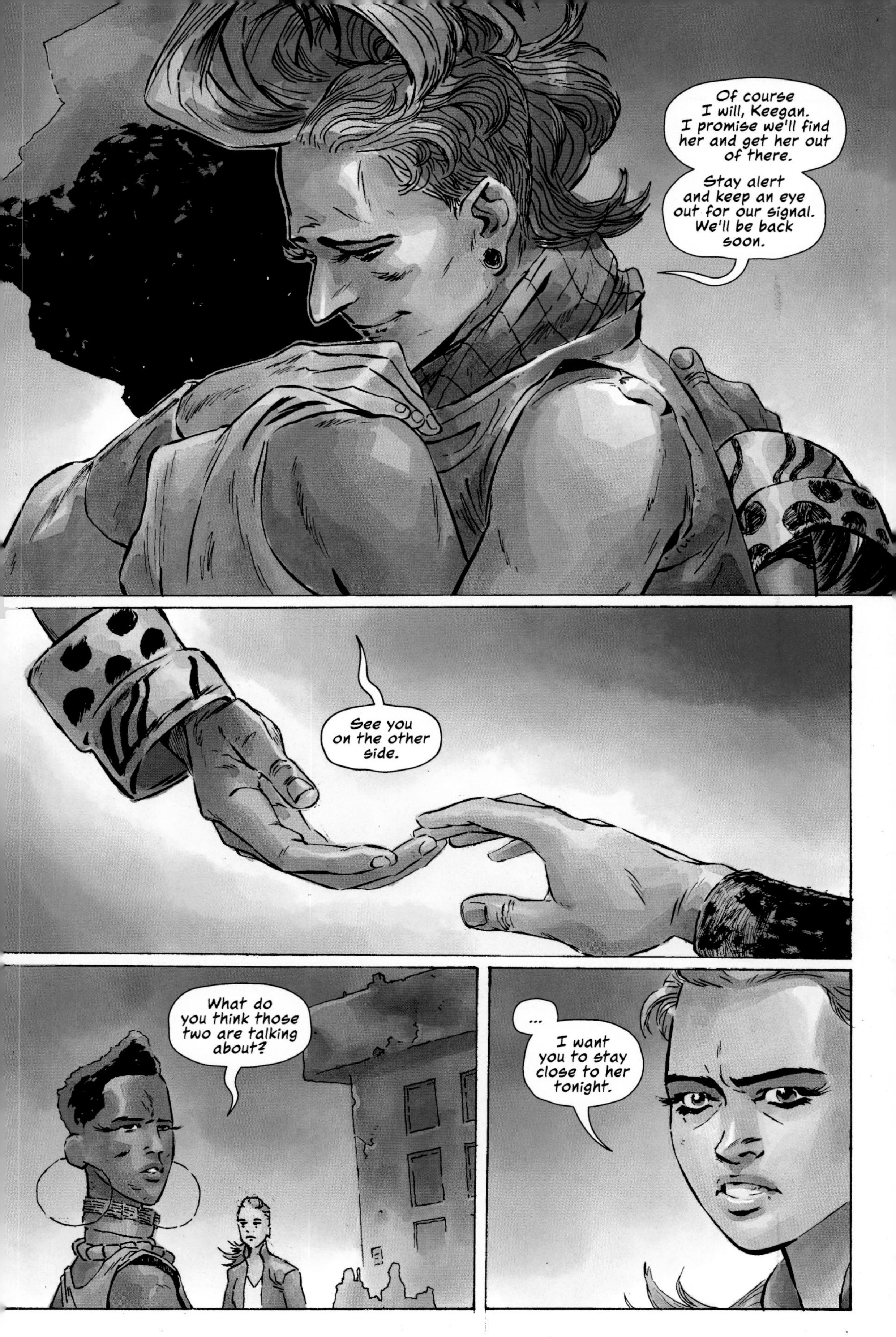
Of course I will, Keegan. I promise we'll find her and get her out of there.
Stay alert and keep an eye out for our signal. We'll be back soon.
See you on the other side.
What do you think those two are talking about?
...
I want you to stay close to her tonight.

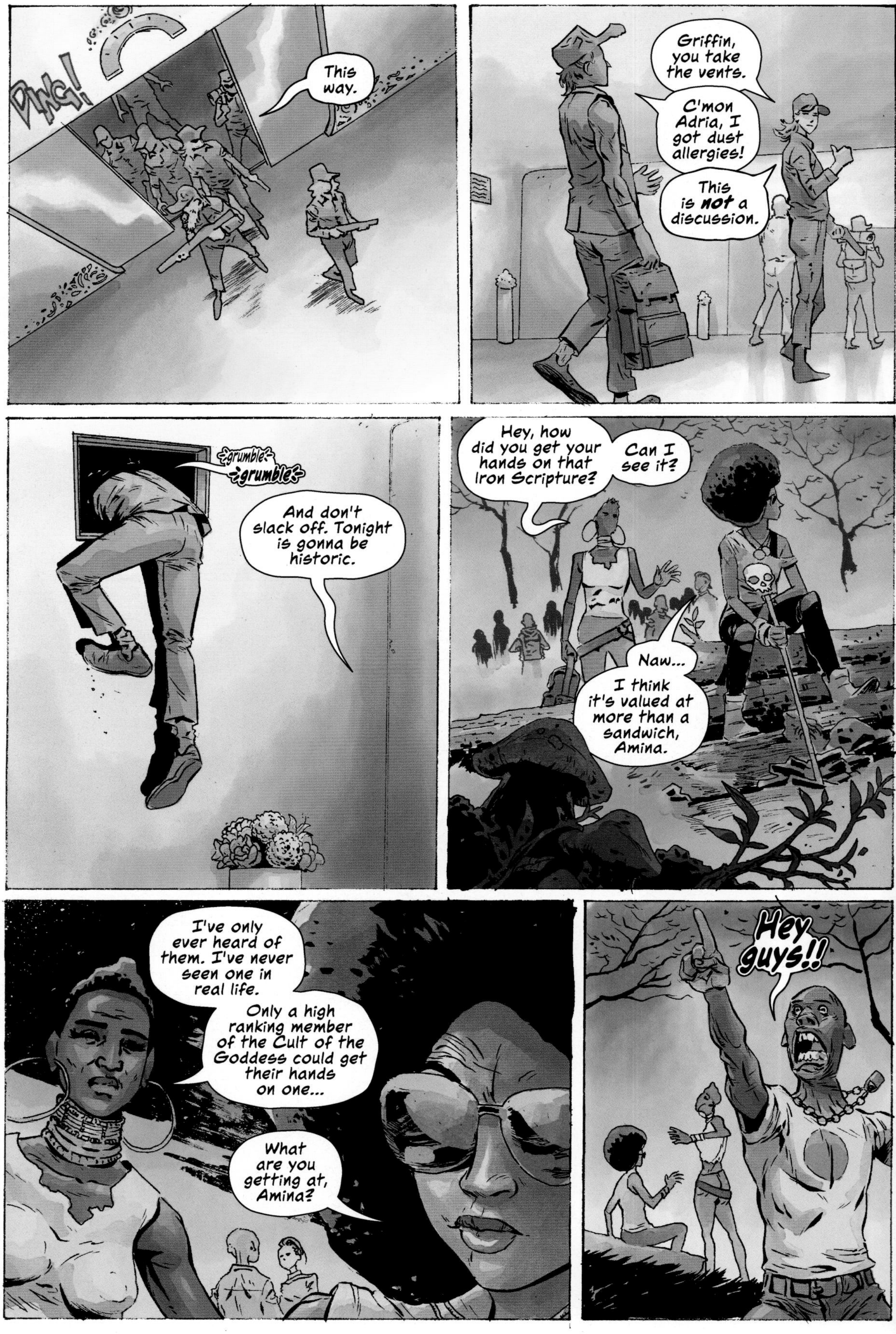
DING!
This way.
Griffin, you take the vents.
C'mon Adria, I got dust allergies!
This is **not** a discussion.
grumble
grumble
And don't slack off. Tonight is gonna be historic.
Hey, how did you get your hands on that Iron Scripture?
Can I see it?
Naw... I think it's valued at more than a sandwich, Amina.
I've only ever heard of them. I've never seen one in real life.
Only a high ranking member of the Cult of the Goddess could get their hands on one...
What are you getting at, Amina?
Hey guys!!

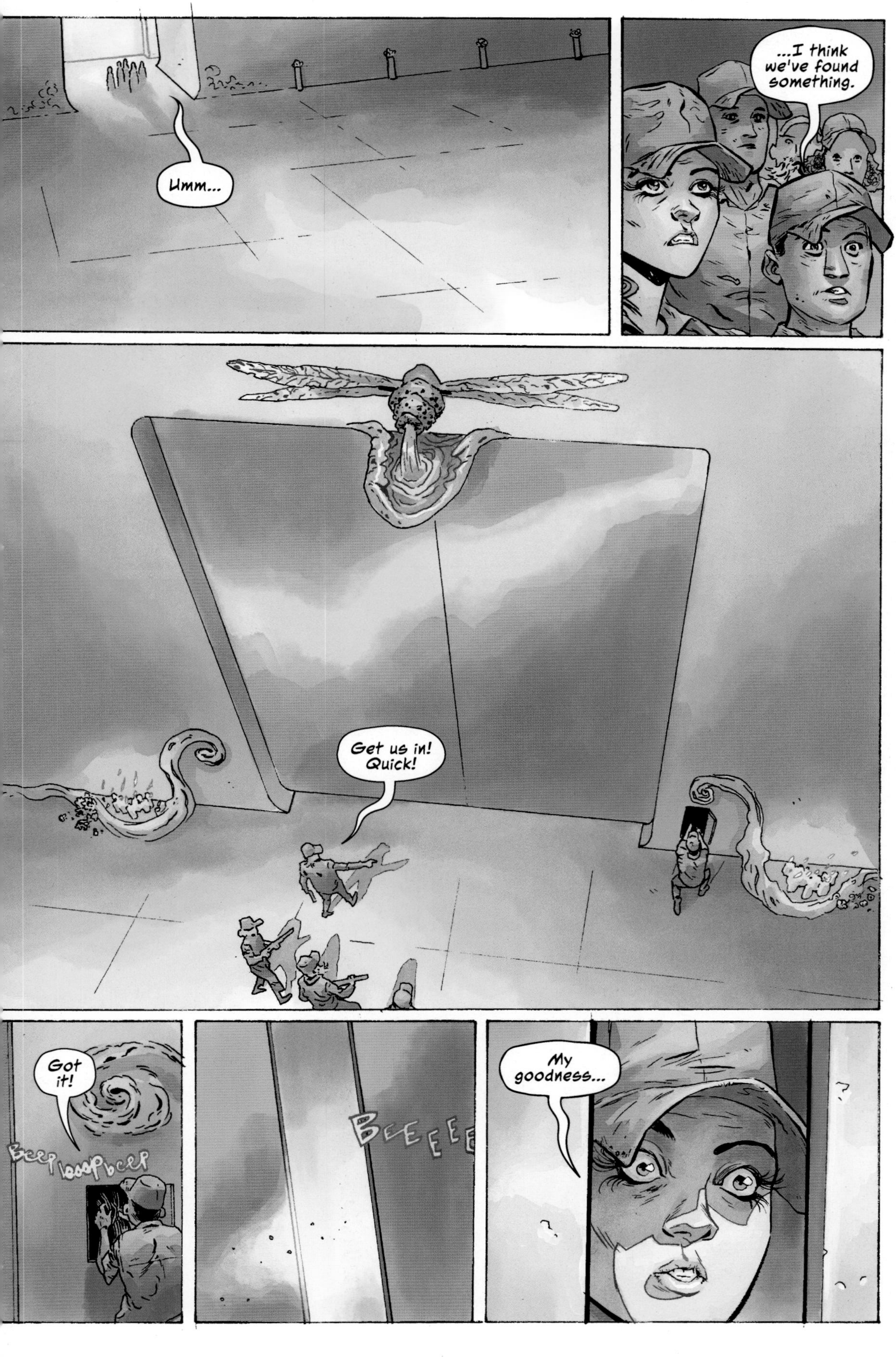
Umm...
...I think we've found something.
Get us in! Quick!
Got it!
Beep boop beep
BEEEEE
My goodness...

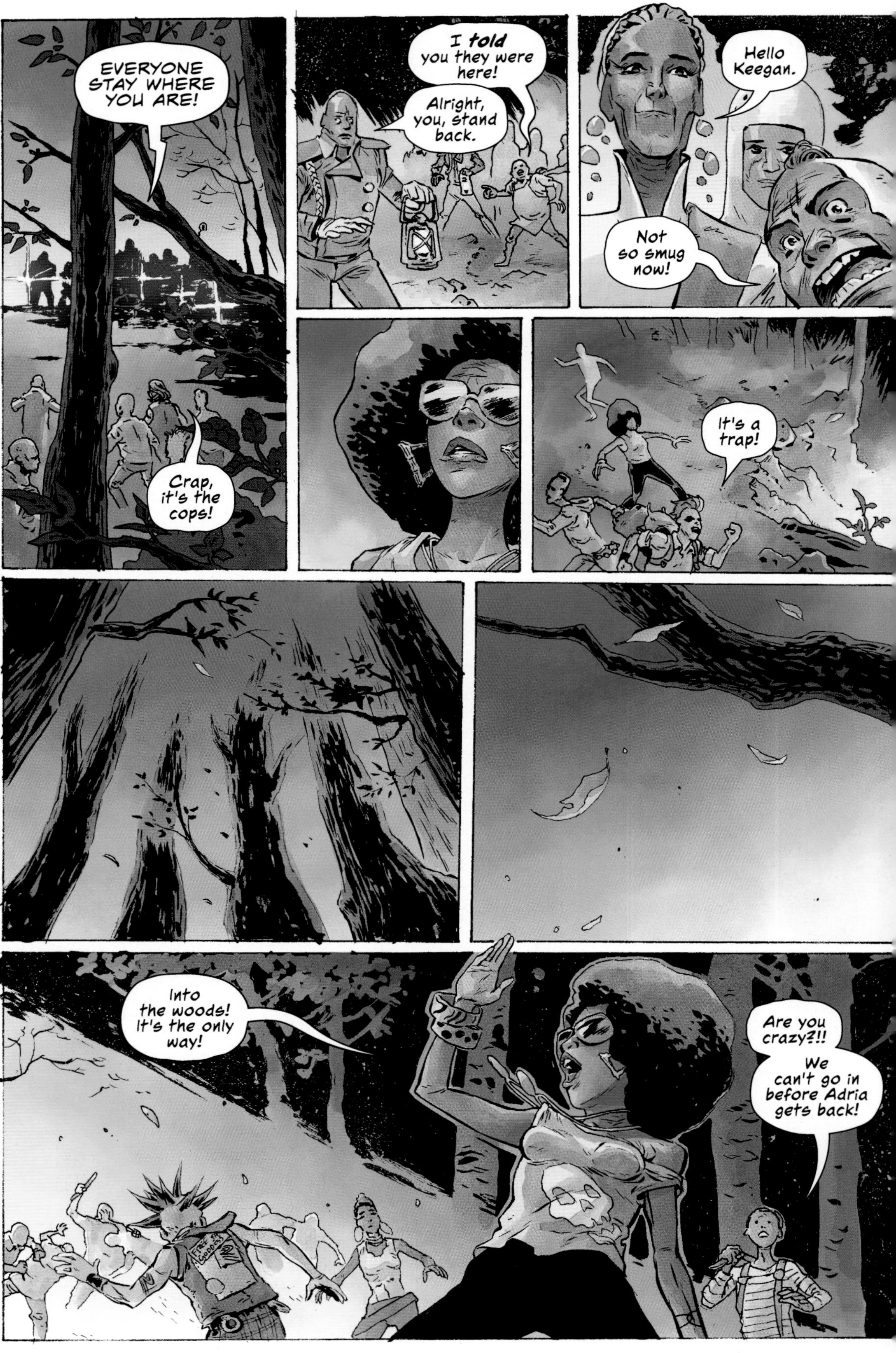
EVERYONE STAY WHERE YOU ARE!
Crap, it's the cops!
I told you they were here!
Alright, you, stand back.
Hello Keegan.
Not so smug now!
It's a trap!
Into the woods! It's the only way!
Are you crazy?!!
We can't go in before Adria gets back!

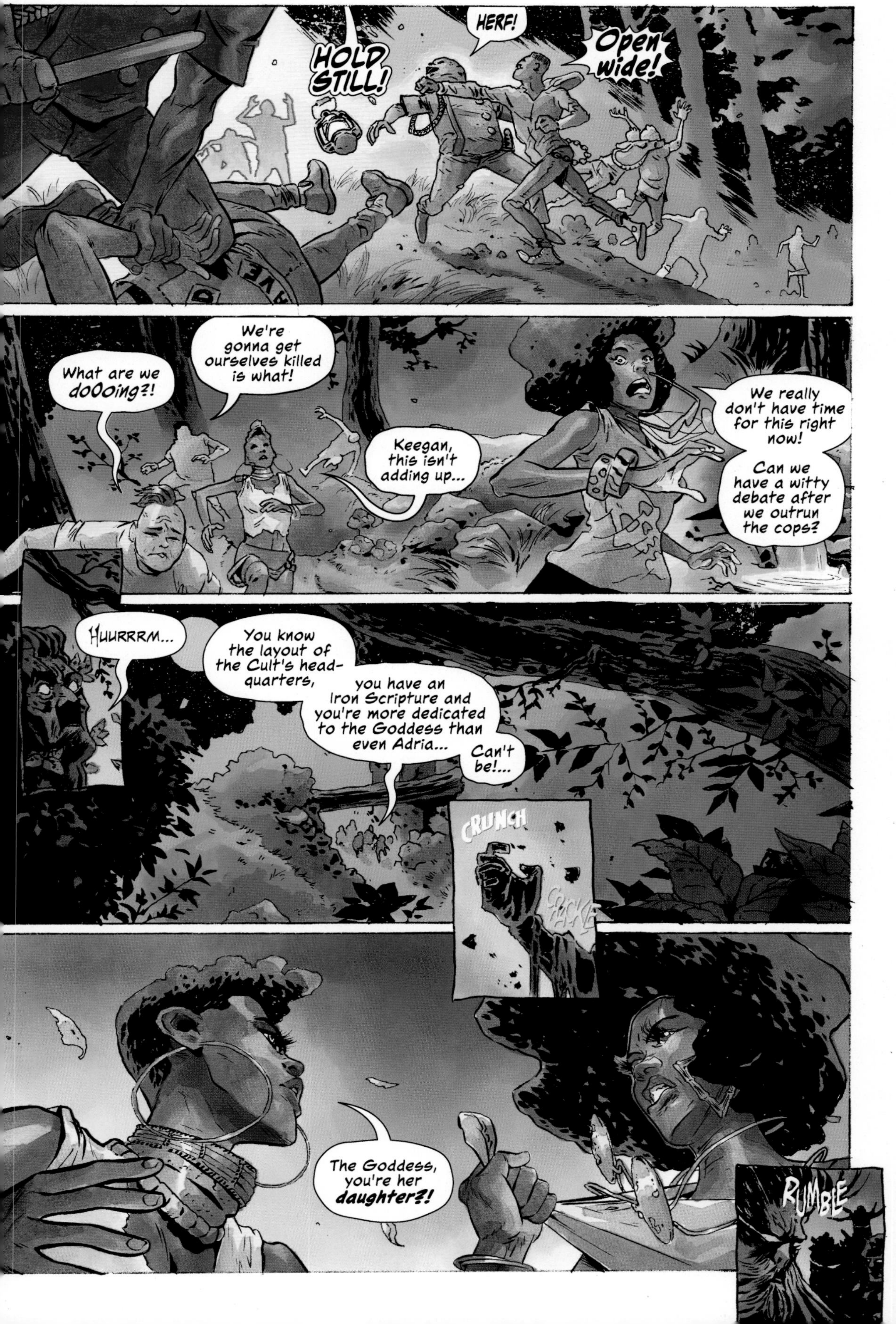
HOLD STILL!
HERF!
Open wide!
What are we doOoing?!
We're gonna get ourselves killed is what!
Keegan, this isn't adding up...
We really don't have time for this right now!
Can we have a witty debate after we outrun the cops?
HUURRRM...
You know the layout of the Cult's head-quarters,
you have an Iron Scripture and you're more dedicated to the Goddess than even Adria...
Can't be!...
CRUNCH
CRACKLE
The Goddess, you're her daughter?!
RUMBLE

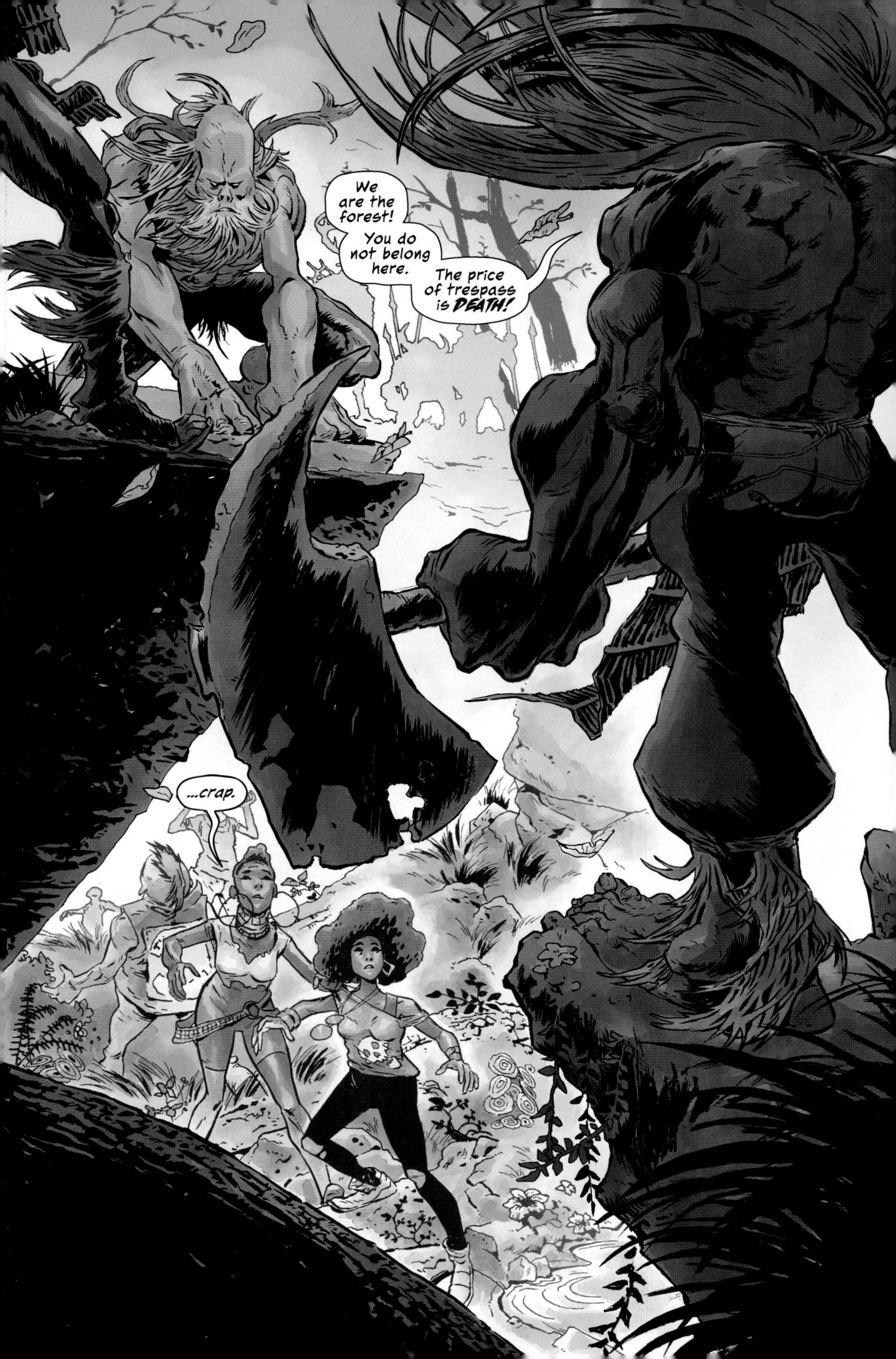
We are the forest!
You do not belong here.
The price of trespass is DEATH!
...crap.

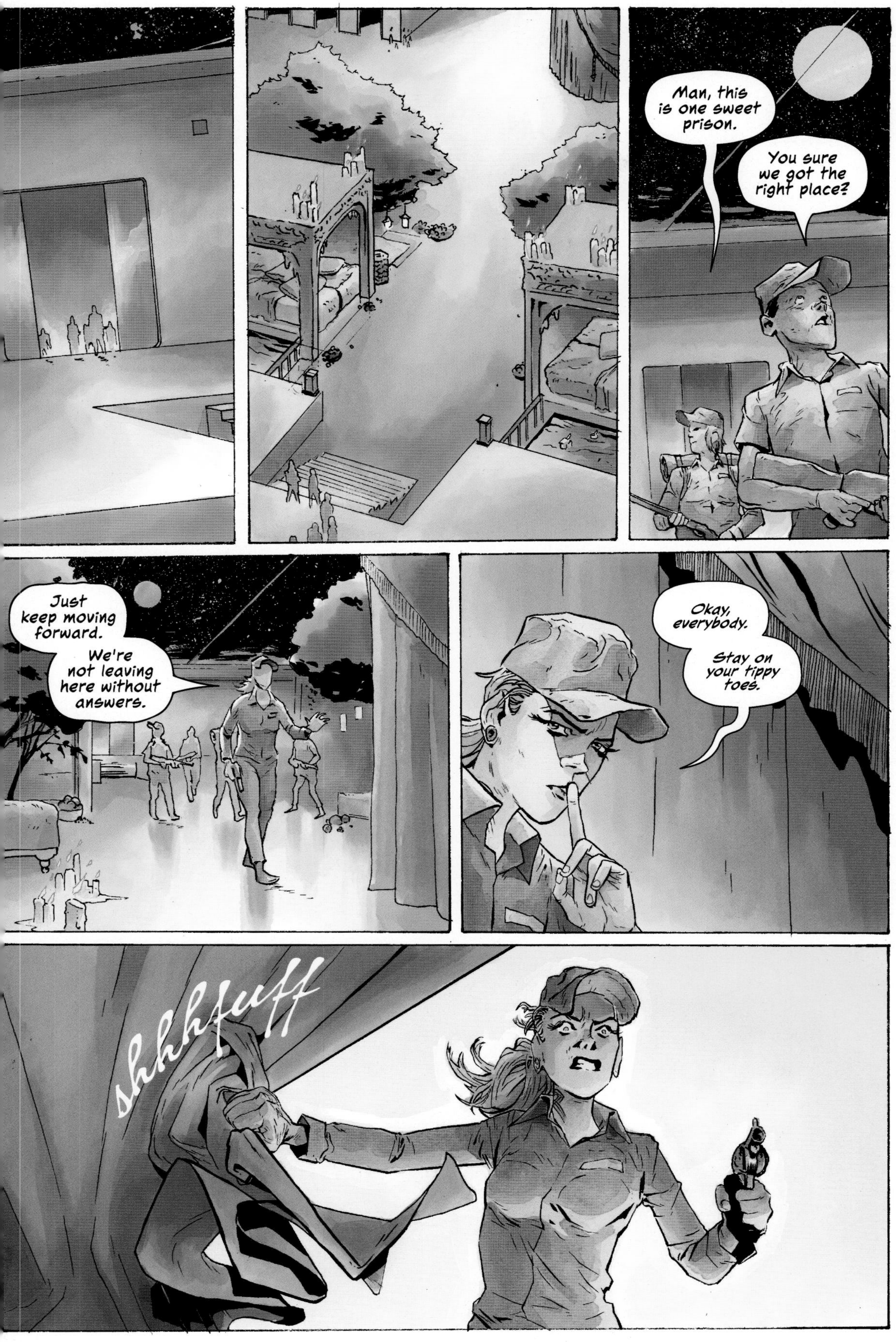
Man, this is one sweet prison.
You sure we got the right place?
Just keep moving forward.
We're not leaving here without answers.
Okay, everybody.
Stay on your tippy toes.
shhhfuff

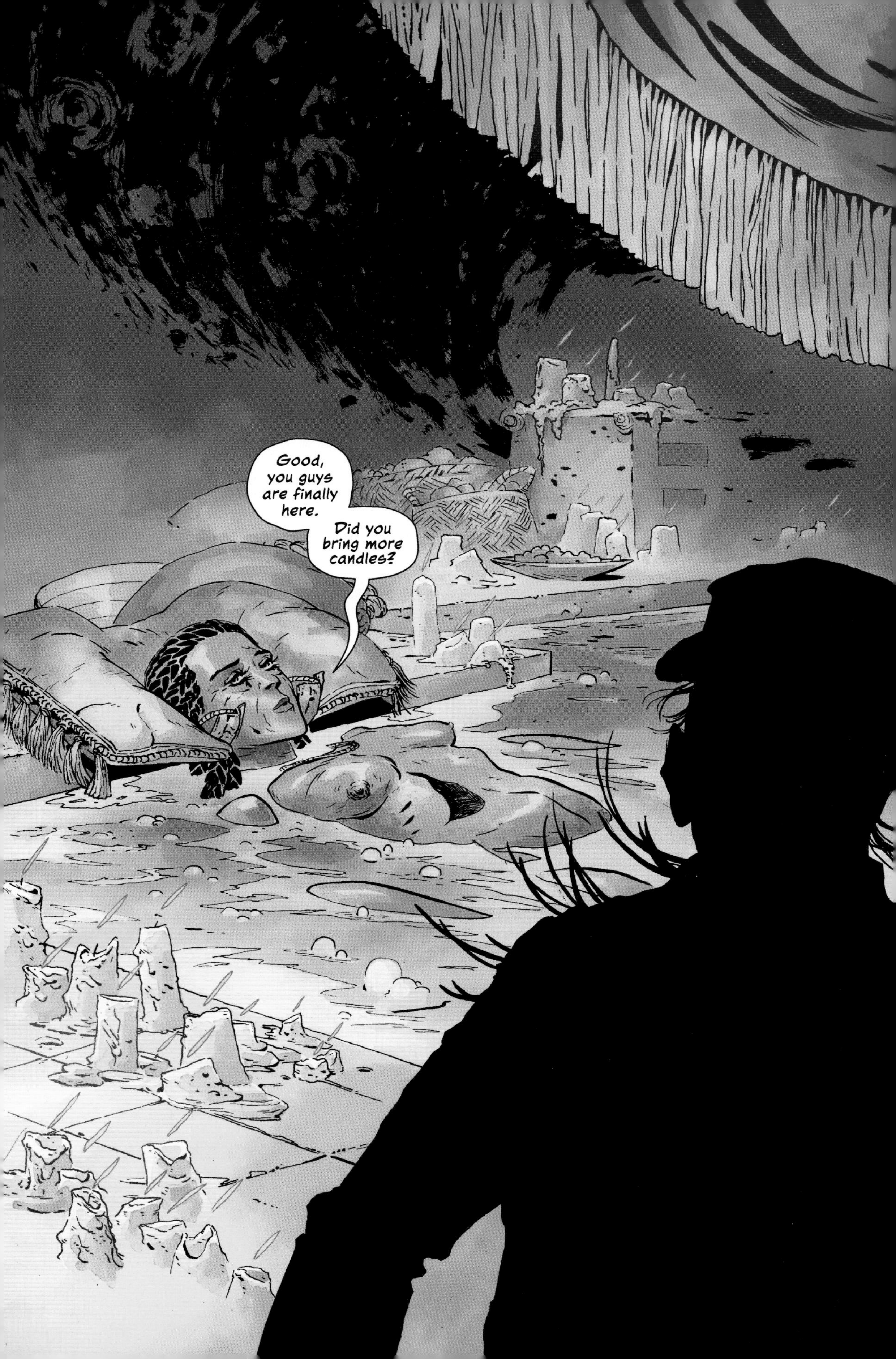
Good, you guys are finally here.
Did you bring more candles?

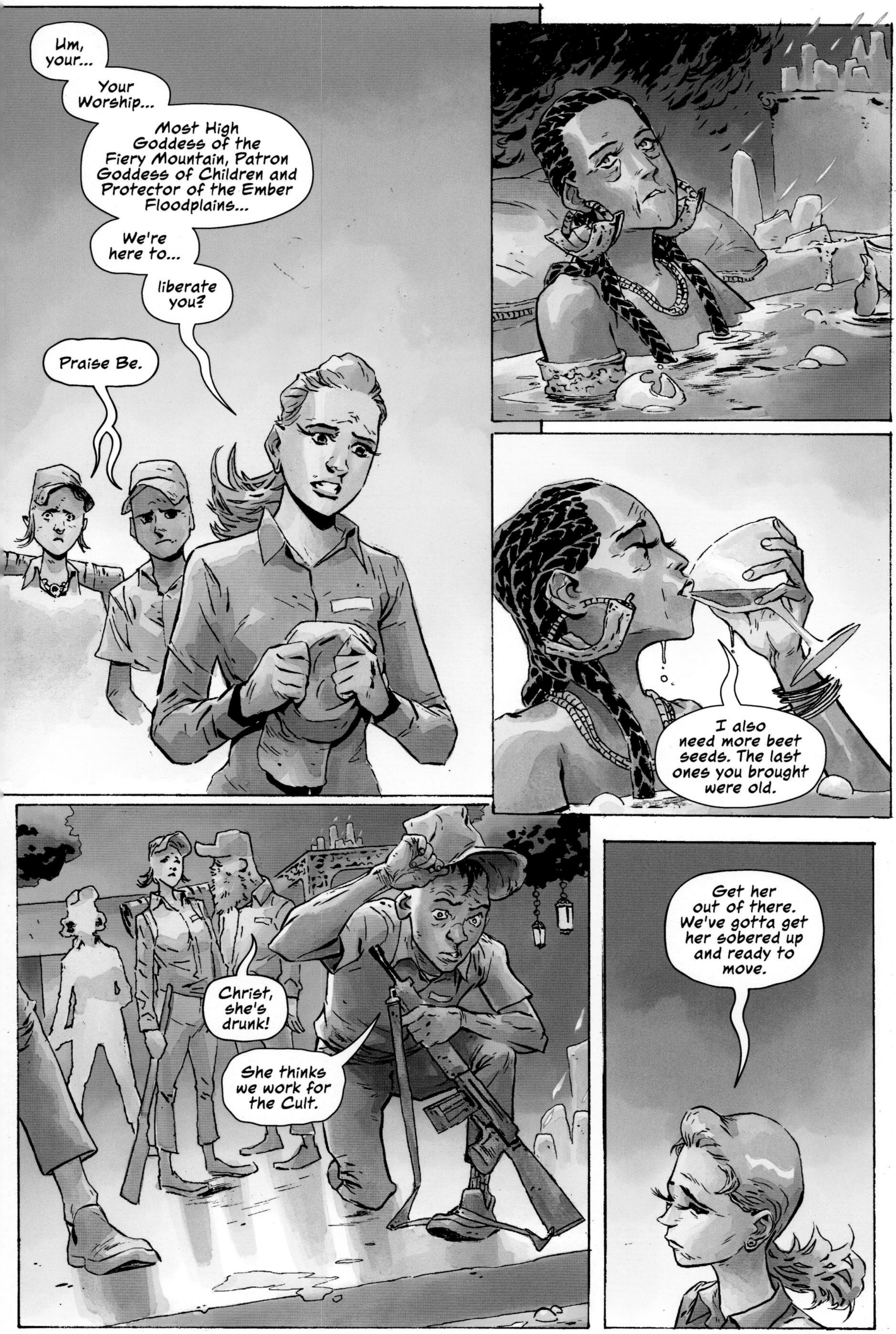
Um, your...
Your Worship...
Most High Goddess of the Fiery Mountain, Patron Goddess of Children and Protector of the Ember Floodplains...
We're here to...
liberate you?
Praise Be.
I also need more beet seeds. The last ones you brought were old.
Christ, she's drunk!
She thinks we work for the Cult.
Get her out of there. We've gotta get her sobered up and ready to move.

Grab her robe.

What the hell are they doing?

Don't! Don't *touch* her!

That's a nice Goddess. We'll have you out of here in no time.

Where did you say you were taking my Keegan? When is she coming back?

Where did you take her?

Foooooooom

Foooooooom

Moooom

Argh!

Bertie!

I'll teach you some respect.

How dare you try and lay hands on me.

You monster!

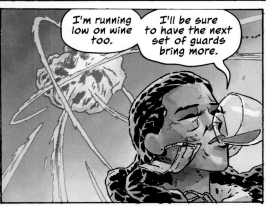

I'm running low on wine too.

I'll be sure to have the next set of guards bring more.

YEEARRRGGH!

FW...OOSH!

Run!

Oh god, stop! Everybody stop!

She killed Tommy!

BOOM

BOOM

Hurk!

SHRRRREEDD

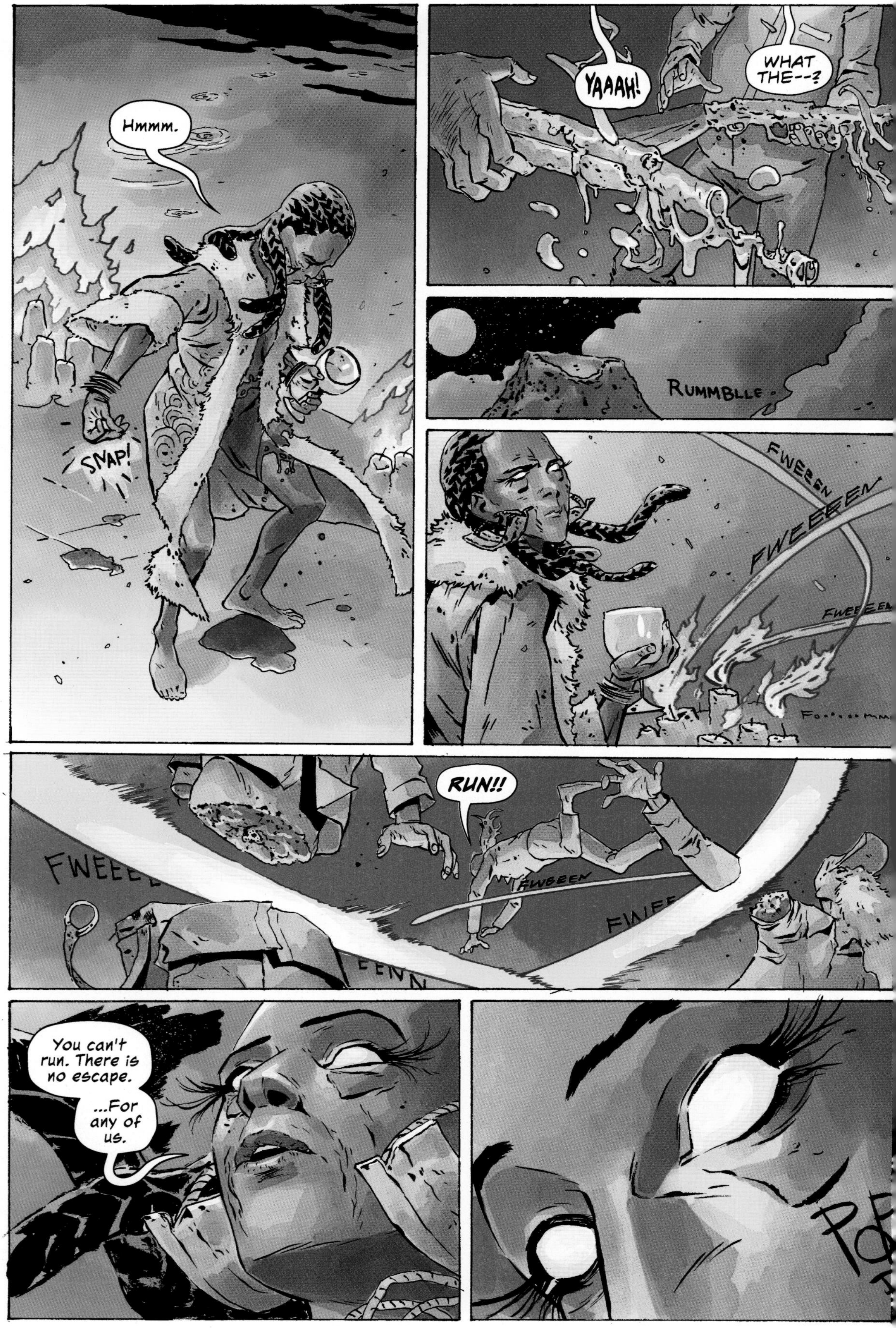
Hmmm.
SNAP!
YAAAH!
WHAT THE--?
RUMMBLLE
FWEEEEN
RUN!!
FWEEEN
You can't run. There is no escape.
...For any of us.

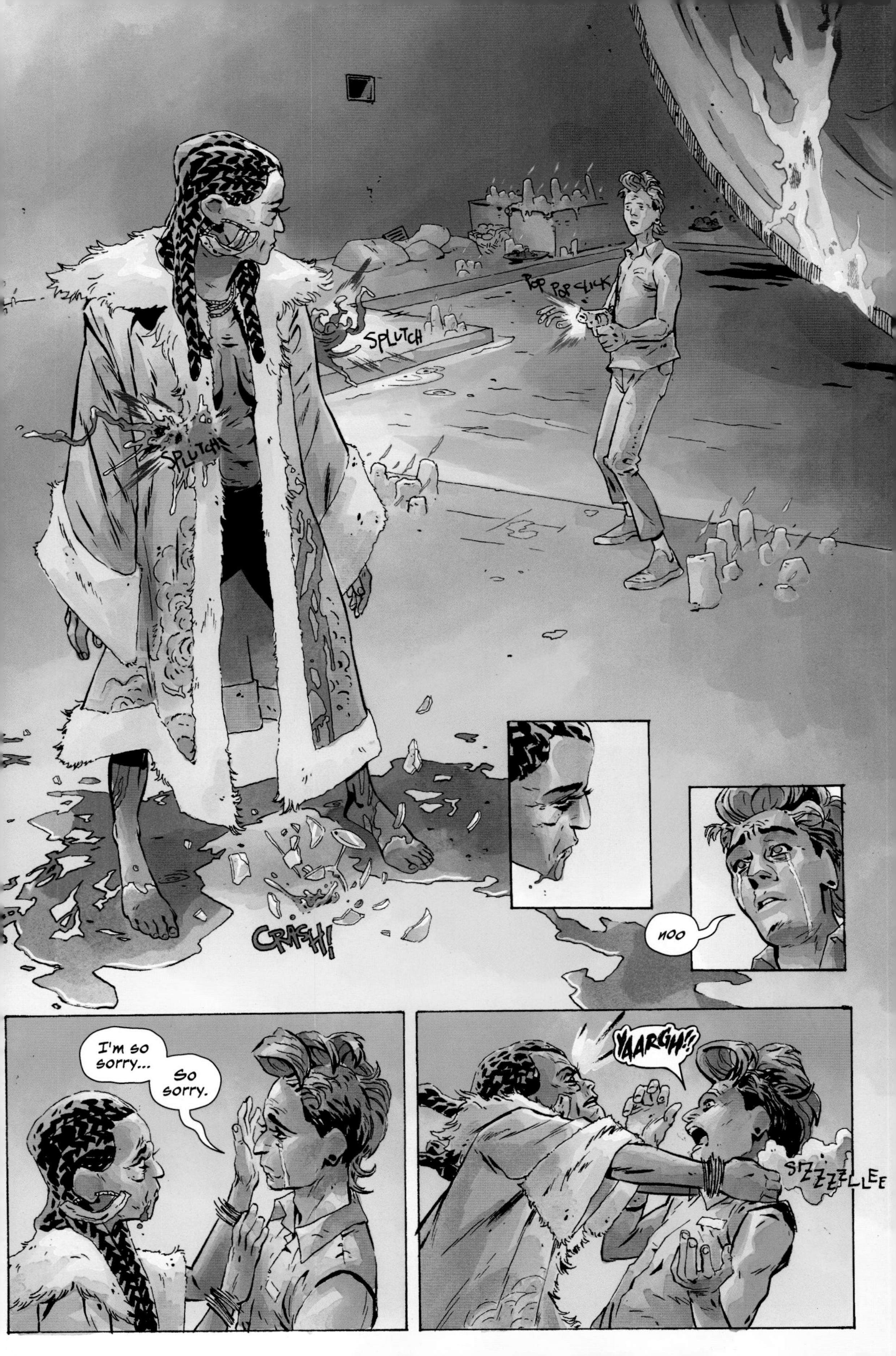

POP POP CLICK
SPLUTCH
SPLUTCH
CRASH!
noo
I'm so sorry...
So sorry.
YAARGH!?
SIZZZZLLEE

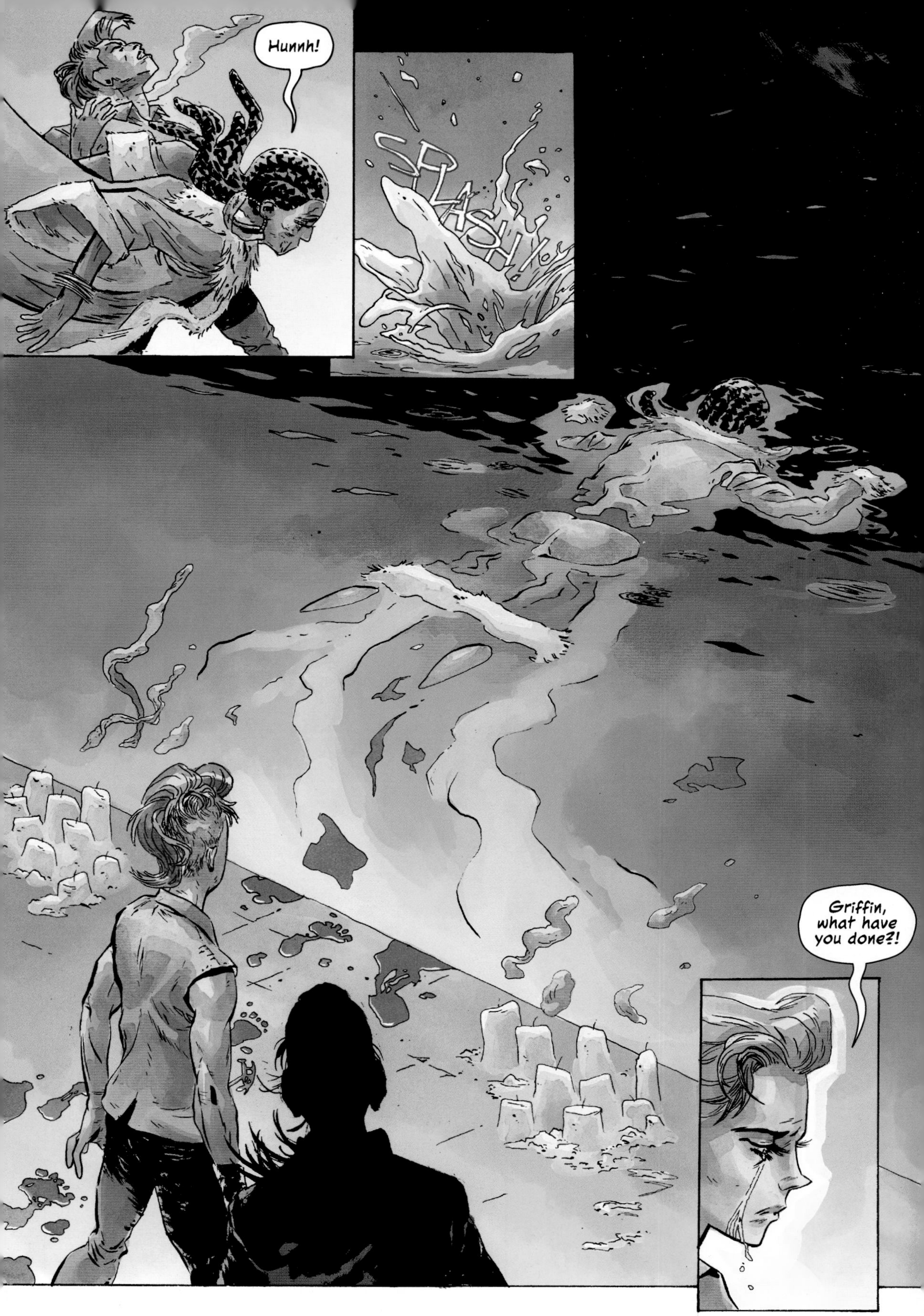

Hunnh!
SPLASH!
Griffin, what have you done?!

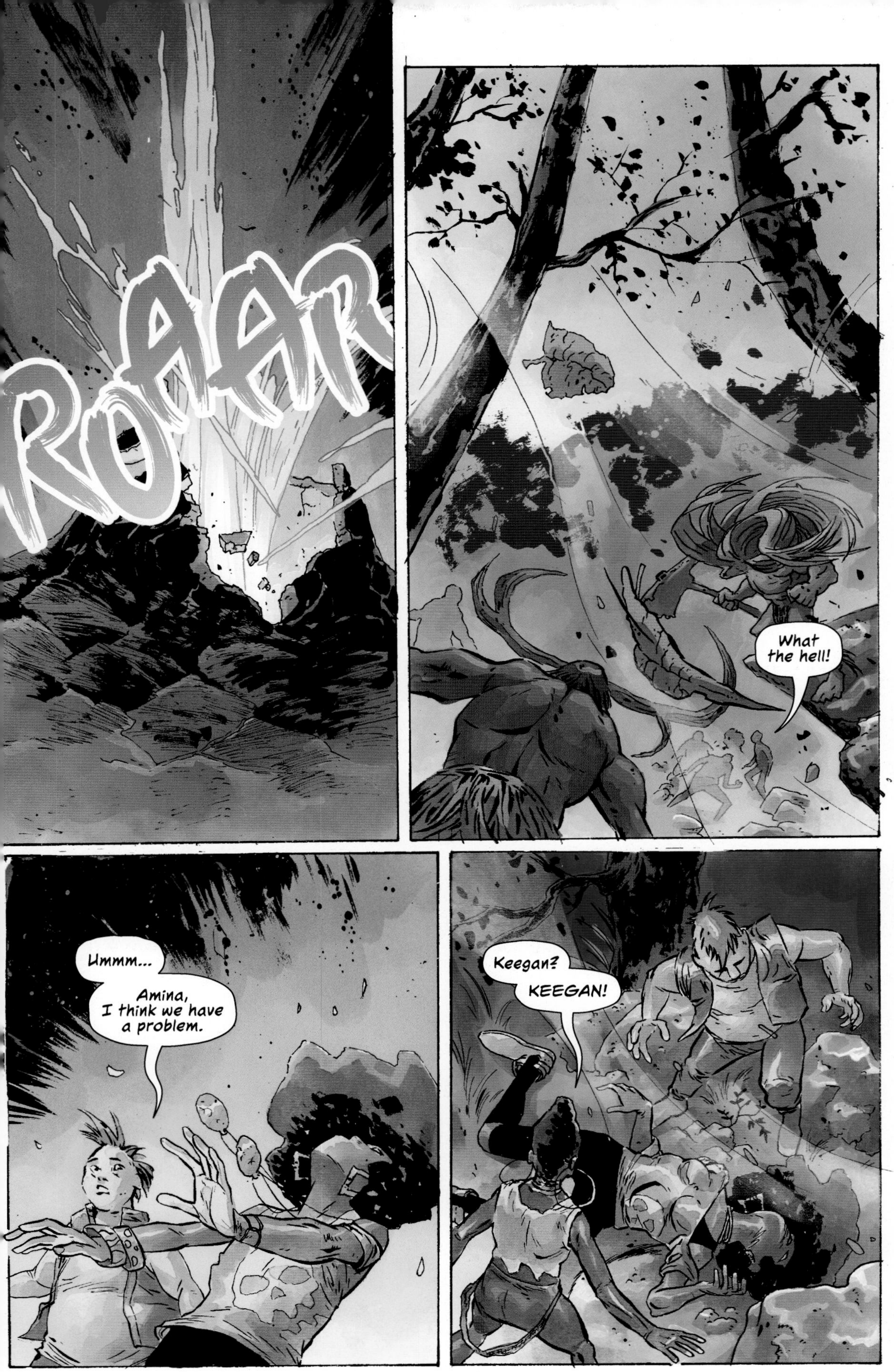
ROAAR
What the hell!
Ummm...
Amina, I think we have a problem.
Keegan?
KEEGAN!

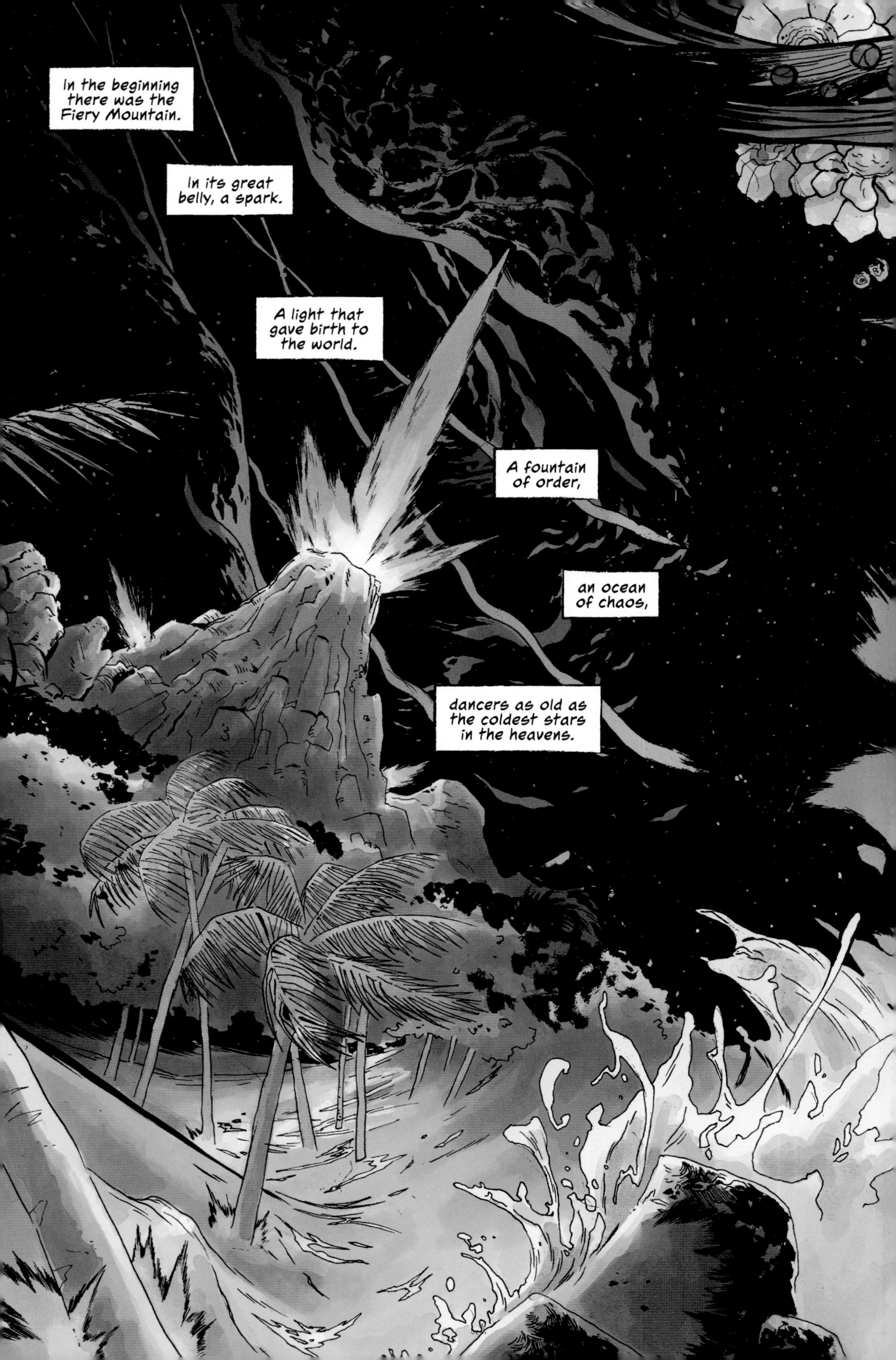
In the beginning there was the Fiery Mountain.
In its great belly, a spark.
A light that gave birth to the world.
A fountain of order,
an ocean of chaos,
dancers as old as the coldest stars in the heavens.

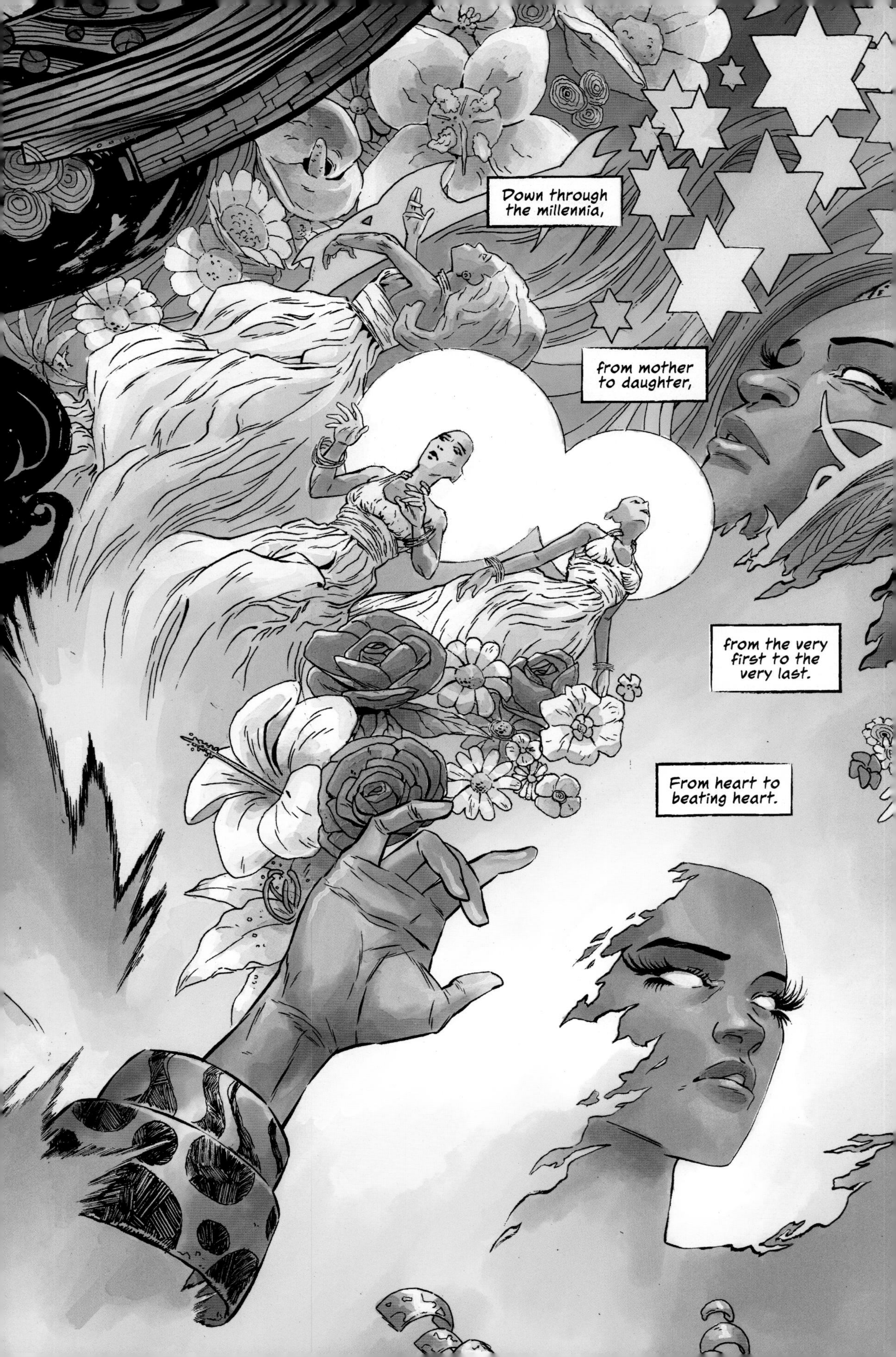
Down through the millennia,
from mother to daughter,
from the very first to the very last.
From heart to beating heart.

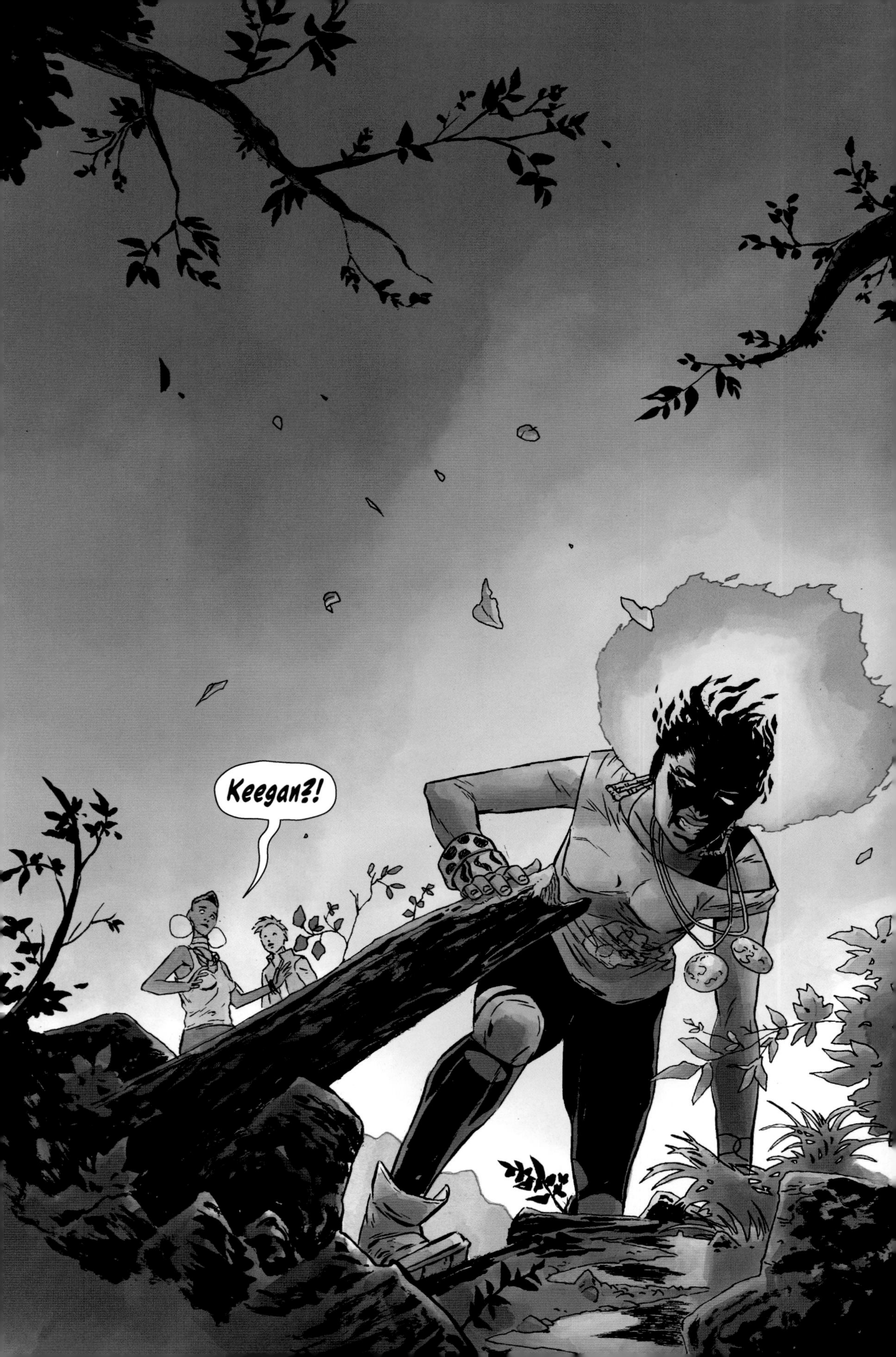
Keegan?!

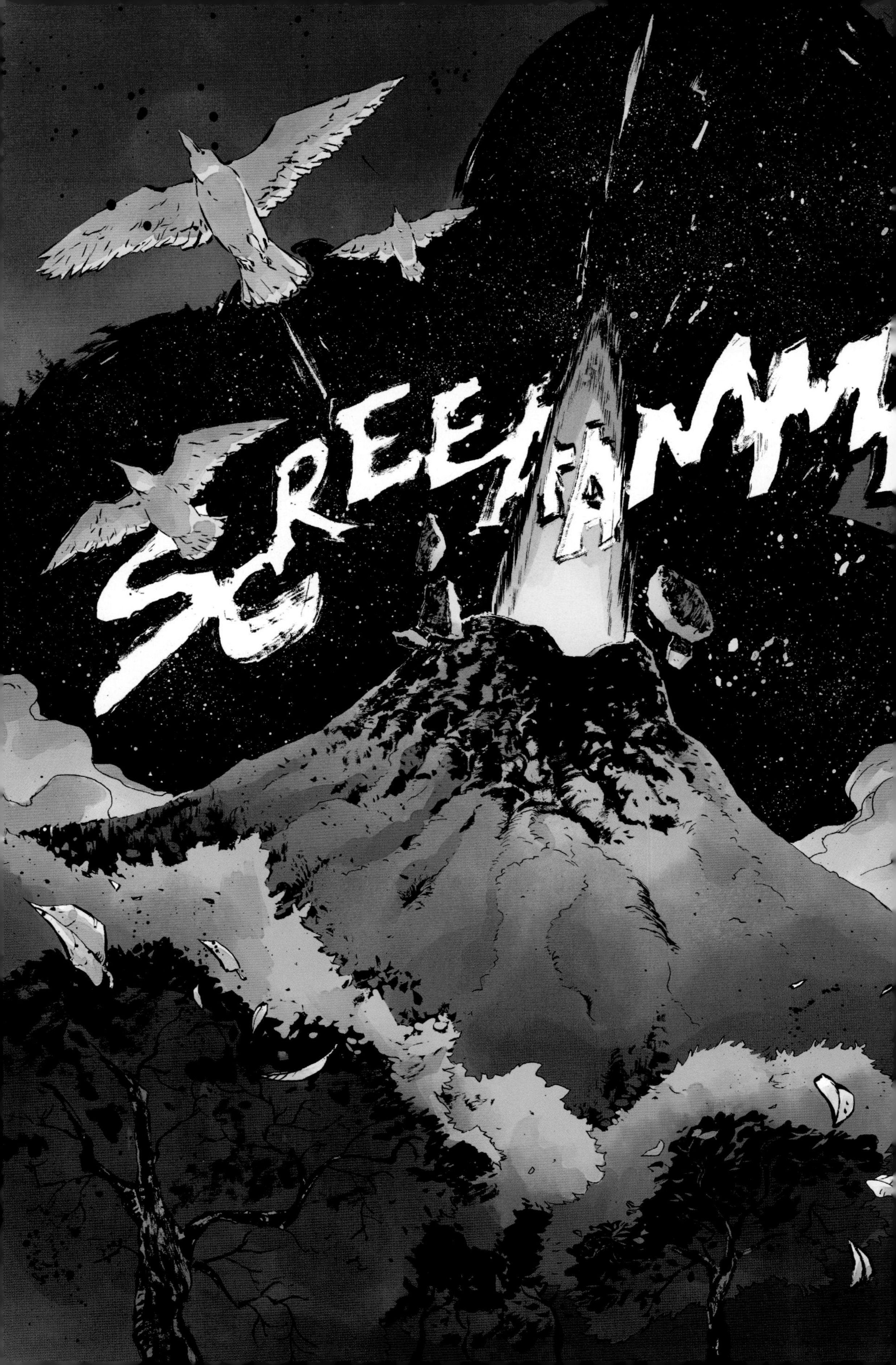
SCREEEAMMM

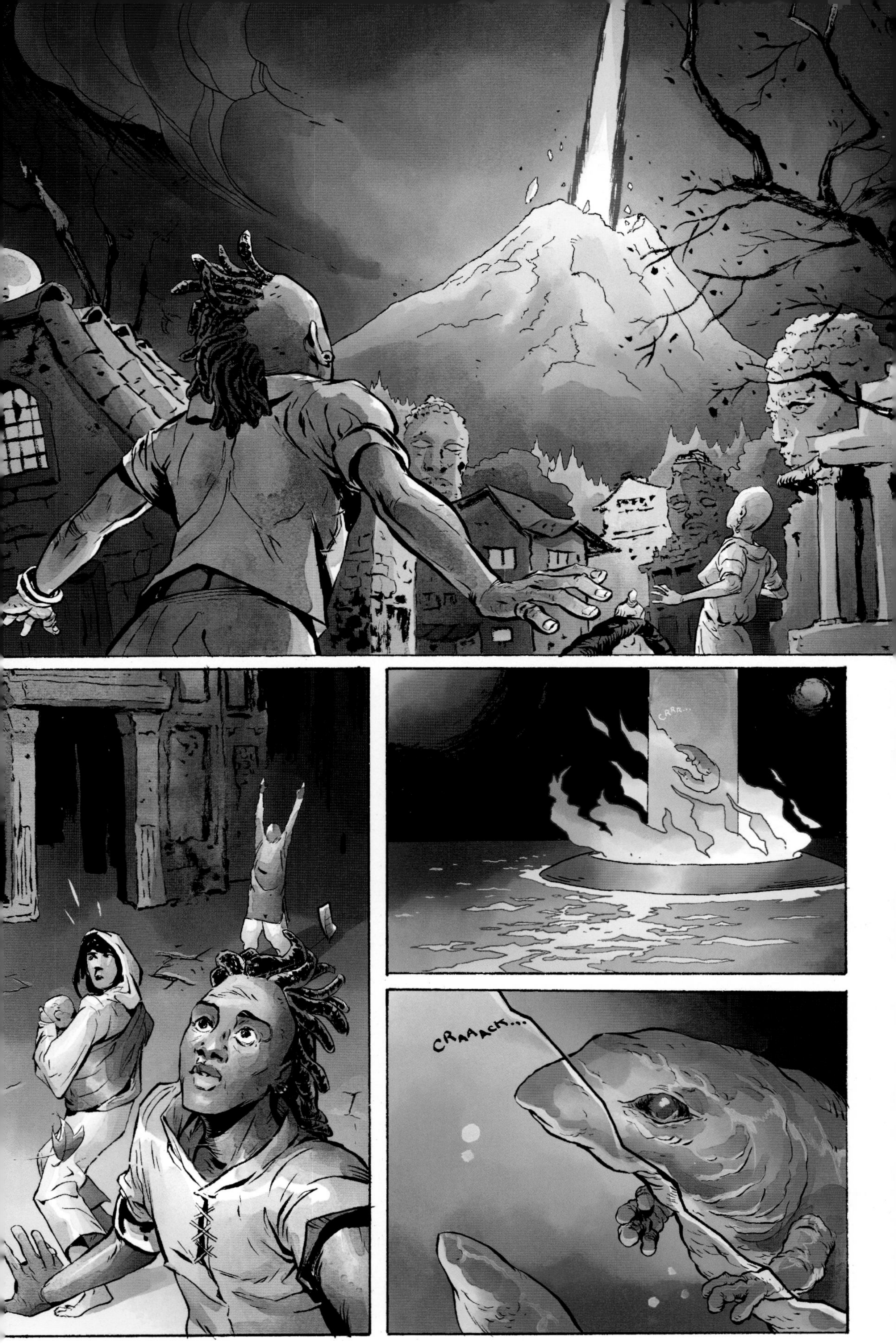
CRRR...
CRAAACK...

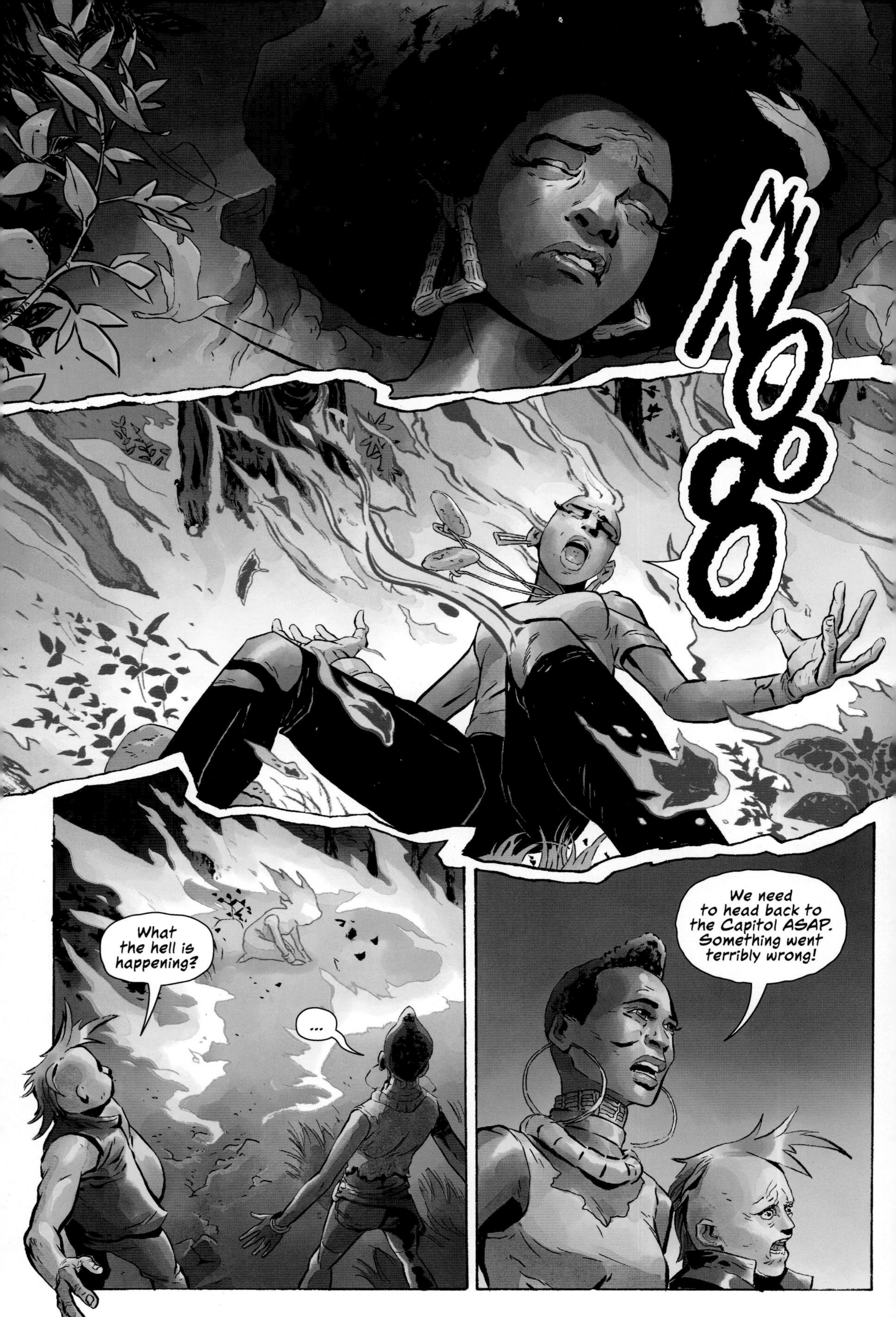
NOOO
What the hell is happening?
...
We need to head back to the Capitol ASAP. Something went terribly wrong!

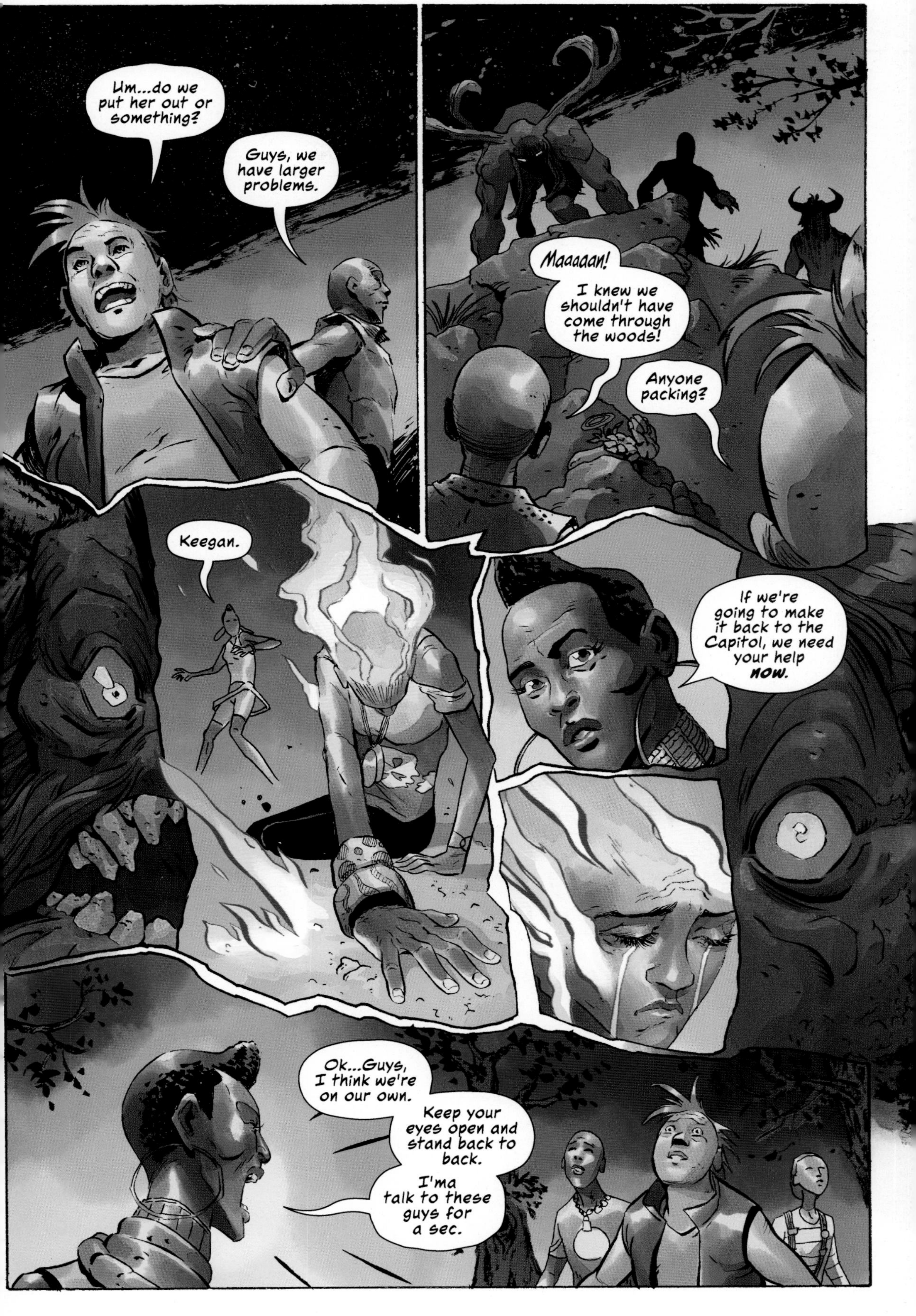
Um...do we put her out or something?
Guys, we have larger problems.
Maaaaan!
I knew we shouldn't have come through the woods!
Anyone packing?
Keegan.
If we're going to make it back to the Capitol, we need your help **NOW.**
Ok...Guys, I think we're on our own.
Keep your eyes open and stand back to back.
I'ma talk to these guys for a sec.

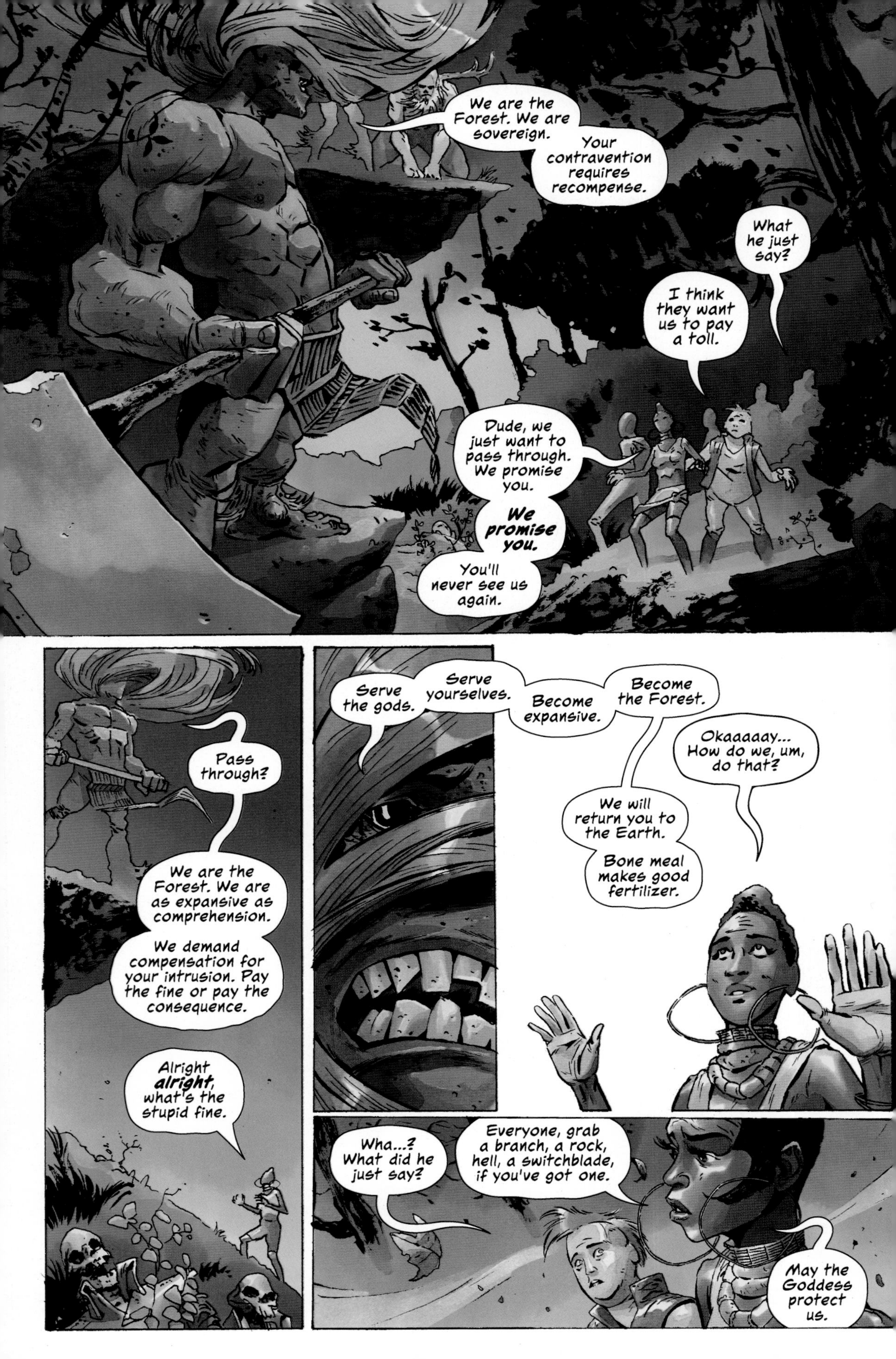
We are the Forest. We are sovereign.
Your contravention requires recompense.
What he just say?
I think they want us to pay a toll.
Dude, we just want to pass through. We promise you.
We promise you.
You'll never see us again.
Pass through?
We are the Forest. We are as expansive as comprehension.
We demand compensation for your intrusion. Pay the fine or pay the consequence.
Alright ***alright***, what's the stupid fine.
Serve the gods.
Serve yourselves.
Become expansive.
Become the Forest.
We will return you to the Earth.
Bone meal makes good fertilizer.
Okaaaaay... How do we, um, do that?
Wha...? What did he just say?
Everyone, grab a branch, a rock, hell, a switchblade, if you've got one.
May the Goddess protect us.

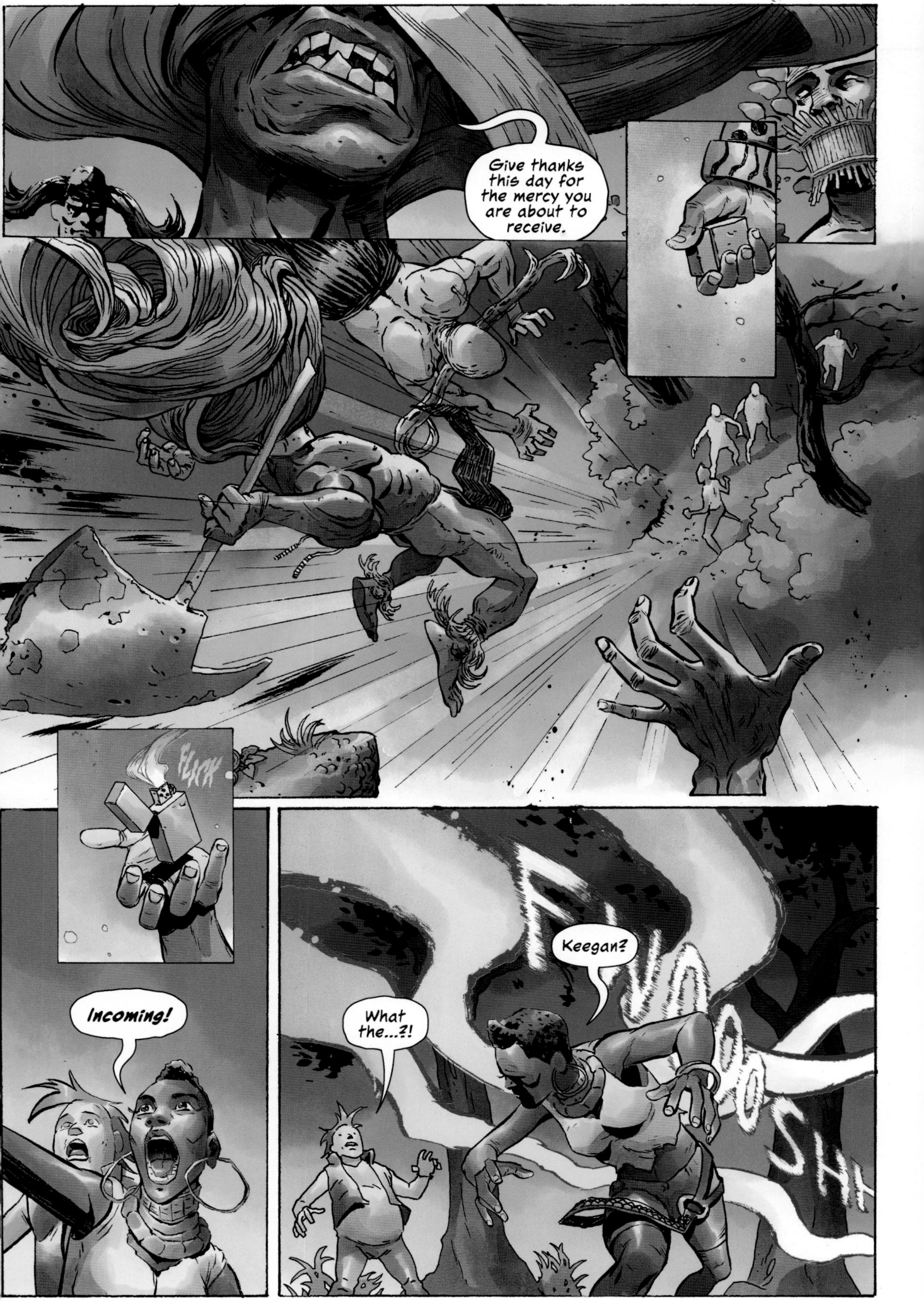
Give thanks this day for the mercy you are about to receive.
FLICK
Incoming!
What the...?!
Keegan?
FWOOOOOSH

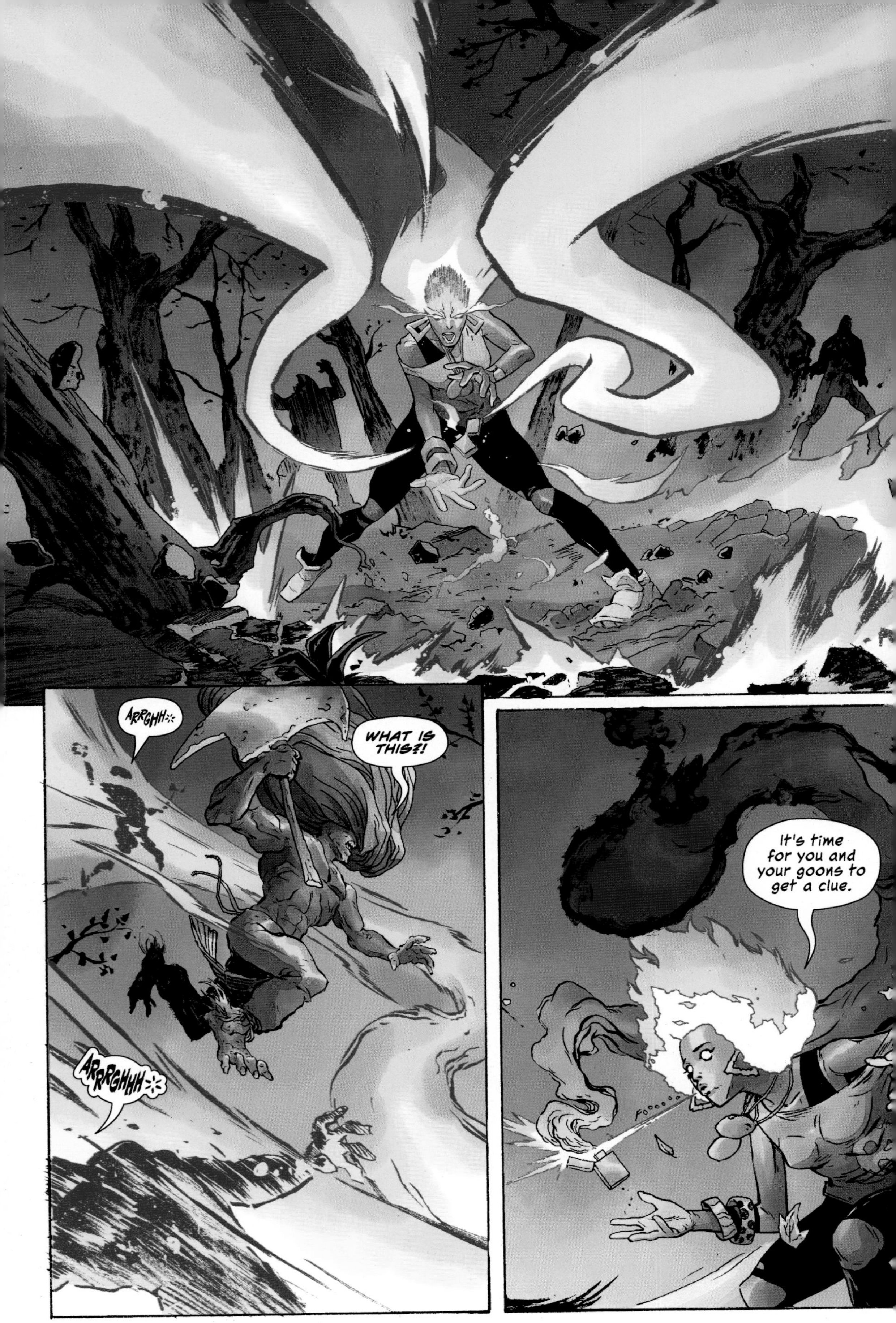
ARRGHH!
WHAT IS THIS?!
ARRRGHHH!
It's time for you and your goons to get a clue.
FOOOOO

ARRGH

WAUGHH

PooOF

We won't have any problems making it back to the Capitol now.

We can get to the bottom of what...

may have... happened...

All hail the goddess of the Fiery Mountain.

Praise be!!

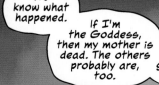

We know what happened.

If I'm the Goddess, then my mother is dead. The others probably are, too.

We can't go back to the Capitol.

The prophecy says the Goddess has to return to Azar, to the mountain...

I have to go to the mountain.

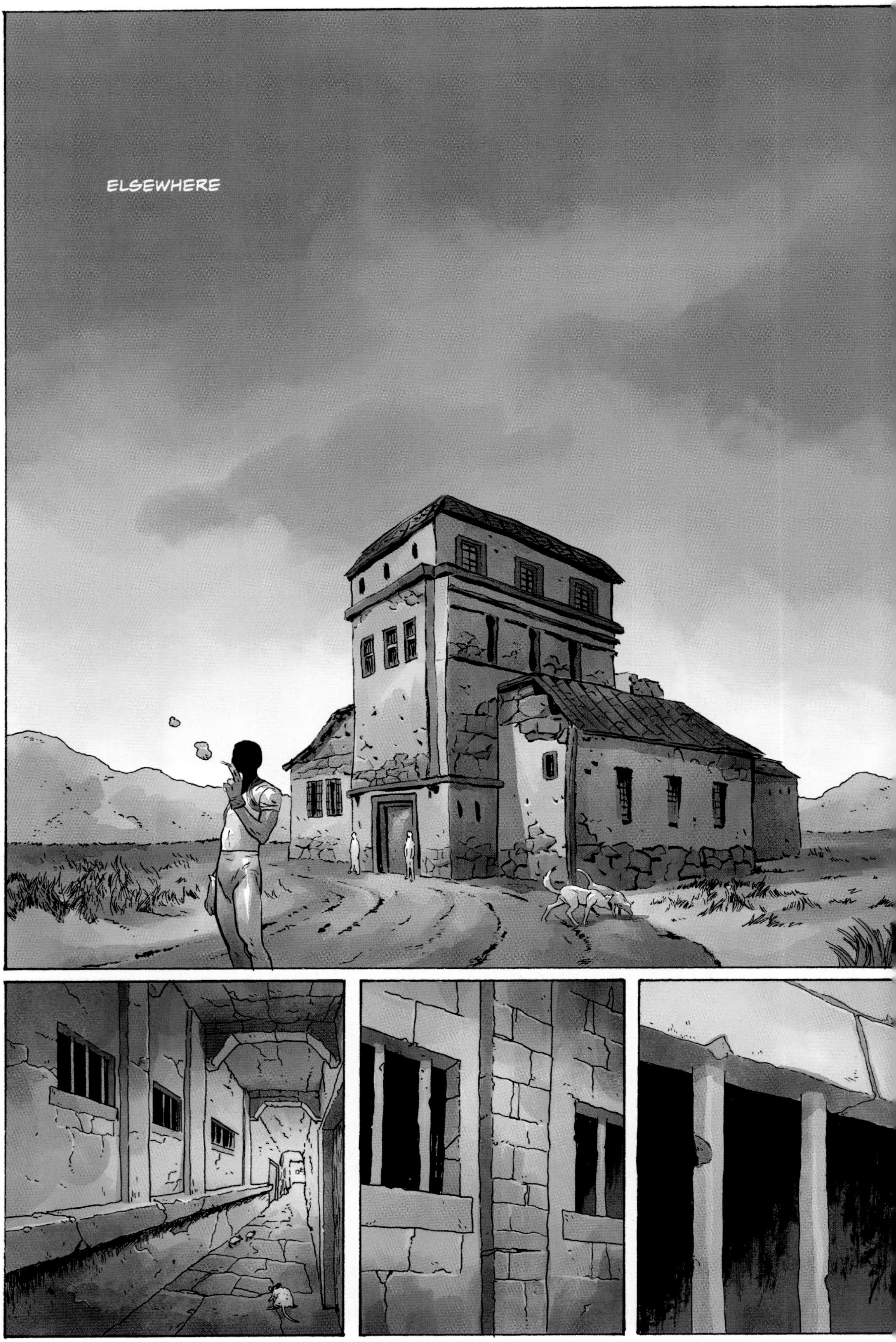
ELSEWHERE

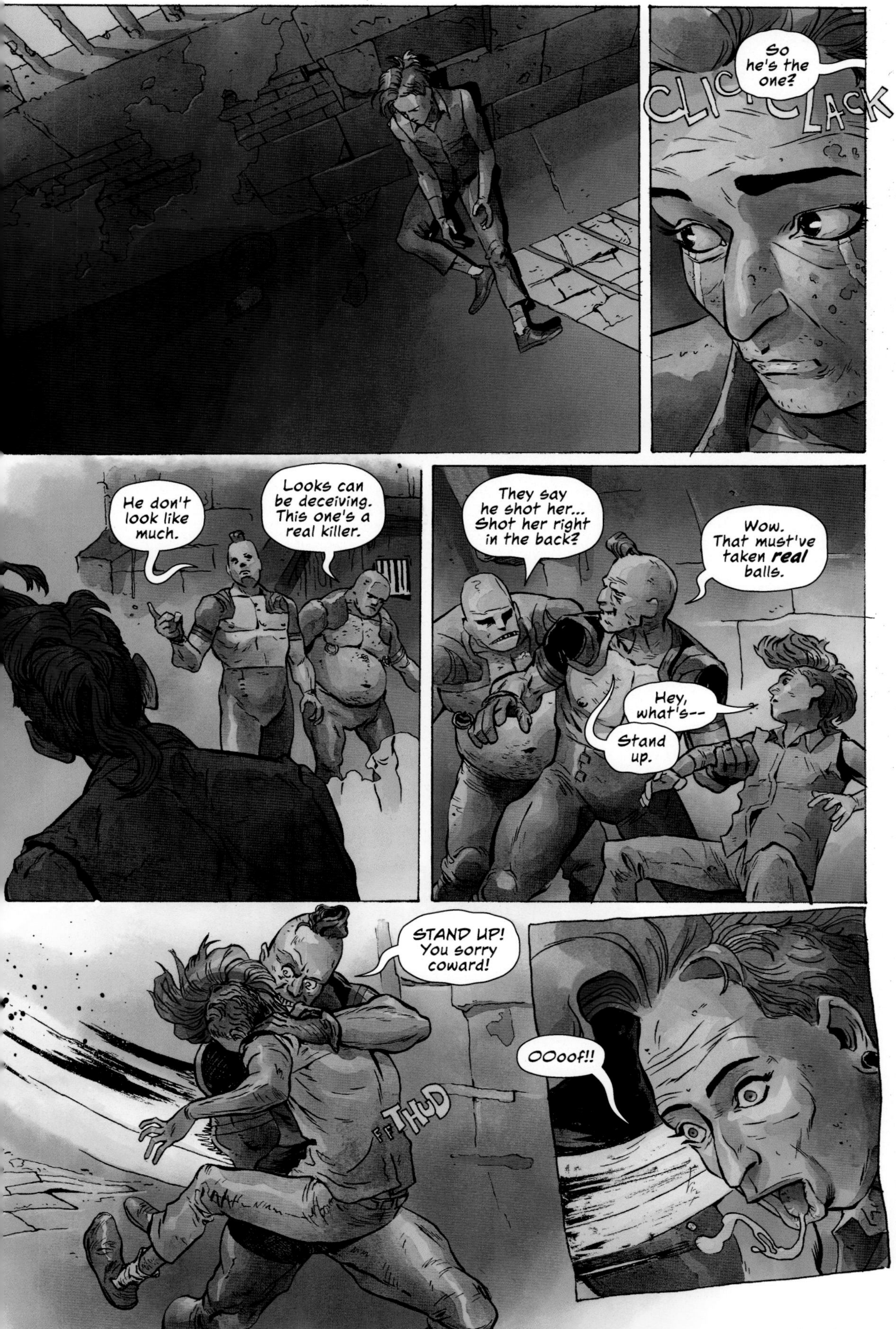

So he's the one?
CLICK CLACK
He don't look like much.
Looks can be deceiving. This one's a real killer.
They say he shot her... Shot her right in the back?
Wow. That must've taken **real** balls.
Hey, what's--
Stand up.
STAND UP! You sorry coward!
FFTHUD
OOoof!!

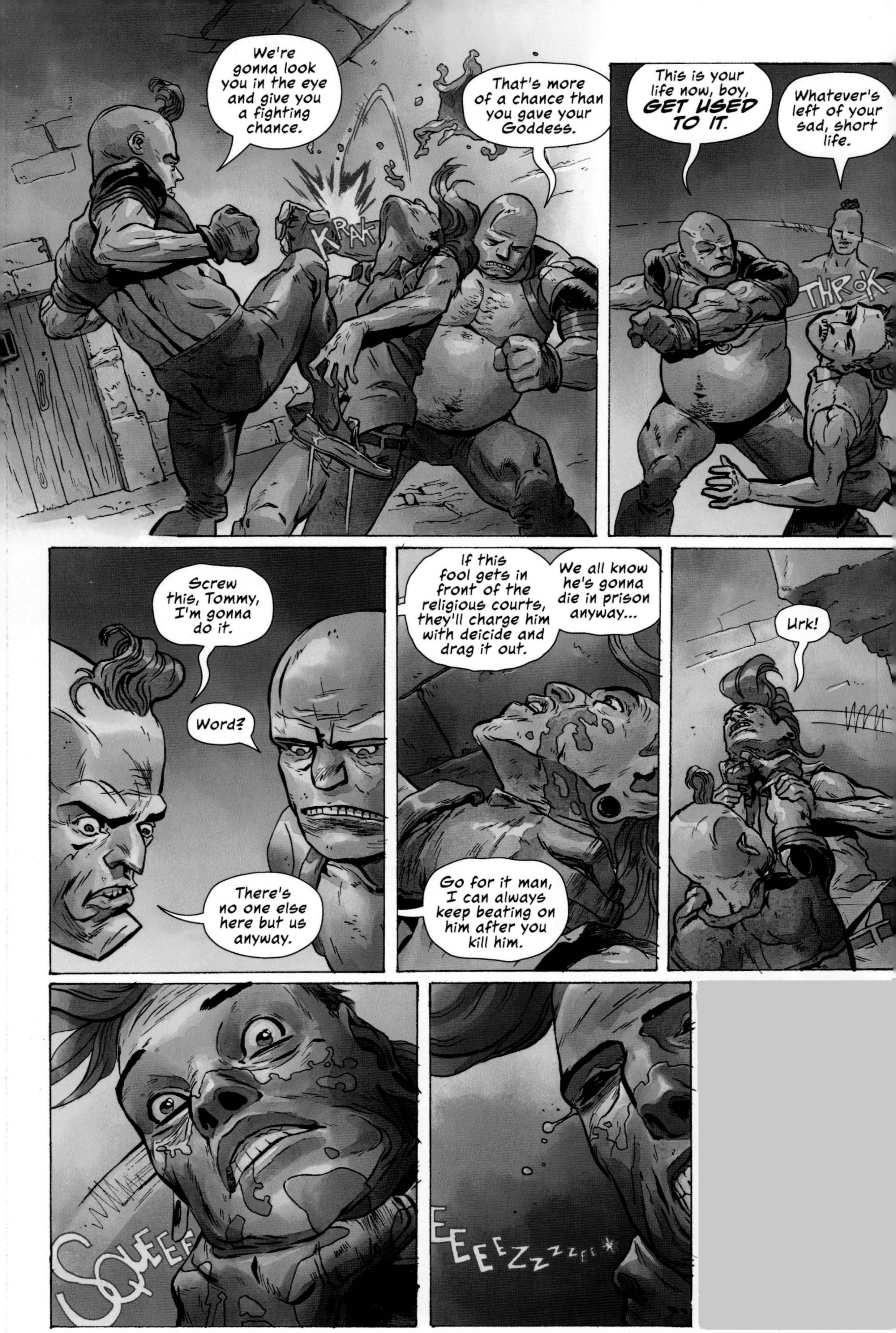
We're gonna look you in the eye and give you a fighting chance.
KRAK
That's more of a chance than you gave your Goddess.
This is your life now, boy, GET USED TO IT.
Whatever's left of your sad, short life.
THROK
Screw this, Tommy, I'm gonna do it.
Word?
There's no one else here but us anyway.
If this fool gets in front of the religious courts, they'll charge him with deicide and drag it out.
We all know he's gonna die in prison anyway...
Go for it man, I can always keep beating on him after you kill him.
Urk!
SQUEEE
EEEEZzzzzEE

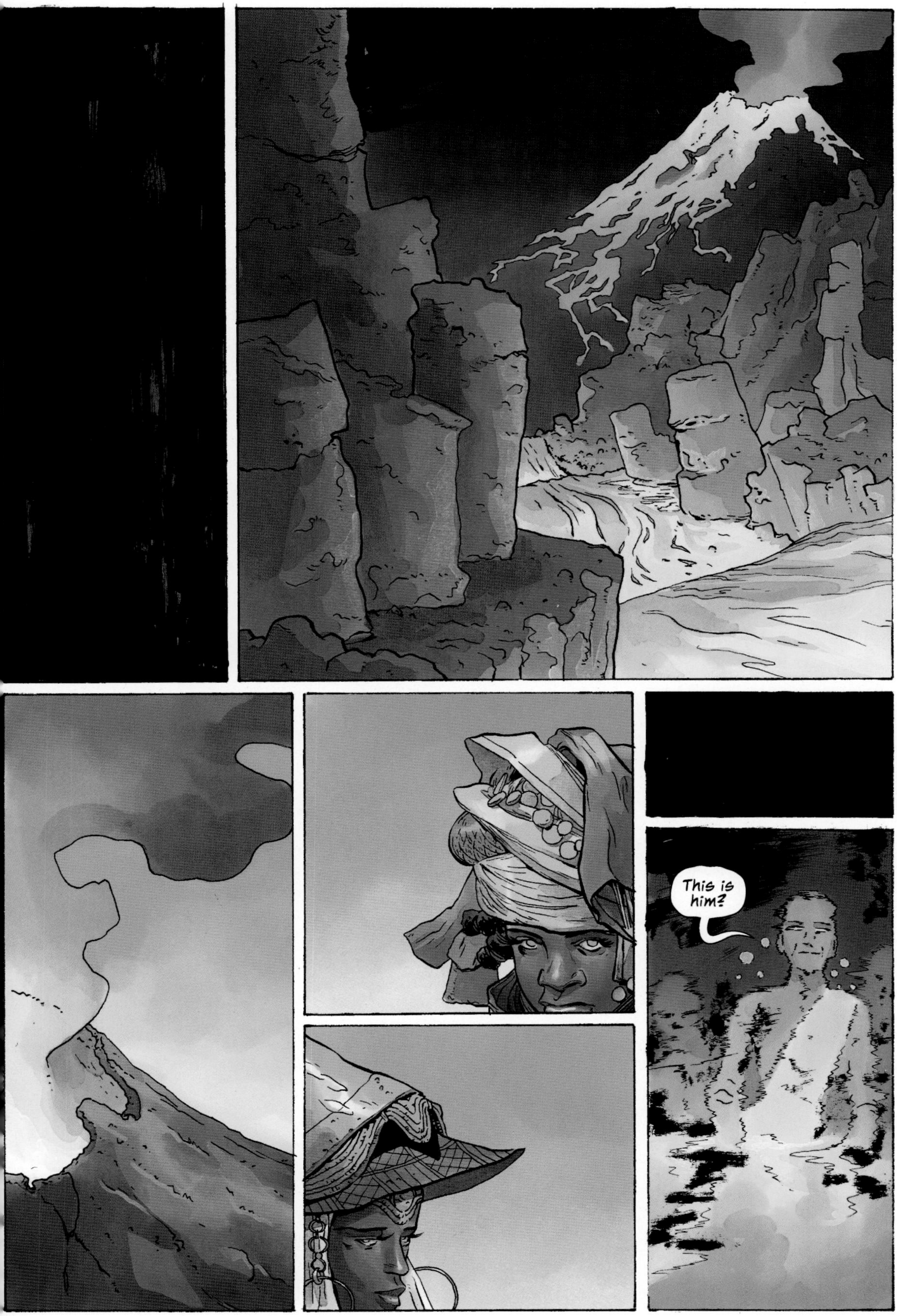
This is him?

Do you know who I am?

You're the High Priestess...

And I'm guessing the person who stopped these goons from murdering me?

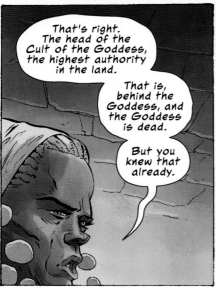

That's right. The head of the Cult of the Goddess, the highest authority in the land.

That is, behind the Goddess, and the Goddess is dead.

But you knew that already.

You are...a vile little ant. A treasonous coward. The Goddess was the light of the world.

It infuriates me to see her brought low by someone so... insignificant.

The Goddess wasn't just the fountain of my faith.

The source of order in my world.

She was my sister...

And Keegan is her daughter.

That's right, boy, as her only daughter, Keegan is now the new Goddess.

You're alive for one reason and one reason only. I'm gonna need you to do it again, Griffin.

I'm going to need you to *kill* her.

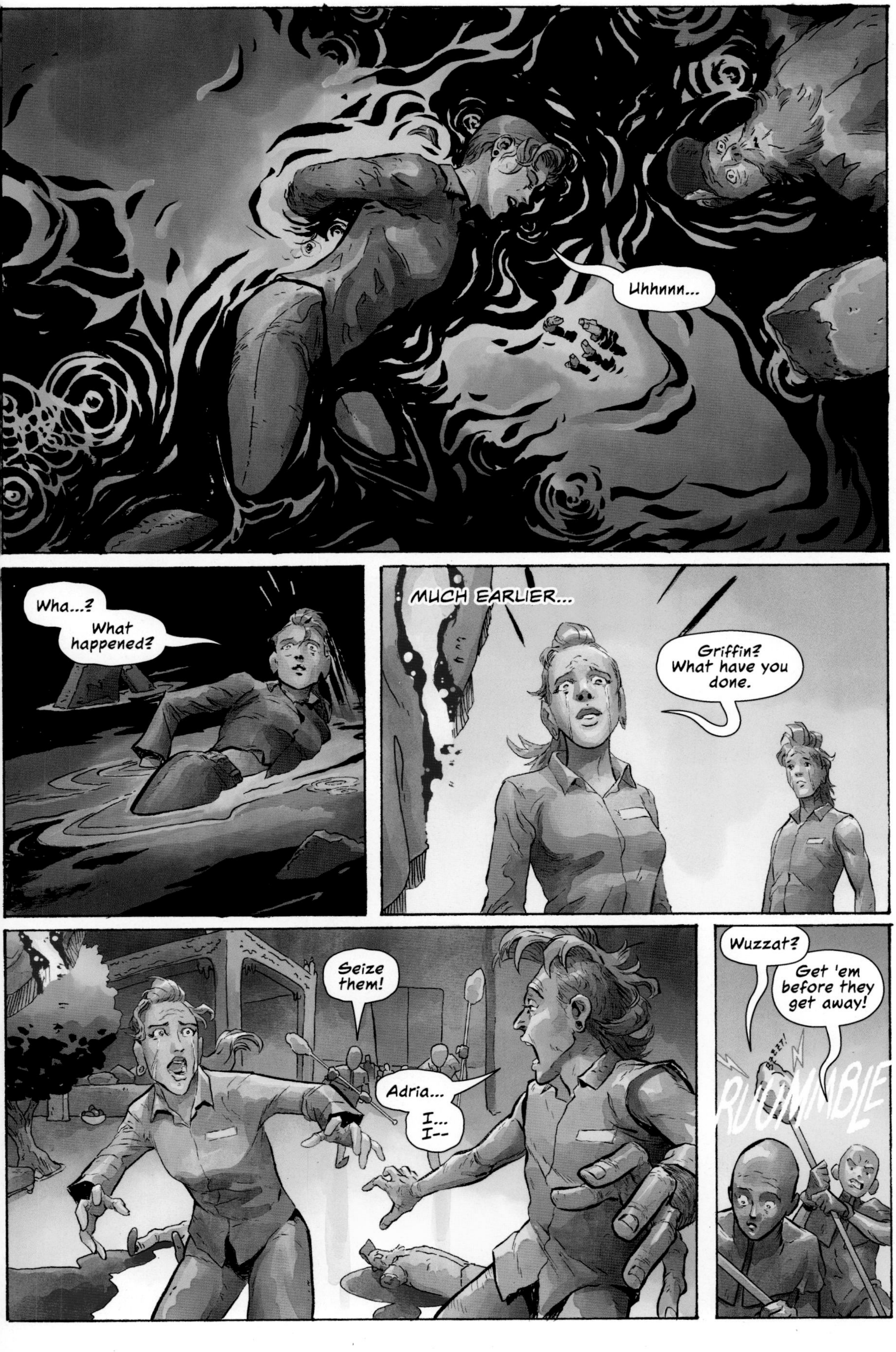
Uhhnnn...
Wha...?
What happened?
MUCH EARLIER...
Griffin? What have you done.
Seize them!
Adria...
I... I--
Wuzzat?
Get 'em before they get away!
RUUMMBLE

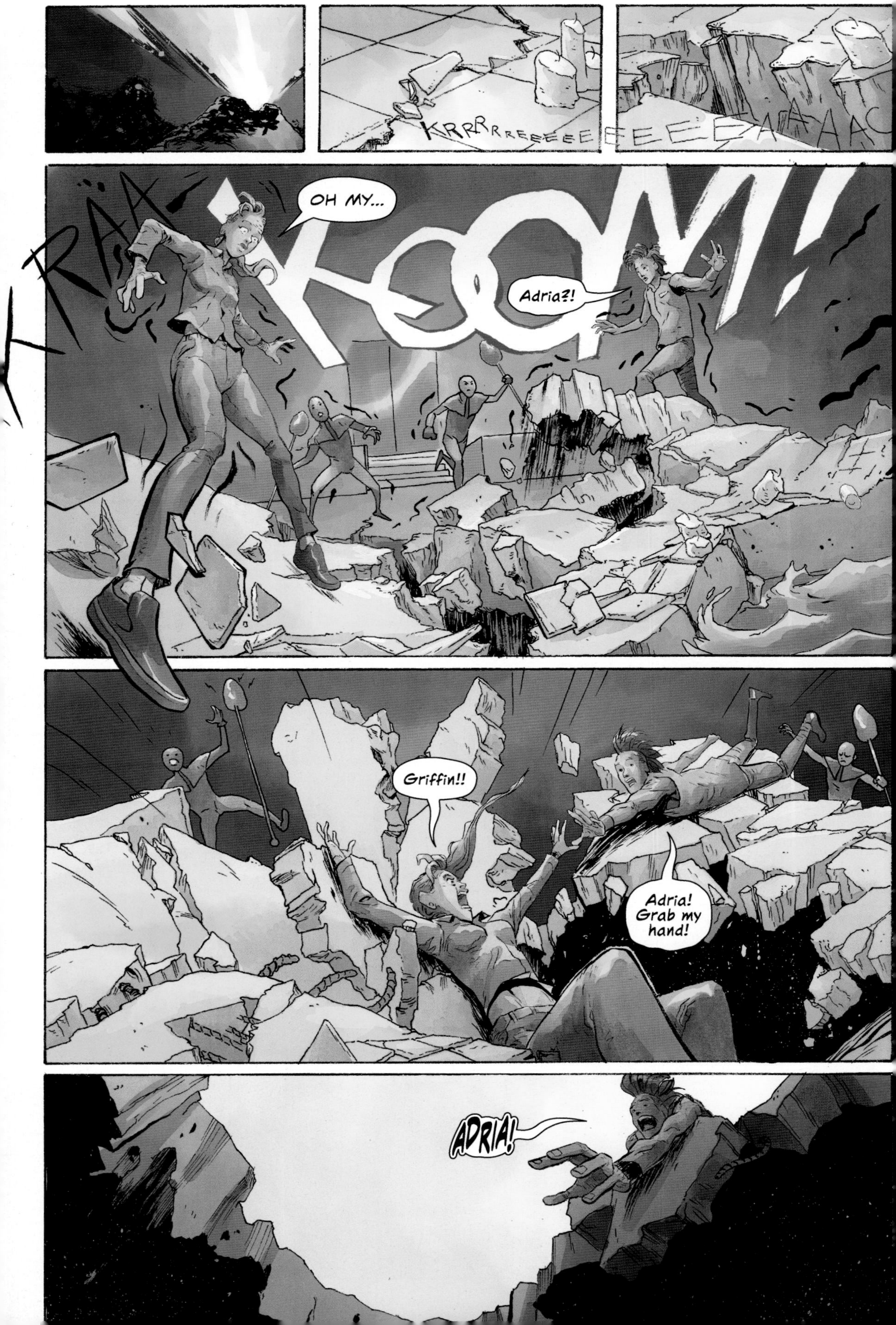
KRRRRREEEEEEEEEEAAAC
KRRÄÄ
KOOM!
OH MY...
Adria?!
Griffin!!
Adria! Grab my hand!
ADRIA!

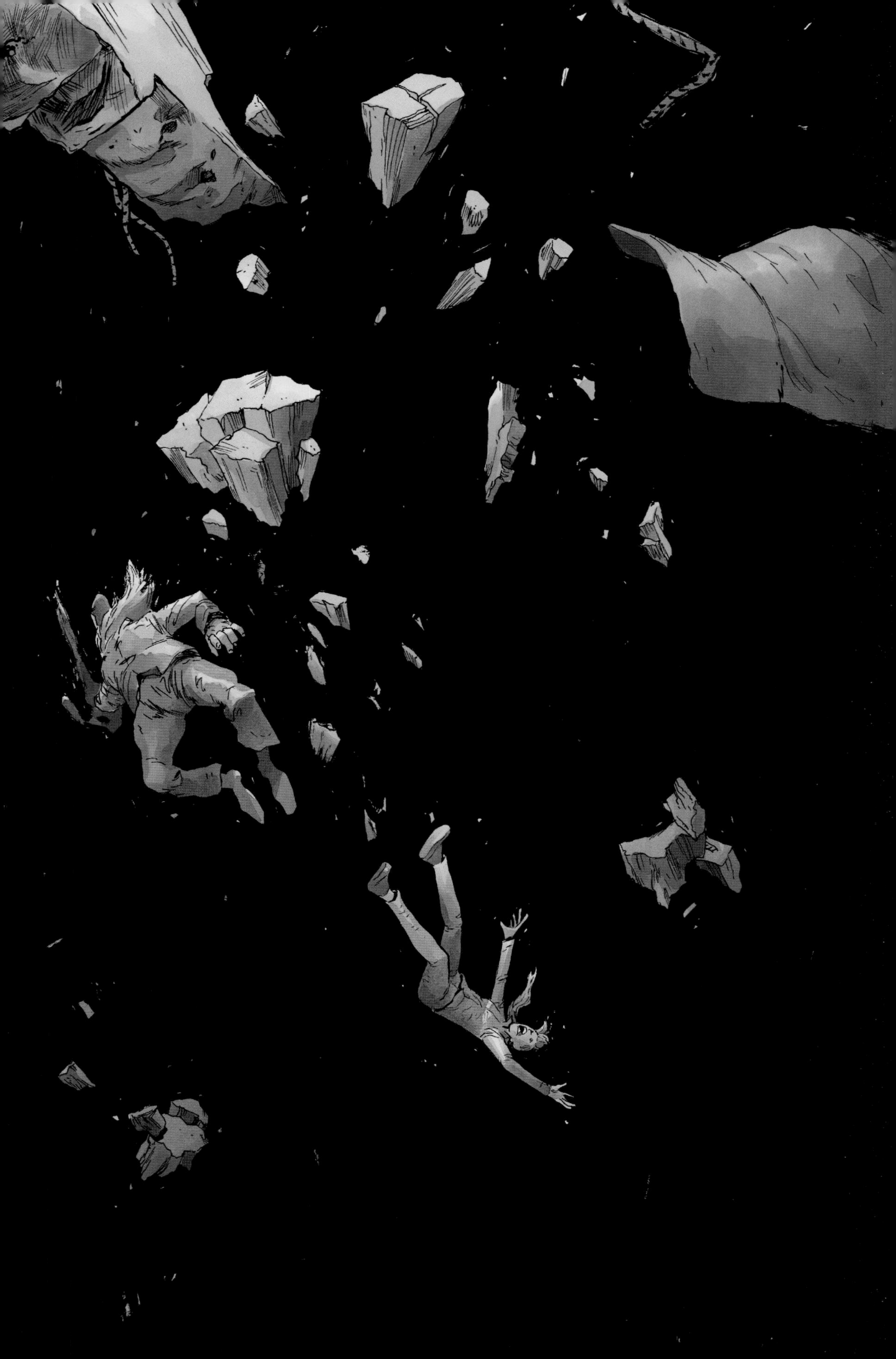

SPLASH

≍GASP≍

!!

NOW.

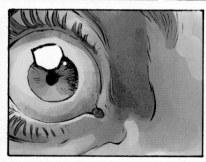

Ouch...

What is this place?

FOOHH...

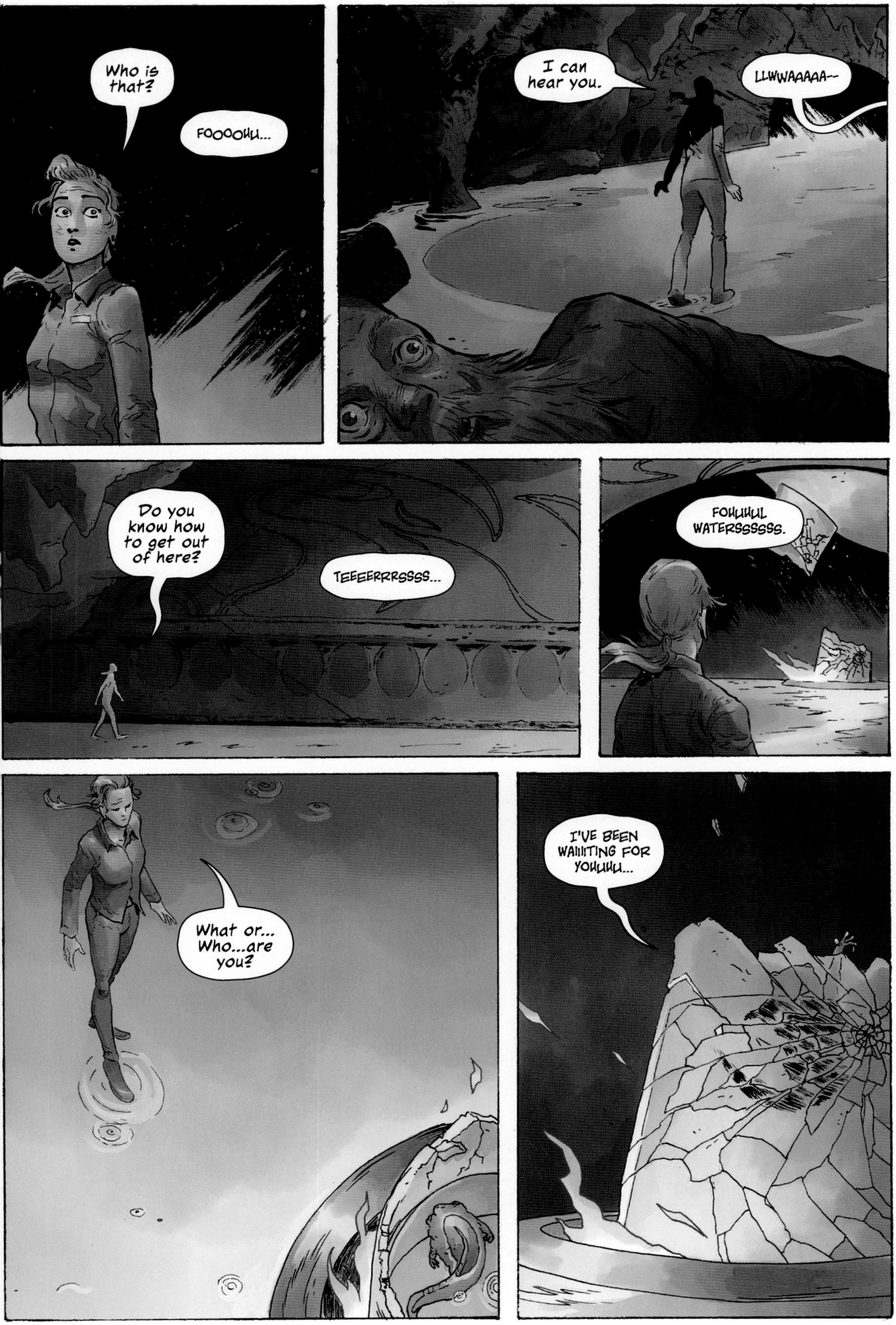
Who is that?
FOOOOUU...
I can hear you.
LLWWAAAAA--
Do you know how to get out of here?
TEEEERRRSSSS...
FOUUUUL WATERSSSSSS.
What or... Who...are you?
I'VE BEEN WAIIIITING FOR YOUUUU...

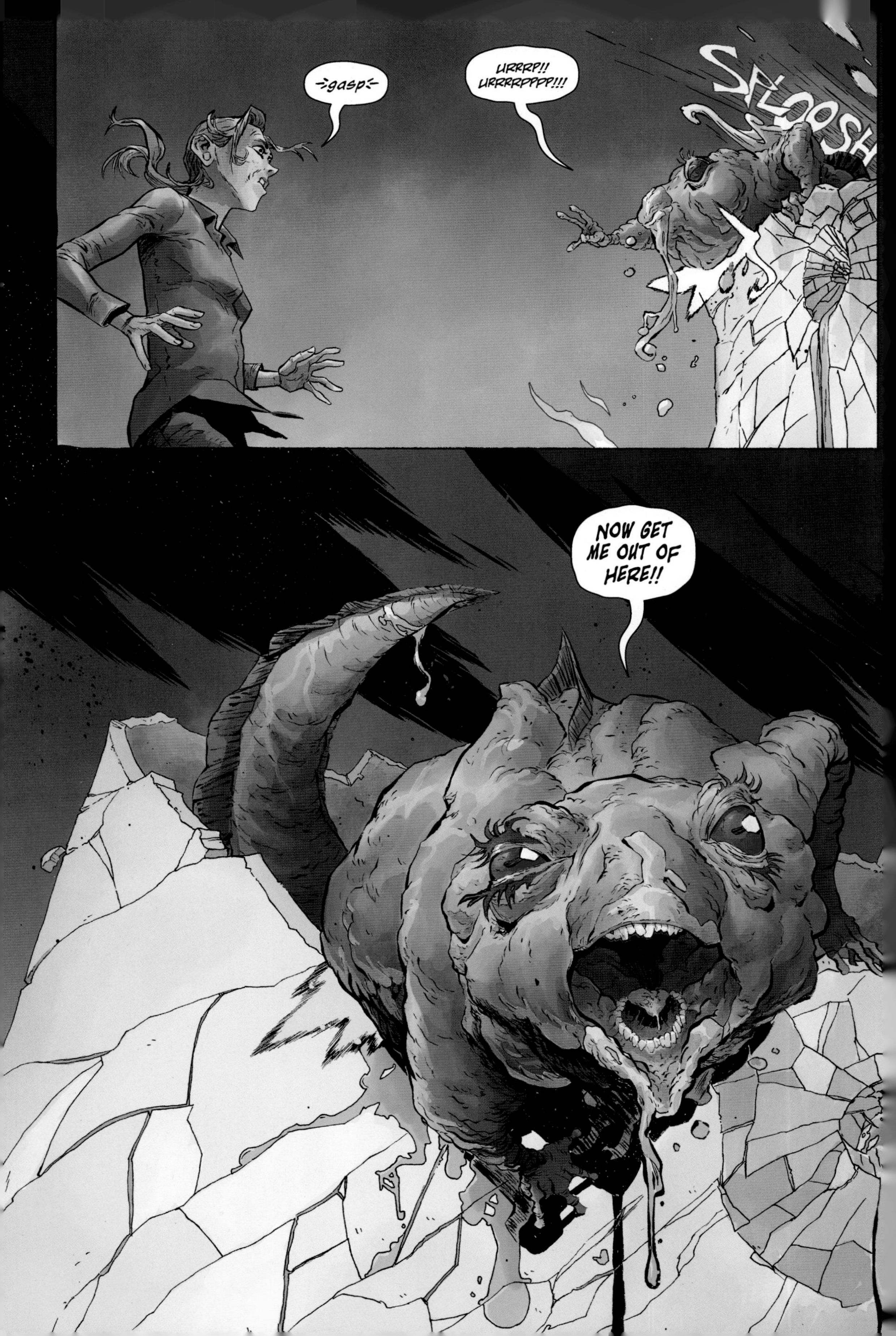

~gasp~
URRRP!! URRRRPPPP!!!
SPLOOSH
NOW GET ME OUT OF HERE!!

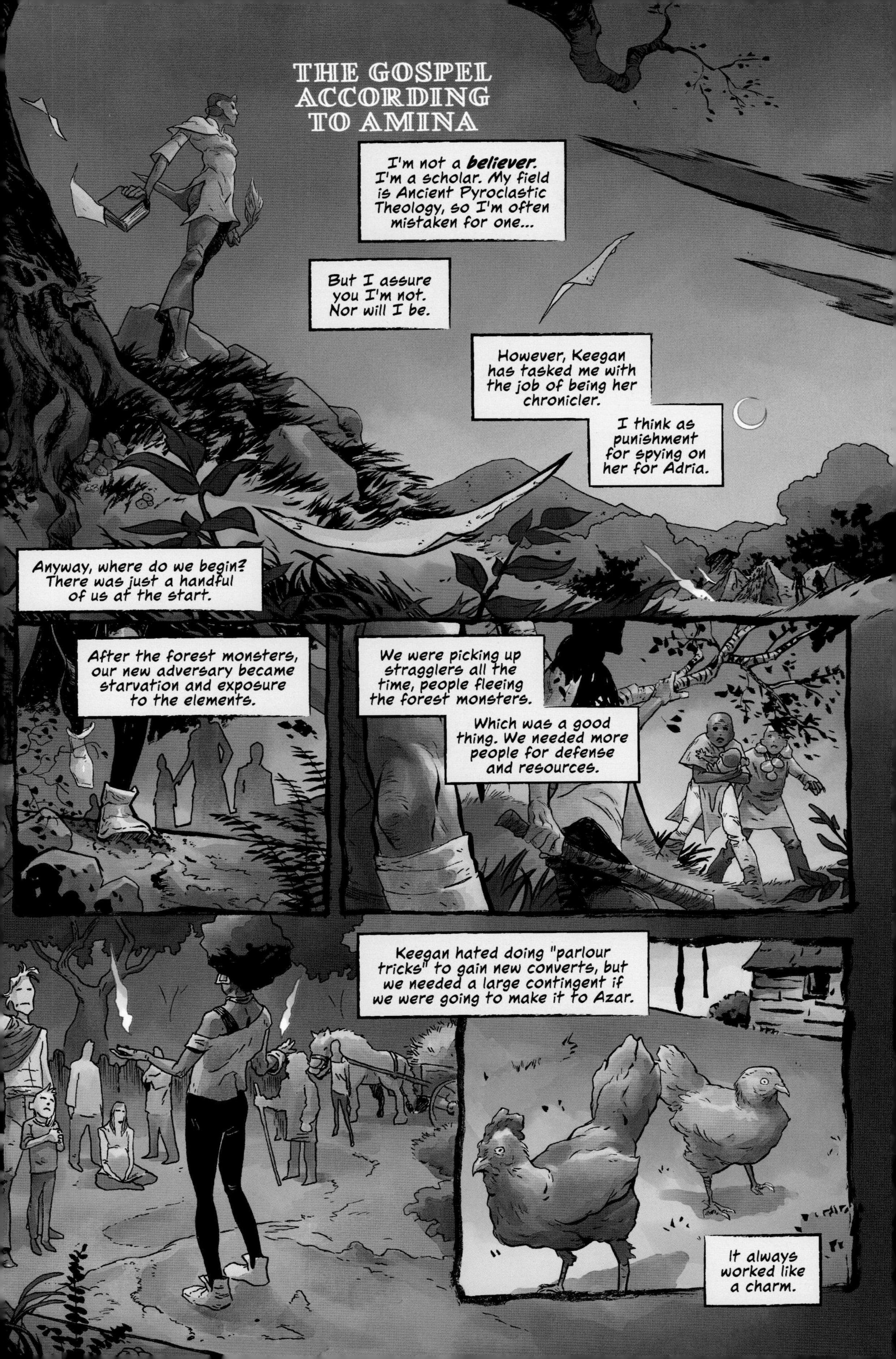
THE GOSPEL ACCORDING TO AMINA
I'm not a believer. I'm a scholar. My field is Ancient Pyroclastic Theology, so I'm often mistaken for one...
But I assure you I'm not. Nor will I be.
However, Keegan has tasked me with the job of being her chronicler.
I think as punishment for spying on her for Adria.
Anyway, where do we begin? There was just a handful of us at the start.
After the forest monsters, our new adversary became starvation and exposure to the elements.
We were picking up stragglers all the time, people fleeing the forest monsters.
Which was a good thing. We needed more people for defense and resources.
Keegan hated doing "parlour tricks" to gain new converts, but we needed a large contingent if we were going to make it to Azar.
It always worked like a charm.

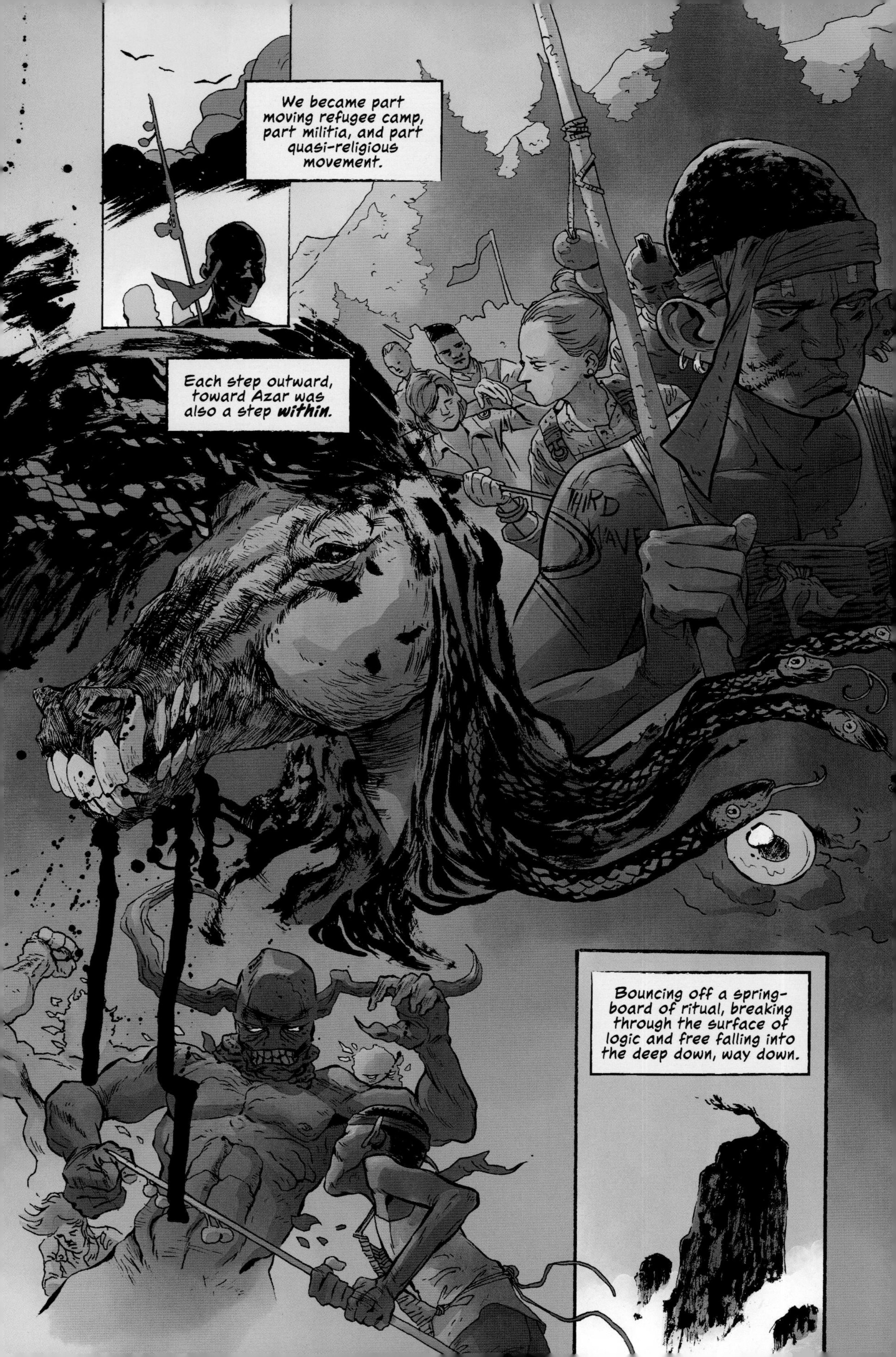
We became part moving refugee camp, part militia, and part quasi-religious movement.
Each step outward, toward Azar was also a step *within*.
THIRD WAVE
Bouncing off a spring-board of ritual, breaking through the surface of logic and free falling into the deep down, way down.

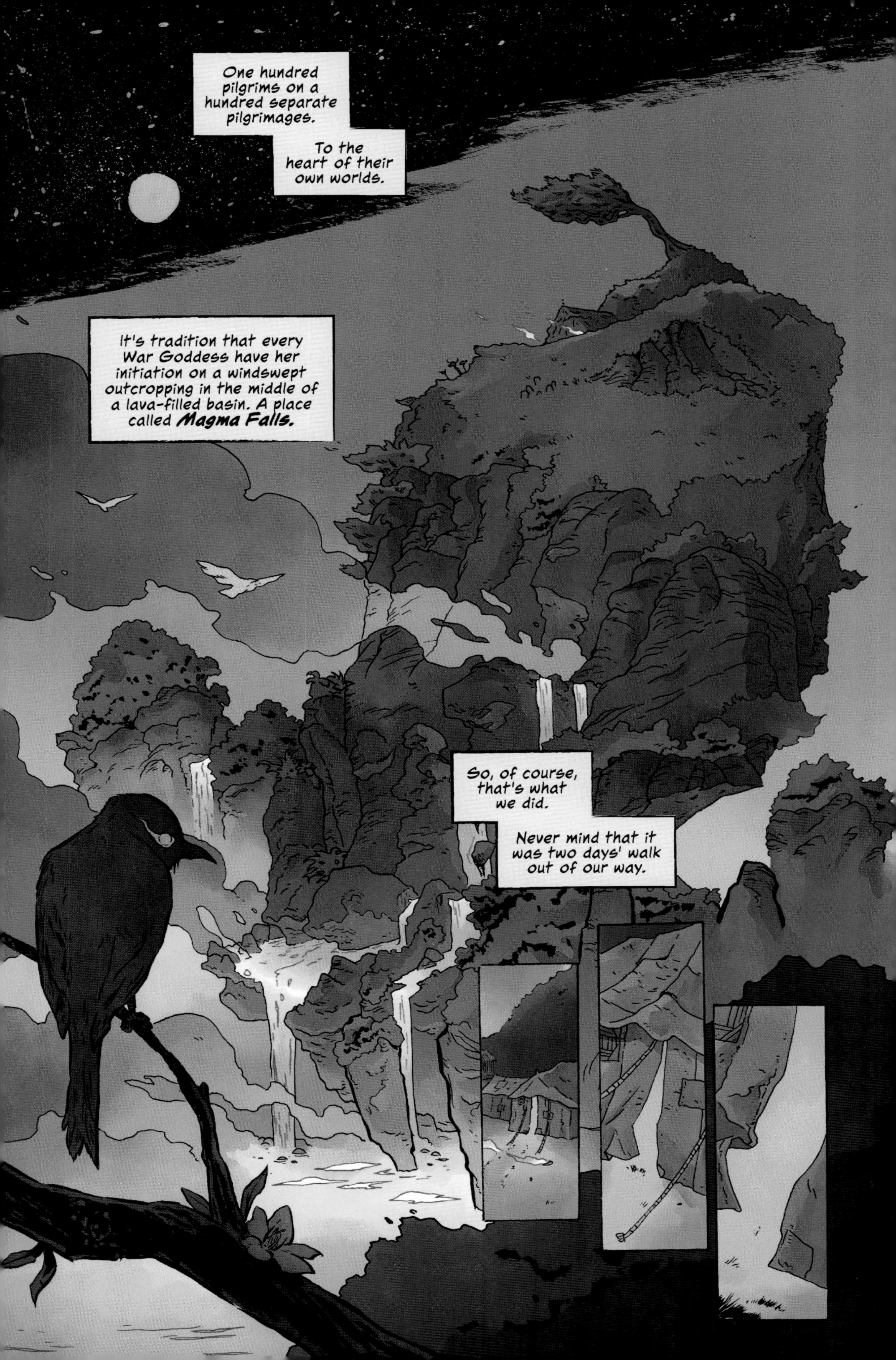
One hundred pilgrims on a hundred separate pilgrimages.
To the heart of their own worlds.
It's tradition that every War Goddess have her initiation on a windswept outcropping in the middle of a lava-filled basin. A place called Magma Falls.
So, of course, that's what we did.
Never mind that it was two days' walk out of our way.

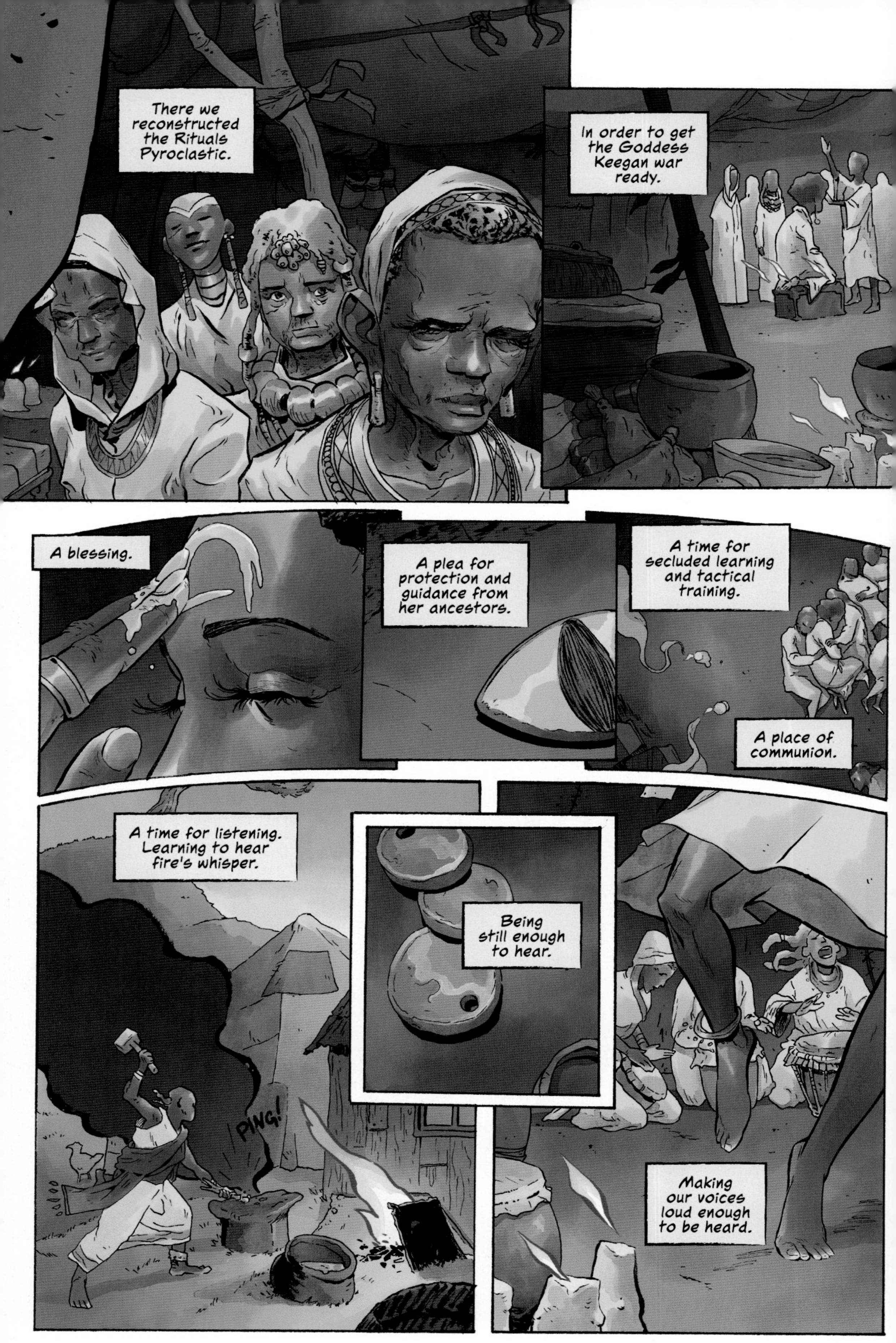
There we reconstructed the Rituals Pyroclastic.
In order to get the Goddess Keegan war ready.
A blessing.
A plea for protection and guidance from her ancestors.
A time for secluded learning and tactical training.
A place of communion.
A time for listening. Learning to hear fire's whisper.
PING!
Being still enough to hear.
Making our voices loud enough to be heard.

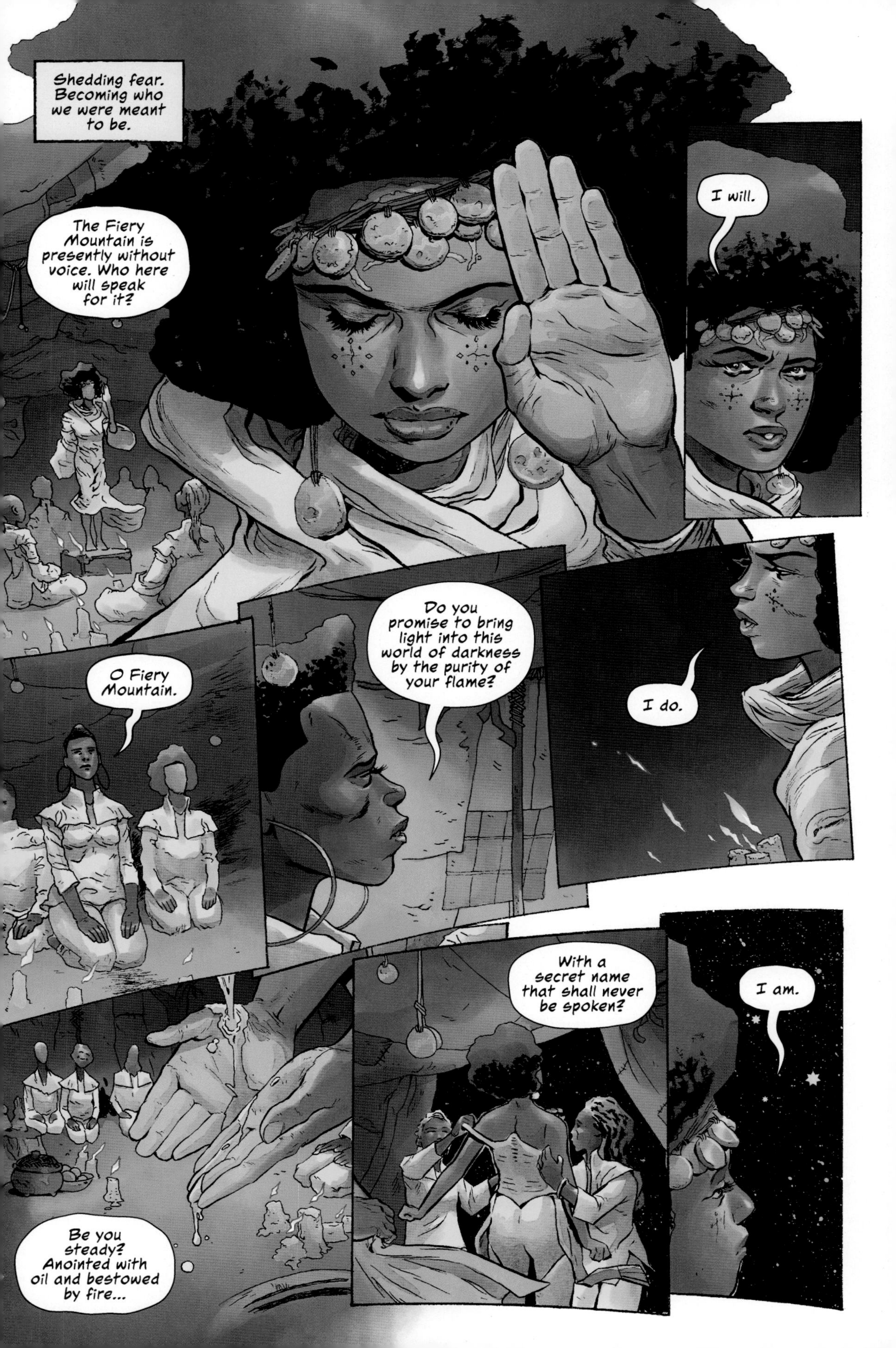
Shedding fear. Becoming who we were meant to be.
The Fiery Mountain is presently without voice. Who here will speak for it?
I will.
O Fiery Mountain.
Do you promise to bring light into this world of darkness by the purity of your flame?
I do.
Be you steady? Anointed with oil and bestowed by fire...
With a secret name that shall never be spoken?
I am.

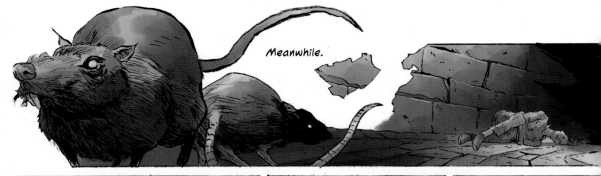

Meanwhile.

Wake up, dummy.

It's time for your shower.

You've got a hot date waiting for you in Azar.

This guy really loves his girlfriend.

ARGH!

Ha! Literally worships the ground she walks on!

Alright, that's enough.

Tell me. You were born in Azar, weren't you, Griffin?

You're a long way from home, bumpkin.

I respect your devotion to Keegan, I do. But, Griffin, you must know.

The Goddess isn't here to help.

Great.

I hope she comes and burns this place to the ground.

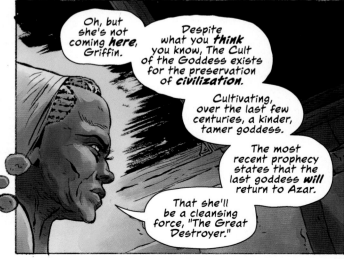

Oh, but she's not coming *here*, Griffin.

Despite what you *think* you know, The Cult of the Goddess exists for the preservation of *civilization*.

Cultivating, over the last few centuries, a kinder, tamer goddess.

The most recent prophecy states that the last goddess *will* return to Azar.

That she'll be a cleansing force, "The Great Destroyer."

But there is still time to stop her.

There have been others, Griffin.

Brave champions who fought the impossible might of the Fiery Mountain.

Stood firm against the tide of chaos and collapse.

Three Short Stories of Four Special Artifacts

Let me tell you how. In three short stories of four special artifacts.

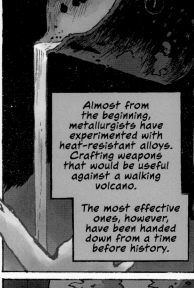

Almost from the beginning, metallurgists have experimented with heat-resistant alloys. Crafting weapons that would be useful against a walking volcano.

The most effective ones, however, have been handed down from a time before history.

After years of burned fields at the hands of the mercurial goddess Zenfa.

A barefoot girl we know only as N'dine, found a special dagger.

She came across the goddess while bathing.

Knowing that the goddesses are most vulnerable in water, she took her chance and struck.

What followed was a generation of peace and stability.

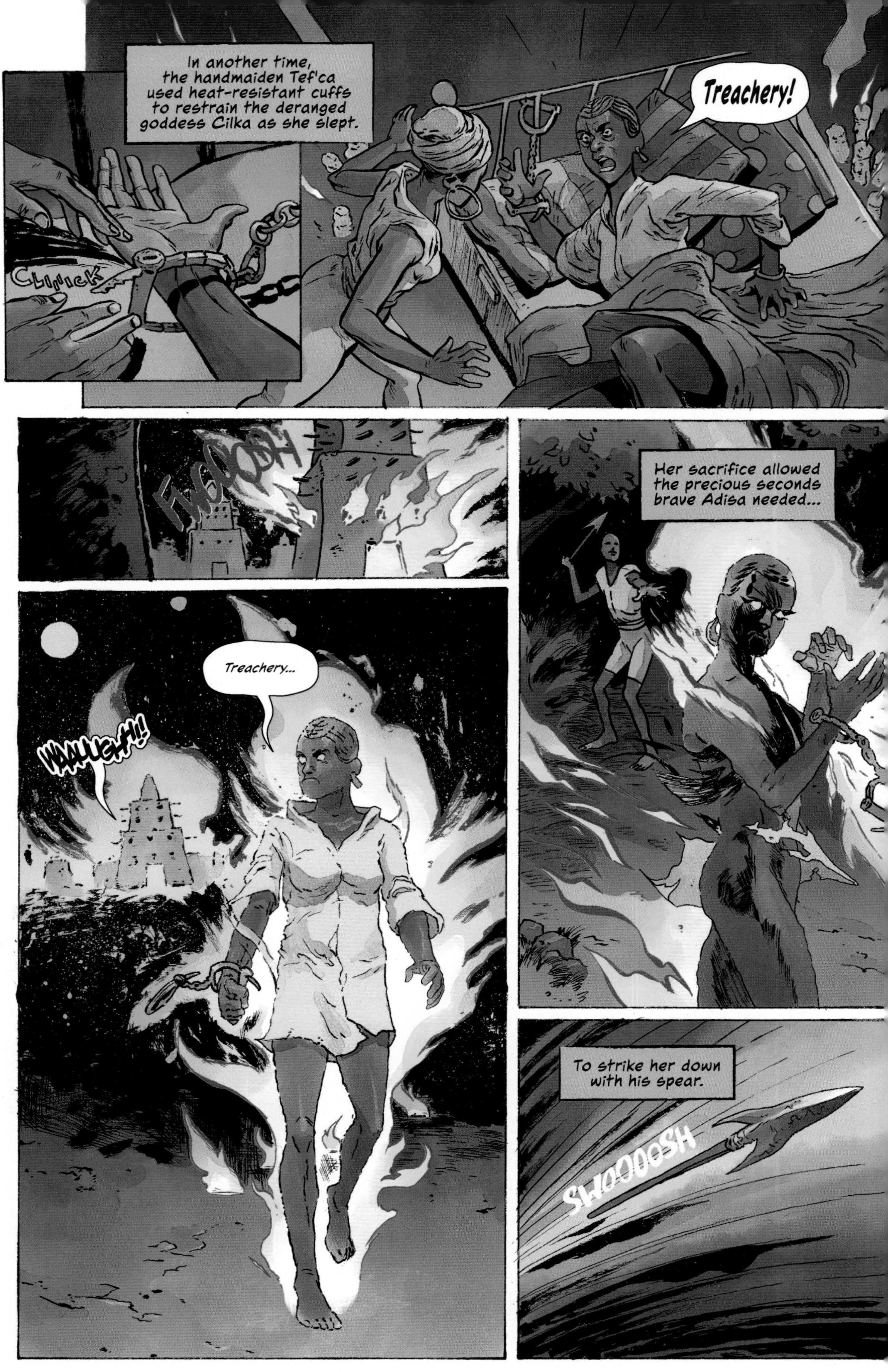
In another time, the handmaiden Tef'ca used heat-resistant cuffs to restrain the deranged goddess Cilka as she slept.
CLINICK
Treachery!
FWOOOSH
Her sacrifice allowed the precious seconds brave Adisa needed...
WAAUGH!!
Treachery...
To strike her down with his spear.
SWOOOOSH

As much as you hate yourself, as much as I hate you...

...your name will go down among the liberators who freed us from the fickle tyranny of a goddess.

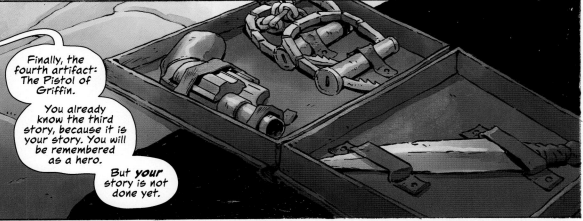

Finally, the fourth artifact: The Pistol of Griffin.

You already know the third story, because it is your story. You will be remembered as a hero.

But **your** story is not done yet.

Keegan **is** the last goddess and she's heading to **Azar** like a flaming arrow towards a paper target.

If she gets there, the prophecy will be fulfilled. Her fire licking clean the bones of a murdered city.

Time to choose, Griffin.

The path of life?

Or the Goddess of Death?

HURRAK

FOOUULL WATERRRS. FOUUUUL WATTERRRSS! DON'T DROP ME IN FOUUUL WAAATERS!!

And is it just me, or are you getting larger by the second?

I just might if you don't stop squirming!

Are you sure you know where you're leading us?

WHY? HAVE MORE IMPORTANT PLACE TO BE, LITTLE URCHIN?!!

Maybe!

THIS WAY...

MUST RETURN TO OCEAN...

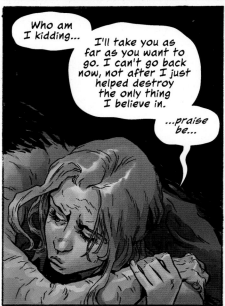

Who am I kidding...

I'll take you as far as you want to go. I can't go back now, not after I just helped destroy the only thing I believe in.

...praise be...

WHAT'S THIS YOU SPEAK OF, URCHIN?

The Goddess of the Fiery Mountain...

...she's...

...she's dead...

CAN IT BE?!

DID URCHIN EVER HEAR TALE OF THE TWO SISTERS?

IN THE BEGINNING, THE TRUE BEGINNING, THERE WERE TWO SISTERS.

THE FIRST GLOWED AS BRIGHT AS THE SUN.

THERE WAS ROOM ONLY FOR HER, AND NOTHING ELSE.

ONLY THE LISSOME CARESS OF THE SECOND SISTER, COULD ASSUAGE THE INTENSITY OF THE FIRST.

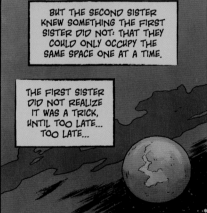

BUT THE SECOND SISTER KNEW SOMETHING THE FIRST SISTER DID NOT: THAT THEY COULD ONLY OCCUPY THE SAME SPACE ONE AT A TIME.

THE FIRST SISTER DID NOT REALIZE IT WAS A TRICK, UNTIL TOO LATE... TOO LATE...

THE COMING TOGETHER OF THE TWO ENCASED THE FIRST SISTER IN A CAGE OF IRON AND STONE.

A STOCKADE OF IMMENSE SIZE. SO LARGE THAT SHE WOULD NEVER AGAIN BE FREE.

THE SECOND SISTER MADE ROOM FOR MORE THAN HERSELF. SHE MADE ROOM FOR LIFE TO FLOURISH.

I AM OF THE SECOND SISTER, OCEAN. I AM ONE OF HER EMISSARIES.

YOUR GODDESS OF FIERY MOUNTAIN IS OF THE FIRST SISTER, FIRE.

I KNOW WHAT YOU ARE THINKING.

NO, WAS NOT ALWAYS THIS WAY.

WAS ONCE BEAUTIFUL... POWERFUL...

LAST I ENCOUNTERED YOUR FIERY GODDESS, THE BATTLE ENDED WITH US BOTH DEPLETED, THEN CAGED.

PLACED IN A CAGE OF FOULLLL WATERSSSS AND BURIED DEEP UNDER THE EARTH.

THIS WAY...

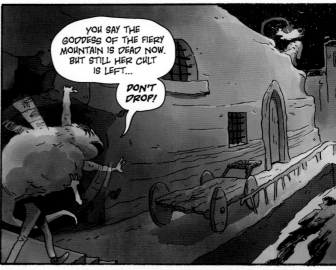

YOU SAY THE GODDESS OF THE FIERY MOUNTAIN IS DEAD NOW. BUT STILL HER CULT IS LEFT...

DON'T DROP!

I CAN DESTROY THEM FOR YOU. GET REVENGE FOR BOTH OF US.

GET ME TO WATERSSS CLEAN AND I WILL SHOW YOU A GODDESS WORTHY OF YOUR DEVOTION.

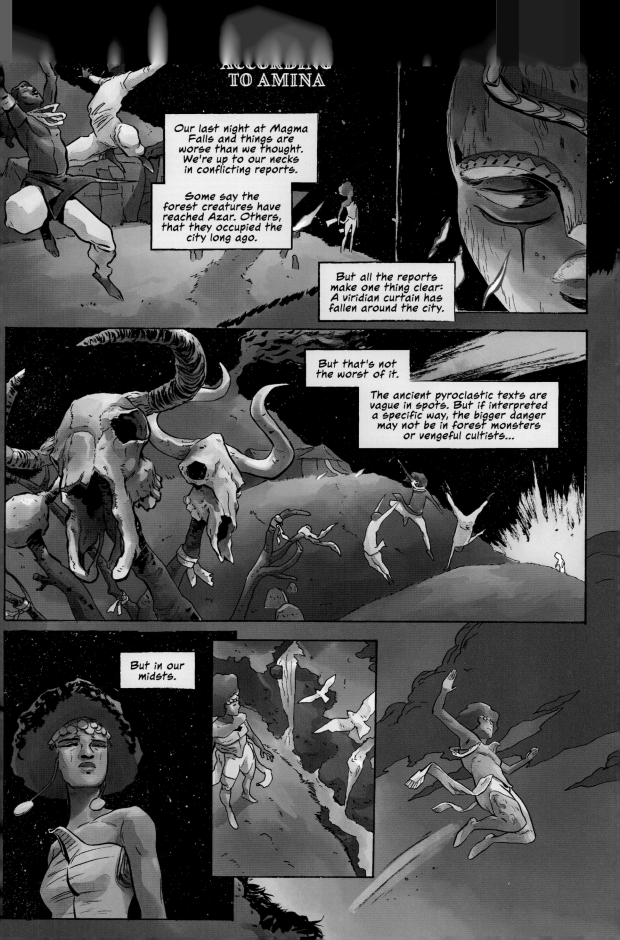

Our last night at Magma Falls and things are worse than we thought. We're up to our necks in conflicting reports.

Some say the forest creatures have reached Azar. Others, that they occupied the city long ago.

But all the reports make one thing clear: A viridian curtain has fallen around the city.

But that's not the worst of it.

The ancient pyroclastic texts are vague in spots. But if interpreted a specific way, the bigger danger may not be in forest monsters or vengeful cultists...

But in our midsts.

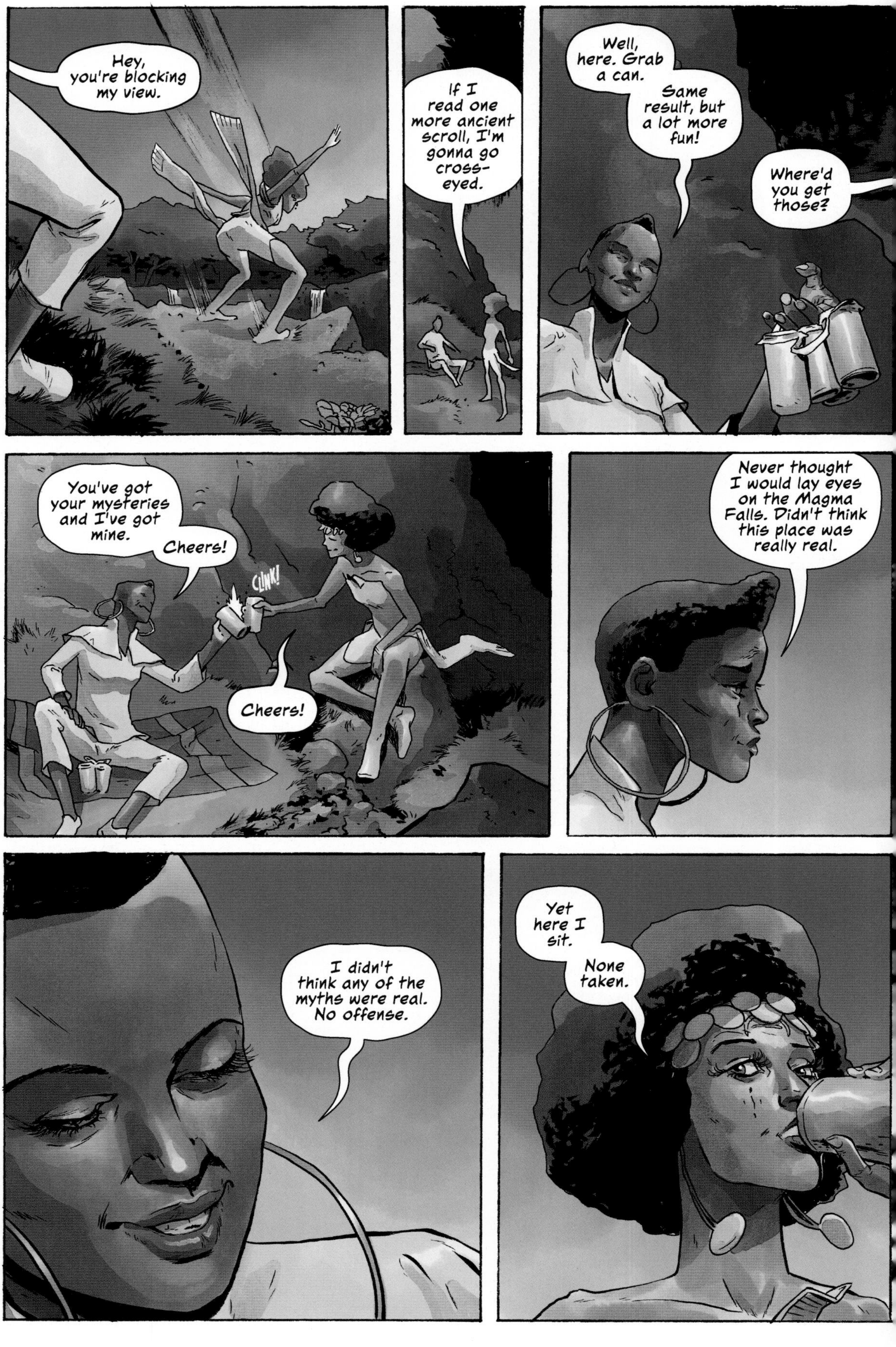
Hey, you're blocking my view.
If I read one more ancient scroll, I'm gonna go cross-eyed.
Well, here. Grab a can.
Same result, but a lot more fun!
Where'd you get those?
You've got your mysteries and I've got mine.
Cheers!
CLINK!
Cheers!
Never thought I would lay eyes on the Magma Falls. Didn't think this place was really real.
I didn't think any of the myths were real. No offense.
Yet here I sit.
None taken.

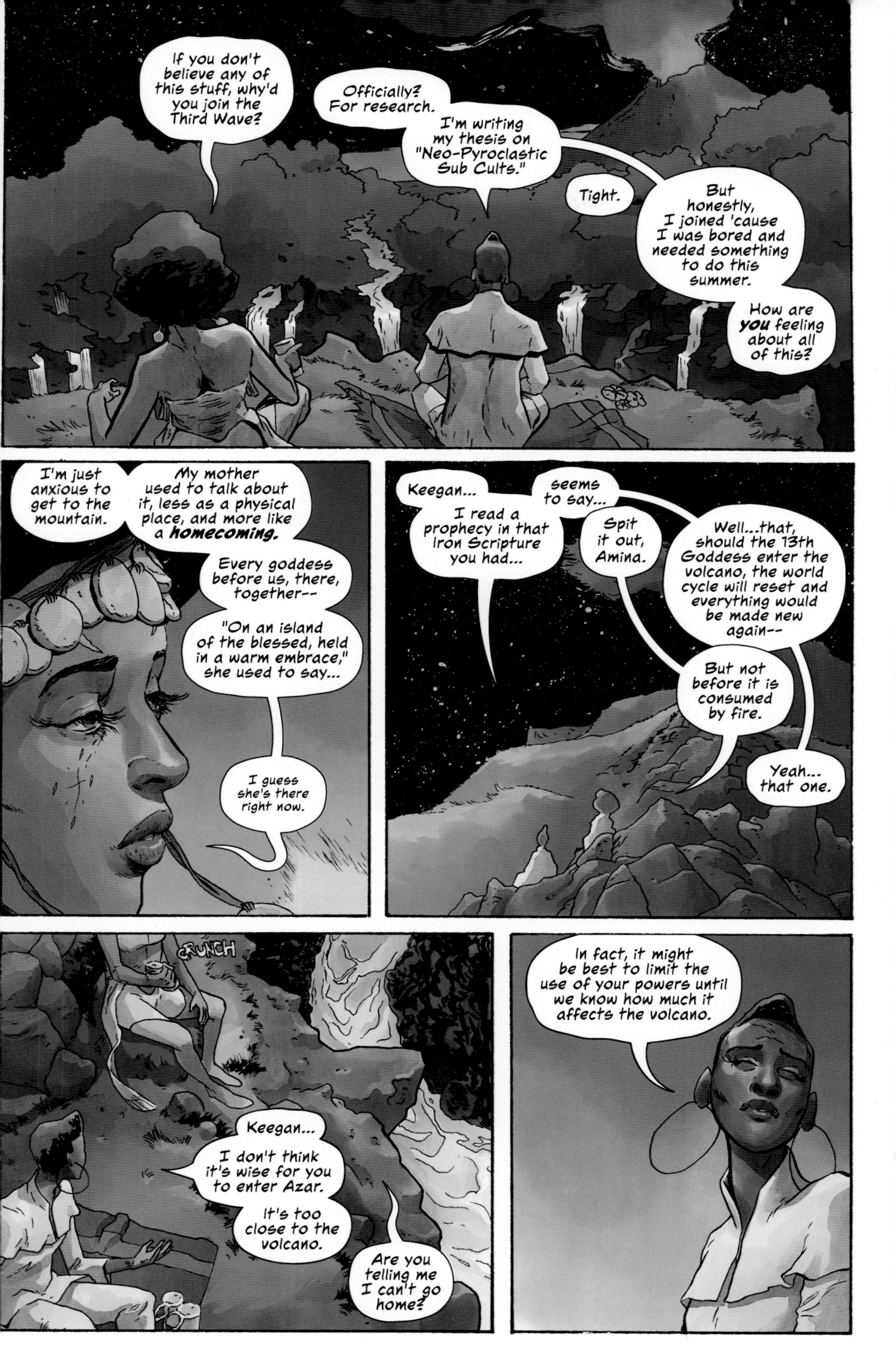
If you don't believe any of this stuff, why'd you join the Third Wave?
Officially? For research.
I'm writing my thesis on "Neo-Pyroclastic Sub Cults."
Tight.
But honestly, I joined 'cause I was bored and needed something to do this summer.
How are **you** feeling about all of this?
I'm just anxious to get to the mountain.
My mother used to talk about it, less as a physical place, and more like a **homecoming.**
Every goddess before us, there, together--
"On an island of the blessed, held in a warm embrace," she used to say...
I guess she's there right now.
Keegan...
I read a prophecy in that Iron Scripture you had...
seems to say...
Spit it out, Amina.
Well...that, should the 13th Goddess enter the volcano, the world cycle will reset and everything would be made new again--
But not before it is consumed by fire.
Yeah... that one.
CRUNCH
Keegan...
I don't think it's wise for you to enter Azar.
It's too close to the volcano.
Are you telling me I can't go home?
In fact, it might be best to limit the use of your powers until we know how much it affects the volcano.

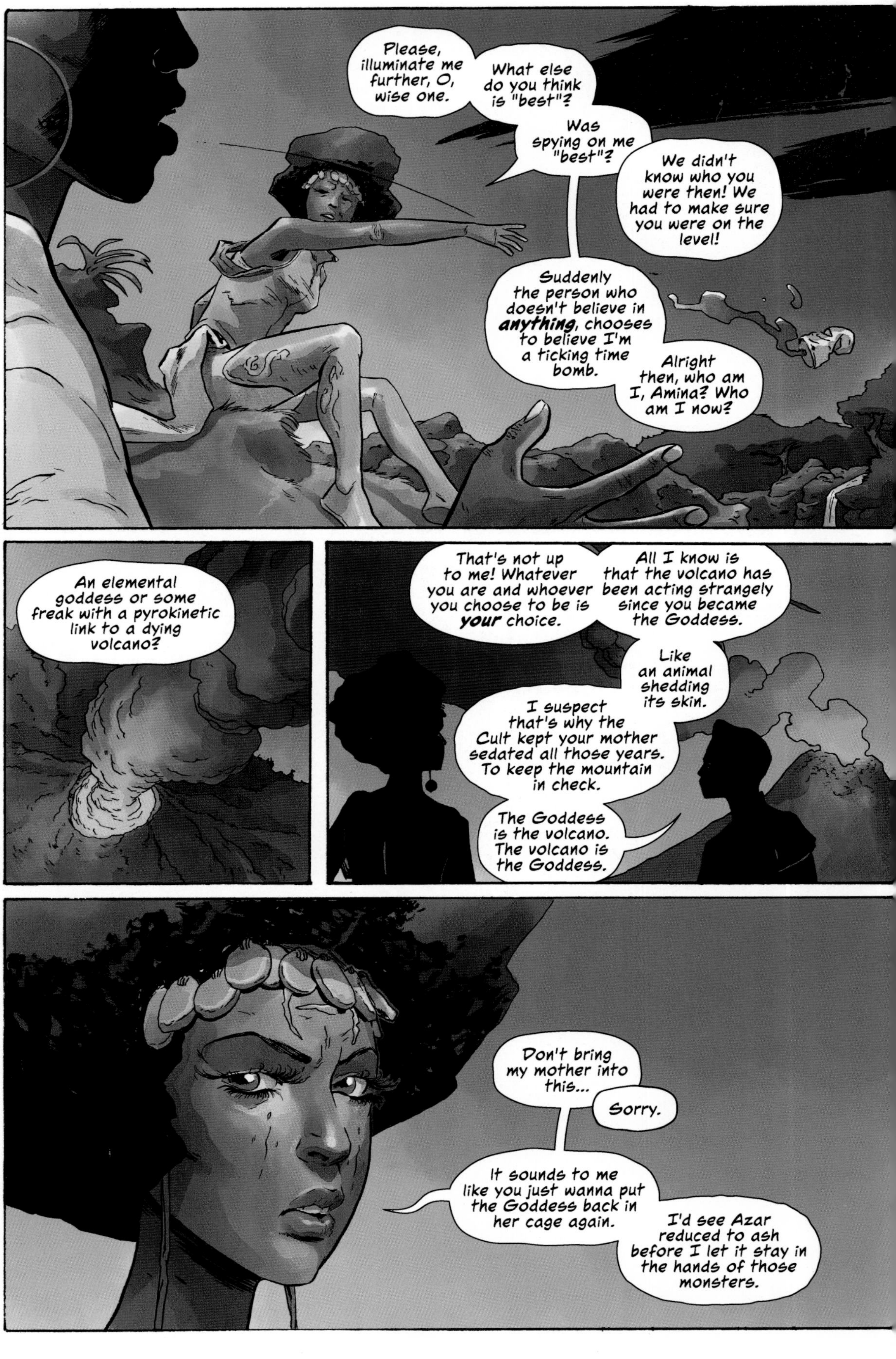
Please, illuminate me further, O, wise one.
What else do you think is "best"?
Was spying on me "best"?
We didn't know who you were then! We had to make sure you were on the level!
Suddenly the person who doesn't believe in **anything**, chooses to believe I'm a ticking time bomb.
Alright then, who am I, Amina? Who am I now?
An elemental goddess or some freak with a pyrokinetic link to a dying volcano?
That's not up to me! Whatever you are and whoever you choose to be is **your** choice.
All I know is that the volcano has been acting strangely since you became the Goddess.
Like an animal shedding its skin.
I suspect that's why the Cult kept your mother sedated all those years. To keep the mountain in check.
The Goddess is the volcano. The volcano is the Goddess.
Don't bring my mother into this...
Sorry.
It sounds to me like you just wanna put the Goddess back in her cage again.
I'd see Azar reduced to ash before I let it stay in the hands of those monsters.

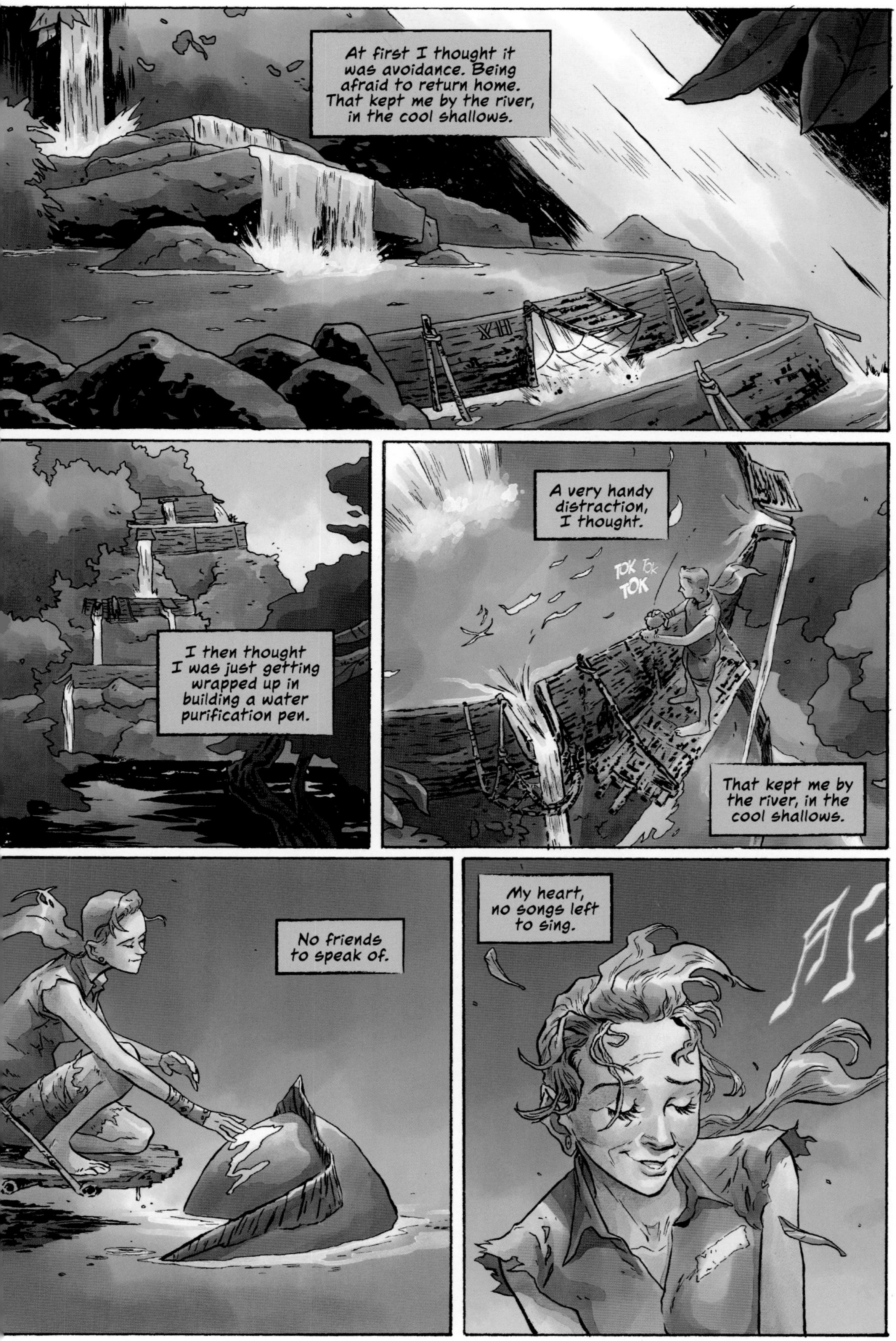
At first I thought it was avoidance. Being afraid to return home. That kept me by the river, in the cool shallows.
I then thought I was just getting wrapped up in building a water purification pen.
A very handy distraction, I thought.
TOK TOK TOK
That kept me by the river, in the cool shallows.
No friends to speak of.
My heart, no songs left to sing.

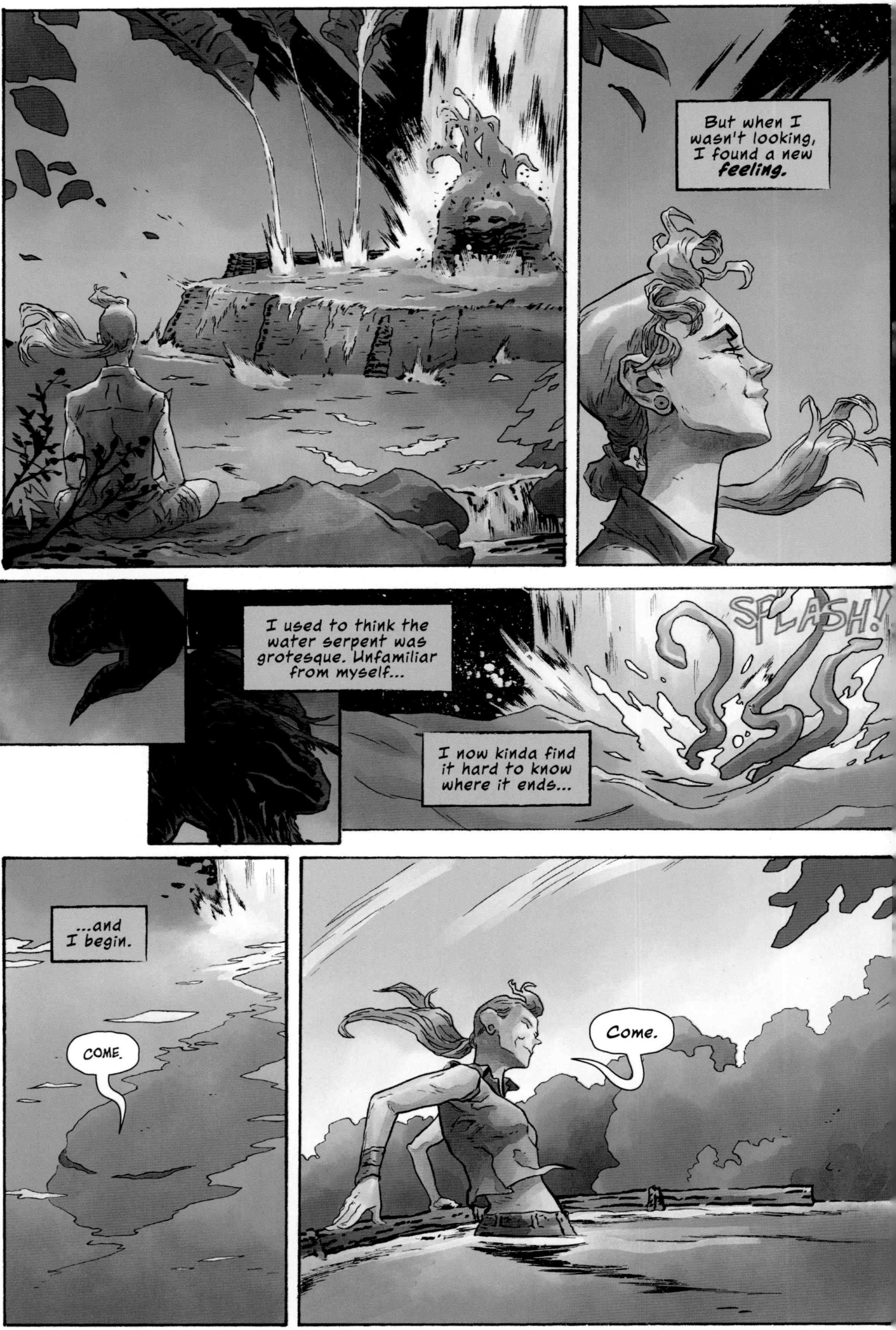

But when I wasn't looking, I found a new **feeling.**
I used to think the water serpent was grotesque. Unfamiliar from myself...
SPLASH!
I now kinda find it hard to know where it ends...
...and I begin.
COME.
Come.

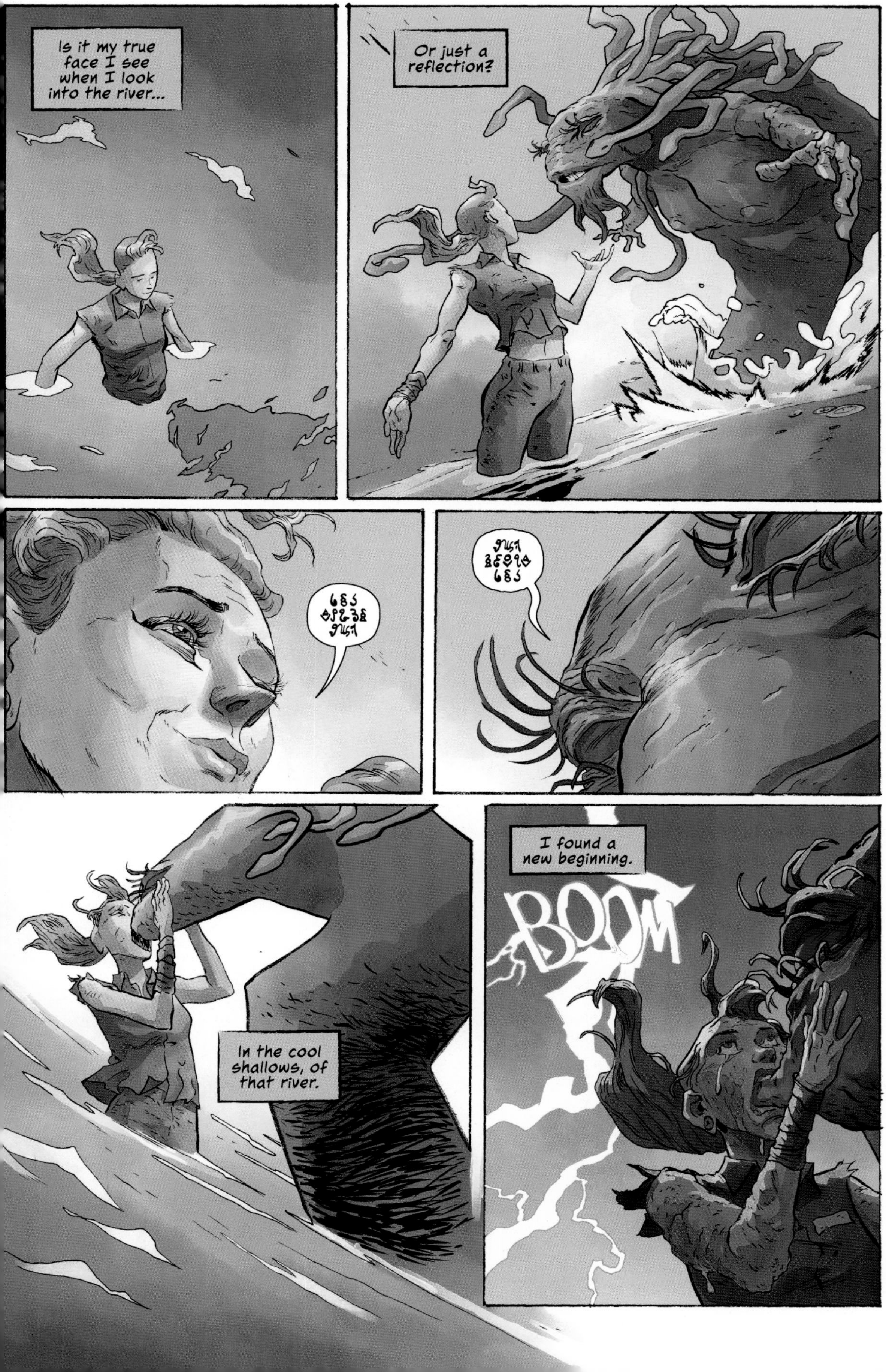
Is it my true face I see when I look into the river...
Or just a reflection?
I found a new beginning.
BOOM
In the cool shallows, of that river.

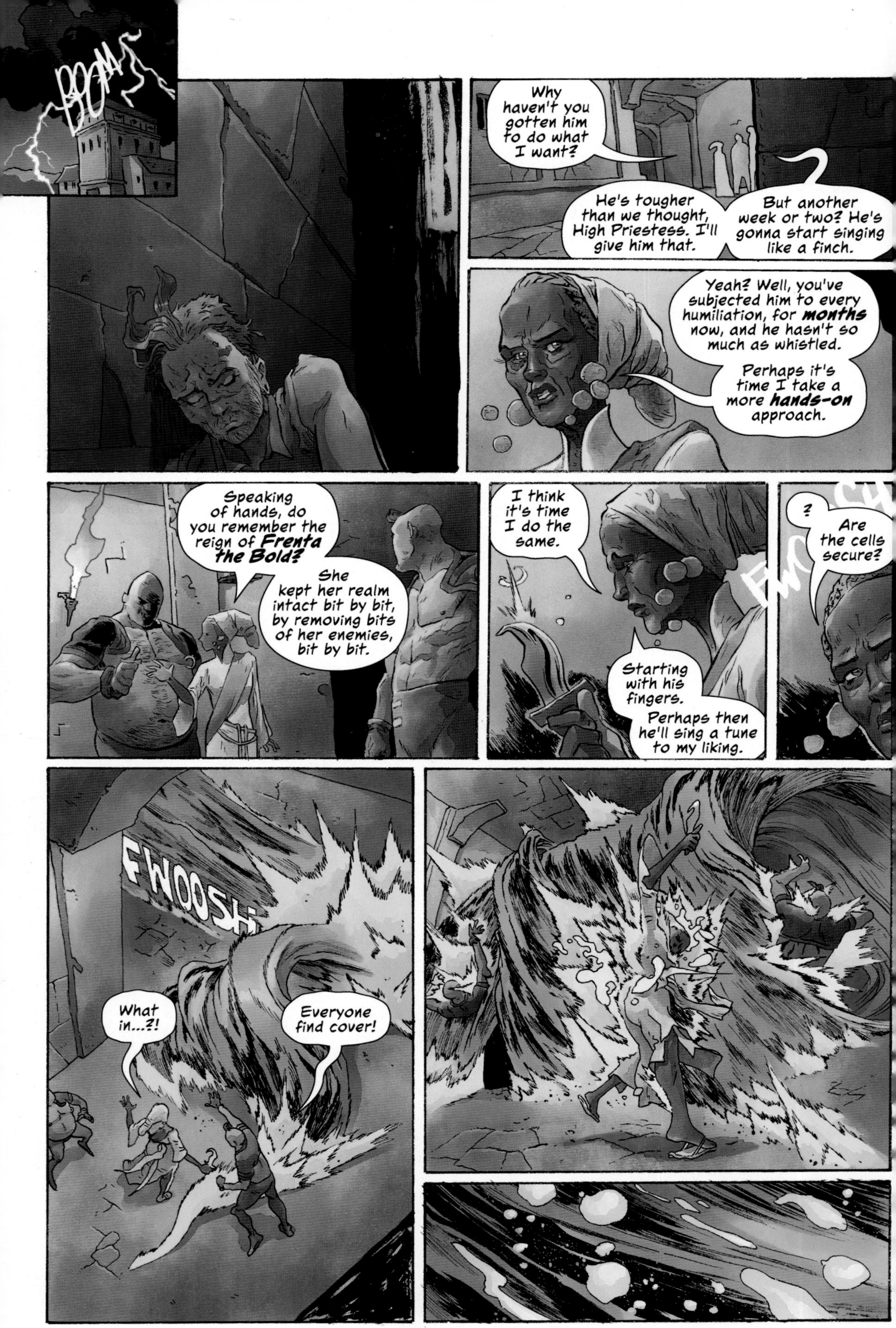
BOOM
Why haven't you gotten him to do what I want?
He's tougher than we thought, High Priestess. I'll give him that.
But another week or two? He's gonna start singing like a finch.
Yeah? Well, you've subjected him to every humiliation, for **months** now, and he hasn't so much as whistled.
Perhaps it's time I take a more **hands-on** approach.
Speaking of hands, do you remember the reign of ***Frenta the Bold?***
She kept her realm intact bit by bit, by removing bits of her enemies, bit by bit.
I think it's time I do the same.
Starting with his fingers.
Perhaps then he'll sing a tune to my liking.
?
Are the cells secure?
FWOOSH
What in...?!
Everyone find cover!

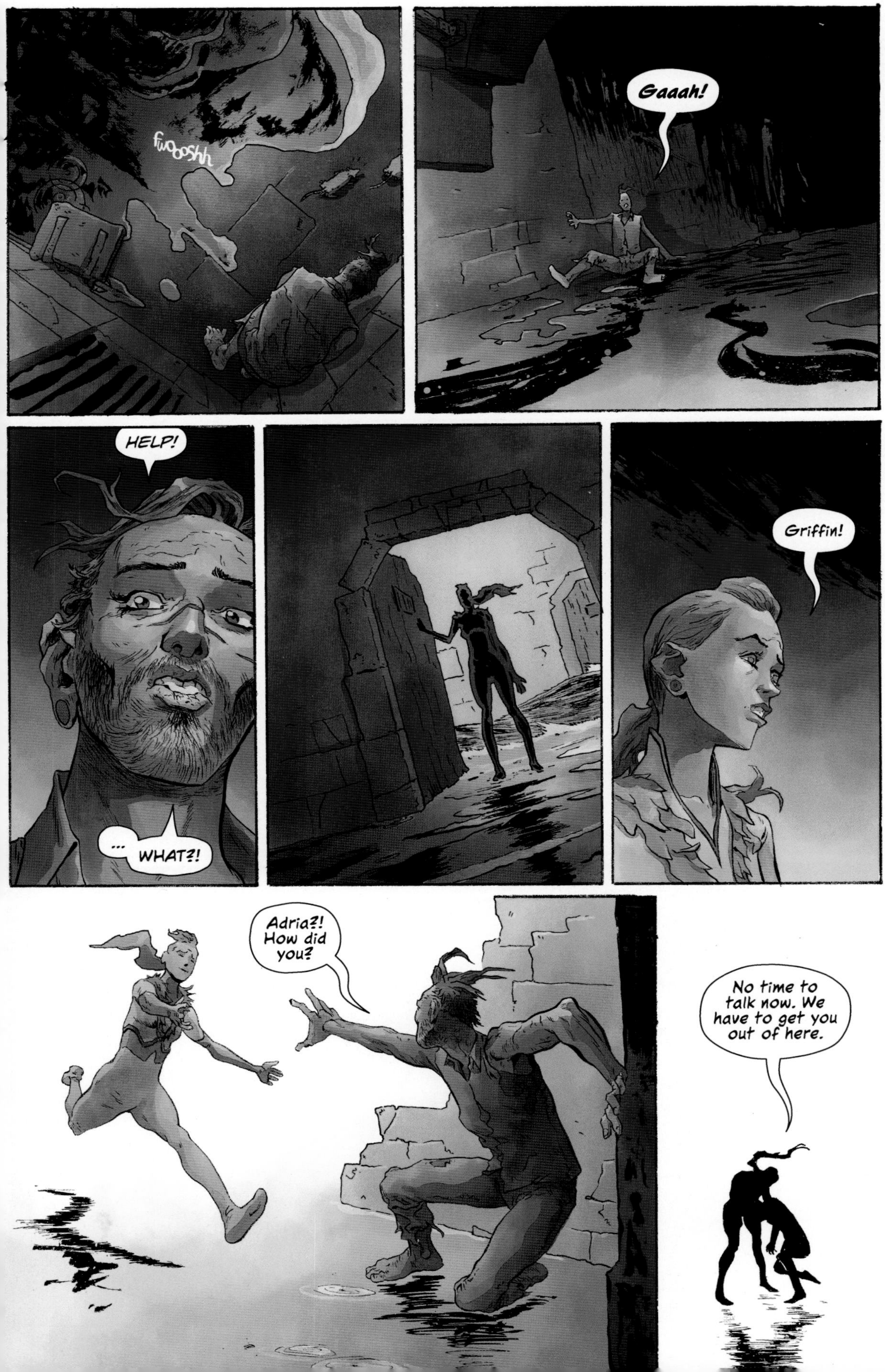
fwoooshh
Gaaah!
HELP!
... WHAT?!
Griffin!
Adria?! How did you?
No time to talk now. We have to get you out of here.

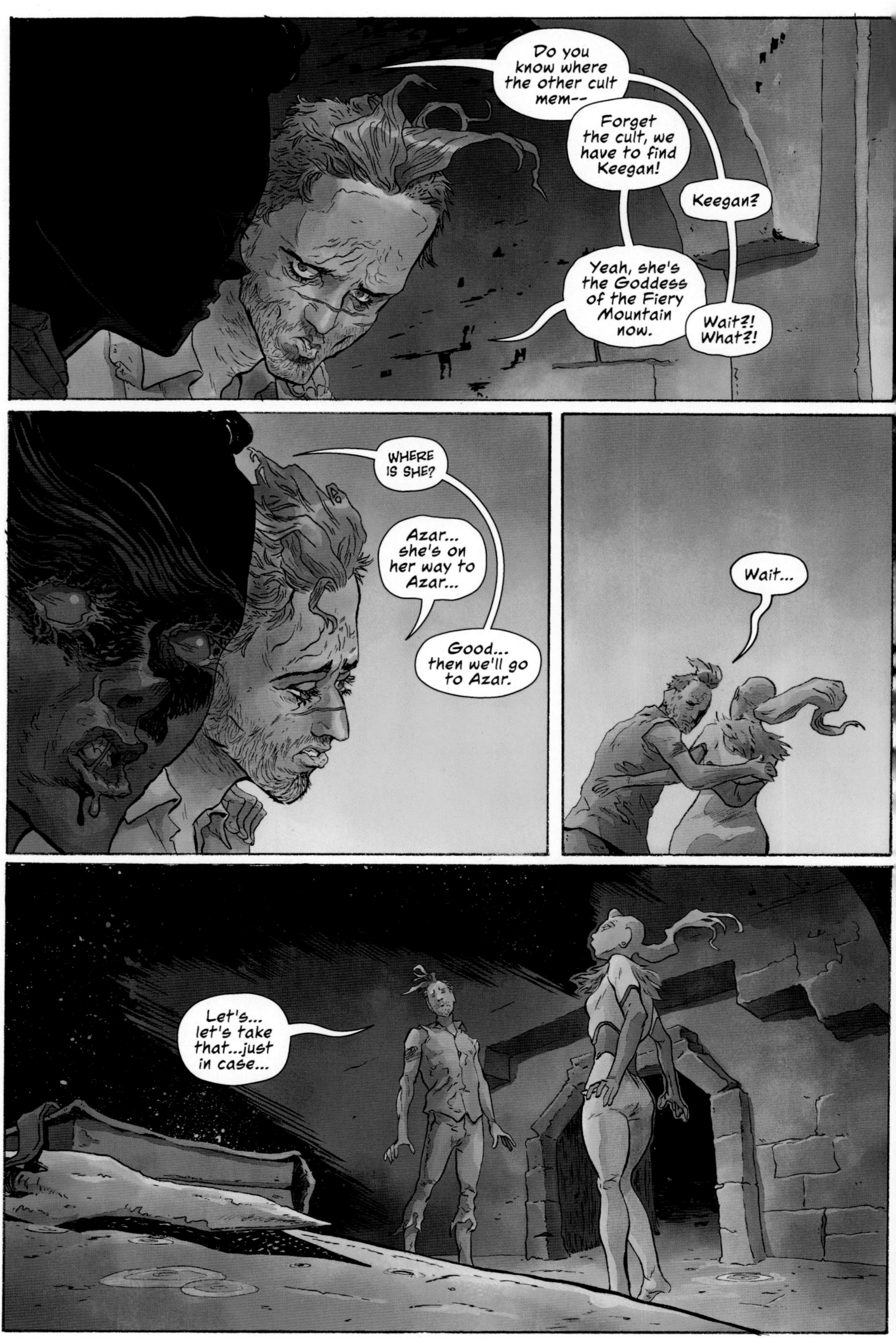
Do you know where the other cult mem--
Forget the cult, we have to find Keegan!
Keegan?
Yeah, she's the Goddess of the Fiery Mountain now.
Wait?! What?!
WHERE IS SHE?
Azar... she's on her way to Azar...
Good... then we'll go to Azar.
Wait...
Let's... let's take that...just in case...

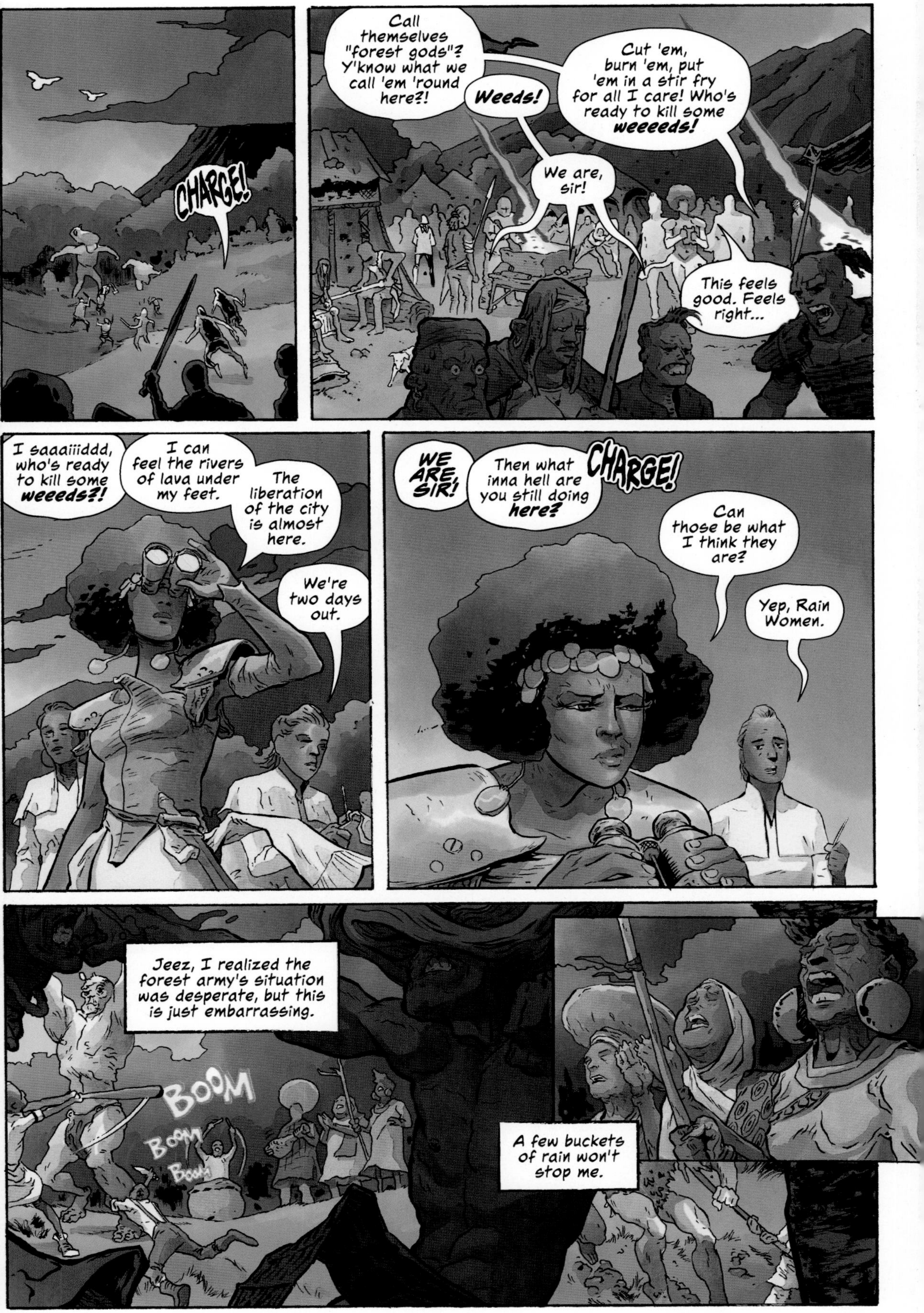
CHARGE!
Call themselves "forest gods"? Y'know what we call 'em 'round here?!
Weeds!
Cut 'em, burn 'em, put 'em in a stir fry for all I care! Who's ready to kill some weeeeds!
We are, sir!
This feels good. Feels right...
I saaaiiiddd, who's ready to kill some weeeds?!
I can feel the rivers of lava under my feet.
The liberation of the city is almost here.
We're two days out.
WE ARE, SIR!
Then what inna hell are you still doing here?
CHARGE!
Can those be what I think they are?
Yep, Rain Women.
Jeez, I realized the forest army's situation was desperate, but this is just embarrassing.
BOOM
BOOM
BOOM
A few buckets of rain won't stop me.

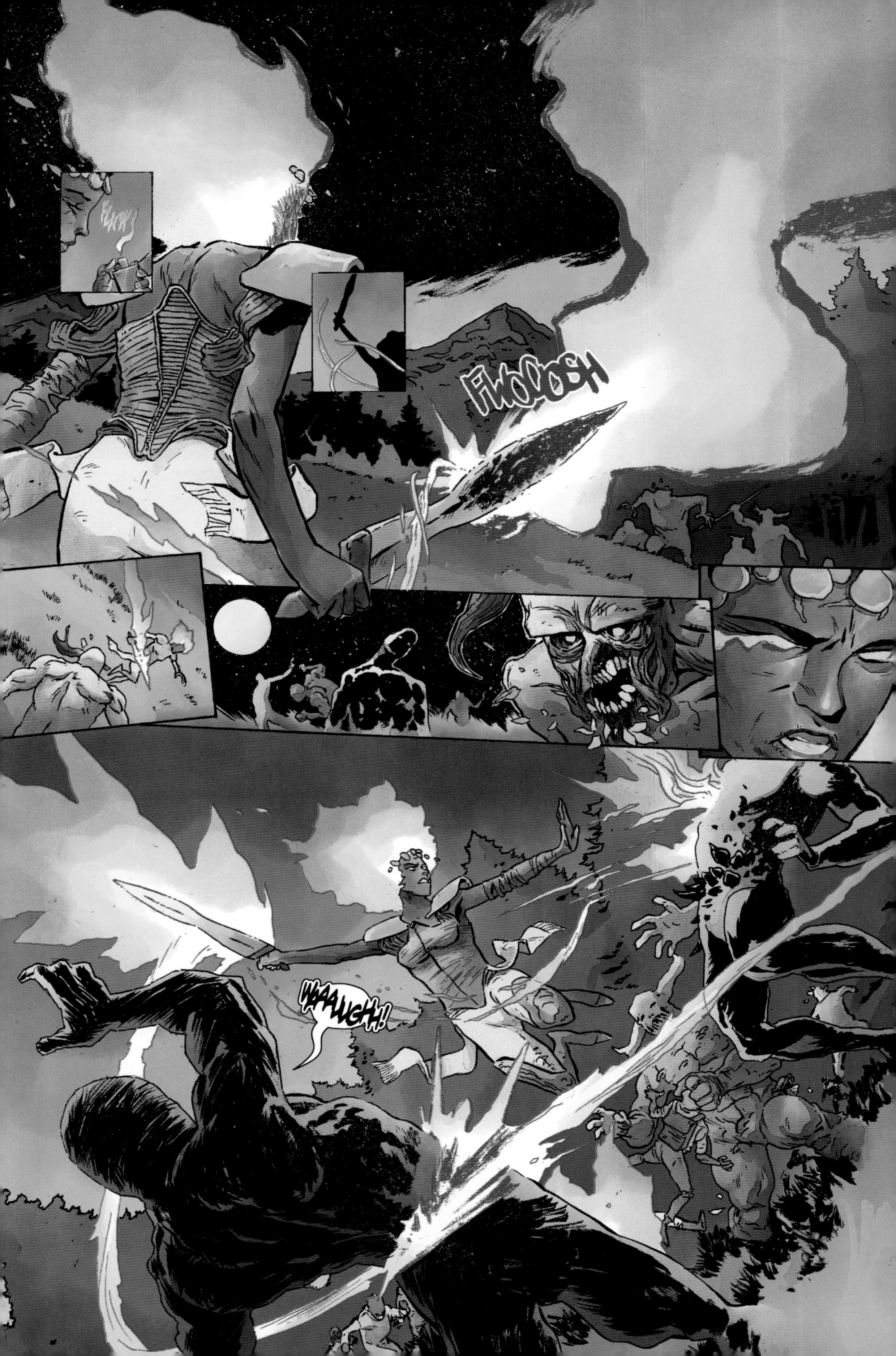
FLICK
FWOOOSH
WAAAUGH!

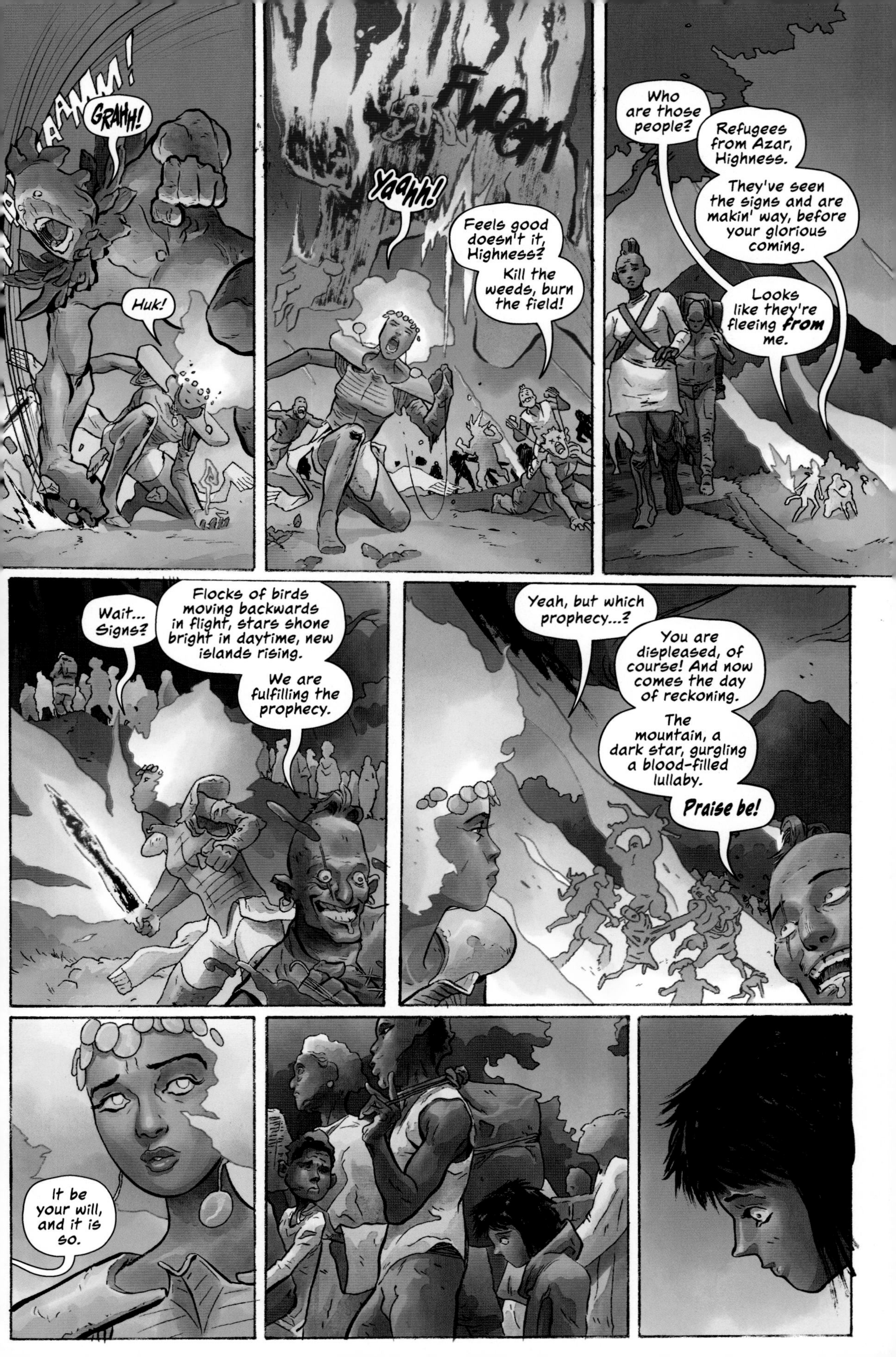

AAMM!
GRAHH!
Huk!
FWOOM
Yaahh!
Feels good doesn't it, Highness?
Kill the weeds, burn the field!
Who are those people?
Refugees from Azar, Highness.
They've seen the signs and are makin' way, before your glorious coming.
Looks like they're fleeing from me.
Wait... Signs?
Flocks of birds moving backwards in flight, stars shone bright in daytime, new islands rising.
We are fulfilling the prophecy.
Yeah, but which prophecy...?
You are displeased, of course! And now comes the day of reckoning.
The mountain, a dark star, gurgling a blood-filled lullaby.
Praise be!
It be your will, and it is so.

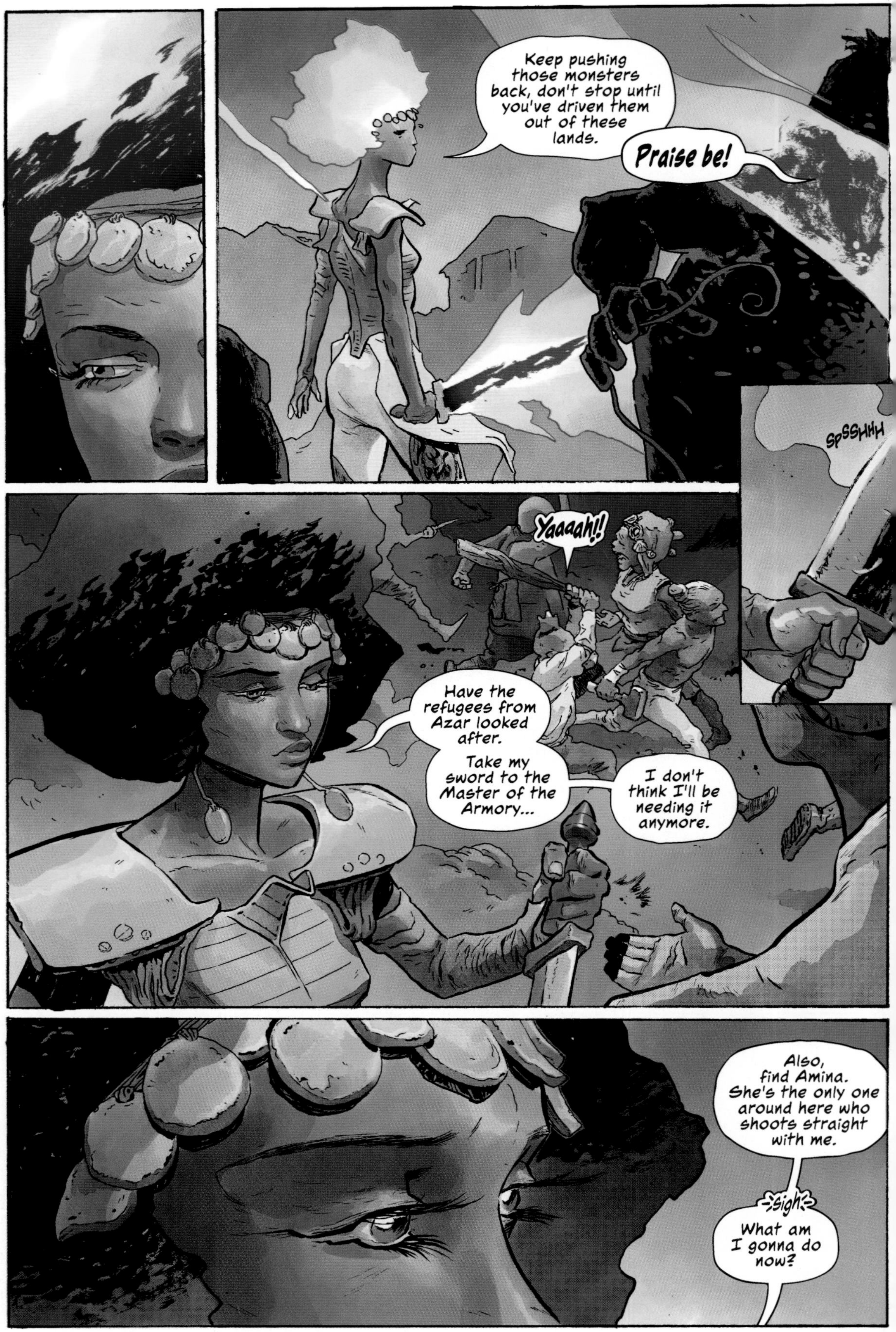
Keep pushing those monsters back, don't stop until you've driven them out of these lands.
Praise be!
SPSSHHH
Yaaaah!!
Have the refugees from Azar looked after.
Take my sword to the Master of the Armory...
I don't think I'll be needing it anymore.
Also, find Amina. She's the only one around here who shoots straight with me.
-sigh-
What am I gonna do now?

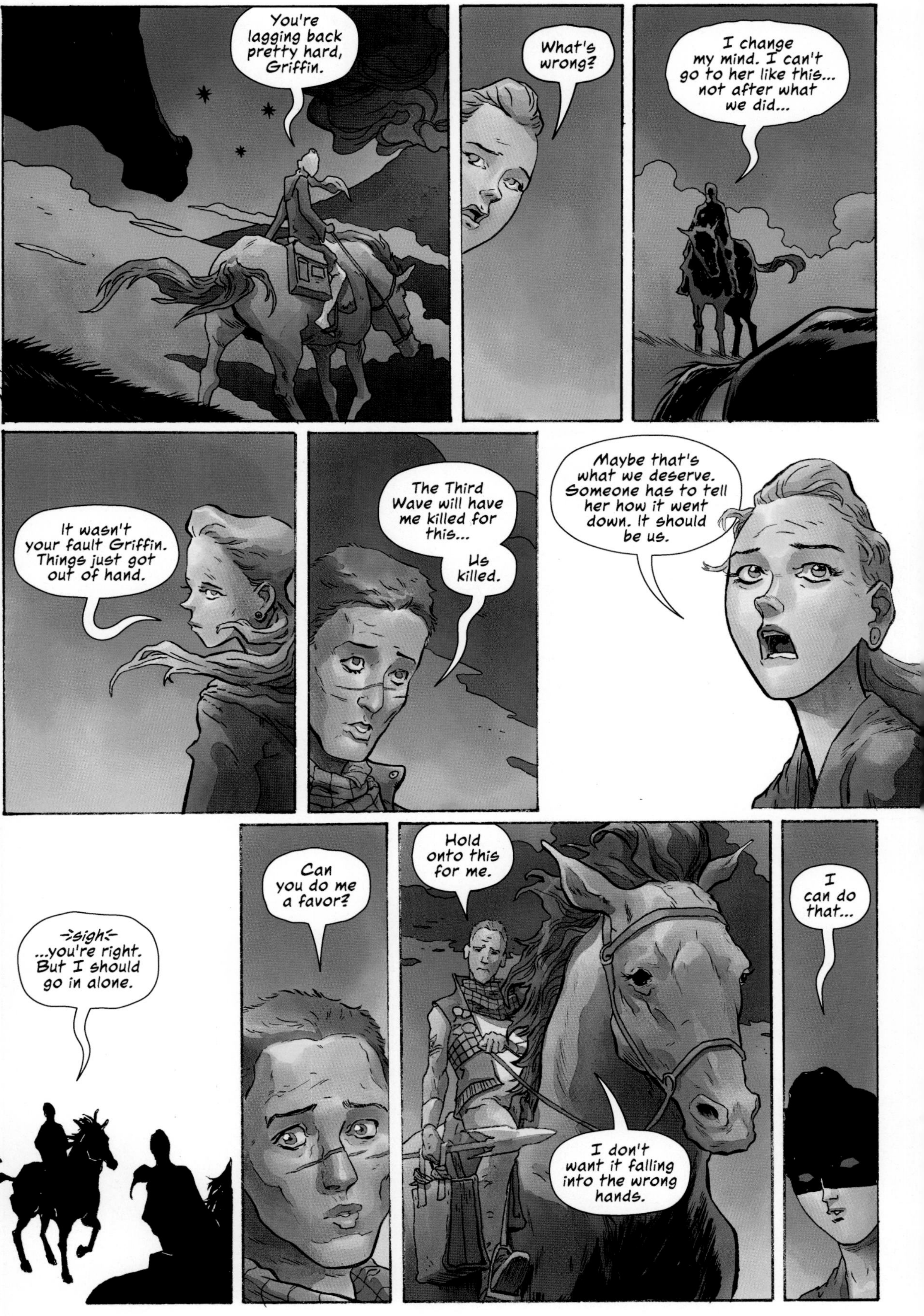
You're lagging back pretty hard, Griffin.
What's wrong?
I change my mind. I can't go to her like this... not after what we did...
It wasn't your fault Griffin. Things just got out of hand.
The Third Wave will have me killed for this...
Us killed.
Maybe that's what we deserve. Someone has to tell her how it went down. It should be us.
-sigh- ...you're right. But I should go in alone.
Can you do me a favor?
Hold onto this for me.
I don't want it falling into the wrong hands.
I can do that...

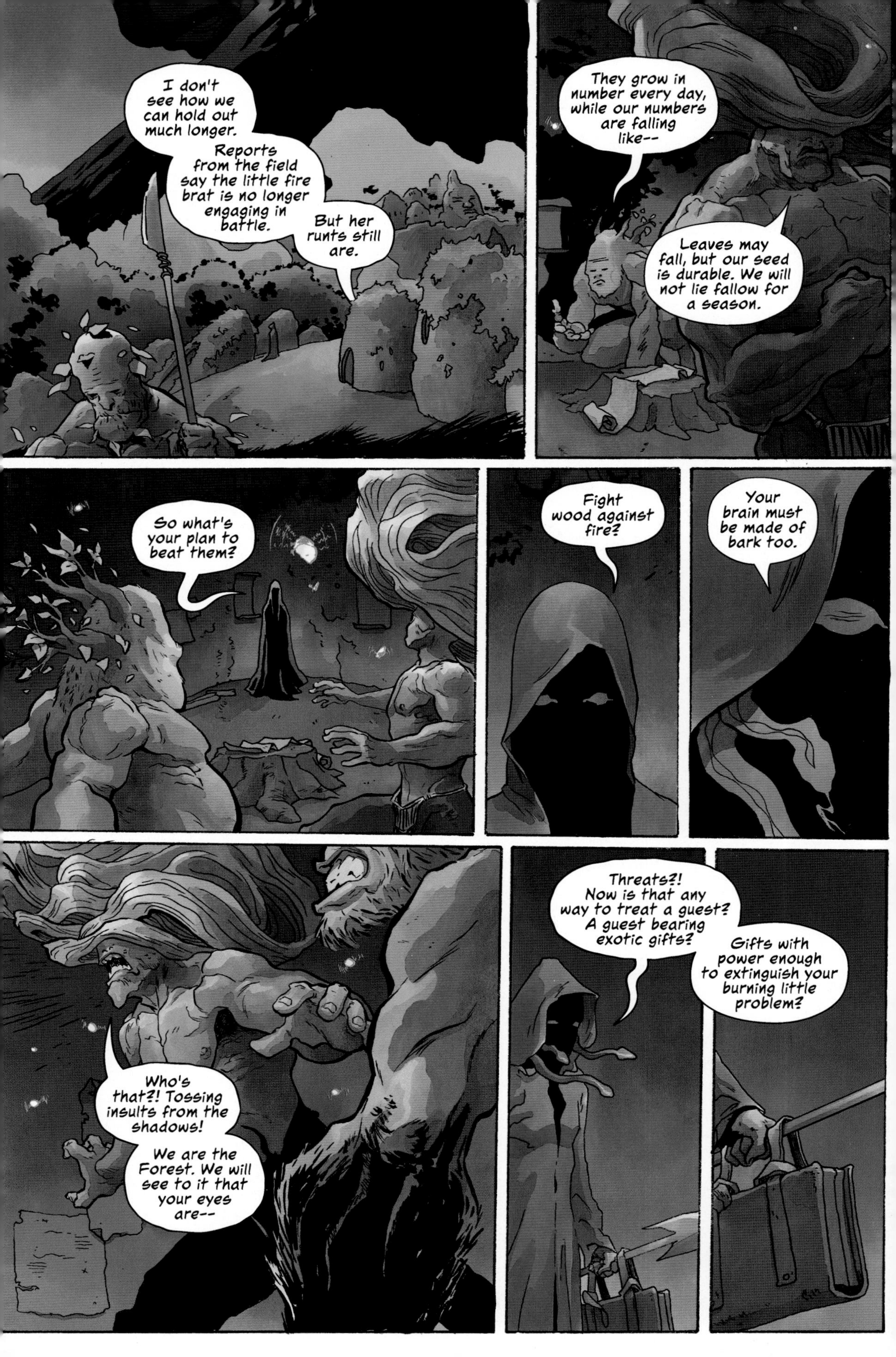
I don't see how we can hold out much longer.
Reports from the field say the little fire brat is no longer engaging in battle.
But her runts still are.
They grow in number every day, while our numbers are falling like--
Leaves may fall, but our seed is durable. We will not lie fallow for a season.
So what's your plan to beat them?
Fight wood against fire?
Your brain must be made of bark too.
Who's that?! Tossing insults from the shadows!
We are the Forest. We will see to it that your eyes are--
Threats?! Now is that any way to treat a guest? A guest bearing exotic gifts?
Gifts with power enough to extinguish your burning little problem?

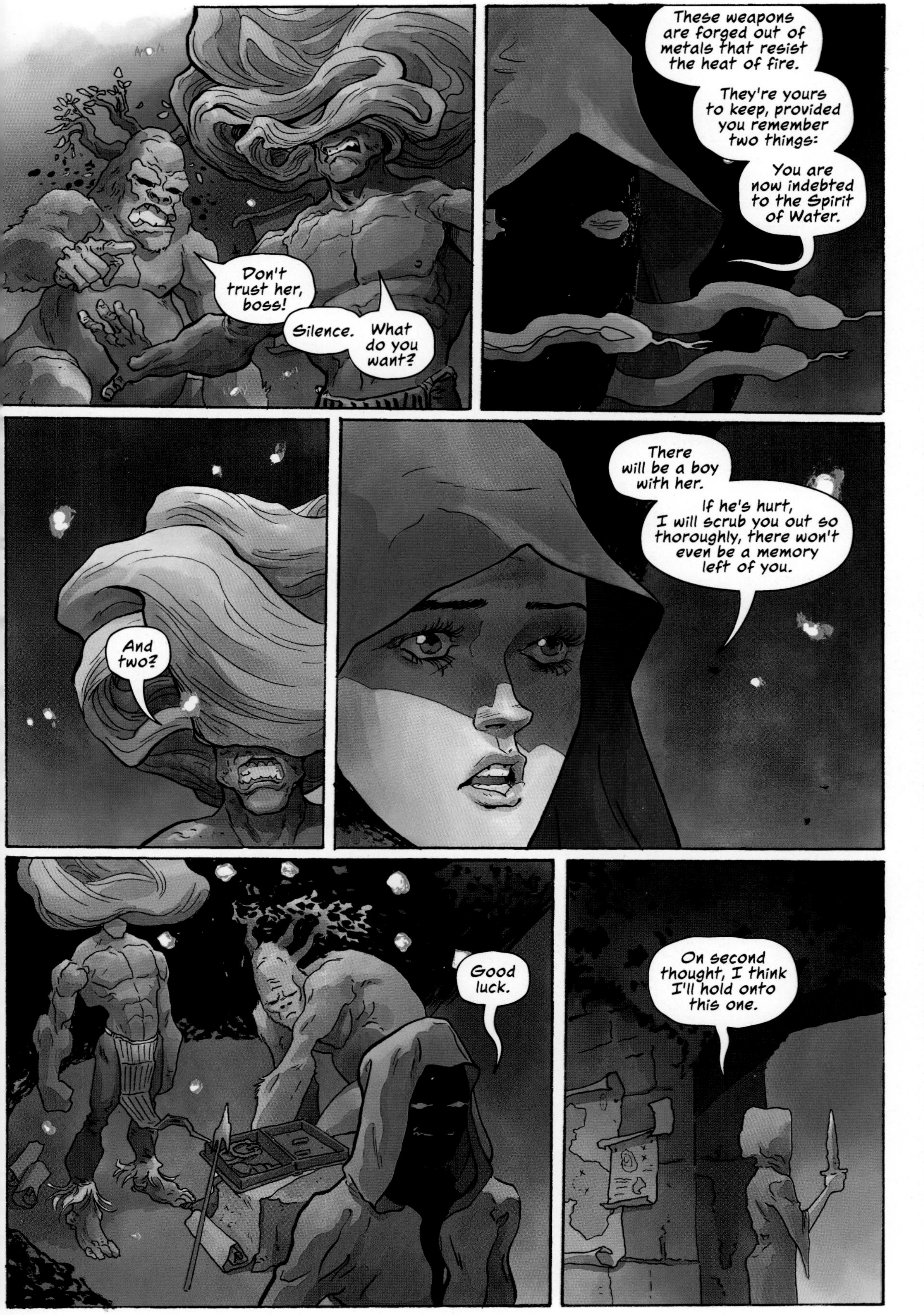
Don't trust her, boss!
Silence.
What do you want?
These weapons are forged out of metals that resist the heat of fire.
They're yours to keep, provided you remember two things:
You are now indebted to the Spirit of Water.
And two?
There will be a boy with her.
If he's hurt, I will scrub you out so thoroughly, there won't even be a memory left of you.
Good luck.
On second thought, I think I'll hold onto this one.

THE GOSPEL ACCORDING TO AMINA

Day 97

Tonight is the first Appeasement of the Goddess Ceremony in hundreds of years.

"Praise and Salutations to the mighty Goddess of the Fiery Mountain...

BOOM

It's being held in the environs, just outside of the city.

"May not your fire rain down on our fields. May not your wrath find us.

"May not our hearts be singed nor our bones turned to ash.

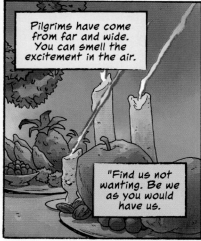

Pilgrims have come from far and wide. You can smell the excitement in the air.

"Find us not wanting. Be we as you would have us.

Our ranks are less excited. Once it came to light that the citizens of Azar aren't **prisoners** of the Forest...

Heh, well, the gruel is **almost** warm tonight.

They're **subjects**. In the Goddesses' absence, the Forest became the city's protectors.

"That your will be done, not ours. We kneel before you."

Our choice: Conquer the city, or walk away. It was an easy choice. We'll announce our withdrawal after the ceremony.

We beseech that you not besiege. We live only to please you.

All of this naturally made Keegan uneasy. But we're keeping our spirits up.

Be we compliant, may we toil to make works that are worthy of your pleasure.

Uggghhh, what's with all this stuff he's ranting?

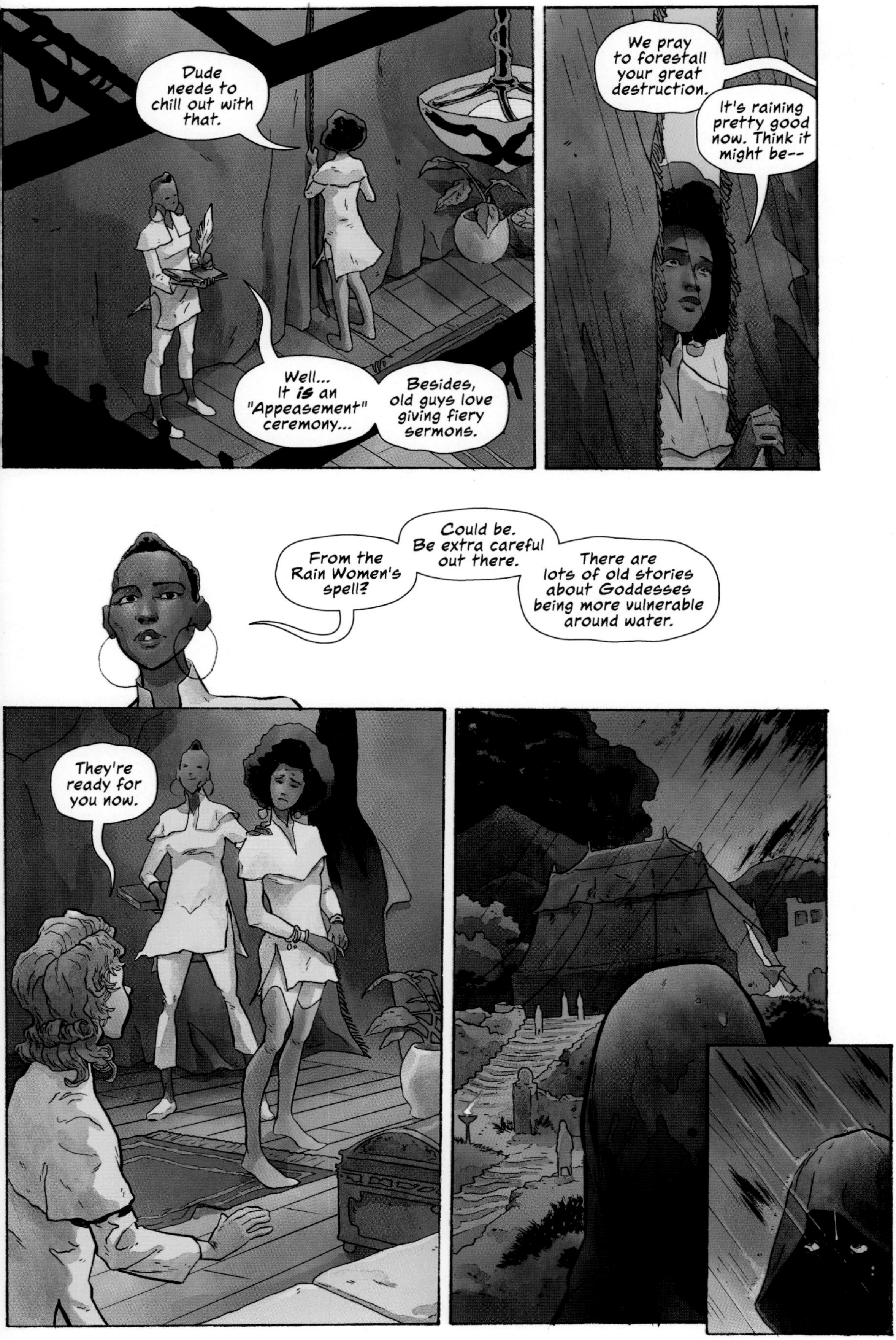
Dude needs to chill out with that.
Well... It *is* an "Appeasement" ceremony...
Besides, old guys love giving fiery sermons.
We pray to forestall your great destruction.
It's raining pretty good now. Think it might be--
From the Rain Women's spell?
Could be. Be extra careful out there.
There are lots of old stories about Goddesses being more vulnerable around water.
They're ready for you now.

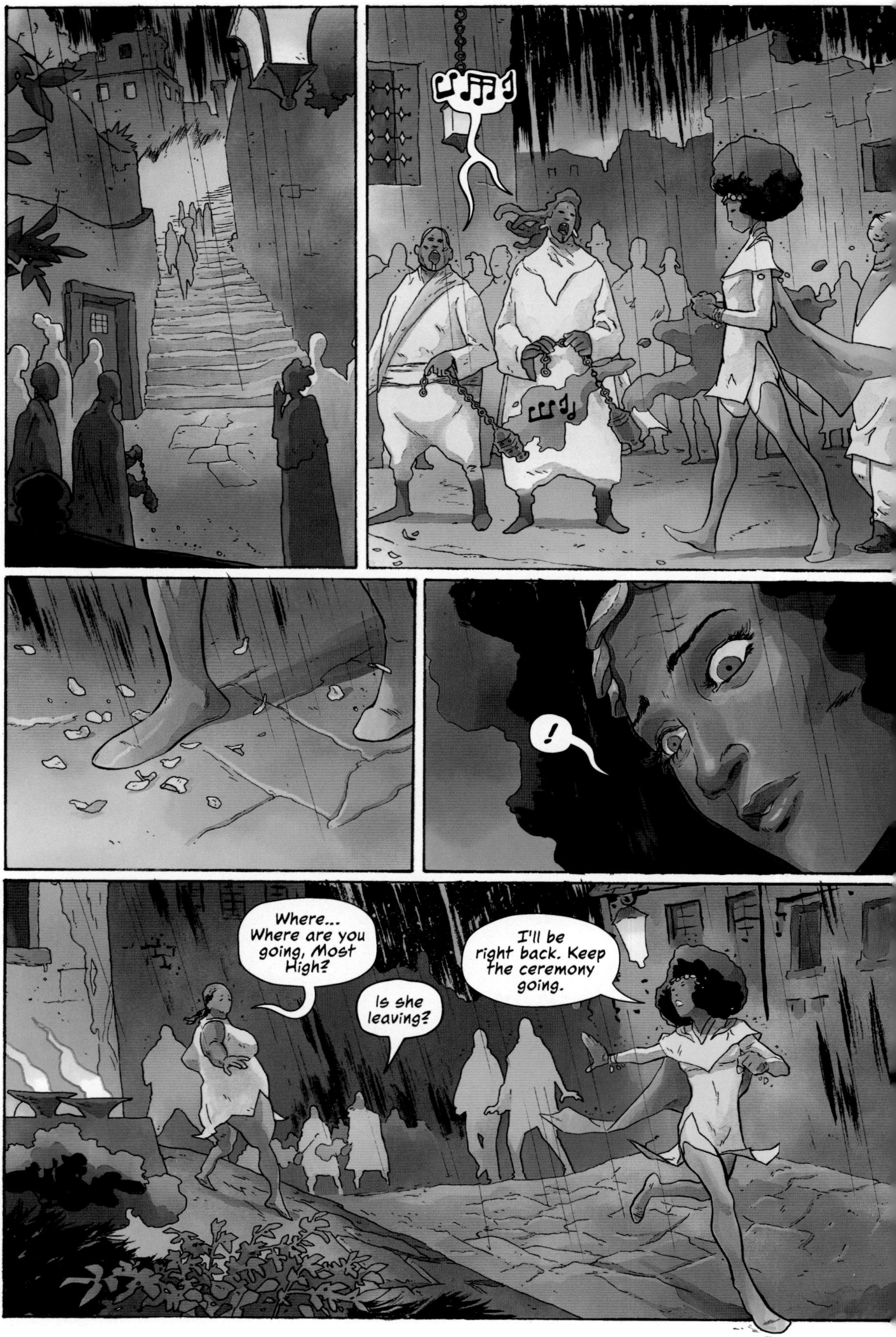
!
Where... Where are you going, Most High?
Is she leaving?
I'll be right back. Keep the ceremony going.

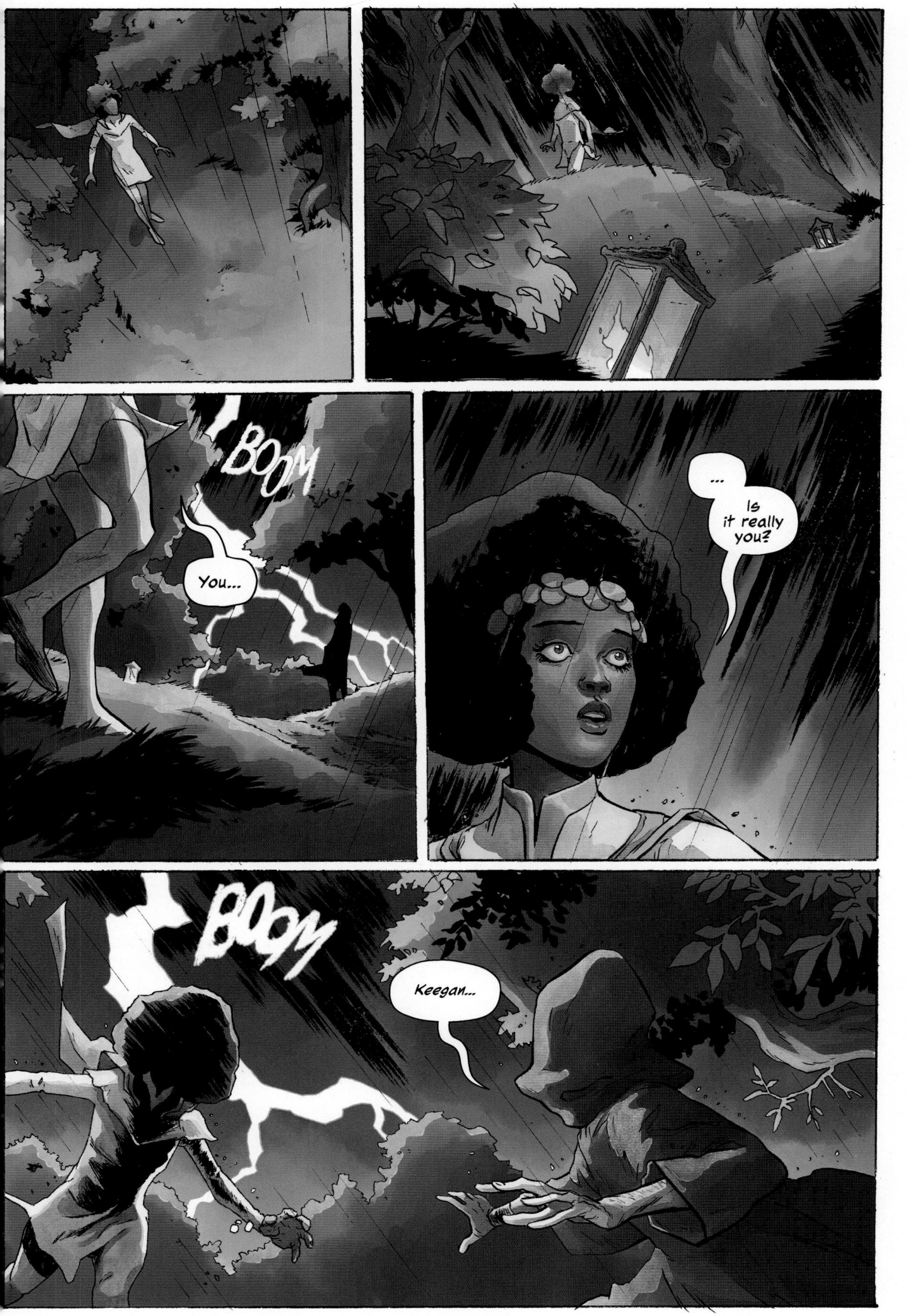
BOOM
You...
...
Is it really you?
BOOM
Keegan...

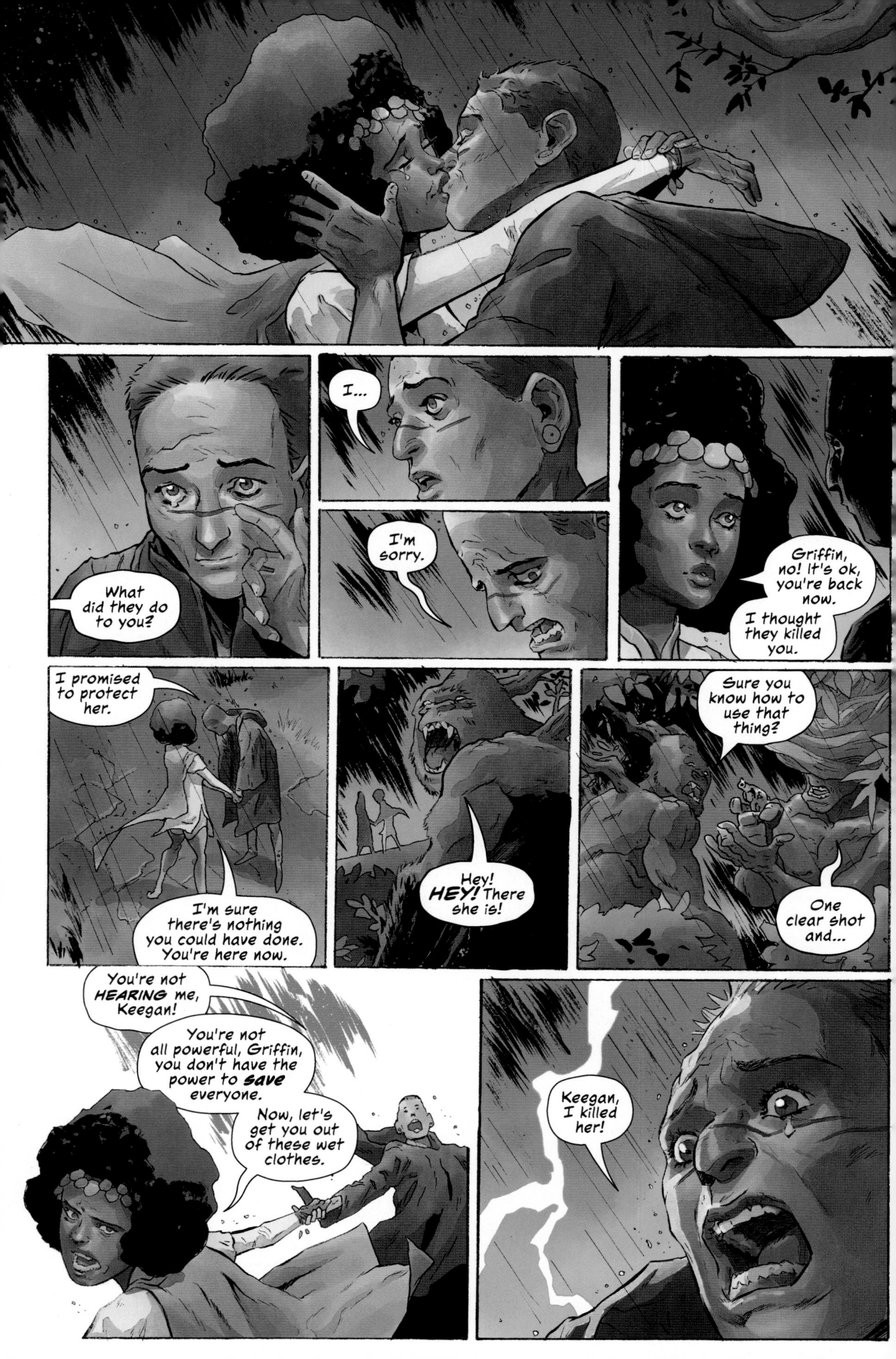

What did they do to you?
I...
I'm sorry.
Griffin, no! It's ok, you're back now.
I thought they killed you.
I promised to protect her.
I'm sure there's nothing you could have done. You're here now.
Hey! HEY! There she is!
Sure you know how to use that thing?
One clear shot and...
You're not HEARING me, Keegan!
You're not all powerful, Griffin, you don't have the power to save everyone.
Now, let's get you out of these wet clothes.
Keegan, I killed her!

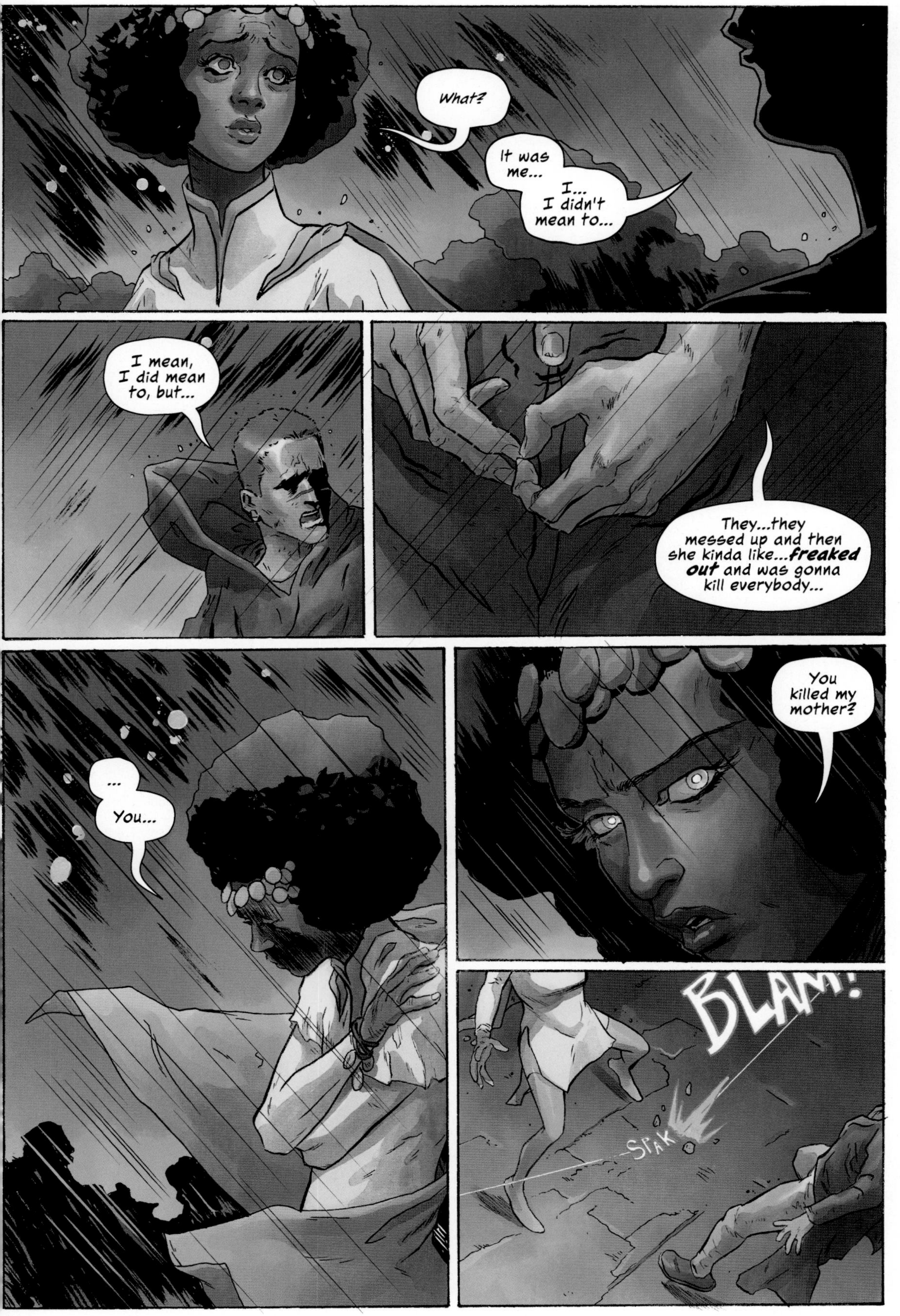
What?
It was me...
I... I didn't mean to...
I mean, I did mean to, but...
They...they messed up and then she kinda like...**freaked out** and was gonna kill everybody...
...
You...
You killed my mother?
BLAM!
SPAK

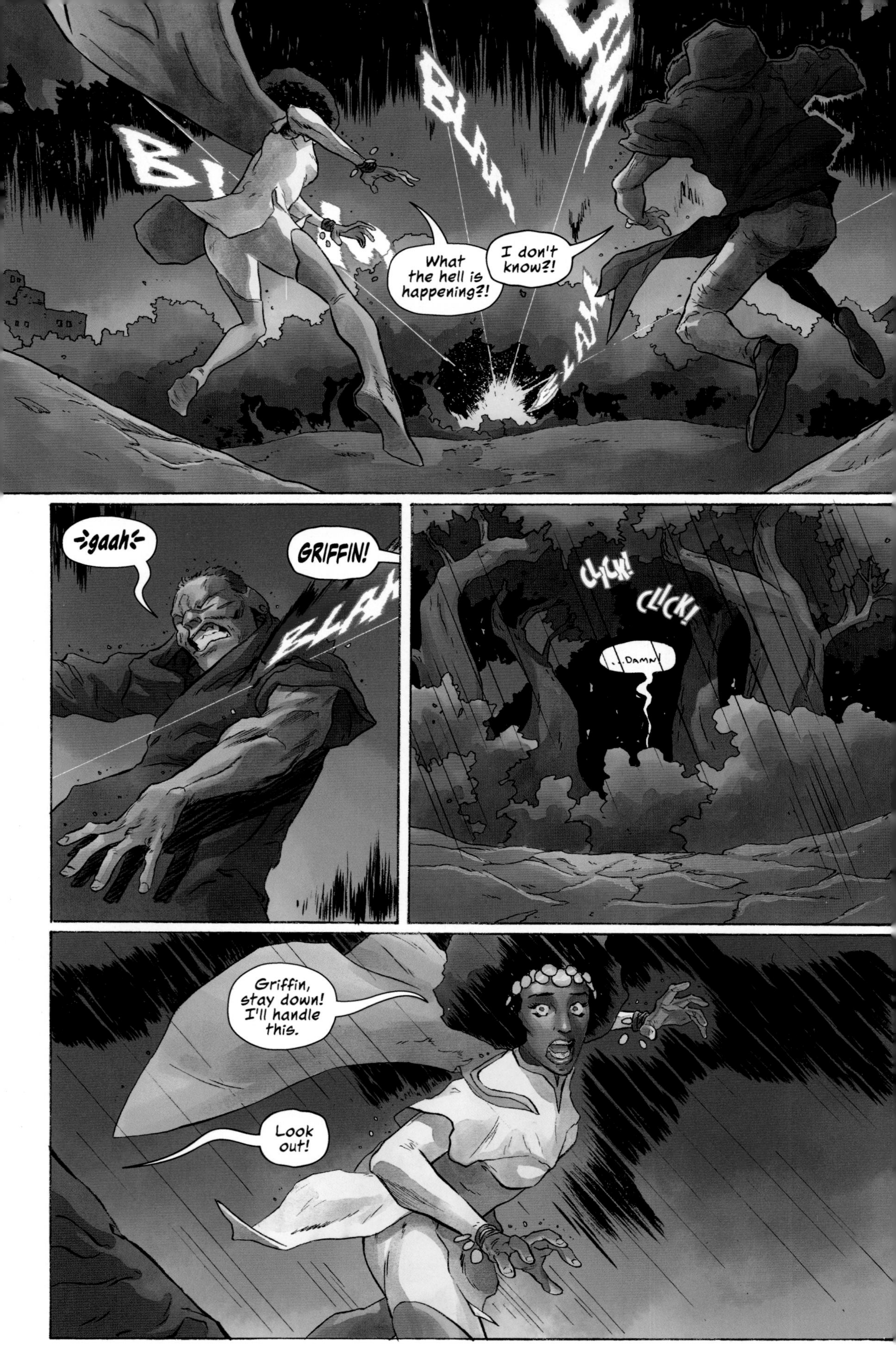
BLAM
What the hell is happening?!
I don't know?!
BLAM
-gaah-
GRIFFIN!
BLAM
CLICK!
CLICK!
...DAMN
Griffin, stay down! I'll handle this.
Look out!

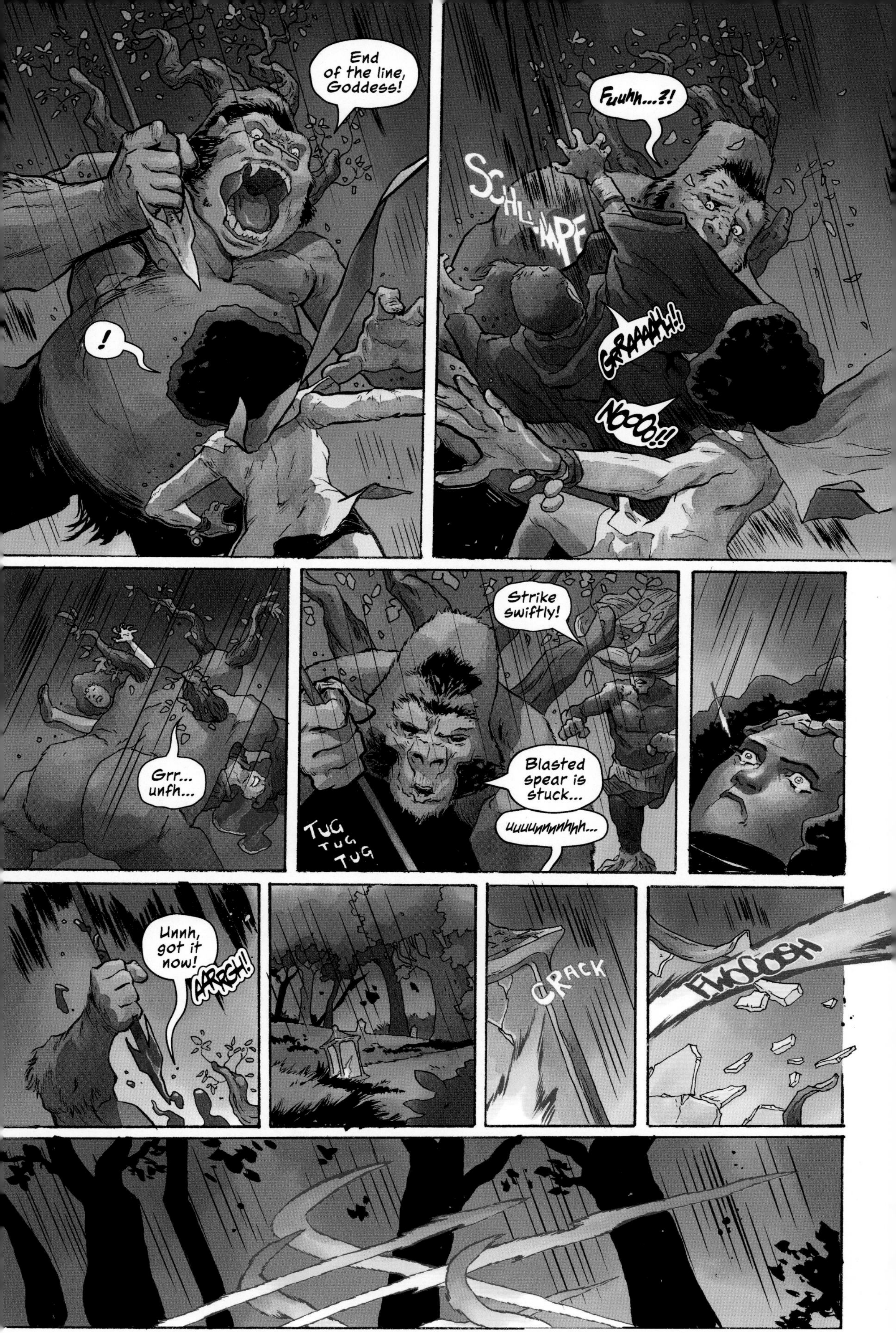
End of the line, Goddess!
!
Fuuhh...?!
SCHLUMPF
GRRAAAHH!!
NOOOO!!
Grr... unfh...
Strike swiftly!
Blasted spear is stuck...
uuuunnnnhh...
TUG TUG TUG
Unnh, got it now!
AARRGH!
CRACK
FWOOOSH

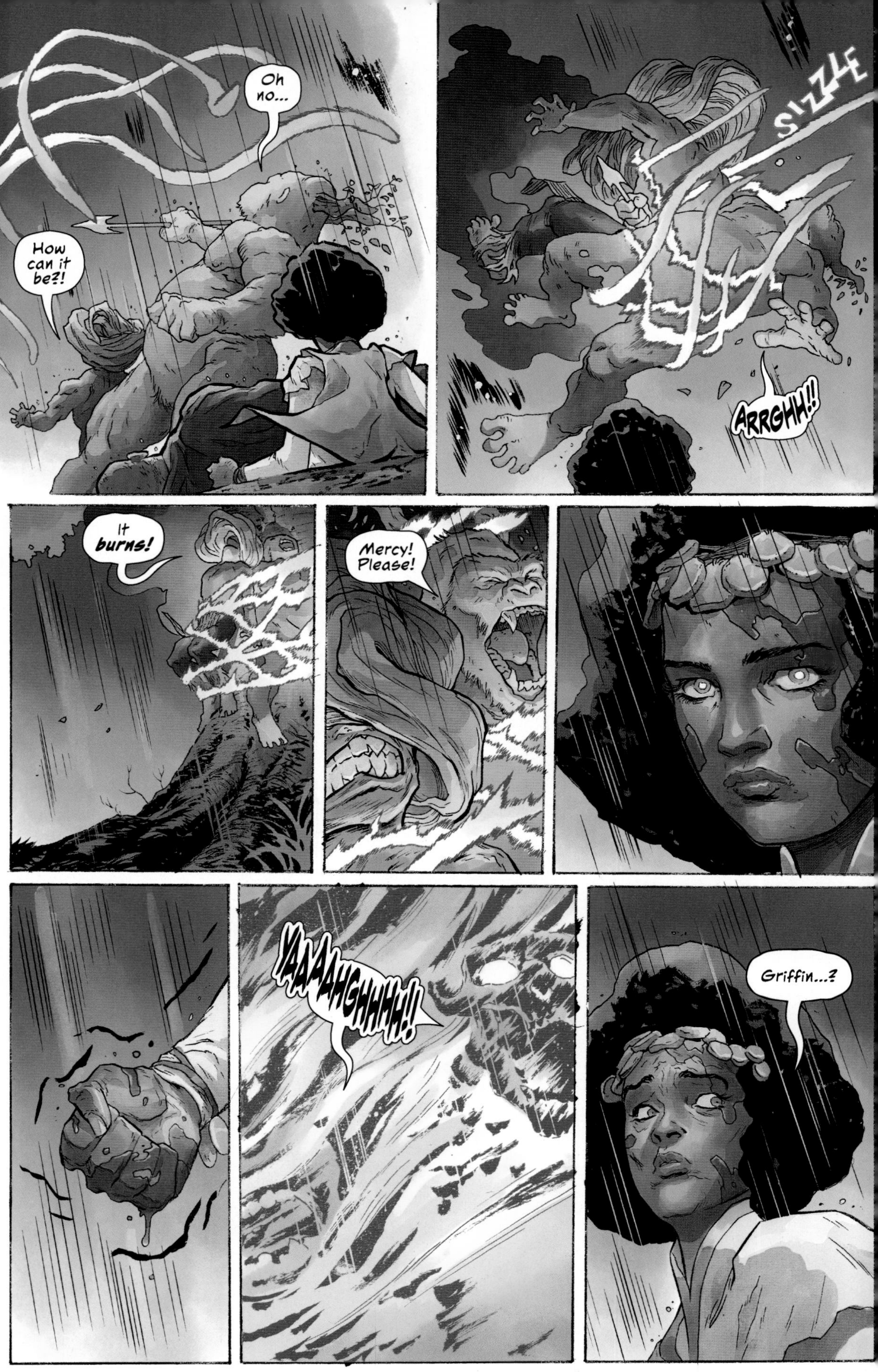

Oh no...
How can it be?!
S'IZZLE
ARRGHH!!
It burns!
Mercy! Please!
YAAAAHGHHHH!!
Griffin...?

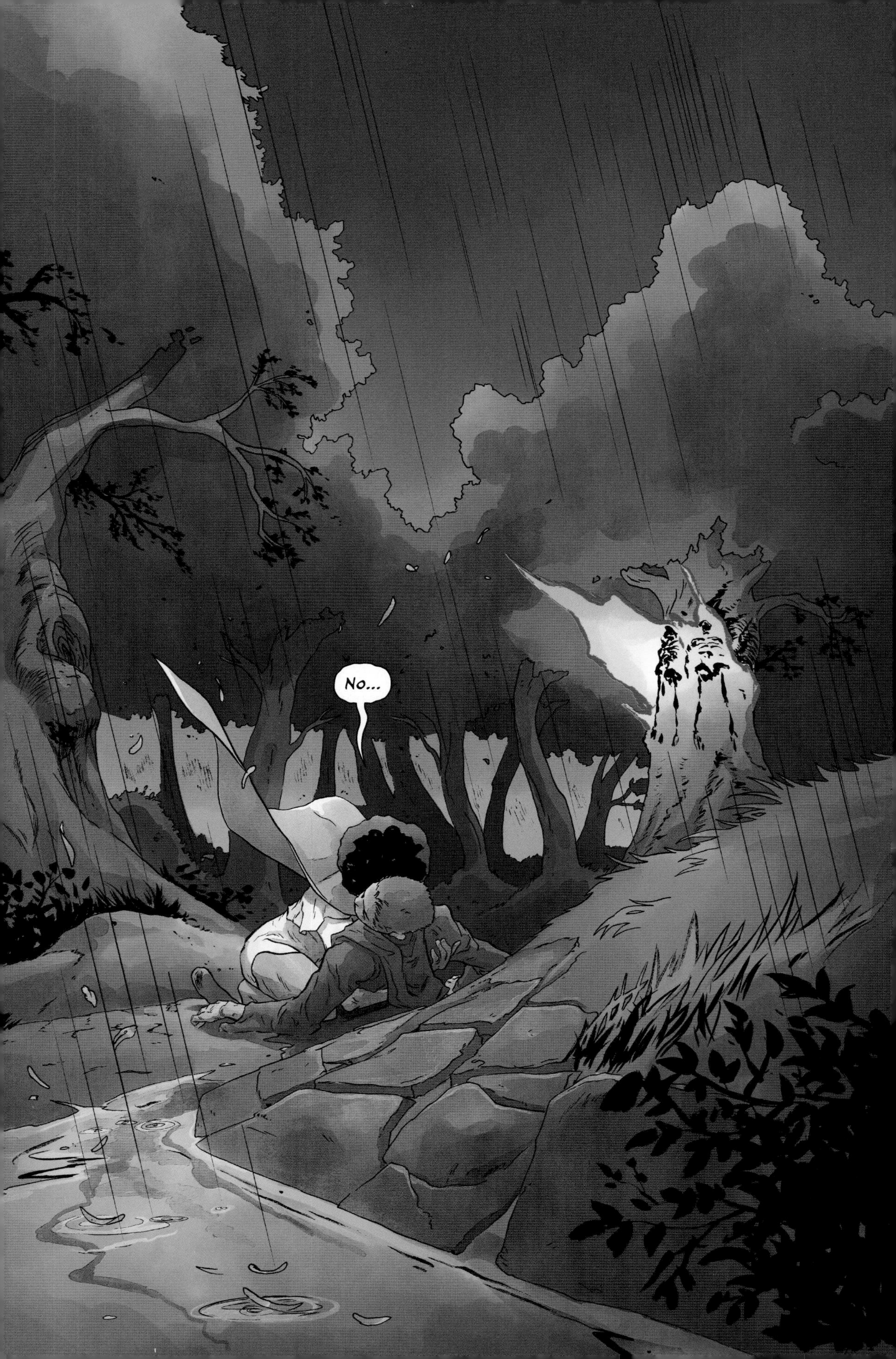
No...

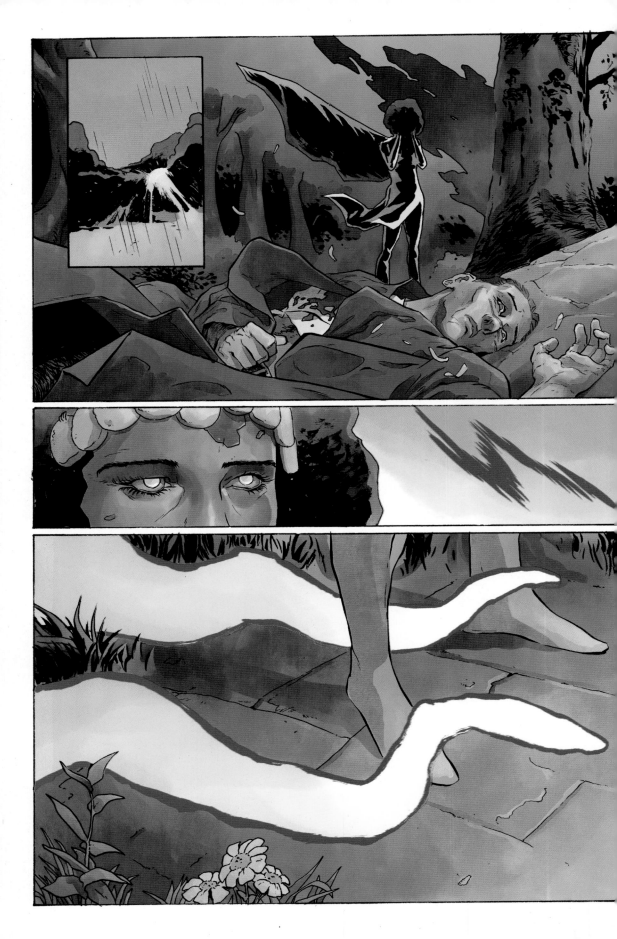

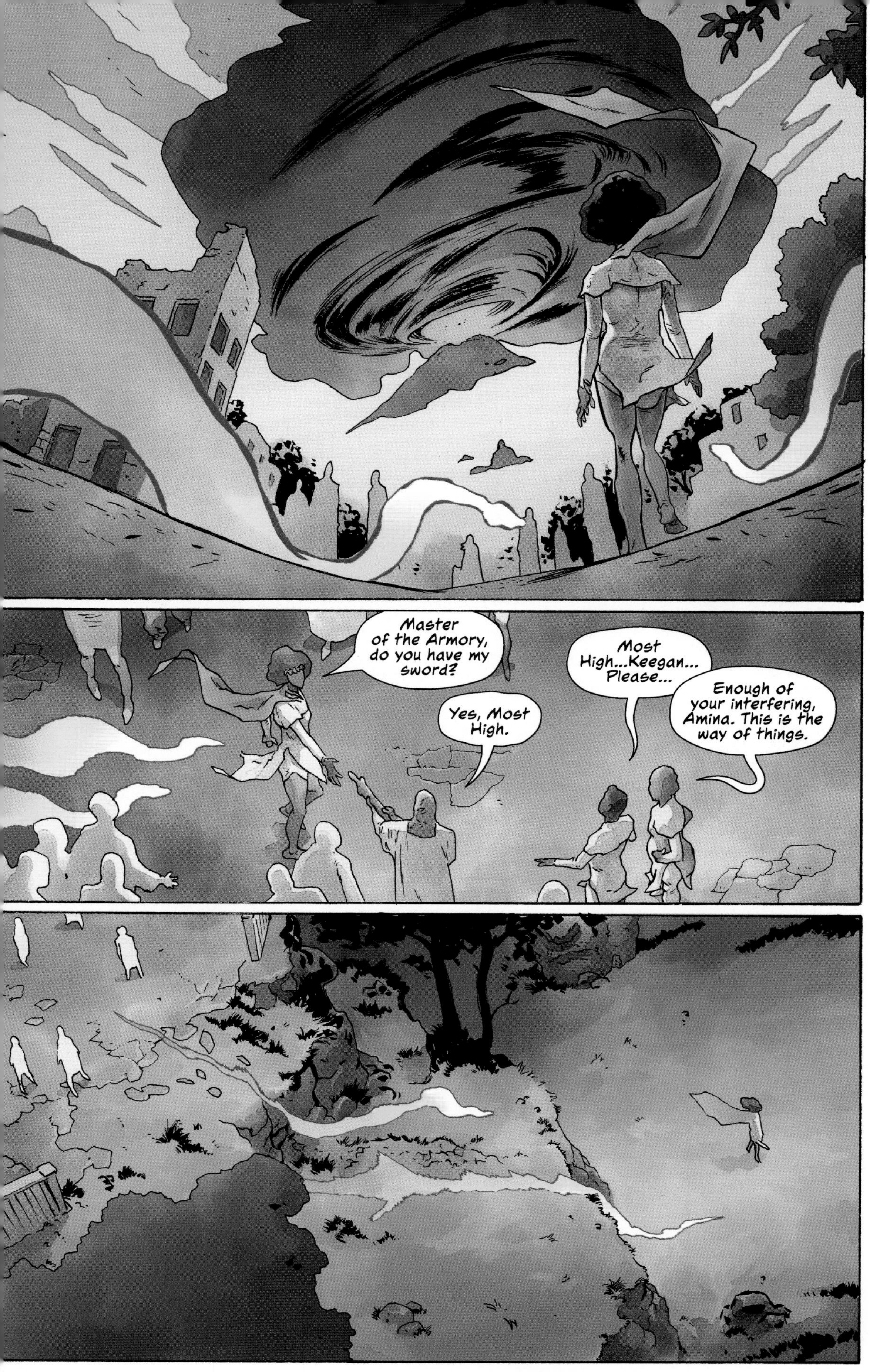
Master of the Armory, do you have my sword?
Yes, Most High.
Most High...Keegan... Please...
Enough of your interfering, Amina. This is the way of things.

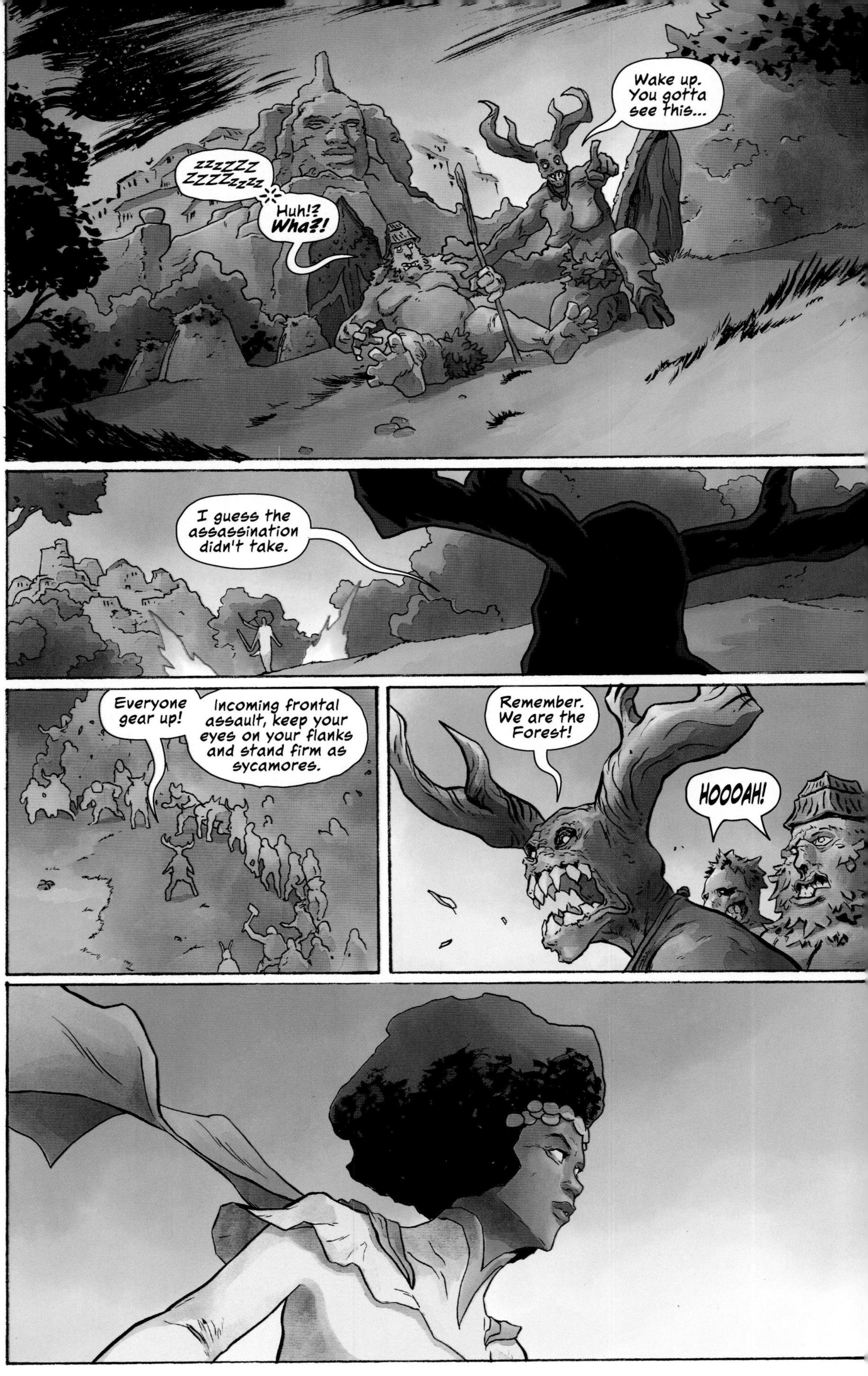
Wake up. You gotta see this...
zzzZZZ ZZZZzzzz
Huh!? Wha?!
I guess the assassination didn't take.
Everyone gear up!
Incoming frontal assault, keep your eyes on your flanks and stand firm as sycamores.
Remember. We are the Forest!
HOOOAH!

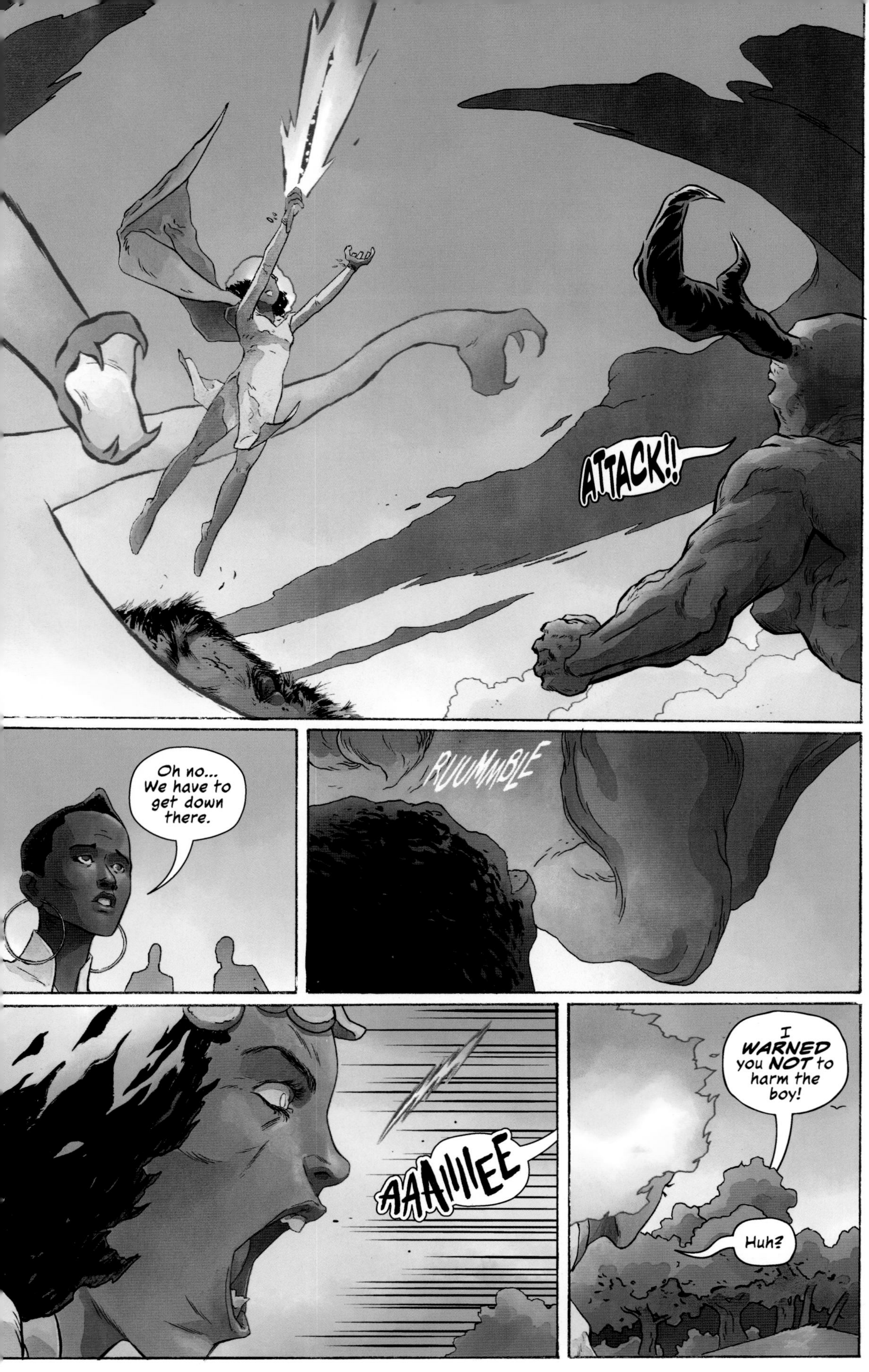
ATTACK!!
Oh no... We have to get down there.
RUUMMBLE
AAAIIIIEE
I WARNED you NOT to harm the boy!
Huh?

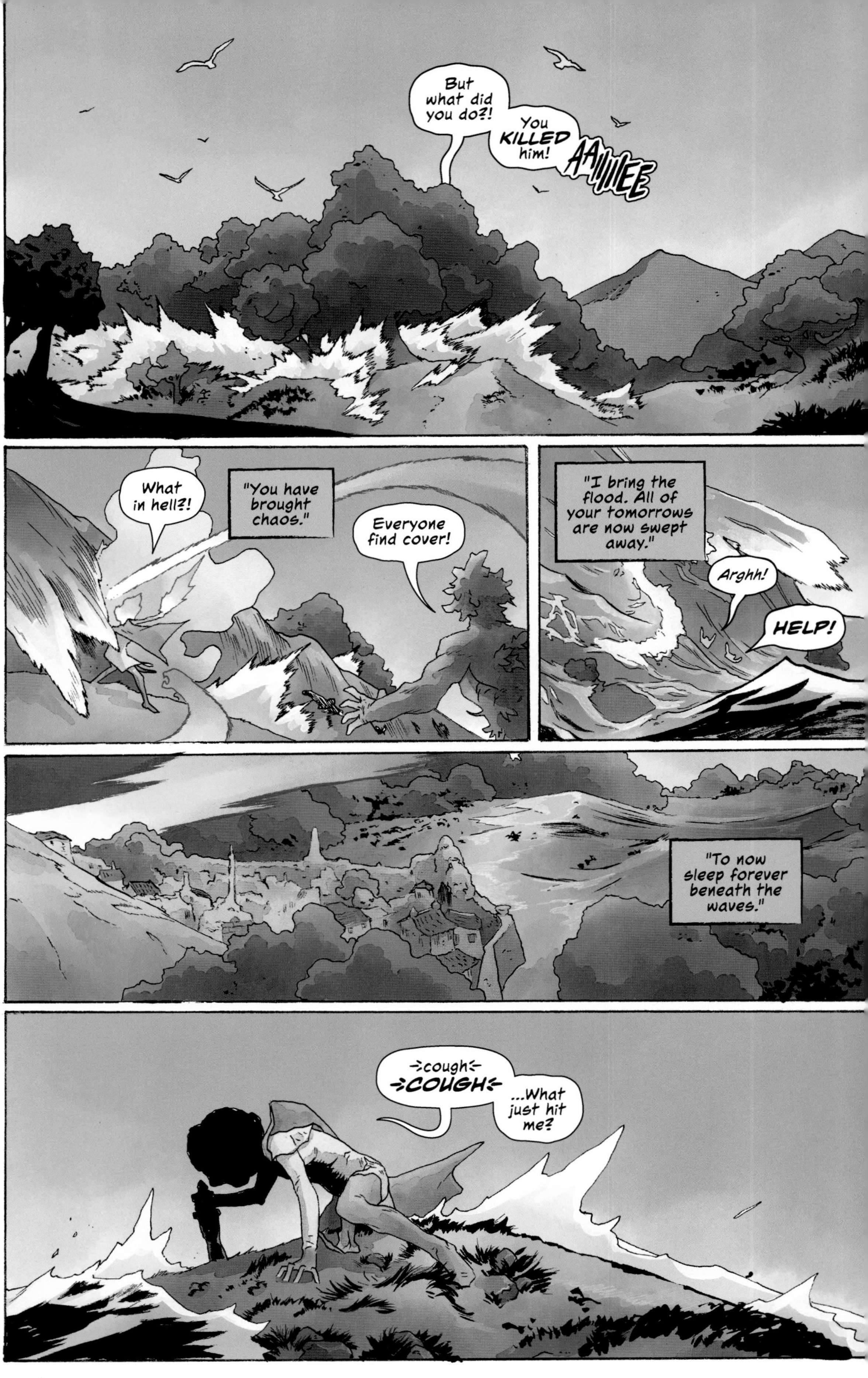
But what did you do?!
You KILLED him!
AAIIIIEE
What in hell?!
"You have brought chaos."
Everyone find cover!
"I bring the flood. All of your tomorrows are now swept away."
Arghh!
HELP!
"To now sleep forever beneath the waves."
cough COUGH ...What just hit me?

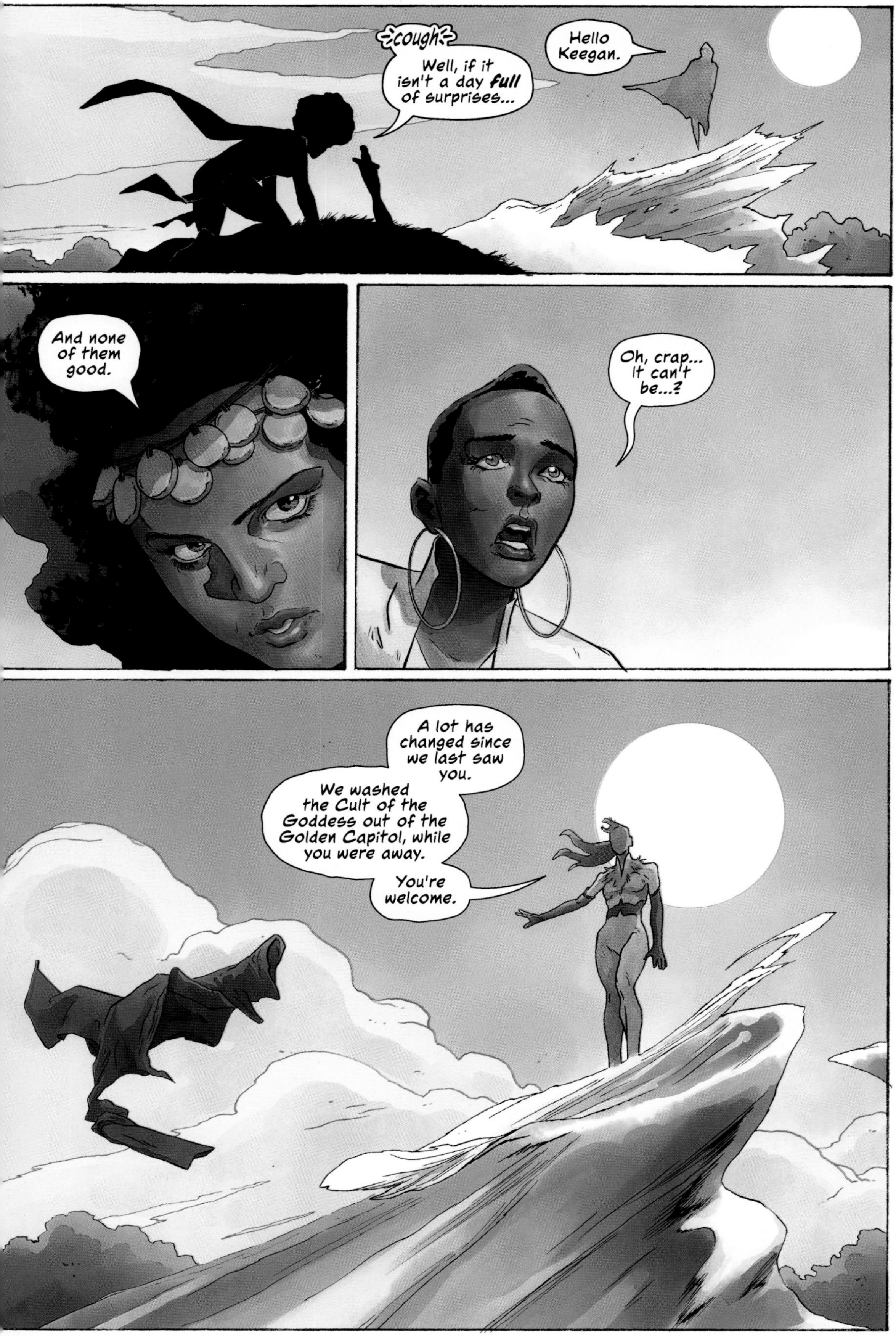

cough
Well, if it isn't a day *full* of surprises...
Hello Keegan.
And none of them good.
Oh, crap... It can't be...?
A lot has changed since we last saw you.
We washed the Cult of the Goddess out of the Golden Capitol, while you were away.
You're welcome.

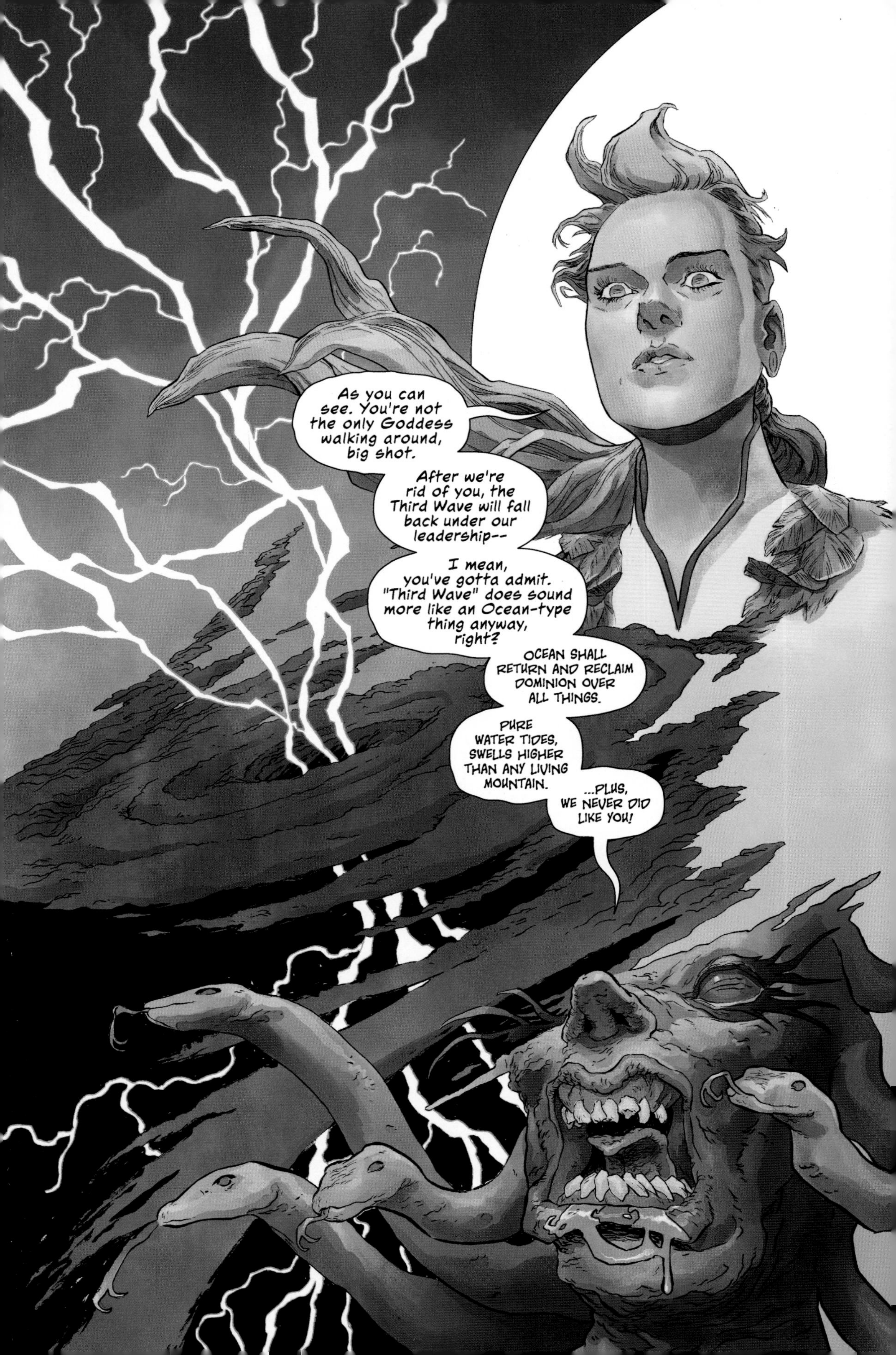
As you can see. You're not the only Goddess walking around, big shot.
After we're rid of you, the Third Wave will fall back under our leadership--
I mean, you've gotta admit. "Third Wave" does sound more like an Ocean-type thing anyway, right?
OCEAN SHALL RETURN AND RECLAIM DOMINION OVER ALL THINGS.
PURE WATER TIDES, SWELLS HIGHER THAN ANY LIVING MOUNTAIN.
...PLUS, WE NEVER DID LIKE YOU!

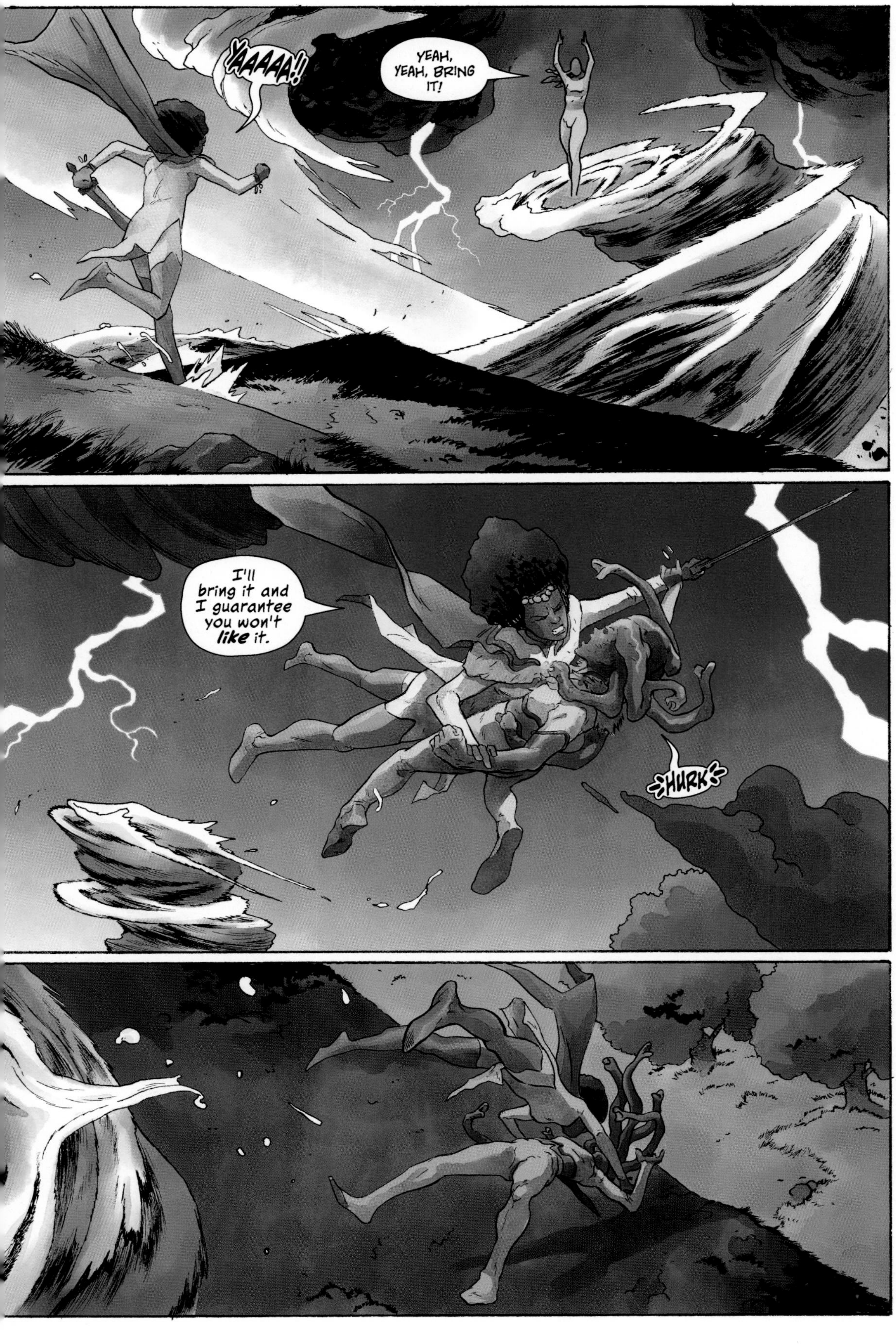
YAAAAA!!
YEAH, YEAH, BRING IT!
I'll bring it and I guarantee you won't *like* it.
HURK

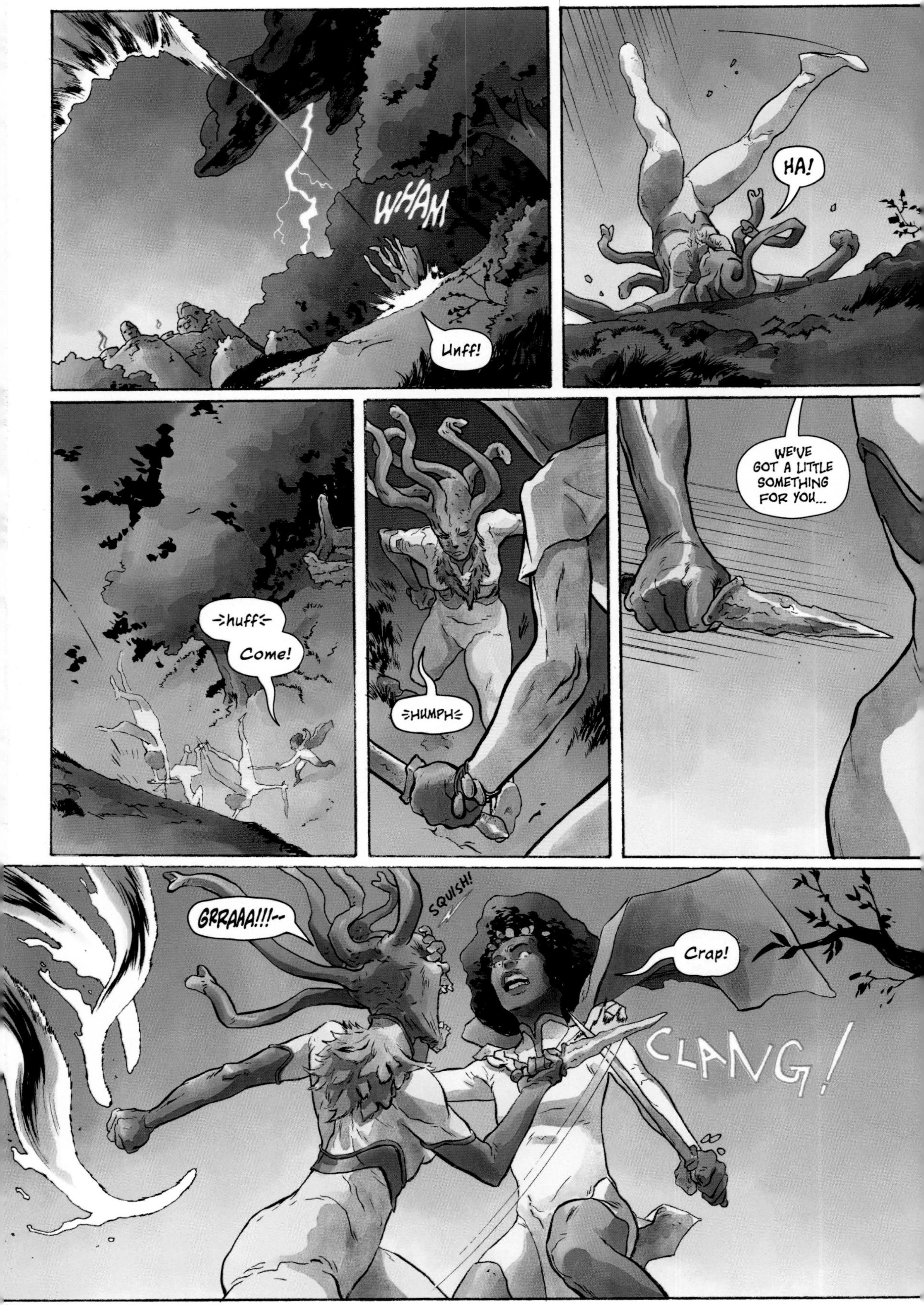
WHAM
Unff!
HA!
huff
Come!
HUMPH
WE'VE GOT A LITTLE SOMETHING FOR YOU...
GRRAAA!!!--
SQUISH!
Crap!
CLANG!

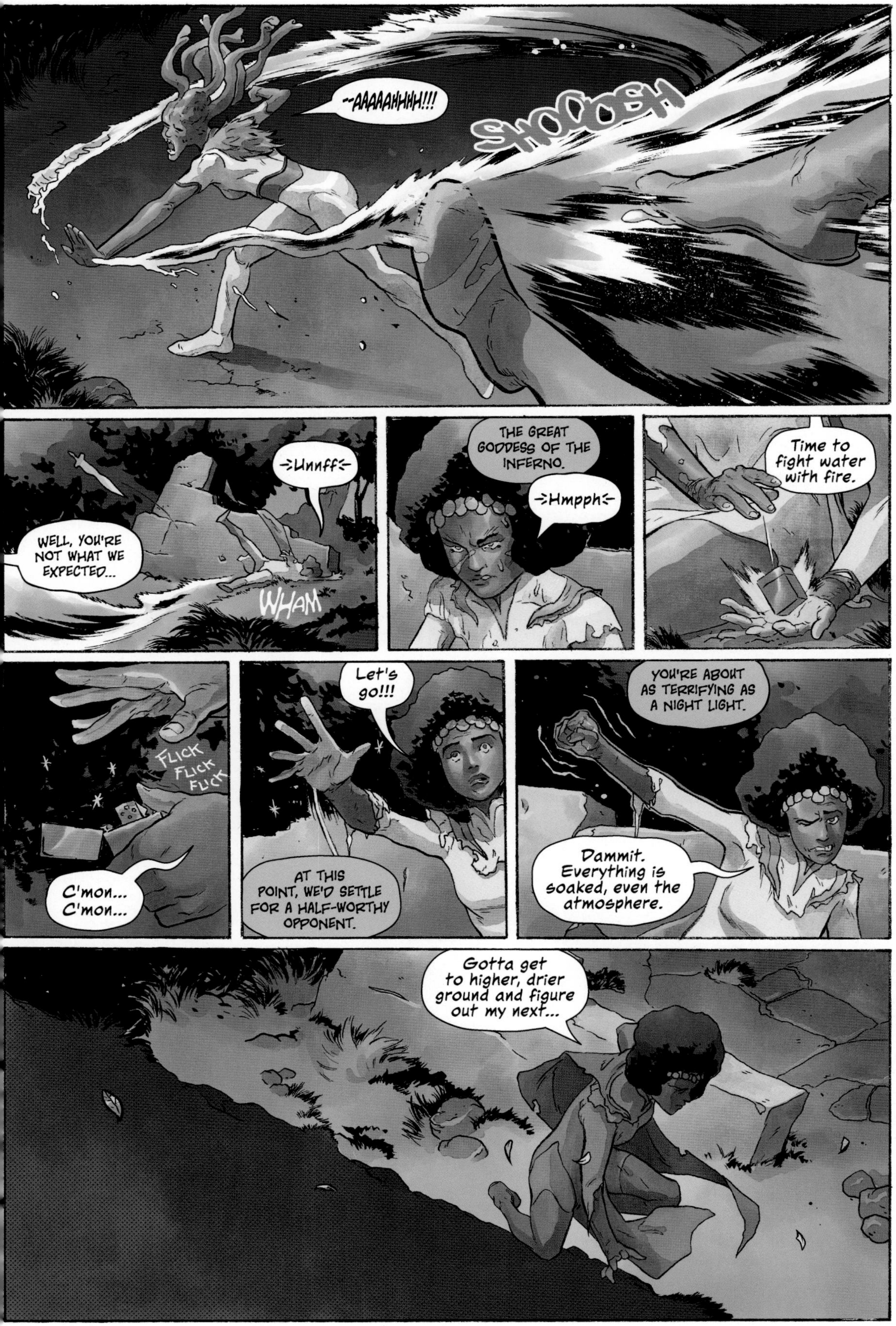
--AAAAAHHHH!!!
SHOOOSH
WELL, YOU'RE NOT WHAT WE EXPECTED...
-Unnff-
WHAM
THE GREAT GODDESS OF THE INFERNO.
-Hmpph-
Time to fight water with fire.
FLICK FLICK FLICK
C'mon... C'mon...
Let's go!!!
AT THIS POINT, WE'D SETTLE FOR A HALF-WORTHY OPPONENT.
YOU'RE ABOUT AS TERRIFYING AS A NIGHT LIGHT.
Dammit. Everything is soaked, even the atmosphere.
Gotta get to higher, drier ground and figure out my next...

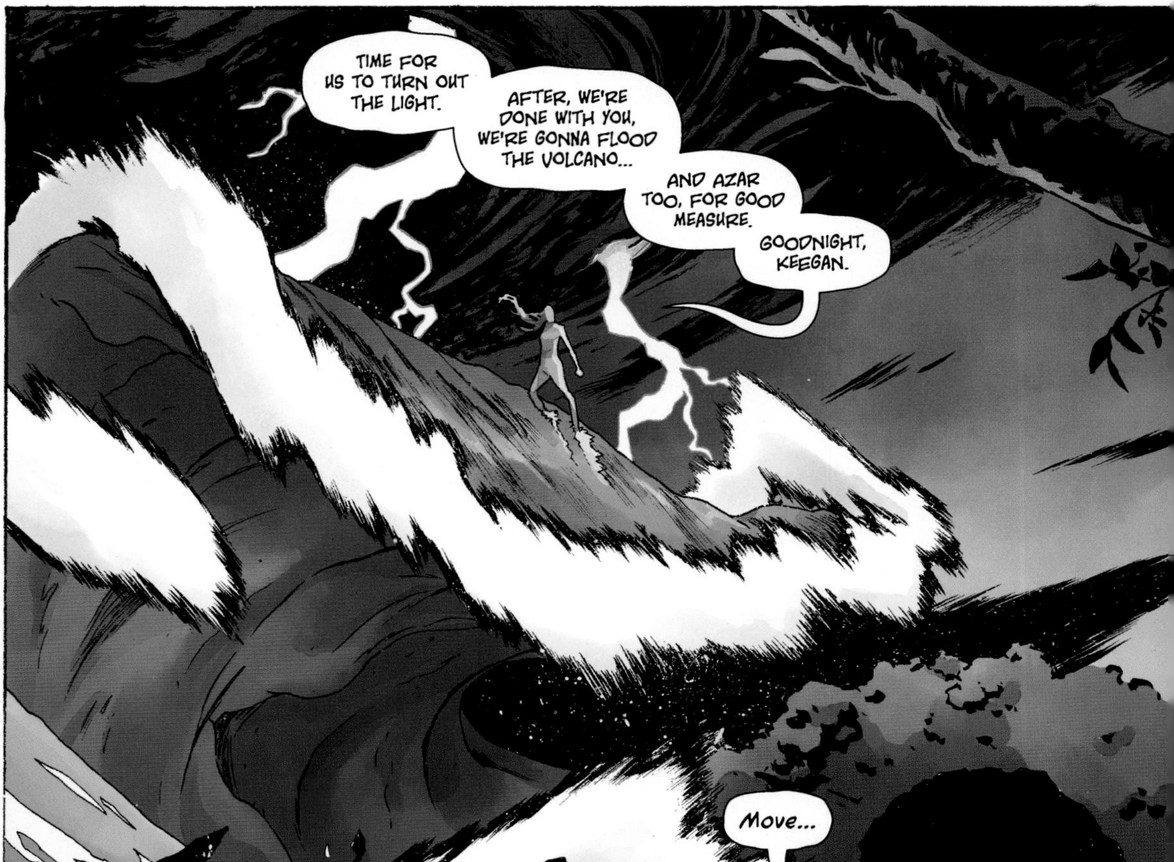
TIME FOR US TO TURN OUT THE LIGHT.
AFTER, WE'RE DONE WITH YOU, WE'RE GONNA FLOOD THE VOLCANO...
AND AZAR TOO, FOR GOOD MEASURE.
GOODNIGHT, KEEGAN.
Move...

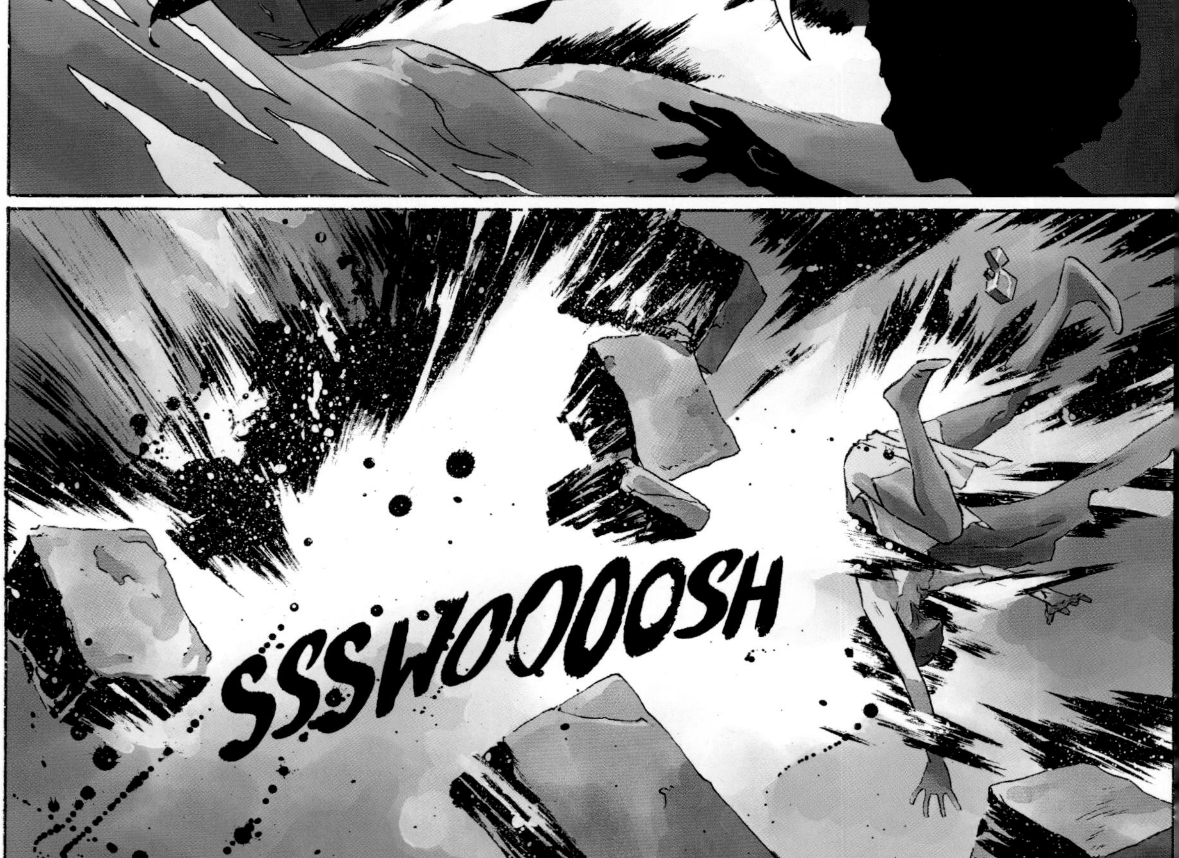
SSSWOOOOOSH

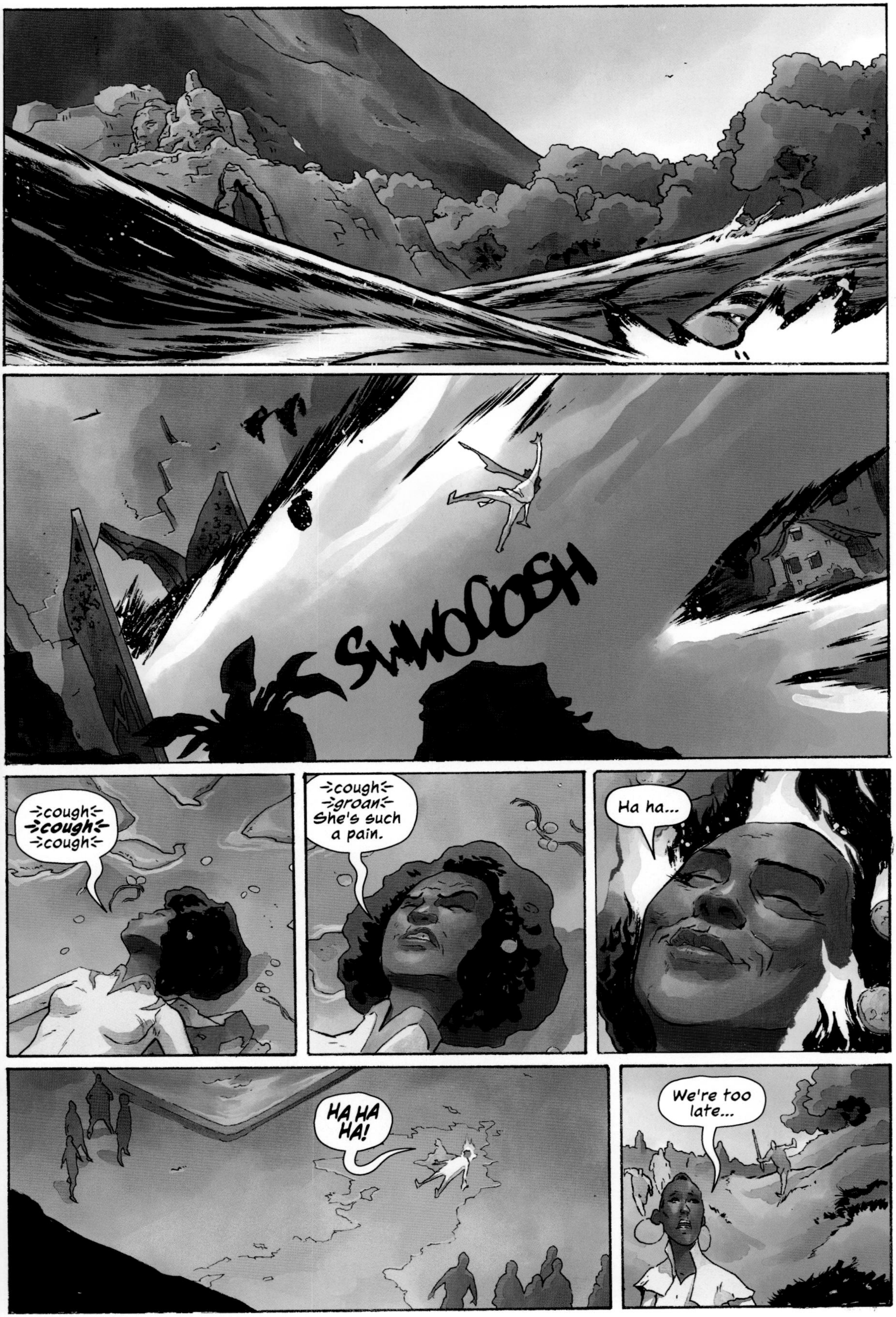
SWOOOSH
cough cough cough
cough groan She's such a pain.
Ha ha...
HA HA HA!
We're too late...

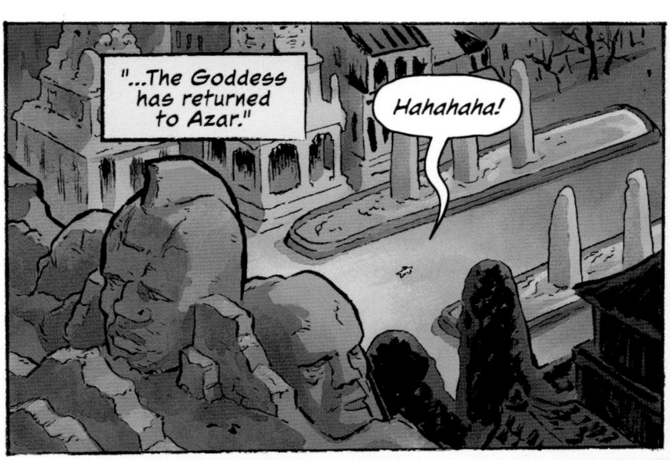
"...The Goddess has returned to Azar."
Hahahaha!
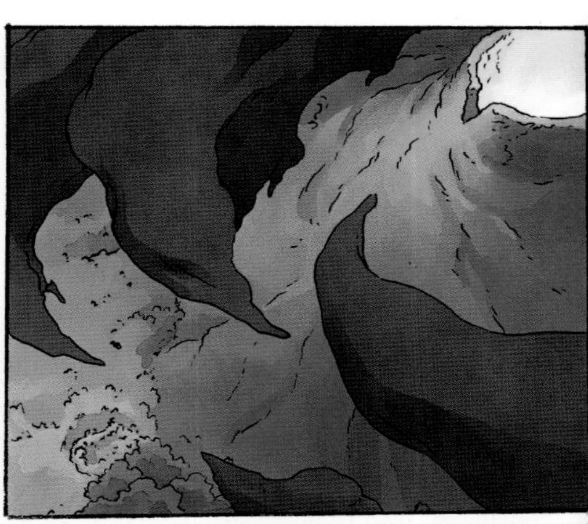
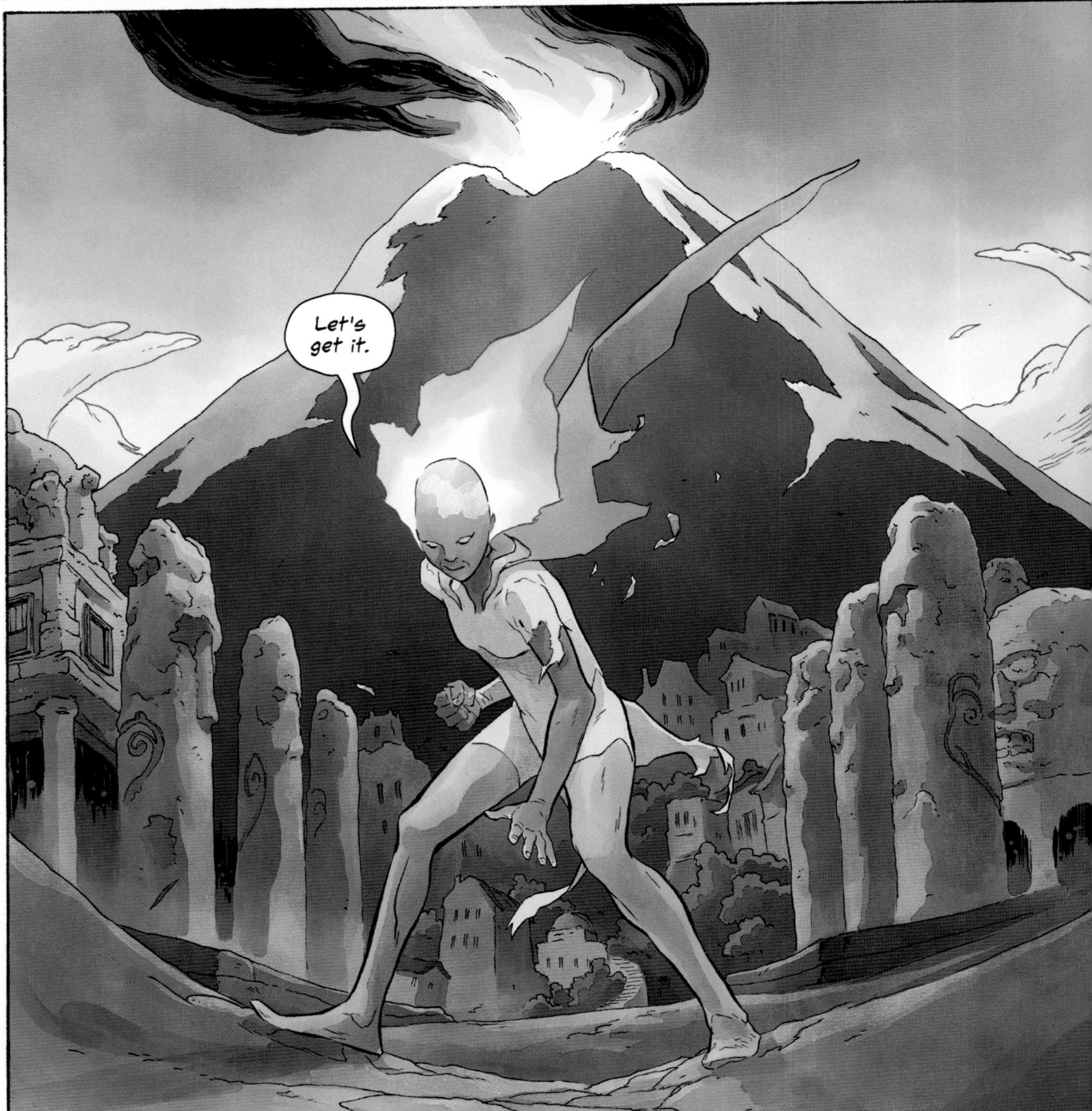
Let's get it.

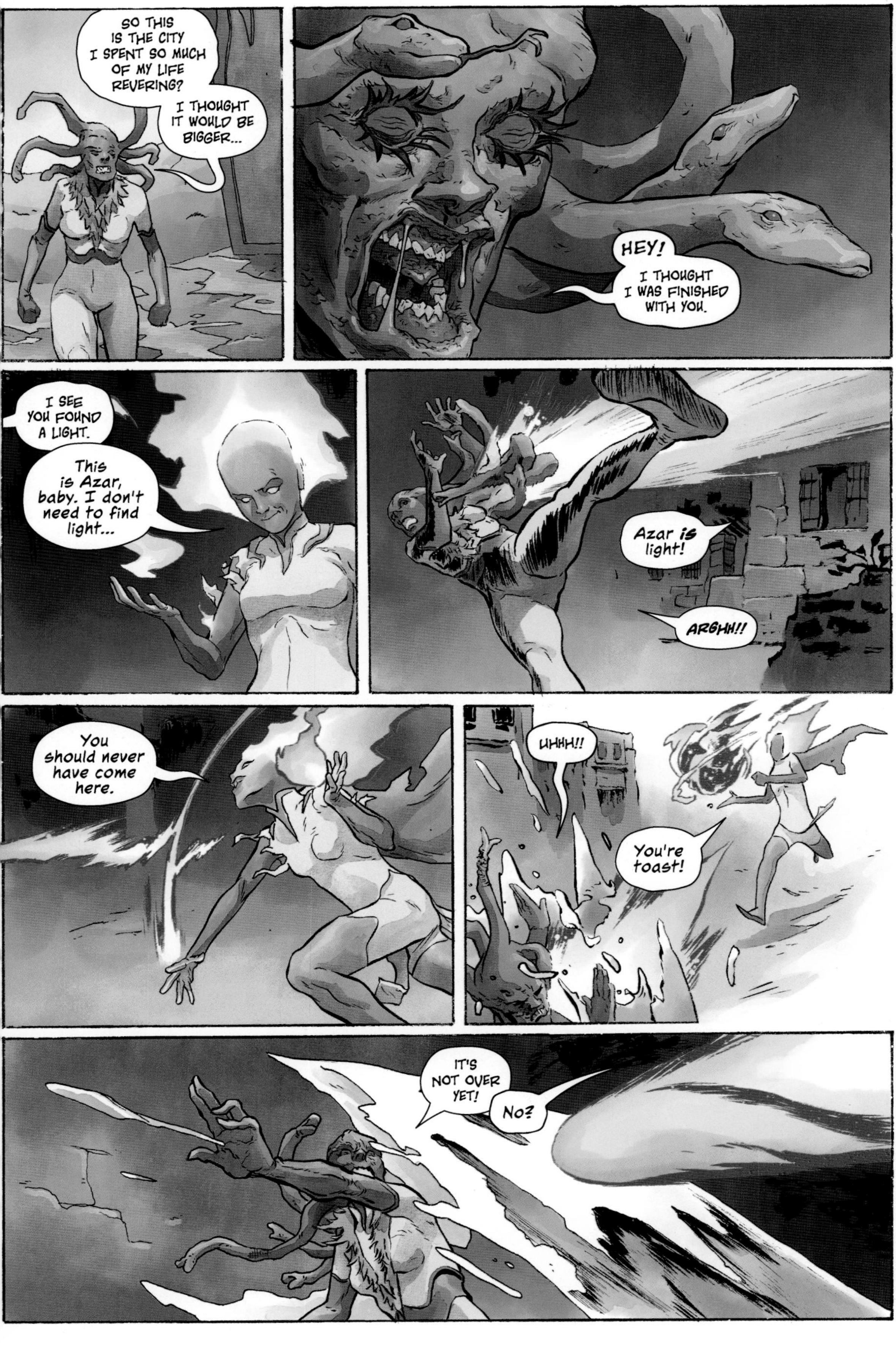
SO THIS IS THE CITY I SPENT SO MUCH OF MY LIFE REVERING?
I THOUGHT IT WOULD BE BIGGER...
HEY!
I THOUGHT I WAS FINISHED WITH YOU.
I SEE YOU FOUND A LIGHT.
This is Azar, baby. I don't need to find light...
Azar is light!
ARGHH!!
You should never have come here.
UHHH!!
You're toast!
IT'S NOT OVER YET!
No?

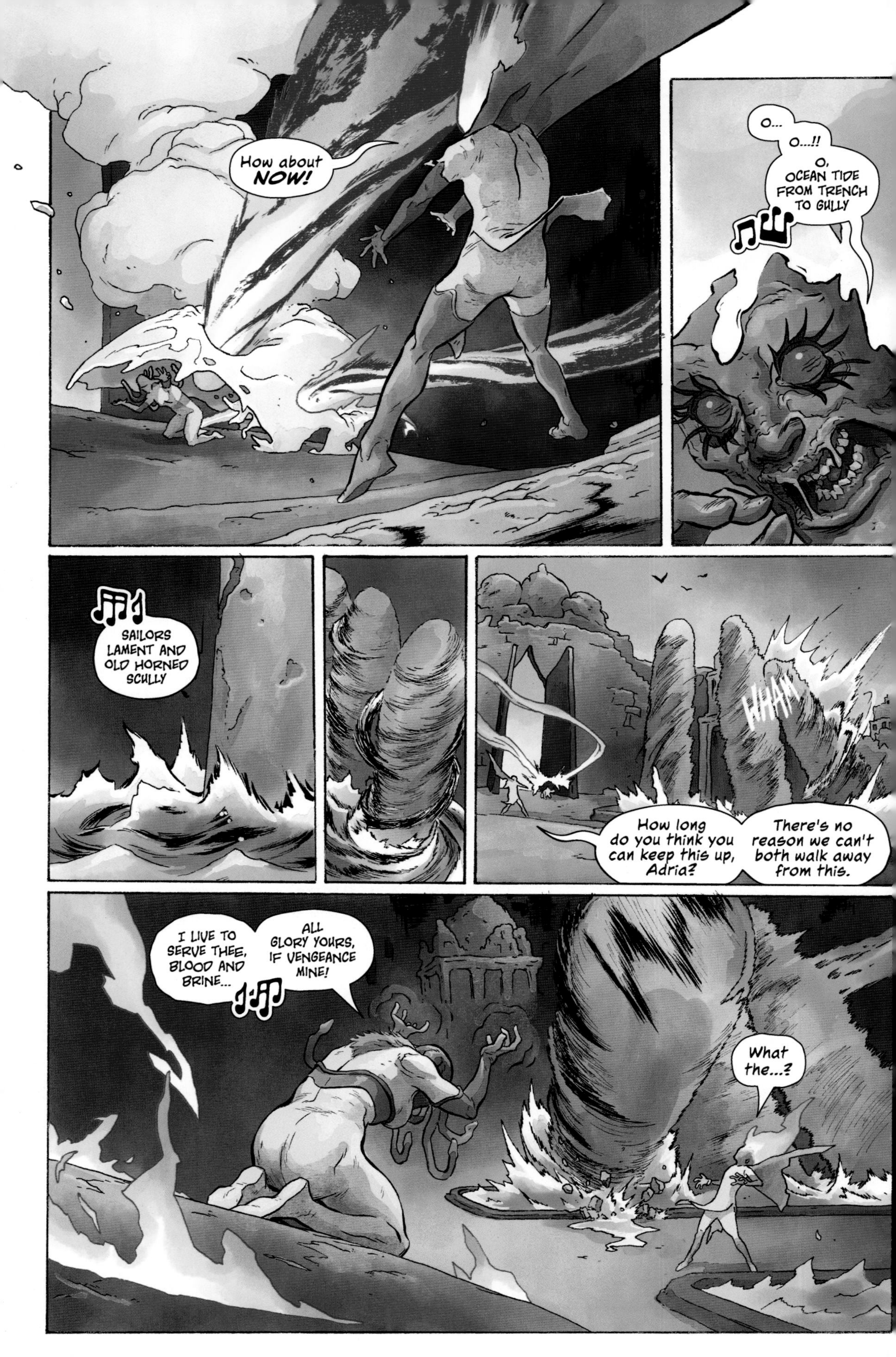
How about NOW!
O...
O...!!
O, OCEAN TIDE FROM TRENCH TO GULLY
SAILORS LAMENT AND OLD HORNED SCULLY
WHAM
How long do you think you can keep this up, Adria?
There's no reason we can't both walk away from this.
I LIVE TO SERVE THEE, BLOOD AND BRINE...
ALL GLORY YOURS, IF VENGEANCE MINE!
What the...?

WHOA!
CRASH!
Huh?!
"ENSNARE"!
SPLASH!
Oh c'mon...
SPLOOSH
HA!
Adria, don't...
GOOD NIGHT, SWEET PRINCESS!
gurgle
SHHHH! SLEEP NOW...
!
SLEEEEEEP...
...

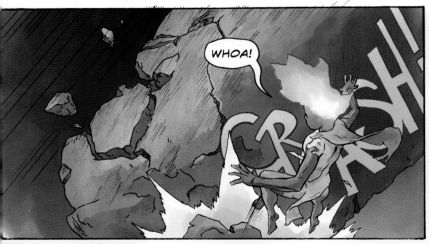

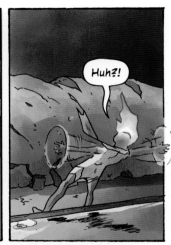

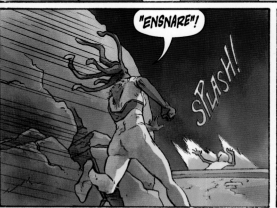

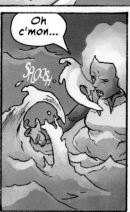

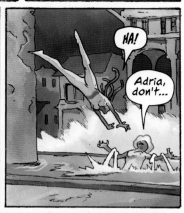

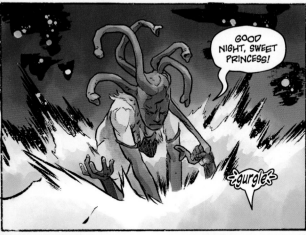

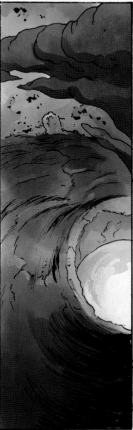

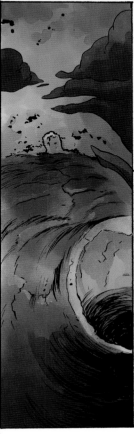

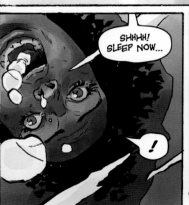

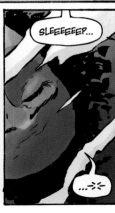

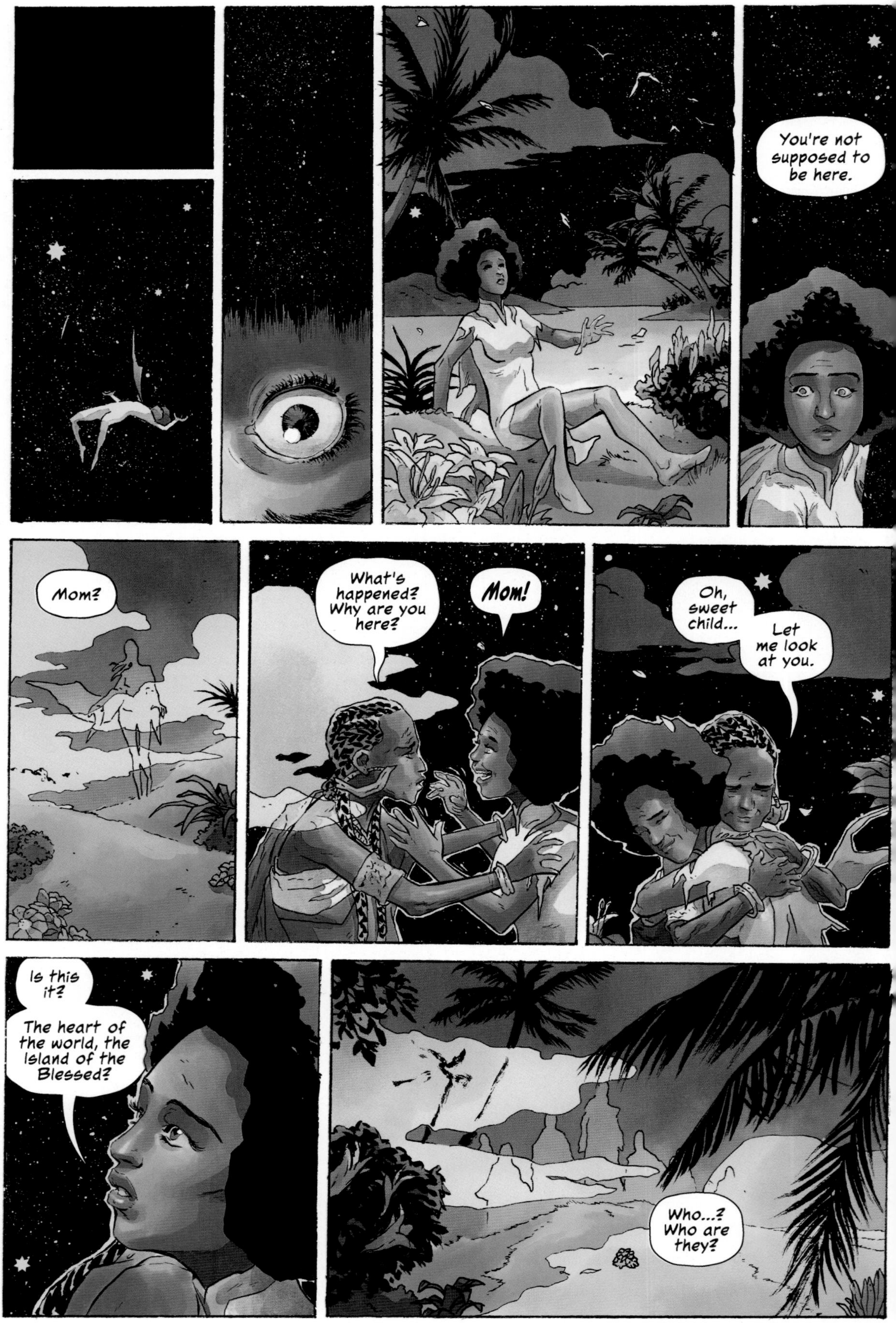
You're not supposed to be here.
Mom?
What's happened? Why are you here?
Mom!
Oh, sweet child...
Let me look at you.
Is this it?
The heart of the world, the Island of the Blessed?
Who...? Who are they?

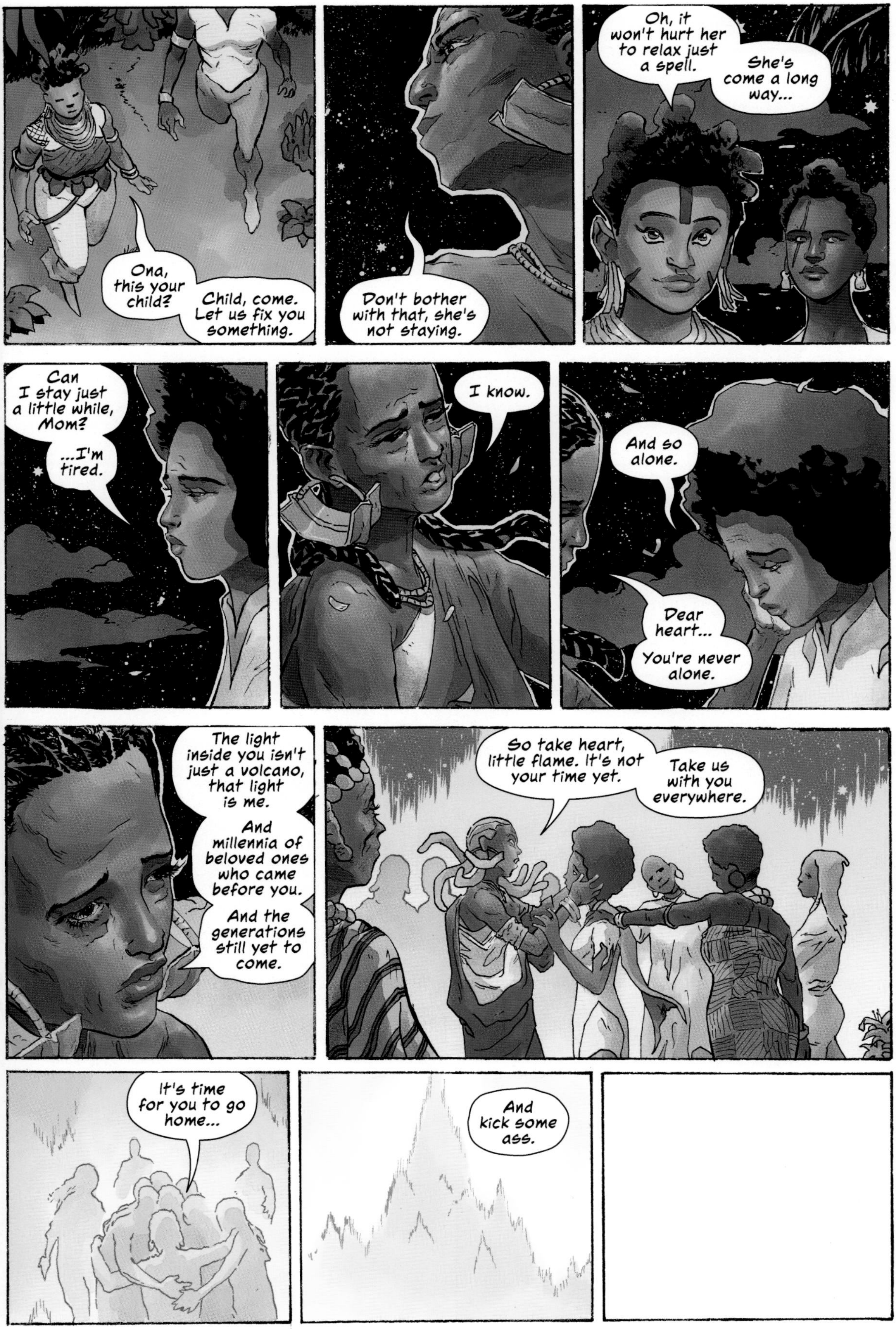
Ona, this your child?
Child, come. Let us fix you something.
Don't bother with that, she's not staying.
Oh, it won't hurt her to relax just a spell.
She's come a long way...
Can I stay just a little while, Mom?
...I'm tired.
I know.
And so alone.
Dear heart...
You're never alone.
The light inside you isn't just a volcano, that light is me.
And millennia of beloved ones who came before you.
And the generations still yet to come.
So take heart, little flame. It's not your time yet.
Take us with you everywhere.
It's time for you to go home...
And kick some ass.

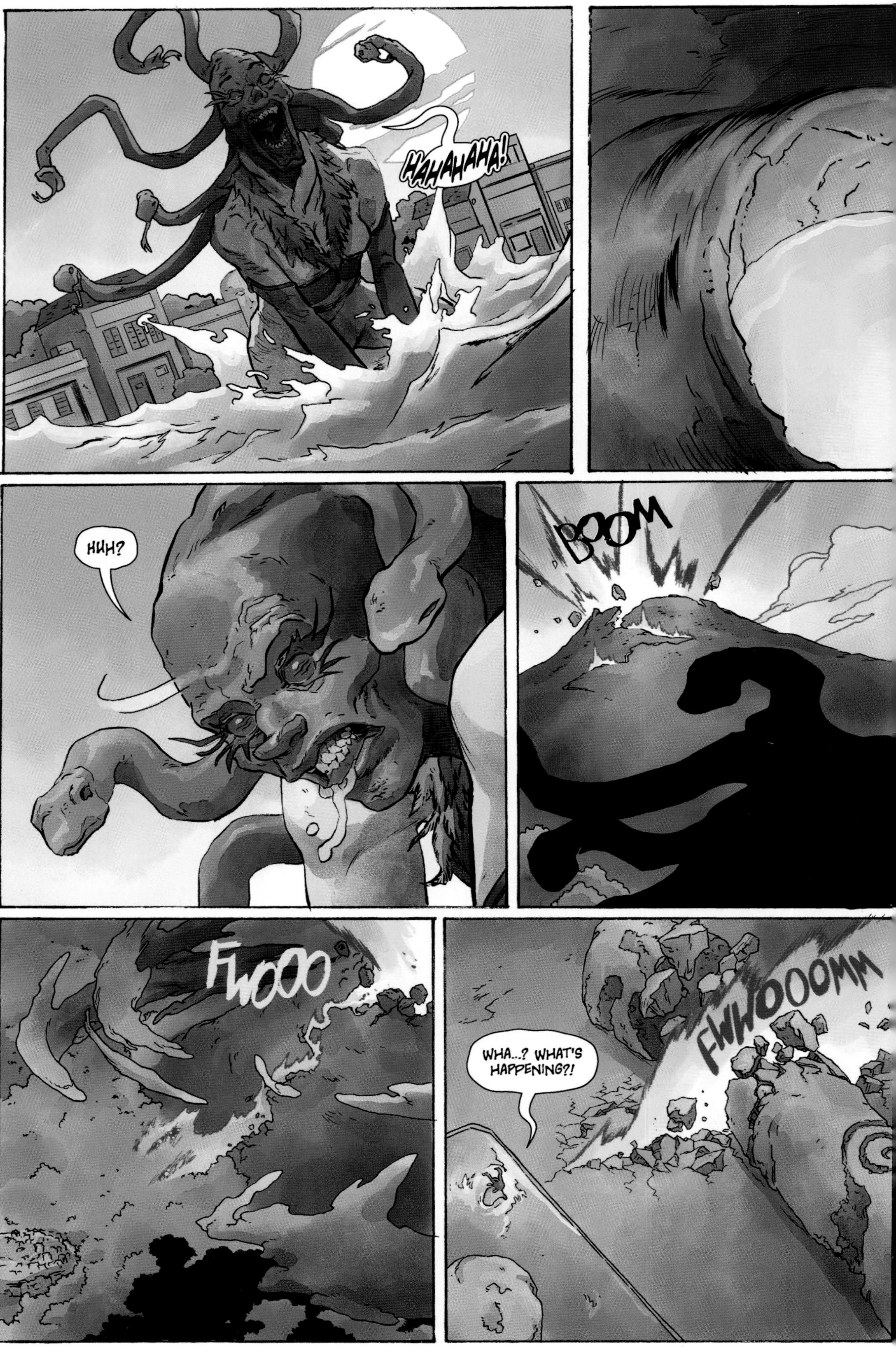
HAHAHAHA!
HUH?
BOOM
FWOOO
WHA...? WHAT'S HAPPENING?!
FWHOOOMM

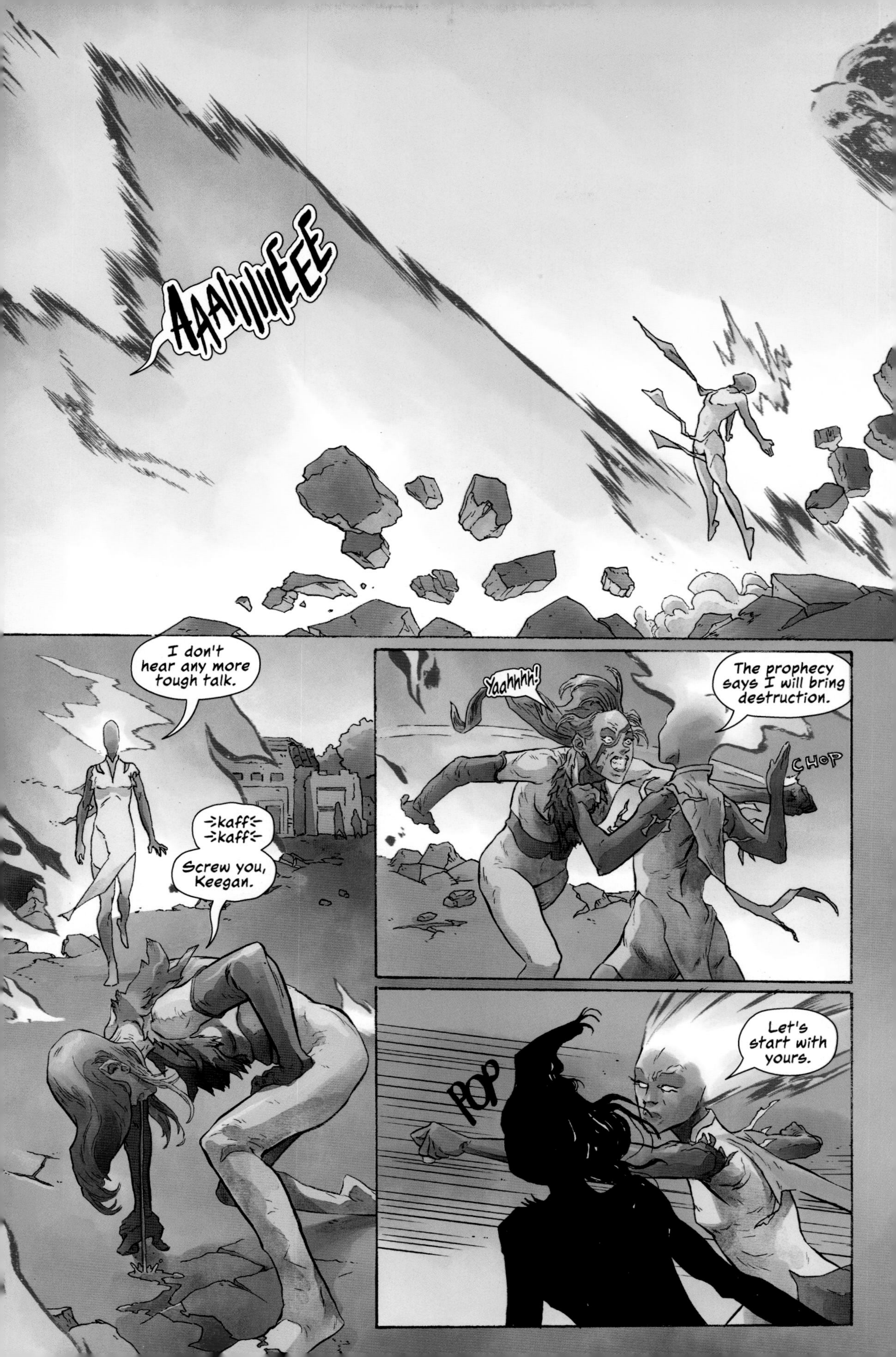
AAAIIIIIEEE
I don't hear any more tough talk.
kaff kaff
Screw you, Keegan.
Yaahhhh!
The prophecy says I will bring destruction.
CHOP
Let's start with yours.
POP

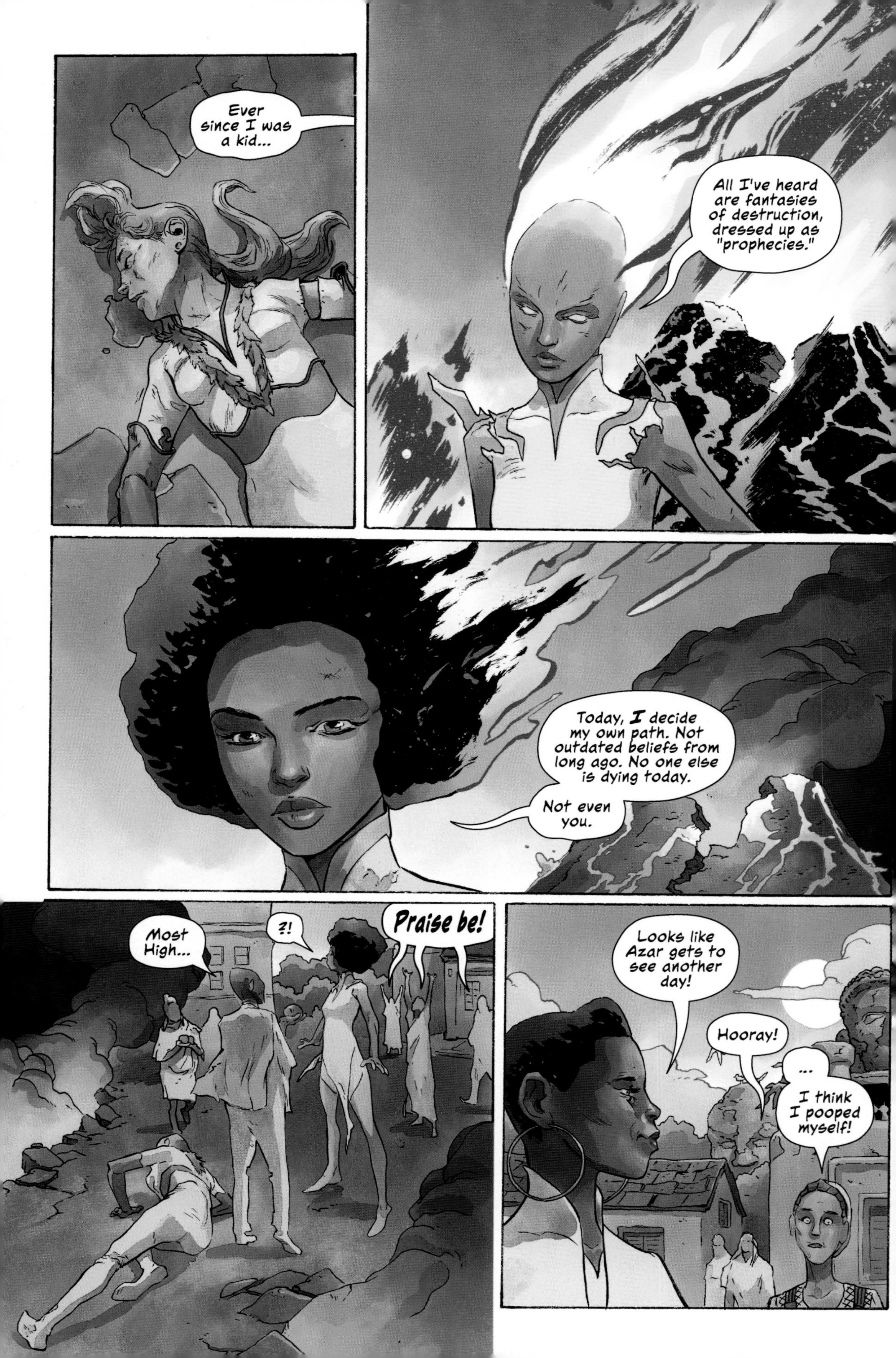
Ever since I was a kid...
All I've heard are fantasies of destruction, dressed up as "prophecies."
Today, I decide my own path. Not outdated beliefs from long ago. No one else is dying today.
Not even you.
Most High...
?!
Praise be!
Looks like Azar gets to see another day!
Hooray!
...
I think I pooped myself!

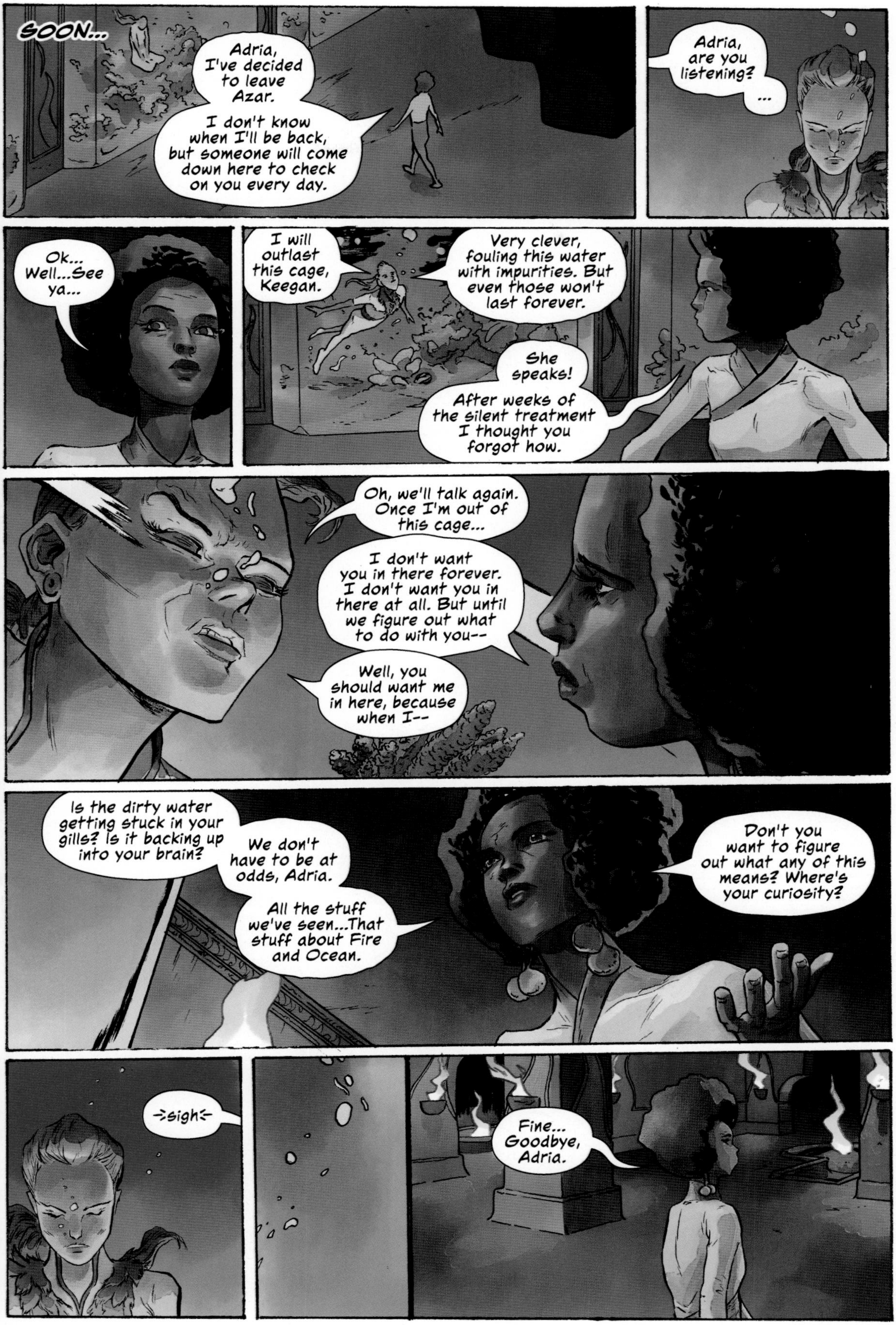
SOON...
Adria, I've decided to leave Azar.
I don't know when I'll be back, but someone will come down here to check on you every day.
Adria, are you listening?
...
Ok... Well...See ya...
I will outlast this cage, Keegan.
Very clever, fouling this water with impurities. But even those won't last forever.
She speaks!
After weeks of the silent treatment I thought you forgot how.
Oh, we'll talk again. Once I'm out of this cage...
I don't want you in there forever. I don't want you in there at all. But until we figure out what to do with you--
Well, you should want me in here, because when I--
Is the dirty water getting stuck in your gills? Is it backing up into your brain?
We don't have to be at odds, Adria.
All the stuff we've seen...That stuff about Fire and Ocean.
Don't you want to figure out what any of this means? Where's your curiosity?
-sigh-
Fine... Goodbye, Adria.

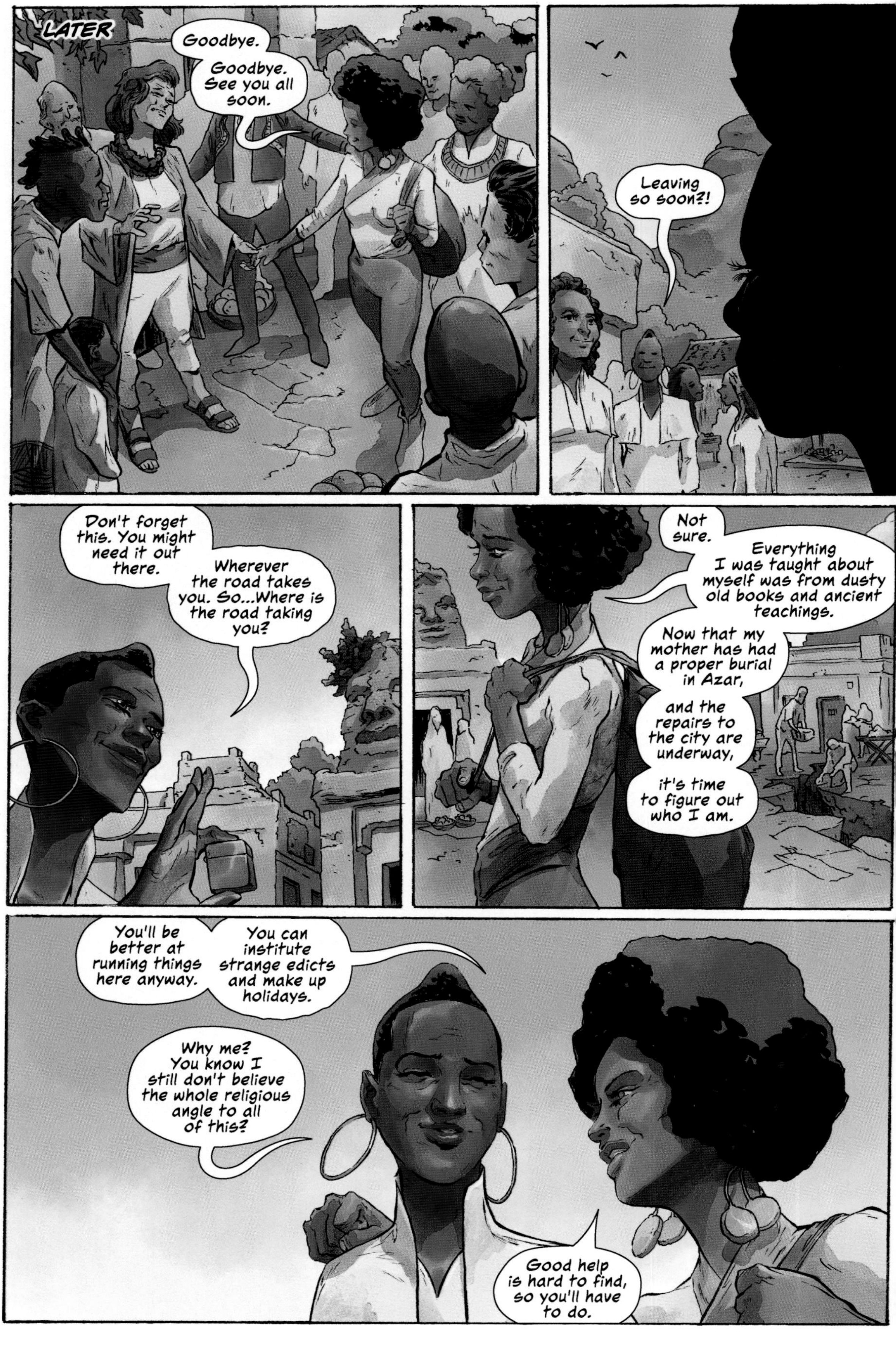
LATER
Goodbye.
Goodbye. See you all soon.
Leaving so soon?!
Don't forget this. You might need it out there.
Wherever the road takes you. So...Where is the road taking you?
Not sure.
Everything I was taught about myself was from dusty old books and ancient teachings.
Now that my mother has had a proper burial in Azar,
and the repairs to the city are underway,
it's time to figure out who I am.
You'll be better at running things here anyway.
You can institute strange edicts and make up holidays.
Why me? You know I still don't believe the whole religious angle to all of this?
Good help is hard to find, so you'll have to do.

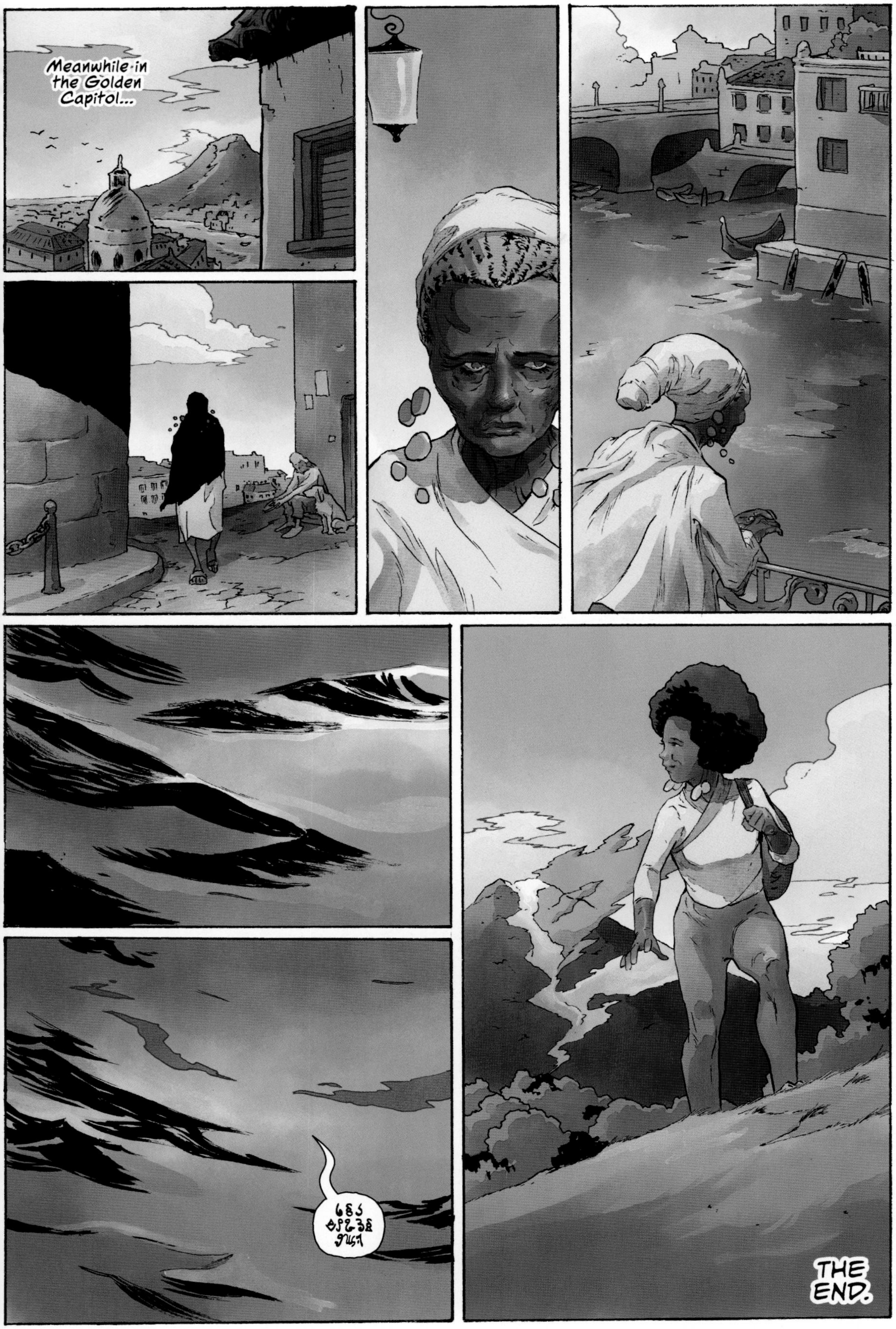
Meanwhile in the Golden Capitol...
THE END.

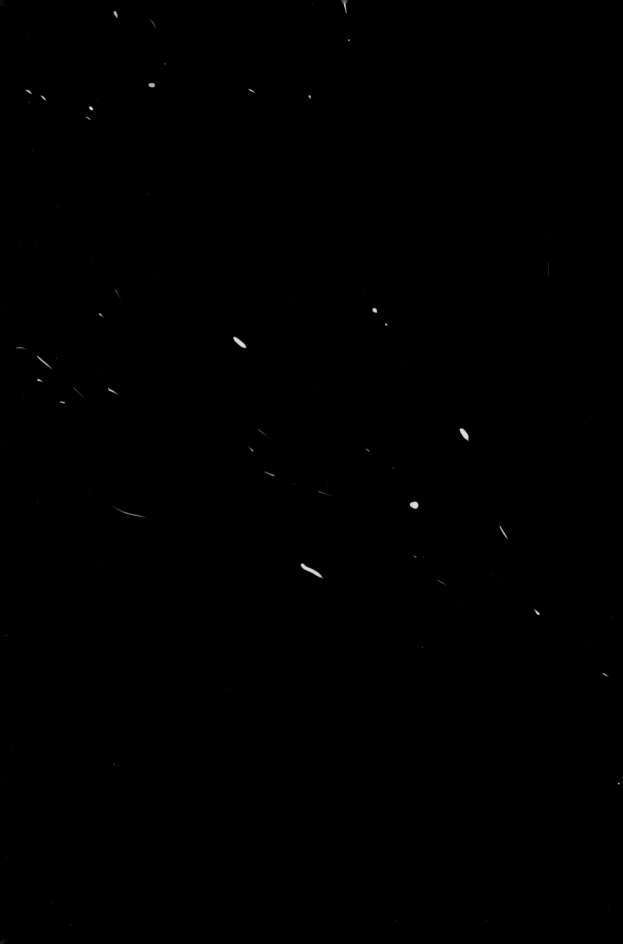

FIREBUG EXTRAS

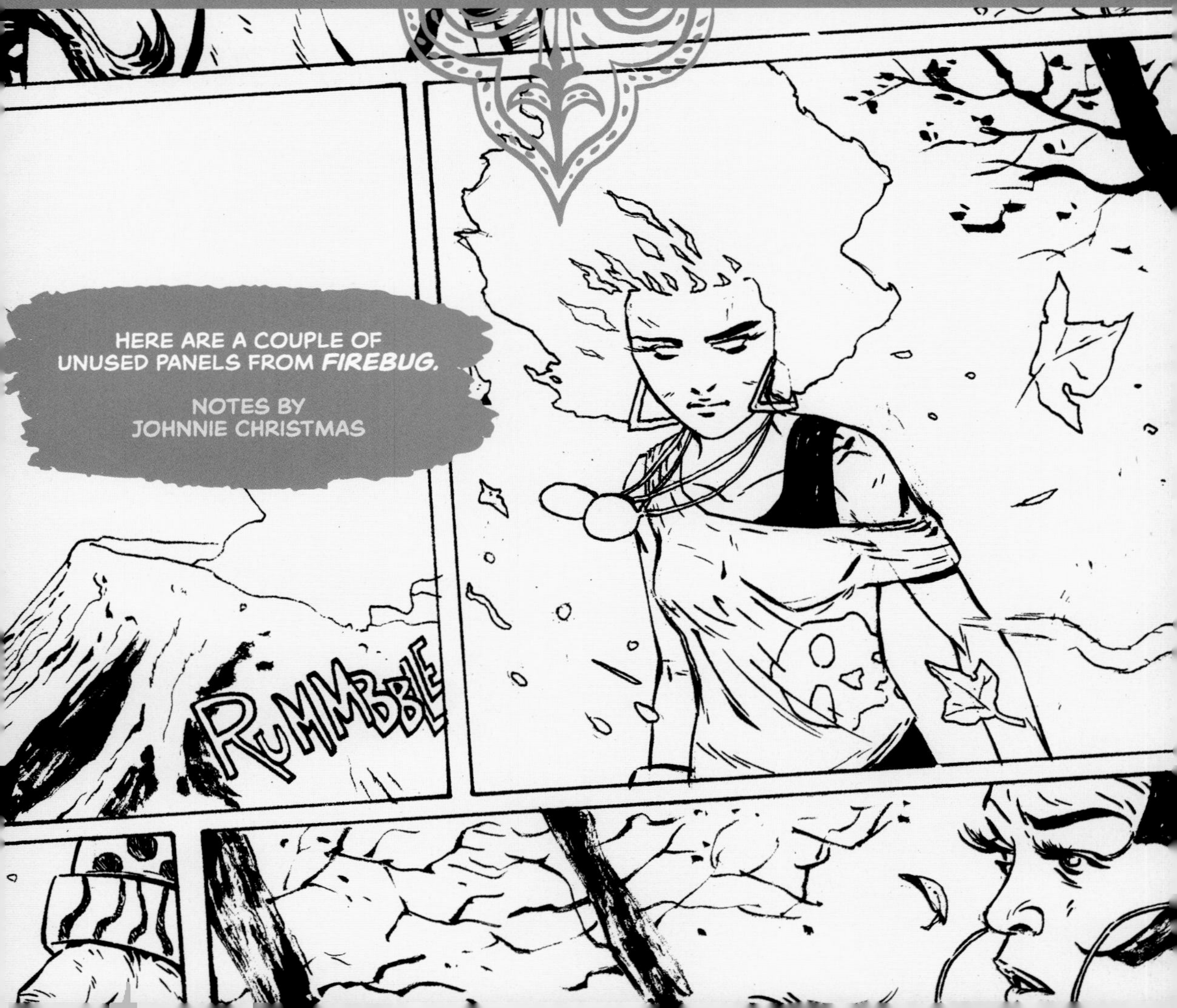
RUMMBBLE

HERE ARE A COUPLE OF UNUSED PANELS FROM ***FIREBUG.***

NOTES BY JOHNNIE CHRISTMAS

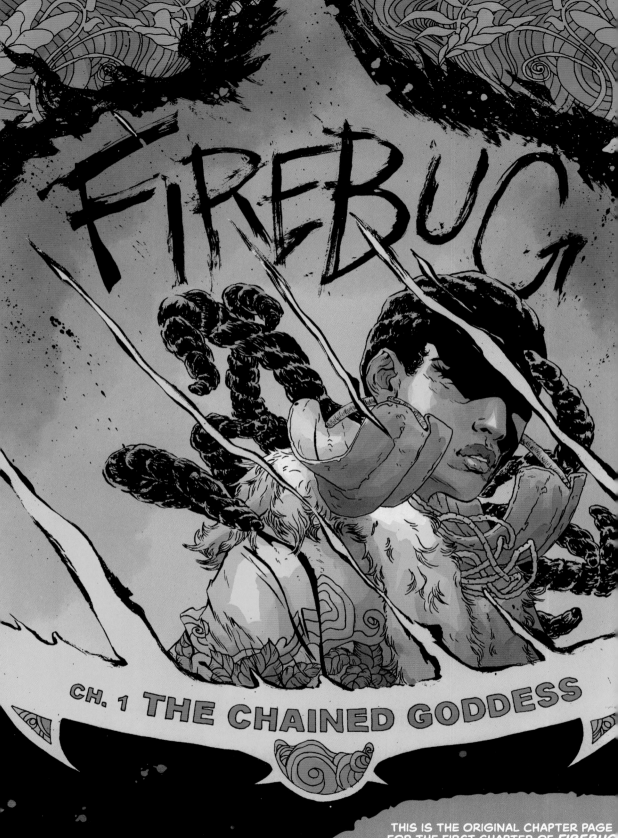

FIREBUG

CH. 1 THE CHAINED GODDESS

THIS IS THE ORIGINAL CHAPTER PAGE FOR THE FIRST CHAPTER OF *FIREBUG* THAT RAN IN *ISLAND* #7. I REDID THE CHAPTER PAGES FOR THIS COLLECTION BUT STILL REALLY LIKE HOW THE EARRINGS AND BRAIDS TURNED OUT.

THIS COVER RAN ON THE COVER OF ***ISLAND* #11**
(THOUGH NO FIREBUG STORY RAN IN THAT ISSUE).

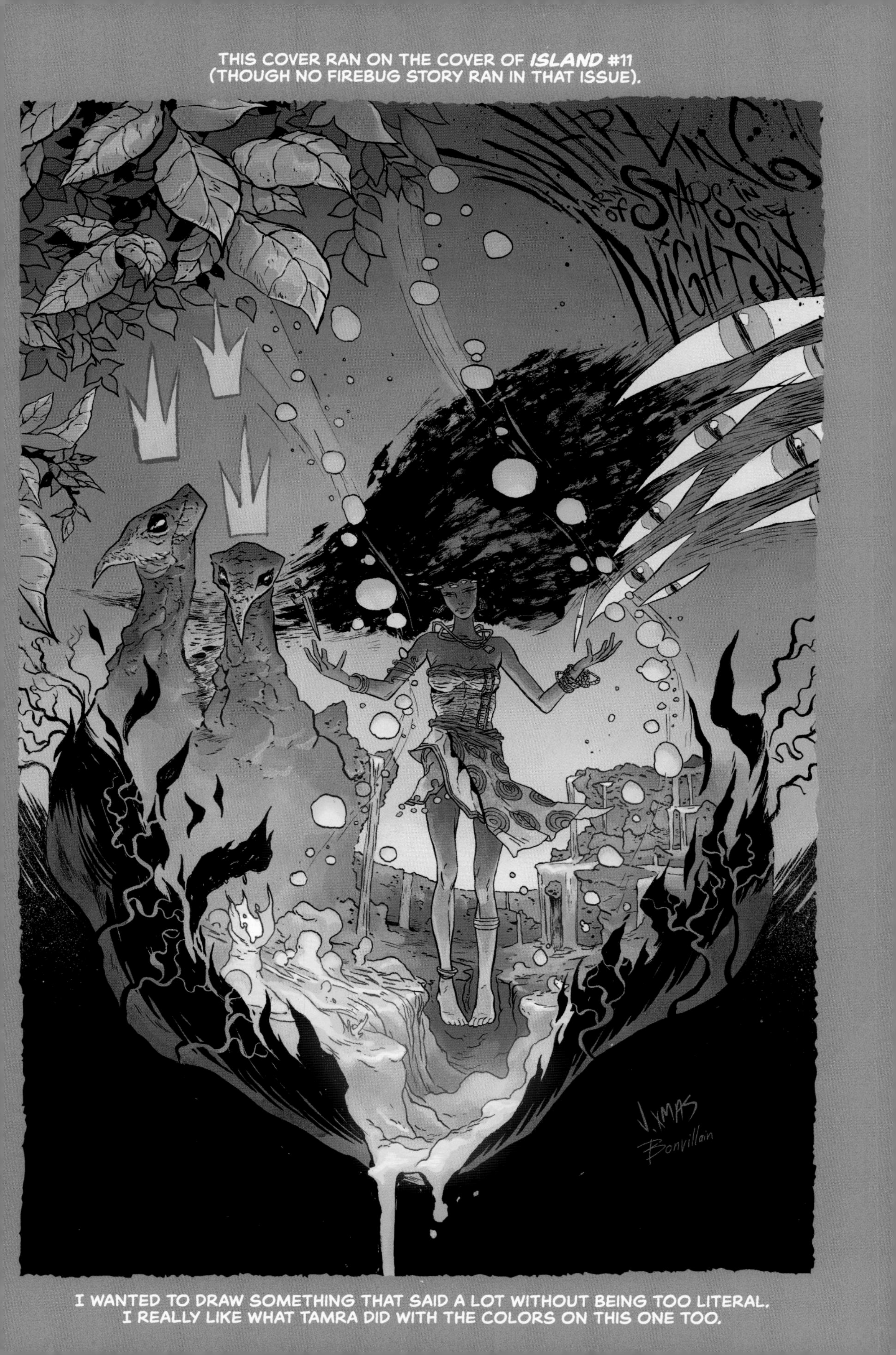
of STARS in the NIGHT SKY
J. XMAS
Bonvillain

I WANTED TO DRAW SOMETHING THAT SAID A LOT WITHOUT BEING TOO LITERAL.
I REALLY LIKE WHAT TAMRA DID WITH THE COLORS ON THIS ONE TOO.

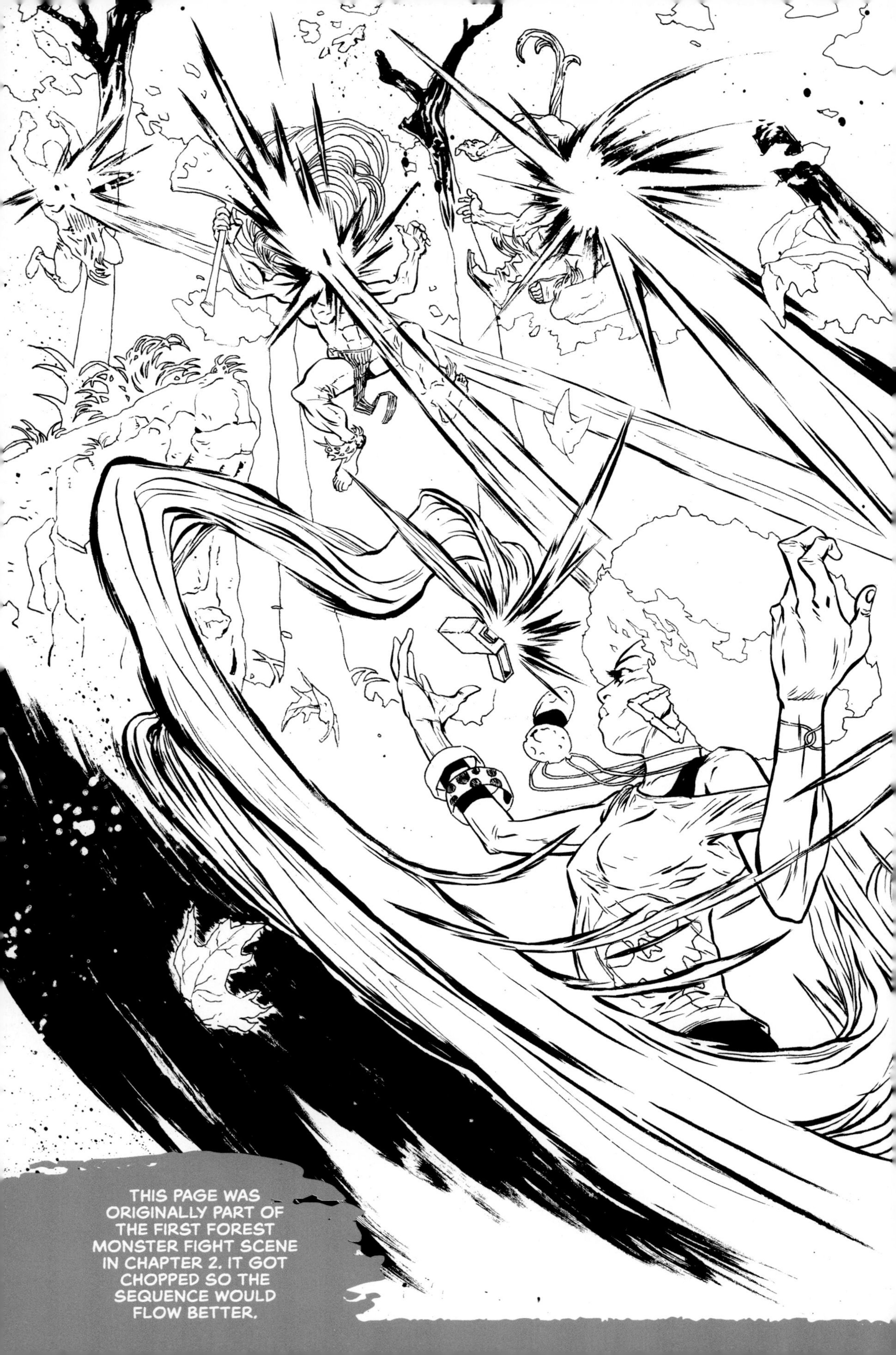

THIS PAGE WAS ORIGINALLY PART OF THE FIRST FOREST MONSTER FIGHT SCENE IN CHAPTER 2. IT GOT CHOPPED SO THE SEQUENCE WOULD FLOW BETTER.

WHEN ***FIREBUG*** WENT FROM SERIALIZATION ON ***ISLAND*** TO A STANDALONE GRAPHIC NOVEL, SOME REWRITING WAS NECESSARY. IT CHANGED THE TRAJECTORY OF STORY FOR THE BETTER, I THINK. AS A RESULT, LOTS OF NEW ELEMENTS WERE INTRODUCED AS THE SCOPE OF THE STORY GOT BIGGER (THE WATER SPIRIT WASN'T IN THE ORIGINAL PLANS!).

HERE'S A PAGE FROM A SUBPLOT THAT DIDN'T MAKE THE CUT.

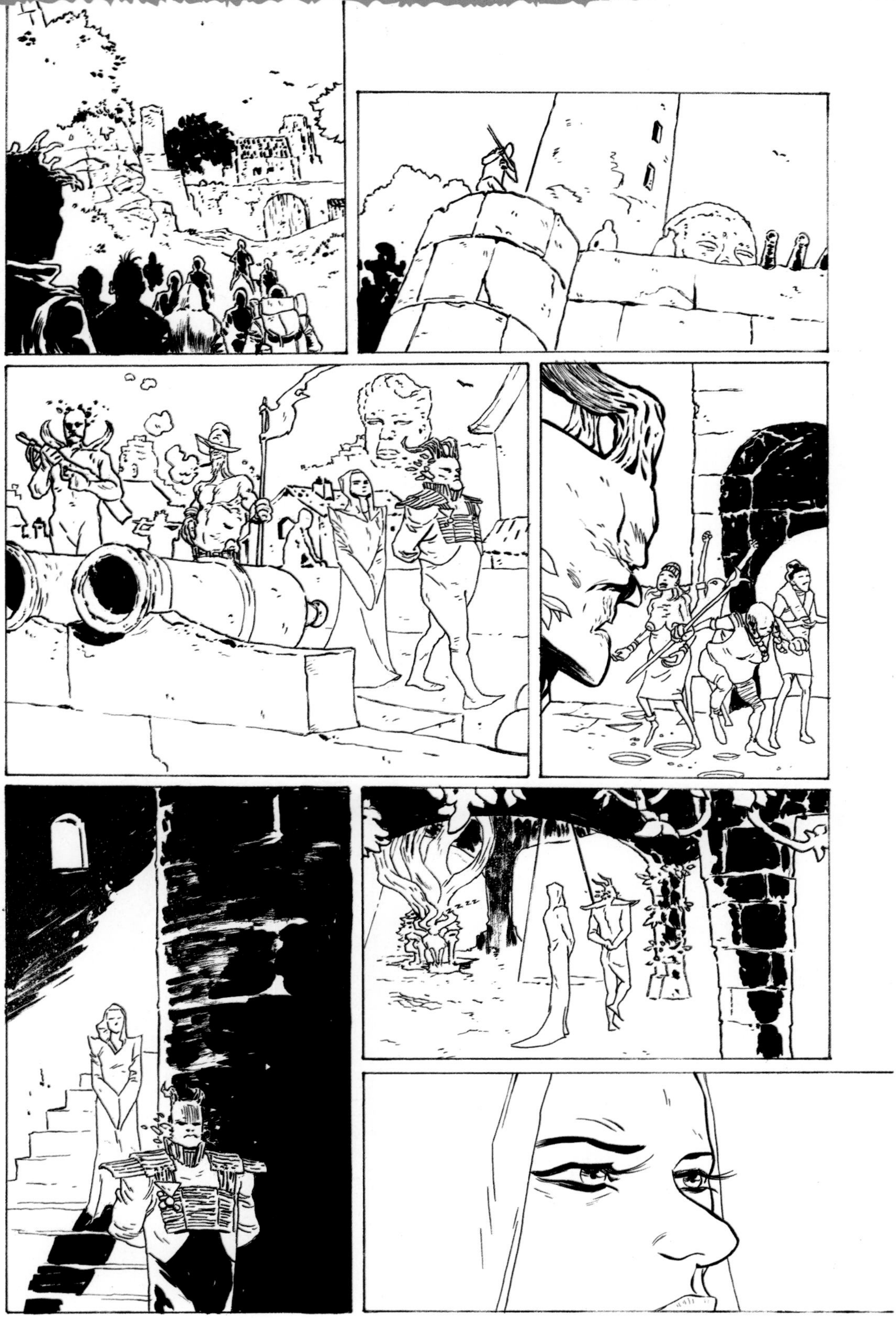

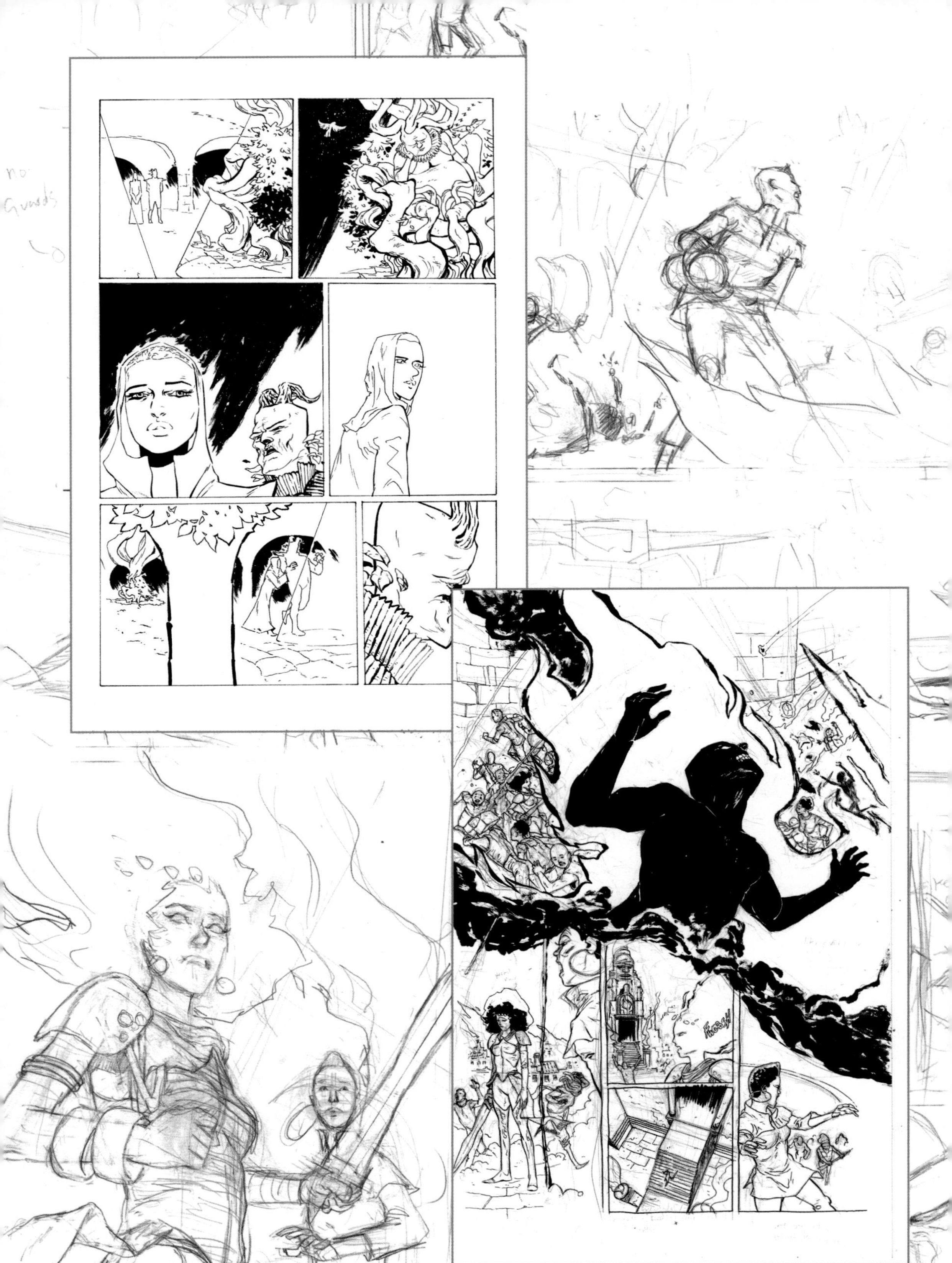
no
Guards

HERE ARE MORE ORPHANED PAGES FROM THE ORIGINAL CHAPTER 2.

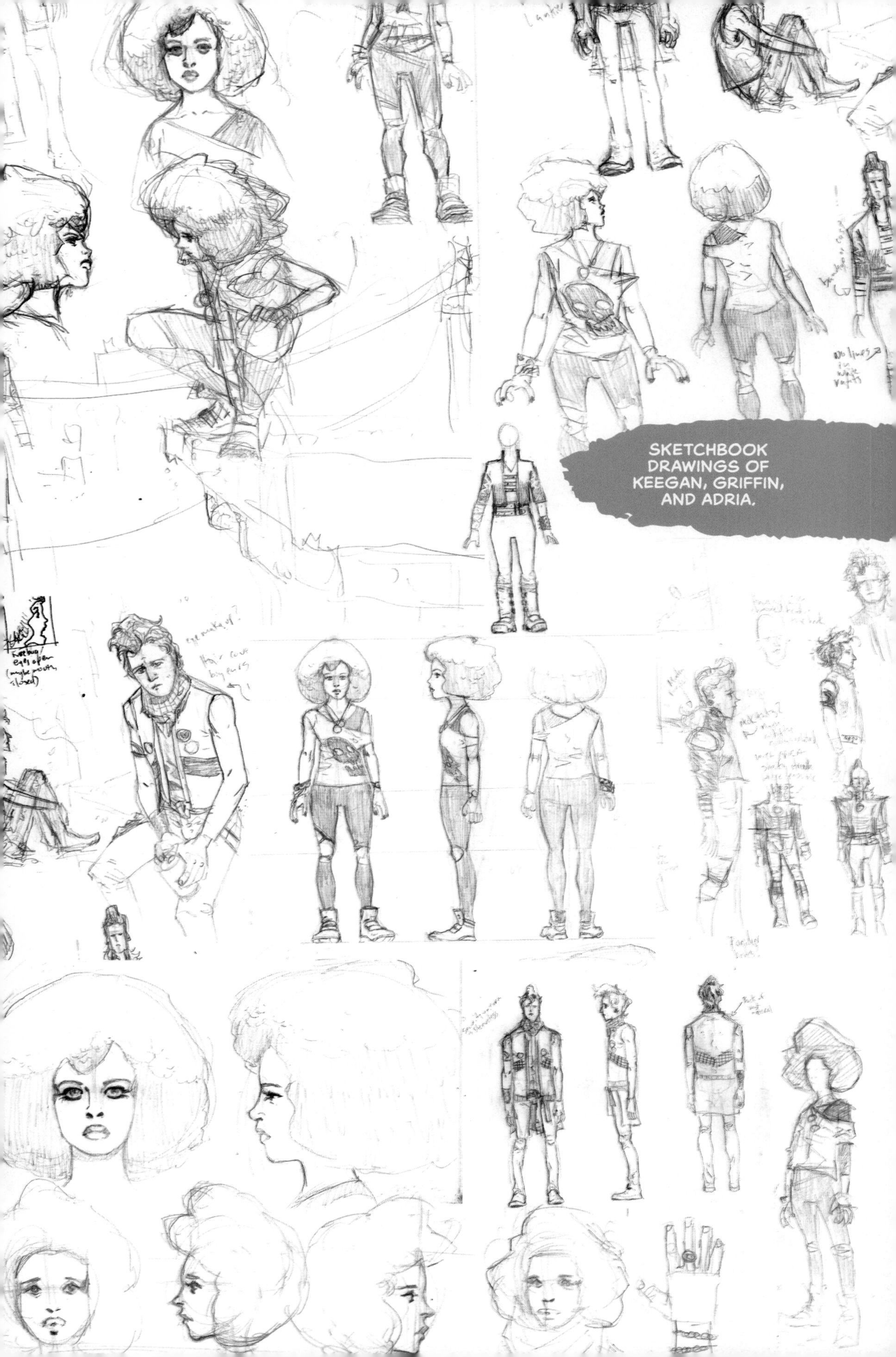

SKETCHBOOK DRAWINGS OF KEEGAN, GRIFFIN, AND ADRIA.

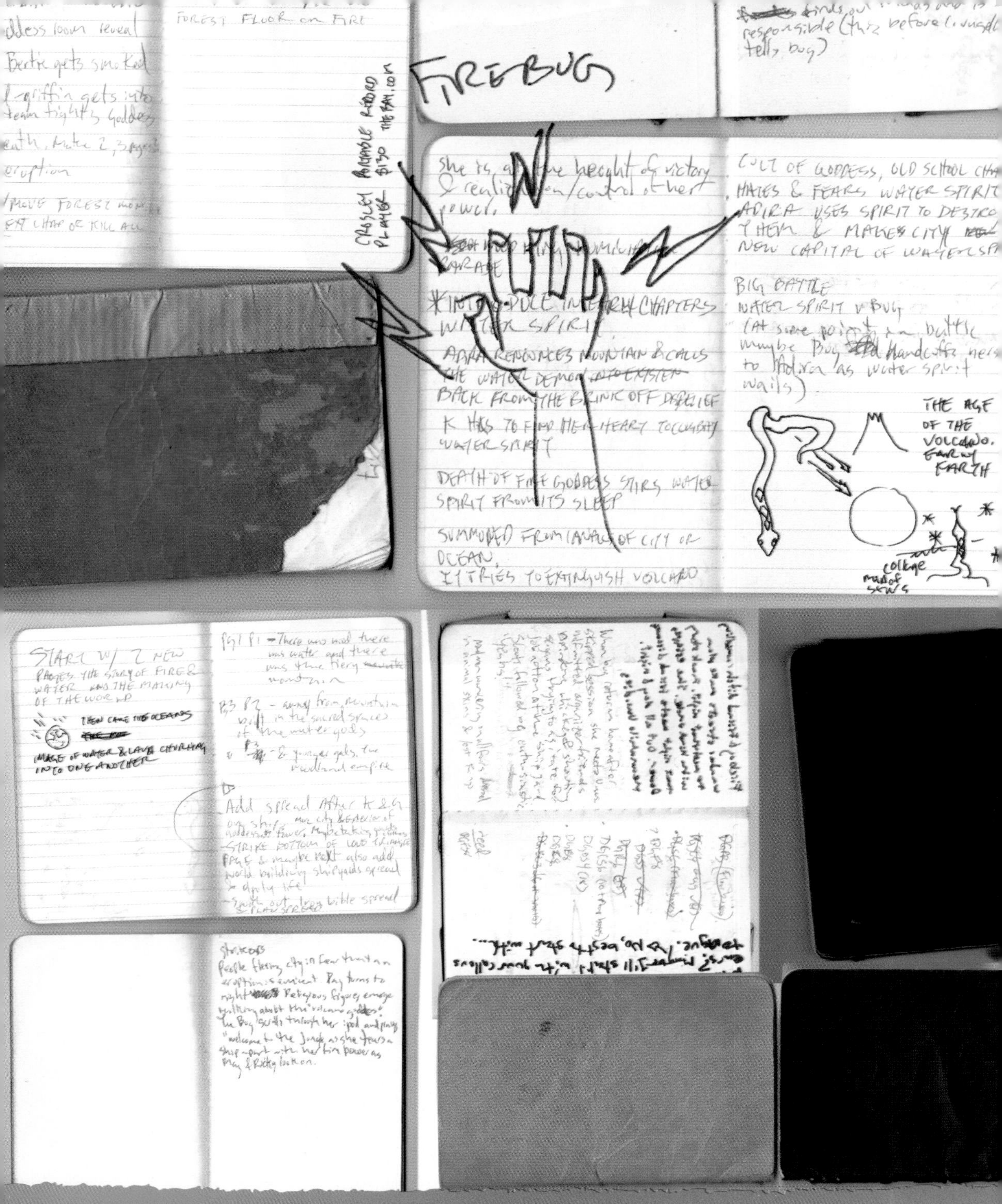
FIREBUG
FOREST FLOOR ON FIRE
CULT OF GODDESS, OLD SCHOOL
BIG BATTLE
THE AGE OF THE VOLCANO. EARLY EARTH
THEN CAME THE OCEANS
IMAGE OF WATER & LAVA CHURNING INTO ONE ANOTHER

THE EARLIEST NOTES I FOUND FOR WHAT WOULD EVENTUALLY BECOME ***FIREBUG*** ARE FROM BACK IN 2011-2012. THE FINAL RESULT IS VERY DIFFERENT THAN WHAT IT STARTED OUT AS, BUT SURPRISINGLY, A LOT OF THE INITIAL IDEAS SURVIVED.

THE UNPREDICTABILITY OF LIFE IS A LOT LIKE LIVING AT THE FOOT OF A VOLCANO. WHAT IF THAT VOLCANO HAD AGENCY?...

I WOULD LAY OUT IDEAS OF BITS OF DIALOGUE, THEN NOT THINK ABOUT IT FOR MONTHS AT A TIME. IT WOULD POP UP IN VARIOUS NOTEBOOKS, LIKE A WHALE SURFACING, ONLY TO DISAPPEAR AGAIN. THEN REAPPEAR AT ANOTHER TIME IN LATER NOTEBOOK, IN A SLIGHTLY DIFFERENT FORM.

JOHNNIE CHRISTMAS IS THE CO-CREATOR OF THE #1 NEW YORK TIMES BESTSELLING GRAPHIC NOVEL SERIES *ANGEL CATBIRD* (WITH ACCLAIMED WRITER MARGARET ATWOOD). HE'S THE CO-CREATER OF THE CRITICALLY ACCLAIMED SERIES *SHELTERED,* WHICH HAS BEEN TRANSLATED INTO MULTIPLE LANGUAGES. HE IS A GRADUATE OF THE PRATT INSTITUTE IN BROOKLYN, NY, EARNING A BFA IN COMMUNICATION DESIGN/ILLUSTRATION.

JOHNNIE MAKES VANCOUVER, BC HIS HOME.

TAMRA BONVILLAIN IS A PROFESSIONAL COLORIST WITH WORK AT IMAGE, MARVEL, DC, DARK HORSE, AND MORE. PAST WORKS INCLUDE *ANGEL CATBIRD,* *MOON GIRL AND DEVIL DINOSAUR,* AND *DOOM PATROL.* A 2009 GRADUATE OF THE JOE KUBERT SCHOOL, SHE NOW RESIDES IN NORTH AUGUSTA, SOUTH CAROLINA.

ARIANA MAHER IS A LETTERER FOR SEVERAL IMAGE COMICS PUBLICATIONS, INCLUDING *FROM UNDER MOUNTAINS, ARCLIGHT,* AND *RINGSIDE.* SHE ALSO LETTERS AND DESIGNS FOR THE INDEPENDENT IMPRINT LITTLE FOOLERY, MOST NOTABLY THE GRAPHIC NOVEL *SMALL TOWN WITCH* AND THE WEBCOMIC *SFEER THEORY.* SHE TENDS TO HANG OUT AT COMIC BOOK CONVENTIONS IN THE PACIFIC NORTHWEST.